OLYMPUS MUST FALL

A NOAH WOLF THRILLER

DAVID ARCHER

VINCE VOGEL

RIGHTHOUSE

ISBN-13: 978-1-63696-439-3

ISBN-10: 1-63696-439-7

Cover design by: Damonza

Printed in the United States of America

www.righthouse.com

www.instagram.com/righthousebooks

www.facebook.com/righthousebooks

twitter.com/righthousebooks

PRAISE FOR THE NOAH WOLF SERIES

NOAH WOLF THRILLERS

ONE

IN THE MIDDLE OF THE ATLANTIC, A GIANT CARGO SHIP sliced through the slate-gray waters. A steel behemoth named *Valkyrie* that seemed both ominous and oddly regal.

Rust streaks hinted at its past life as a simple cargo freighter, but those old scars were nearly lost beneath the sleek modifications. Its towering superstructure bristled with concealed weaponry and sensor arrays—silent declarations that this was no ordinary ship.

Helicopter pads had replaced rows of shipping containers, and reinforced hull plating added bulk beneath the waterline. From a distance, it was just another Panamax-class freighter, but up close, it revealed itself as something far more dangerous: Noah Wolf's floating fortress.

Once known by a mundane designation lost in commercial shipping logs, the *Valkyrie* had been hijacked by Noah and his team in the chaos following the downfall of E & E. In a daring, near-bloodless operation, they'd seized control of the vessel, stripped its identifiers, and rebuilt it piece by piece. Whole sections of cabins were gutted to make way for state-of-the-art surveillance suites, armories, and sleeping quarters.

Over time, the old cargo holds were converted into labs and training spaces. The result was a roving stronghold that allowed Noah's people to remain perpetually out of reach of any nation's jurisdiction—an ideal vantage point from which to strike at the Council.

A five-man crew worked tirelessly to keep the ship running at all hours. Each had overlapping skill sets that blended mechanical, navigational, and combat expertise. At the helm stood Captain Marlow, a quiet man with decades at sea under a variety of flags. Two engineers, an electronics specialist, and a ship's quartermaster rounded out this skeleton team, maintaining everything from the *Valkyrie's* twin engines to the highly classified stealth technology that kept them hidden from the Council's prying eyes.

Supplies had to be continuously sourced, often through black markets or coded trades with sympathetic insiders. Fuel, spare parts, and fresh food all arrived in carefully arranged drops, orchestrated by the ever-watchful gaze of the ship's intelligence suite.

Scattered across the globe, the remnants of E & E's staff had been left in chaos when the Council declared open season on them. Some had been captured, others had disappeared without a trace, and far too many had turned up dead in grisly, staged accidents that bore the Council's invisible signature.

Only a lucky few escaped, using back channels and encrypted signals to find their way to the *Valkyrie*. They came aboard battered and haunted but resolute—and determined to avenge their fallen comrades. For all of them, this converted ship was more than a safe haven; it was the only place left where they could fight back.

With every passing day, the Council's noose tightened. Patrol ships, satellite sweeps, and infiltration agents haunted the open seas, searching for any sign of Noah or his fugitive allies. Only

Wally's cloaking devices—a patchwork of jammers, decoy transponders, and advanced radar-evading modifications—kept the *Valkyrie* shrouded.

Hidden beneath swirling Atlantic fog and cloaked from every modern eye, the ship carried both the living embers of E & E's resistance and the unbreakable resolve of those who refused to bow. No port to call home, no country to grant them shelter. Yet they had each other—and the *Valkyrie* herself—to fight a war that the rest of the world never even realized was being waged.

One year to the day after the fall of E & E, Noah Wolf stood on the bridge of the *Valkyrie*. Arms folded behind his back, he gazed out through reinforced windows at the endless expanse of water. The churning gray of the Atlantic stretched before him, restless and unrelenting. Somewhere beyond that horizon—somewhere far beyond his reach—was his daughter, Norah. Taken one year ago to the day. The day her mother was murdered by a woman he had once called a friend: Allison Peterson. Once the head of E & E, she had betrayed them in the most brutal way—and by the end, E & E was in flames, his wife was dead, and his daughter was gone.

That day, in blood and iron, he had made a vow—to destroy Allison, to burn the Council to the ground, and to bring his daughter home.

And now, aboard the *Valkyrie*, that vow edged closer to reality. Because something was coming. A piece of intel that just might turn the tide.

Below decks in the surveillance room, the drone of electronics was broken by a sudden chirp—the quantum surveillance array had picked up something. Seated in front of the console, Neil Blessing jerked upright, eyes flicking across scrolling lines of encrypted code. At the same time, Wally Lawson, who had been idly pacing behind him, snapped to attention.

"Another random scramble from the Council's data net?" Wally asked, leaning over Neil's shoulder.

Neil shook his head as he tapped at the keyboard. "No," he

murmured. "This is different. Looks like a transmission signature I haven't seen in weeks."

He typed a rapid string of commands, focusing the array's entanglement sensors onto the faint signal. On the screen, fragments of text began to coalesce into something intelligible. Neil's face went pale for a second, then hardened.

"It's him," he said quietly, half to himself.

Wally's brow furrowed. "Who?"

"The ghost we've been chasing. My Council mole on black site intelligence. If I'm reading this right..." He paused, rechecking the data. "They're forwarding a location. Possibly instructions."

Wally leaned in, scanning the lines of text. His eyes widened. "That's—this is big, Neil. We need to get this to Noah and the others."

Neil nodded, already saving and encrypting the data to a secured drive. "Let's go."

They bolted from the surveillance console.

On the bridge, Noah registered their arrival before he turned around. Jenny Blessing stood near the console, scanning radar readouts, while Katya worked alongside the navigation officer, her sharp green eyes flicking over the data on the screen.

As Wally and Neil stepped forward, Noah stepped away from the railing. "Talk to me," he said.

Neil held up a portable drive. "We picked up a Council transmission. It's from that operative we've been tracking."

Noah's gaze flicked to the small device in Neil's hand, then back to his face. "Coordinates? Orders?"

"Both, I think," Neil replied. "We have to decode the rest of the message first. But one thing is clear: They're on the move—and it's happening soon."

Noah didn't need to hear any more details to know what this meant: a new lead, a chance to strike back, and the potential for a trap.

Still, they had no choice but to follow the thread.

"All right," Noah said at last. "Gather everyone in the war room. We don't wait on this."

One way or another, the hunt was about to begin in earnest.

TWO

THE *VALKYRIE'S* WAR ROOM WAS A PLACE OF organized chaos: maps taped to metal walls, monitors looping satellite feeds, and a sprawling table strewn with laptops, tablets, and scattered dossiers. At the head of the table stood Noah, eyes flicking between Neil and Wally. Jenny and Katya flanked him.

Neil cleared his throat, stepping forward to address the group. "We've spent the last couple of days monitoring new chatter on the quantum array," he began. "We started picking up Council transmissions referencing someone requesting extraction. At first, we had no idea who—it was just coded designations."

Wally jumped in. "I cross-referenced that with some older data we had—stuff we pulled during the Swiss Alps raid. It mentioned 'Project Mountaintop,' a research division overseen by a man named Dr. Adrian Knox."

Noah's gaze sharpened at the name. He recalled it from E & E's archives, back before everything crumbled. A brilliant mind, rumored to be behind some of the Council's most advanced tech. "So let me get this right," Noah said. "Knox is requesting extraction?"

"Yes."

Katya crossed her arms. "But he's the Council's golden scientist. Why would he request extraction?"

"Because he's defecting," Neil answered. "At least that's what it looks like from intercepted communications. Nevertheless, we need to be fast."

"Why?"

"The Council has found out. His encrypted messages have been picked up by their internal channels. It looks like he's now found his way into their security apparatus. The chatter I've picked up uses words like 'containment,' 'suppression,' and 'immediate disposal.'"

"They're going to kill him," Jenny said bluntly.

Neil nodded. "Yes. It looks like the Council wants him quiet —permanently."

"A clear sign that they're scared of what he might tell us," Katya added.

Neil nodded again.

"So where are they taking him?" asked Noah.

Wally moved to a large map on the wall, tapping the region in question. "A black-site prison facility in the Colombian jungle. We matched the coordinates from the Council's chatter to the location. Everything points to Dr. Knox being there."

Katya's mouth tightened. "Could be a trap—he tips us off, we walk in, and the Council comes crashing down on us. His detainment could just be more spycraft."

Noah studied the map in silence. "You're right. The Council knows we're desperate to gain any intel, any advantage. Hanging Knox like bait in a place as isolated as a Colombian black site would be effective."

The flicker of a smile formed on Neil's lips despite the tension. "There's only one way to find out," he said.

THREE

NIGHT PRESSED HEAVILY ON THE COLOMBIAN JUNGLE, an inky darkness broken only by moonlight filtering through the canopy. Beneath the thick humidity and chorus of insects lay a secret: a Council black site disguised as a long-abandoned military base. Rusted chain-link fences and vine-choked concrete masked the reality—a fortified prison burrowed deep into the mountainside.

Guard towers swept the jungle with floodlights and infrared cameras, each manned by mercenaries in dark tactical gear. Overhead, silent drones patrolled, their thermal imaging picking up the faintest hint of movement. Beyond the towers, an electrified fence cut through the jungle like a scar, its occasional sparks—often when hit by bats or birds—illuminating the night.

At the mountain's base, a gate led into the hidden compound, guarded by automated turrets and armed sentries.

Jenny eased the truck toward the rusted chain-link gate, its tires crunching over gravel and potholes. Overhead, towering floodlights swept arcs through the black jungle. The faint hum of a surveillance drone drifted over them, its camera lens swiveling to track their approach.

Both she and Neil knew better than to look up—they had to maintain the illusion of being no more than two low-level arms traffickers fulfilling a lucrative shipment.

A pair of guards stood at the entrance, rifles slung across their chests. One stepped forward, signaling them to stop. Jenny rolled down the window.

An officer in dark fatigues, sporting a neatly trimmed mustache, materialized from the shadows.

"You're late," he grunted, his gaze shifting to the paper manifest Jenny held out.

"The roads were a nightmare," Jenny responded with a shrug. "How about we don't waste any more time?"

The officer scanned the documents, a flashlight beam flickering across the harsh angles of his face. A bead of sweat glistened at his temple as he read.

"Shotguns, batons..." he muttered, flipping the page.

"And riot shields," Jenny added smoothly.

A heavy moment passed before the officer thrust the papers back. "Move along," he muttered, waving them forward. "Follow the road. The warehouses are right ahead."

"Sure thing," Jenny said, putting the truck into gear.

At the officer's signal, the two guards opened the gate. Jenny rolled the truck inside, passing armed patrols as they entered the compound.

Rising out of the darkness, a squat, concrete barracks came into view. Two soldiers flagged them to a stop near a group of crates stacked beneath a corrugated metal awning.

As Jenny pulled the truck to a halt, a stern-faced guard approached the driver's side window. "Stay in the cab," he barked, tapping the metal door for emphasis. "We'll unload everything."

Jenny raised her hands in a show of compliance. "No problem. We've been on the road all night; we'll just grab some shut-eye while you're at it. Knock on the window when you're done, and we'll be out of your hair."

The guard nodded and stepped away from the truck. Without waiting another beat, Jenny cranked the window up and pulled the curtains around all the inside windows, blocking out the glare of the compound's floodlights.

Neil exhaled softly in the darkness, his voice barely above a whisper. "Let's get to work."

He reached under the dash and pulled out a compact tablet, its screen glowing faintly green. Wally had already prepared the device with a custom hacking suite, optimized to break into the Council's security network. In the hush, Jenny could hear muffled voices and the thump of crates as workers began unloading the shotguns from the back.

"Loading the Trojan now," Neil breathed, his eyes fixed on the code crawling across the tablet's interface. He tapped a few virtual keys, and the device pinged softly. "We have a backdoor connection for Wally."

Far out in the Atlantic, Wally was hunched over a console aboard the *Valkyrie*, ready to exploit this freshly opened gateway into the black site's systems. If all went according to plan, he'd soon have limited control over cameras, perimeter sensors—maybe even automated turrets.

"Done," Neil announced. The tablet's screen gave one final flash of confirmation. "Wally's in."

Outside, the scrape of pallets and the grunts from the unloading team punctuated the night.

Jenny glanced at Neil, who nodded once.

Hidden behind the curtains, they both slid off their seats, crouching on the floor of the cab. Neil pulled aside a section of rubber matting, revealing a concealed hatch beneath the passenger seat. He unlatched it. Below, the jungle night seeped through, thick with the scent of damp earth and rotting vegetation.

"Let's go," Jenny whispered.

Neil squeezed through first, disappearing into the darkness below the truck. Jenny then slipped through the hatch after him, carefully closing the secret door behind her.

FOUR

THE JUNGLE SEEMED TO BREATHE AROUND THEM IN hushed, humid waves. Noah and Katya slipped through the tangled vines and towering palms like jungle cats, dressed in dark, form-fitting gear that masked both their heat signatures and human outlines.

Overhead, two drones patrolled in a slow, deliberate circuit, their rotors faintly buzzing in the heavy air.

They were grateful for the suits, but to access the black site from this side, they needed to take out the drones first.

Katya lifted a compact thermal monocular to her eye, scanning for the drone operators. A small beep indicated two stationary heat signatures nearly half a kilometer away, perched in a low camouflaged tower.

"Got them."

She lowered the scope, sliding it into a thigh pouch. Then, with practiced ease, she unslung a suppressed SR-25, resting it against a fallen log. The rifle's matte-black barrel barely caught the moonlight as she chambered a subsonic 7.62mm round, the movement near-silent.

"Wind's moving left to right, slight cross-breeze," she murmured, adjusting the rifle's optic.

Noah crouched behind her, watching as Katya lined up the shot. She exhaled slowly, her breathing steady.

The suppressor gave only a dull *thwip* as she squeezed the trigger.

Four hundred meters away, the first operator jerked violently, then slumped forward, sliding off the observation stool.

One down.

Katya barely shifted, already lining up the second shot.

Almost simultaneously, the second drone pivoted, whirring in a lazy arc above the canopy. Katya adjusted her aim, her heartbeat steady, her mind clear. The second operator had flinched at the sudden slump of his partner but hadn't yet reacted.

A fraction of a second.

That was all she had.

She exhaled and squeezed the trigger.

The rifle gave another muted *thwip*. Four hundred meters away, the operator's head snapped back, and he crumpled into the shadowed depths of the tower.

Two down.

The drone hesitated in midair, its flight pattern erratic, as if searching for new input. Without a guiding hand at the controls, it drifted, its rotors stabilizing just long enough to start veering away.

Katya's hand was already shifting, her fingers brushing over her rifle's selector switch. She flicked to semi-auto, leading the shot as the drone banked left. Another suppressed round spat from the barrel.

The impact caught the drone at its rear stabilizer, sending it into a sudden, spiraling descent. It clipped the edge of a tree, then tumbled through the branches before smashing into the jungle floor with a sharp crack.

Katya exhaled and lowered the rifle. "Drones are down."

Noah was already moving.

They advanced deeper into the jungle. Eventually, they reached the low-slung silhouette of a security shed near the compound's perimeter. Vines wound their way around corrugated steel walls, and a dim light glowed inside.

Noah edged up to the doorway, peering through a grimy window. One lone technician sat at a console watching camera feeds of the base's perimeter, eyes jumping nervously between multiple monitors.

Noah slipped through the partially ajar door without a sound. In two silent strides, he was behind the unsuspecting technician. A swift jerk of Noah's arms, and the man's neck snapped in a single, brutal motion. The body slackened in Noah's grip, and he carefully lowered it to the floor.

Intel indicated that this security substation sat directly atop the compound's main power grid. Taking it out would disable the entire security system.

Katya crouched by the shed's electrical conduits, quickly setting charges of C4. She pressed them against the main power relays, her nimble fingers trailing wires to a compact detonator. "It's done," she whispered, eyes flicking over to Noah in confirmation.

They slipped into the jungle gloom. Barely had they put a few dozen meters between themselves and the shed when a contained *phoomp* rattled the air, immediately followed by a louder, concussive boom. The explosive charges tore through the electrical grid, sending a brief flash of light skyward before snuffing it out.

A second later, the entire compound went dark. Guard towers, floodlights, and fence lights blinked off in unison, plunging the fortress into blackness. Sirens wailed, an urgent, discordant alarm. Searchlights flickered on. A handful of backup generators kicked in, sputtering enough power to illuminate corridors and key defense systems.

Noah turned to Katya, a faint smile of grim satisfaction ghosting across his features. "We're in business."

FIVE

With the power down, all the electronic doors unlocked, allowing Jenny and Neil to slip inside the main building with ease.

Together, they moved toward the holding cell of Dr. Adrian Knox.

Old emergency lighting flickered here and there, bathing the subterranean halls in a sickly, pulsing red. They paused at a heavy steel door labeled Interrogation Sector C, listening for any sign of guards.

Hearing none, Jenny gave Neil a curt nod.

He tapped furiously on his tablet, bypassing the lock's electronic control—which was still being powered by the backup generators.

With a soft click, the door slid open.

Inside, the chamber was lined with reinforced cells on either side. Some sat dark and empty; others contained hollow-eyed figures who stared listlessly through barred windows. In the cell at the far end, a dull light revealed a single occupant: Dr. Adrian Knox.

Stripped of anything but a soiled jumpsuit, he looked gaunt and haggard, days of stubble lining his face. His thinning gray hair clung to his scalp in disordered tufts, and wire-rimmed glasses sat crookedly on a nose that looked recently broken. Yet there was a keen awareness in his eyes—an undercurrent of anger that flared when he saw them.

Jenny pressed a gloved hand against the security panel, and the cell door hissed open. "Dr. Knox," she whispered. "We're here to get you out."

He rose unsteadily. "Thank God," he exhaled, a shudder of relief passing through him. "I thought you'd never come." As Neil stepped forward, Knox's tone became urgent. "However, we need to hurry."

Neil frowned. "Why?"

"Because they're sending a team of Elites to retrieve me."

"Elites," Neil muttered. "Great. Nothing we love more than fighting those freaks."

The Council's genetics program had engineered the ultimate combatants—Elites. Assassins bred for strength, speed, and obedience. Trained from childhood, they were tougher, faster, and deadlier than any soldier the team had ever faced.

Every encounter with them so far had nearly ended in death. They'd paid for each fight with blood—and with lives they couldn't replace.

"They're taking me back to the labs," Knox went on. "They're going to make me continue my work." He swallowed hard. "They could be here any minute."

As if on cue, Wally's strained voice crackled over their comms. "Guys—we have a problem. Unknown helicopter inbound, on final approach. It's not responding to standard Council comms. They're using a classified band."

Jenny tapped her earpiece. "Looks like the Elites the doc mentioned," she muttered.

"I think you're right," Wally said. "I'm picking up advanced weapons signatures from the chopper. They're now coming over the compound. From the satellite I'm getting five heat signatures inside. A pilot and four rather large individuals."

Neil exchanged a quick glance with Jenny. "Time to move, Doc," he said quietly. "Can you run?"

Knox nodded. "I can manage."

Jenny led the way back down the corridor, scanning for any signs of security response. With the main power sabotaged, emergency klaxons wailed sporadically, lights flickering in and out. The whole facility felt like it was teetering on the edge of collapse.

Once this Elite squad got here, it would only get worse.

SIX

A THUNDEROUS ROAR BROKE THROUGH THE NIGHT AS an all-black helicopter descended over the compound, its rotors whipping up a violent gust of wind and debris. The side doors slid open, revealing four figures in sleek, armored exo-suits.

Hooking themselves onto rappelling lines, they dropped into the fray below—each landing in a precise formation.

These were the Elites. Raised, honed, and perfected into living weapons.

Moving in unison, they advanced into the compound, their exo-suits absorbing the darkness—each a variation of the same cutting-edge design: black ballistic plating contoured to the body, augmented by servo motors at the joints that gave them enhanced strength and agility.

At the front was Luca, the eldest brother. Tall and broad-shouldered, his exo-suit boasted extra plating across the chest and shoulders, making him a walking tank.

Next to him strode Nadia, a slender figure whose suit bore custom modifications for speed and stealth: a whisper in the dark, a blade pressed to an unsuspecting throat.

Flanking them was Marius, whose exo-suit showcased a sophisticated targeting suite, complete with a multi-lens visor for his helmet that constantly analyzed range, wind, and trajectory for his high-powered sniper rifle.

At the rear, Elena sported an exo-suit that glimmered with integrated tech. Embedded sensors spanned her arms and chest, controlling an advanced drone that hovered at her shoulder.

As the four assassins entered a corridor, a wide-eyed Council soldier rushed up, stammering, "This way... please, this way!"

He led them toward Sector C, the siblings following without a word, their formation tight, weapons ready. They had a clear objective: retrieve Dr. Adrian Knox. Whether that meant dragging him back alive or leaving a path of bodies in their wake hardly mattered.

SEVEN

Jenny and Neil hurried Dr. Adrian Knox through the labyrinth of corridors.

"Left here," Neil hissed, one hand firmly gripping Knox's arm to keep him moving. With his free hand, he tapped the controls on his tablet, feeding command prompts to Wally aboard the *Valkyrie*. Security doors ahead slid open with a grinding whirr, allowing them through—then slammed shut behind them, sealing off any pursuers.

Jenny scanned the next stretch of hallway, looking for movement in the half-light. "Clear," she murmured before throwing a look over her shoulder at Knox. "You hanging in there?"

Knox managed a grim nod. "Better than I was sitting in that cell," he said between ragged breaths.

They pressed on, each footstep a tense beat in a silent countdown. Ahead, another door hissed open at Neil's command. Jenny pushed Knox through into a long corridor and followed close behind, shutting the door quickly behind them.

"We should be—" Neil stopped short as four figures materialized like phantoms ahead of them.

It was the Elites: Luca, Nadia, Marius, and Elena, exo-suits pulsing under the red lights, Elena's drone hovering at her shoulder like a pet bird.

Jenny and Neil froze mid-step. Dr. Knox's face paled, and he huddled close behind them.

"Run!" Jenny barked.

Luca raised his rifle. The corridor erupted in gunfire. Jenny yanked Knox's arm, dragging him with them as they sprinted through a half-open door to a large cell block. Bullets tore through the air, sparking against metal walls, punching through where they had stood moments before.

They dove inside the cell block, slamming into cover behind a low wall as rounds chewed through the metal.

"Wally, open the cells!" Neil shouted into his comms.

A pause. Then, all at once, electronic locks disengaged. Cell doors clanged open. Dozens of prisoners spilled into the central hallway—confused and hesitant. Then came the bullets as the assassins entered.

Nadia fired at the low wall, cutting down a man in the front as he strayed into her path. The room erupted into chaos. Panic surged through the prisoners, and suddenly they were stamping, shoving past each other, screaming.

Jenny grabbed Knox, weaving through the frenzied mob. The assassins disappeared behind the flood of bodies, momentarily overwhelmed.

Jenny, Neil, and Knox burst out the opposite door, shoving it closed behind them. They ran. Footsteps pounded behind them, the assassins regrouping.

Then Neil swore.

The gate ahead was chained and padlocked. They were trapped in a large storage yard. A tall fence surrounded them, topped with razor wire.

"Shit."

They spun, pressing against a container, hearts hammering.

The door to the cell block swung open.

Elena's drone glided out, ascended into the air, then hovered over them, feeding their exact position back to her visor.

The assassins emerged from the door.

"Dr. Knox?" Luca called out, voice calm. "Dr. Knox, it would be better if you simply came with us now. No need to hide."

Knox swallowed. "Eh... I'm good," he stammered back.

Jenny spotted the drone's red eye staring down at them. Without hesitation, she raised her pistol and shot it out of the sky.

Elena flinched as the feed cut out.

Luca clenched his jaw. The assassins signaled to one another silently, breaking off to surround the container.

The moment stretched, a breath before violence.

Then—

Something landed not far from the Elites' feet.

A grenade.

BOOM!

An explosion ripped through the yard, filling the air with thick, choking smoke.

Through the swirling haze, two figures surged forward—Noah and Katya. They fired at the Elites, but their bullets were deflected by the armor-plated suits.

The Council assassins were thrown back slightly, but they didn't panic. They adapted.

They switched their visors to thermal.

Luca charged first, a massive figure in the smoke, his exo-suit absorbing bullets as he barreled toward Noah. Noah sidestepped, but Luca was faster than any normal man his size had a right to be.

As Noah dodged, a massive fist flicked out into his ribs, sending him skidding backward into a crate. Pain flared.

Katya met Nadia head-on, her combat knife flashing. But Nadia was faster. Her enhanced reflexes let her dodge Katya's first strike, then her second. She twisted mid-air, planted a kick into Katya's chest, and sent her flying back.

Emerging from behind the container, Jenny parried Elena's

blade, trying to land a strike, but Elena's exo-suit moved like a second skin—every block, every attack was too fluid, too sharp.

Marius engaged from range, his multi-lens visor analyzing every movement, waiting for an opening.

As for Neil, he knew they couldn't win this fight head-on. Especially with him being the weakest in hand-to-hand. Instead, this would need brains as well as brawn.

Leaving Knox, he ducked behind a row of storage containers, brain racing. *Think, think.*

Then he saw it.

A crane loomed above the yard, its cab just meters away.

Its chains were already attached to a container, ready to be lifted up—dropped.

Meanwhile in the fight, Noah gritted his teeth and lunged back at Luca, driving an uppercut straight into his jaw. The impact barely staggered him—Luca retaliated, swinging a heavy elbow that Noah barely dodged.

Katya recovered, launching into a relentless series of knife strikes—but Nadia was an inhuman blur, evading with ease. Then, with a sudden shift, Nadia ducked inside Katya's guard and smashed an elbow into her ribs.

Katya gasped, stumbling. Nadia twisted her wrist, sending Katya's knife spinning into the dirt.

Jenny, meanwhile, was losing ground to Elena.

Elena used her enhanced strength to grip Jenny's wrist, forcing her karambit down. Jenny twisted, kicked off a nearby container, and spun mid-air, throwing Elena off balance.

Still, it wasn't enough. They weren't winning.

Neil reached the crane controls and scrambled inside, his fingers flying over the levers.

The assassins were regrouping.

Nadia had Katya pinned. Luca was closing in on Noah. Elena and Marius were boxing in Jenny.

Neil's pulse hammered. They were losing. Even with all their skill, they couldn't fight exo-suited, genetically enhanced killers head-on.

Then he spotted it—the perfect opportunity.

The container swayed above the yard—forty feet of solid steel. If he could drop it at the right moment, it wouldn't just slow them down. It would trap them.

"Guys!" he barked through comms. "I'm gonna need you to get them all grouped up in the middle of the yard!"

Noah understood first. He feinted left, forcing Luca toward the others.

Jenny ducked a slash from Elena and kicked backward, driving her toward Marius.

Katya, gritting her teeth, twisted free from Nadia's grip and maneuvered her into the group.

The Elite assassins, unaware, closed in around each other—seconds from finishing the fight.

Neil yanked the lever.

"GET OUTTA THERE!"

Noah, Jenny, and Katya dove away just as the massive steel crate plummeted.

It crashed down with a thunderous impact, kicking up dust and debris.

When the smoke cleared, Marius and Elena were pinned beneath the twisted wreckage.

Luca and Nadia had barely rolled free, scrambling back, furious. But the container blocked their path to Noah and the others.

Jenny hauled Knox to his feet.

"Move!" Noah barked.

Katya took point, leading them deeper into the yard.

"This way," she called.

A few meters ahead, Katya veered right, skidding to a stop near a narrow opening in the chain-link fence—a section she and Noah had cut through earlier to infiltrate the compound.

"One at a time," she ordered.

Neil shoved Knox through first, then followed. Jenny slipped through next. Noah watched their backs, weapon raised, scanning the yard for any sign of pursuit.

As he crawled through last, Wally's voice crackled over their comms.

"Bad news, guys—your ride's been torched."

Noah's stomach dropped.

"Say again?"

"Council patrols just found your evac chopper. They hit it with an RPG."

Noah turned toward the jungle and spotted it—thick black smoke curling through the treetops. Beyond the foliage, flickers of orange fire licked at the night sky.

Their way out was gone.

"Shit," Jenny muttered.

Knox ran a trembling hand over his face. "So what now?"

Noah scanned their surroundings, thinking fast. Then, through the trees, he caught the dull sheen of black metal—a chopper sitting on a helipad just past the fence line.

Not theirs.

The Elites' helicopter.

A slow grin spread across his face.

"We're taking that."

Katya followed his gaze and gave a sharp nod. "Cover me."

She unslung her SR-25, dropping to a knee. The pilot was still inside, scanning the jungle from his seat. He wouldn't see it coming.

Katya's breath steadied.

She squeezed the trigger.

A sharp *thwip* cut through the night. The pilot's head snapped forward against the control panel.

"Clear," she muttered, standing.

Noah didn't waste a second. "Move."

They broke into a sprint, vaulting fallen logs and tearing through undergrowth.

They burst onto the helipad, the chopper's rotors still idling.

Noah climbed in first, dragging the dead pilot's body out of the seat and onto the ground.

"Get in!" he barked.

Neil helped Knox up. Jenny jumped into the co-pilot seat.

Katya swung in last, slamming the door shut just as Noah powered up the controls.

The chopper lurched into the air, dust kicking up beneath them.

Just as they lifted off, the Elites freed themselves.

From the air, Noah saw Luca and Nadia sprinting toward the helipad. Luca raised his rifle. Noah jerked the chopper left as bullets sprayed past the hull.

Neil peered down and smirked. He lifted a hand, wiggling his fingers in a small wave.

Jenny laughed and mirrored him, waving to the Elites as they vanished beneath the jungle canopy.

They were free, Knox with them, the mission complete.

EIGHT

BACK ON THE *VALKYRIE*, THE BUZZING OVERHEAD lights cast a sterile glow over the converted medical bay.

Katya sat on the edge of an examination table, her left shoulder bare, streaked with drying blood. Jenny worked quickly, stitching her up with a needle and surgical thread.

Across from them, Dr. Adrian Knox reclined against another examination table, his face pale, his wrist hooked up to an IV drip. He was gaunt, bruised, and exhausted, but he was alive.

Noah stood against a bulkhead, arms crossed, watching him. Not with sympathy. Not with anger. Just waiting.

Wally hovered near a console, occasionally glancing at a tablet. Neil sat on a crate nearby, tapping a finger against his knee, his eyes sharp.

Finally, it was Knox who broke the silence.

"How much do you know about Project Mountaintop?" His voice was raw.

"Not enough," Noah replied. "But I know the Council doesn't keep defectors like you alive unless you're worth something to them."

Knox exhaled, rubbing his eyes. "That's because for the past twenty years, I and my team at Mountaintop have been working on the Council's greatest weapon. Olympus."

Wally lifted his head. Jenny paused mid-stitch. Neil's finger froze over his knee.

"That's what they call it," Knox continued. "Not a project. Not a protocol. A system. A super AI. And it's already started."

A deep silence fell over the room.

Knox shifted on the examination table. "I wasn't part of the whole thing. My expertise was programming and interface—Phase Two. But Olympus is bigger than me. Bigger than any of us. It's designed to be unstoppable. You can kill Council members, you can blow up data centers, but Olympus... if it's allowed to go fully online, it will keep going. No matter what."

Noah's jaw tightened. "Explain."

Knox licked his lips, his voice turning clinical, almost detached—the voice of a scientist dissecting a specimen.

"It works in three phases. Phase One is already in motion—subversion. The Council has been pulling strings for centuries, restructuring global economies, installing leaders, creating controlled instability. Every supply chain disruption, every food shortage, every market crash—it's the Council working behind the scenes." Knox looked up, eyes rimmed red. "But all of that... all that manipulation took armies of personnel. Decades of work. Placing people in position. Bribing, blackmailing, killing. Constant maneuvering just to keep control of the world's economy."

He shook his head slowly. "And now, they don't need any of it."

No one spoke.

"With the rise of automation, of AI, of digital infrastructure —never before has the entire system been so easy to hijack. Olympus is designed to do what took the Council generations to accomplish. But faster. Cleaner. Permanent."

He drew in a shaky breath. "It will manipulate everything—

markets, taxation, trade flows, even the perceived worth of curren-cies. It doesn't just observe the system; it becomes the system."

Wally frowned. "It's a trading algorithm?"

"No," Knox said flatly. "It's the end of free will in global economics. Olympus is designed to learn and adapt, rewrite its own code, and spread itself like a virus into the bones of every digital institution. Banking, insurance, investment firms, govern-ment databases—anywhere with a signal."

He shifted, wincing at the IV in his arm. "The servers it needs are massive. We're talking floors of buildings. Power grids have already been rerouted to support them. And they're building more—underground this time. Shielded. Hardened. Even if you destroy one, the rest survive. You'd need to take down the entire network simultaneously to have a chance."

Noah's jaw tightened.

"If Olympus goes fully online," Knox said, "we won't be able to stop it. Not with EMPs. Not with code. Not with guns. It'll lock down systems across the globe. Drain digital accounts. Trigger crashes. Manipulate elections. Rewrite ownership of land and assets. It will cause an economic implosion on a scale we can't begin to model."

He looked around the room, his eyes haunted.

"And the Council will be the only ones holding the keys."

"Jesus Christ..." Neil muttered, rubbing his face.

Knox shook his head. "No. Not Jesus. The gods of Olympus. The Council sees themselves as deities, reshaping civilization in their image."

Katya scoffed, wincing as Jenny tied off the final stitch. "Nothing new. Just another empire trying to play God."

Knox turned his tired eyes to her. "Then you'll love Phase Two."

Katya didn't blink. Neither did Noah.

Knox swallowed. "Olympus will take down the world."

The words hung in the air like poison.

"Define 'take down,'" Noah said, voice cold.

Knox sighed. "It's not just hacking. It's annihilation. The AI is designed to infiltrate every system on the planet. Not just financial markets. Power grids. Water supplies. Media. Communication networks. Satellites. Radar. Everything. The moment Phase Two activates, it will erase all existing code—every program, every backup, every failsafe. A total technological blackout."

The weight of the words settled like ice.

"No Internet. No power. No emergency response. No global defenses," Knox continued. "Planes will fall out of the sky. Automated factories will shut down. Banks will be wiped clean. Every piece of data in existence—gone. A full technological blackout. Billions thrown back into the dark ages. No power. No communication. No currency. The world will descend into pitch black darkness. And when it does..." He hesitated. "That's when they send in Phase Three."

Wally's face was pale. "What will they send in?"

Knox turned to him, a grim expression on his face. "Bioweapons. With no satellites, no radio, no government coordination, no one will even know what's happening. The world will be blind. And in that blindness, the Council will release their weapons—targeted nanotech bioweapons. Not viruses. Not chemical agents. Something far worse."

Jenny's hands clenched into fists. "We've seen them in action. Firsthand."

Knox exhaled slowly. "Then you know how quickly they'll exterminate entire populations. After the blackout, it'll be pretty easy." His voice dropped. "Then the golden future begins. A new world order. No nations. No governments. No resistance. Only the Council. Olympus running everything."

Silence.

Noah glanced at Wally. "Can we stop it?"

Wally's eyes flickered with thought, but his voice was grim. "I don't know. But if Olympus goes fully live as our friend here says, the fight is over before it begins."

The room fell deathly silent.

Jenny's knuckles were white. Neil's finger pressed into his knee. Wally had gone utterly still.

Finally, Noah spoke. "When?"

Knox met his gaze, something haunted behind his bloodshot eyes.

"Phase One is already in progress. Phase Two starts within a month."

Noah turned to Wally. "Can you shut it down?"

The tech genius let out a slow breath. "If you can get me inside their systems, maybe. But I need direct access to their mainframe. Wherever they're running Olympus from."

Knox shifted again. "I know where to start."

Noah's gaze snapped back to him.

Knox nodded grimly. "There's a Council hub in Hong Kong. A data center that feeds Olympus real-time inputs. If you can access the building's mainframe, you might be able to set up a link —something that lets you hack in remotely. It's the only way."

"A link?" Jenny asked.

Knox sighed. "You'd need to get in and out of the building without being noticed. Even then, it'll take a day or two to break through their security—then who knows how long to upload a virus strong enough to do any real damage. You'll be sitting on a time bomb, hoping they don't catch you before it's done."

Noah's eyes never left Knox's face.

"Then we do that. Burn it all down."

Knox fixed him with a bloodshot stare. "I hope you do. Because if you don't, in thirty days, half the world will be dead."

Noah turned, his gaze sweeping across his team. Jenny. Neil. Wally. Katya. Each one held his stare, no hesitation.

He exhaled, his decision final.

"Prep the ship. We leave for Hong Kong tonight."

NINE

A SUBARCTIC WIND RATTLED THE IRON DOORS OF THE facility, but inside the vast concrete chamber, the air hung thick with the sour tang of fear and blood. Fluorescent bulbs ringed the domed ceiling, casting stark halos of light on the floor far below.

Allison Peterson—known here only as "Mother"—stood at the edge of the open floor. Her posture was deceptively calm, arms folded behind her back. She wore a black tactical uniform: close-fitting, practical, devoid of rank insignias or patches. An almost motherly smile touched her lips, but her eyes held no warmth. Instead, they surveyed the scene like a hawk.

A circle of children sat cross-legged along the perimeter, their heads shaved, each wearing plain gray T-shirts, cotton trousers, and worn canvas shoes.

Their gazes were fixed on the two in the center: a boy and a girl of around ten years old, circling each other on the reinforced mat. Despite their youth, their movements bore the hallmark of deadly training: precise footwork, lethal stances, a coldness to their eyes.

Above them, a narrow balcony followed the curve of the

dome. Two scientists in stark white lab coats peered through a camcorder, panning over the scene. On a nearby console, red lights flickered—recording vital data from biometric monitors attached to the children's ankles.

"Fight!" Allison snapped.

The two went at each other in rabid furry, a blur of fists and feet.

Allison prowled around the fighting duo. "Faster," she barked, voice echoing in the dome.

The boy darted in with a sharp strike, testing the girl's defense. She slipped aside, eyes cold, waiting for an opening.

Their small bodies collided, fists and elbows cutting through the air, each blow delivered with more ferocity than any child should possess. Around them, the other trainees watched, expressionless—no one dared flinch or avert their eyes. They all knew the penalty for failing to follow "Mother's" lessons.

A flurry of blows ended with the girl managing a sweep that sent the boy sprawling. He landed hard, and she wasted no time seizing his arm and yanking it into a tight hold. The boy thrashed, teeth gritted against the pain. The girl's grip tightened, but she hesitated, flicking a glance toward Allison as though seeking permission.

Allison's voice cut like a blade. "Break it."

Fear flickered across the girl's face for half a second—just long enough for Allison to see it. Then, with a sharp twist, the girl broke the boy's arm.

A wet crack echoed in the dome.

The boy's choked scream reverberated, followed by a whimpering moan as he curled up on the mat, cradling his ruined limb.

Two medics in plain gray smocks rushed in, hoisting the injured child onto a stretcher. The circle of onlooking kids parted silently, unblinking. It was an everyday horror here—another lesson in cruelty.

As the girl rose, trembling from adrenaline, she approached Allison with her head bowed.

A sharp backhand struck her cheek, snapping her head to one side.

"You hesitated," Allison hissed as she retracted the hand. "Hesitation gets you killed!"

A hush settled over the dome. The girl swallowed hard, blinking back tears. She dared not lift her eyes.

Allison turned from her without further comment, looking back at the circle of waiting trainees. No child so much as flinched under her scrutiny. She gave a small, curt nod at the scientists observing from the balcony. Their camera still rolled, capturing every brutal second for the Council's research logs.

"Next two," she ordered. "One-One-Nine and Three-O-Two!"

A wiry boy of about nine stepped forward, clenching his fists in anticipation of another grueling match.

However, after a brief pause, it became clear there would be no second challenger. The children seated along the curved walls exchanged wary glances, but no one spoke.

Allison's gaze scanned the small figures. She caught sight of Three-O-Two, a frail-looking girl slumped with her back against the concrete.

It was Norah. Noah's daughter.

She was now eight—and nothing like she had been when her father had last seen her one year ago. Her head was shaved like all the others, one eye swollen to a purple bruise, her lip split and caked with dried blood. Yet in that moment, she radiated a silent defiance.

Allison's eyes narrowed. "Three-O-Two," she repeated, impatience lacing each syllable. "Are you refusing to fight *again*?"

Norah slowly raised her face. Even with one eye nearly shut, her expression burned with a resolve that belied her slight frame. She spoke through clenched teeth. "Yes, Mother. I am refusing to fight again."

A heavy hush fell over the dome. The other children didn't move a muscle. They knew what was coming all too well.

Allison's nostrils flared in anger. "Then you shall be taught a lesson—once again."

She let out a piercing whistle.

As if triggered by a reflex, the ring of children sprang up in unison. Norah's body went rigid, but she did not rise. The children advanced like a disciplined pack, eyes locked on her. One after another, they began kicking and punching her, each blow landing with a sickening thud.

Norah coiled into herself, arms wrapped around her head as best she could, silent aside from ragged gasps of pain. She refused to fight back, even as each child delivered their strike.

It was a ritual by now—this wasn't the first time she had defied "Mother."

After a minute that felt like an eternity, Allison whistled again. The children immediately halted, returning to their places around the walls with eerie obedience.

In the center, Norah lay curled in a limp ball, her breathing ragged, blood trickling across the floor.

Allison's expression was a mask of cold detachment. "Take her away."

A soldier emerged from a side door. Seizing Norah's arm, he dragged her bruised, half-conscious body across the floor, leaving a faint smear of blood as he passed. The other children kept their eyes forward, betraying no emotion.

Just as the soldier reached the doorway, another entered the chamber going the other way, stopping a few paces behind Allison.

She didn't turn.

"Mother." The voice was low, deferential.

She let a beat of silence pass before responding. "Speak."

"You have a call waiting for you."

Allison exhaled sharply, turned on her heel, and walked past the waiting trainees without another word.

She strode down a stark, narrow corridor, flanked by guards who stiffened at her presence.

A reinforced steel door slid open as she approached her office. Inside, she stepped behind a sleek, black-tinted monitor, tapping a command into the terminal.

The screen flared to life.

Number Twenty-Seven stared back at her.

His face was shadowed, his figure backlit by the sterile glow of a Council war room. His tone was emotionless, but there was a flicker of urgency in his expression.

"Noah Wolf has taken Dr. Knox."

Allison tilted her head slightly, considering the information, the faintest hint of a smirk emerging on her lips.

"Then we should have a good guess at what his next move might be."

TEN

HONG KONG, KOWLOON FINANCIAL DISTRICT | 02:30 HKT | FEBRUARY 18

A LIGHT DRIZZLE GLOSSED THE STREETS OF HONG Kong's Kowloon Financial District, turning neon signage into a kaleidoscope of pinks and blues that reflected off every slick surface.

It was half-past two in the morning, and though the late hour thinned the crowds, the city never fully slept. Night-shift workers and insomniacs bustled through the glistening sidewalks, umbrellas bobbing under the warm glow of street lamps.

The Council's prized Olympus data hub was stored inside a sleek glass skyscraper. Towering fifty-five stories above the neon-soaked streets, its upper floors vanished into a low-hanging cloud bank, giving the entire structure an ethereal glow.

The plan was to enter the building in two ways. Jenny and Neil would enter through the lobby and create a distraction while Noah and Katya would slip in from a neighboring building. Once Noah and Katya reached the mainframe, they would install a device linking Olympus remotely to *Valkyrie*. From there, Wally would hack into the mainframe. As soon as he was in, the team would make its escape.

While Noah and Katya rode the elevator to the roof of an adjoining building, Jenny and Neil assumed their roles for the diversion. Both stumbled across the pavement with exaggerated clumsiness, arms around each other's shoulders, feigning the sloppy joy of inebriated tourists. Jenny—barefoot for effect, holding her stilettos in one hand—rapped the thin heel of one against the pristine glass doors.

Inside the lobby, a handful of security guards manned a semi-circular reception desk. Behind them stretched a wall of monitors displaying hallway feeds, office corridors, and elevator banks. One monitor bank, to the far left, showed a large mainframe room lined with data racks—the fortieth-floor server farm that was their real charge.

As Jenny's tapping echoed on the glass, two of the guards glanced over with disinterest. It was almost three in the morning; they clearly wanted nothing to do with a pair of soggy, loud Westerners making a scene.

One of them motioned in annoyance for the "tourists" to leave, but Jenny persisted, tapping harder, her expression morphing into a clueless, drunken grin.

At last, a guard with a ring of keys hanging at his belt heaved a weary sigh and strode over. He slid a key into the door's electronic lock, which emitted a sharp click. As soon as the door swung open, Jenny and Neil practically tumbled inside.

"Oh, thank you, thank you!" Neil slurred, swaying theatrically. He pretended to fumble for a phone in his pocket. "We are so lost. We were, like... out for... for drinks... somewhere." He spoke in a loose drawl, stumbling over his words just enough to be convincing. "D'you guys, like, speak English?"

One of the guards, a slightly older man with a neat mustache, stepped forward, speaking up with noticeable reluctance. "I do," he said in crisp but accented English. "You're not supposed to be here at this hour. Do you need directions?"

Jenny giggled, running a hand through her wet hair while balancing precariously on one heel. "We're in Hong Kong for a... a big business conference thingy. Went out for cocktails with a... a client? And then—" she patted Neil's chest—"my silly fiancé here lost our phone's GPS."

"Okay," the mustachioed guard sighed, gesturing them farther into the lobby. "We can call you a taxi if you want."

"That... that would be amazing," Neil gushed, feigning relief. He stumbled in a half-circle before "catching" himself on the front of the reception desk. His eyes crossed comically, drawing chuckles from the rest of the security detail.

As for Jenny, she was all smiles and slurred words—except for the moment when the guards' attention locked on to Neil's antics. Under the desk, out of their line of sight, she slipped a tiny black device out of her handbag. With a practiced flick of her fingers, she adhered it to the underside of the reception countertop.

The device emitted no sound or telltale light. But in Jenny's earpiece, Wally's voice came through in a clipped whisper: "Okay. I'm in. Placing the cameras into a loop now."

The tiny device was a network tap, designed to silently jack into the building's security feed, intercepting camera footage, keycard logs, and alarm protocols, feeding everything back to Wally aboard the *Valkyrie*.

Jenny straightened, painting a look of drunken confusion on her face. "Um, sorry... where can I—like—sit down?" she asked, turning on a wobbly heel.

At that instant, the bank of lobby monitors jittered. The real-time video feeds flickered, then stabilized, now stuck on footage from an hour before—a quiet, empty building.

The glitch went unnoticed by the guards, who were too busy watching Neil lurch sideways, almost falling, prompting another round of laughter.

ELEVEN

A DAMP WIND SWEPT OVER THE ROOFTOP OF THE neighboring skyscraper, brushing against Noah's and Katya's dark clothing. High above Kowloon's neon-lit streets, the two of them stood at the edge of the building. Rain beaded on the carbon-fiber surfaces of their harnesses and compressed gas guns.

Katya took a single step forward and raised her gun—a sleek launcher that fired suction-cup grapples. She lined up the angle on the skyscraper across the street.

With a soft *pfft*, the grappling cup shot out, trailing a thin cord behind it. It struck the glass façade, latching on with a sharp hiss.

Noah did the same a few meters away, establishing a second line. Both reels locked tight, the wires creating a slight downward angle between the two buildings.

A shared nod signaled their readiness. They clipped harnesses to the lines, then leaned over the edge without hesitation. The wind whipped at their clothes, and for a moment, they were suspended in midair over the dizzying drop.

Before—

They zipped down toward the skyscraper's fortieth-floor windows, silent as shadows sliding through the dark.

Rain splattered on the tinted glass as they braked to a controlled stop. Katya pressed a compact cutting device to the surface, the device humming as the glass parted in a neat circle.

Together, they slipped inside, boots landing on plush carpet in an unoccupied office space. Noah tapped his earpiece, voice hushed yet resolute.

"We're in."

TWELVE

Neil leaned heavily against the lobby's marble reception desk, a wide, glassy-eyed grin pasted across his face. "No, no, listen—" he slurred, his voice reverberating slightly in the high-ceilinged space, "I swear, we were in the taxi, and the driver was all... all... speaking, like, Chinese—or Cantonese, or, or... is it Mandarin? And I told him, I said, 'Buddy, just drop us off at the big building... you know, the, the big one.'"

The older guard with the mustache couldn't hold back a chuckle. Another guard, younger and less amused, scowled from his seat behind the monitors. "Let's hope your taxi is here soon."

"Oh, sure, sure!" Neil swayed dangerously, his hands flailing as though to steady himself. "I'll wait right... here." He thumped the desk as if to prove his point, letting loose a manic little laugh. "Hey, can you believe it? We're here in Hong Kong for a... a— what's it called, babe?" He turned to Jenny, who had perched herself on a leather bench near the door.

Jenny flicked her gaze up from her phone. "A... a business... summit, I think?" she mumbled, as though barely coherent. "Some conference with, like... bigwigs."

The old guard leaned forward. "You two must've had quite the night."

Neil launched into a theatrical sigh. "You have no idea. Like, we went to this bar—it had a giant fish tank in the middle! I mean, imagine! A fish tank in a bar. The fish, they were glowing!"

Behind the desk, the bank of monitors continued to display the looped footage Wally had set in motion, none of the guards suspecting that two intruders were roaming the building's upper floors.

THIRTEEN

Silence reigned over the fortieth floor as Noah and Katya glided between towering racks of servers—the entire floor one big server room. The space glowed with the faint pulse of status LEDs, blue lights cascading in regular intervals across polished aluminum housings.

Reaching the main relay panel, Noah knelt down and ran a gloved hand along its base, searching for the right access point. Finding a maintenance port tucked beneath the housing, he pried open the panel just enough to work. He withdrew a slim, disc-like uplink device from a protective pouch on his vest, then fished out a thin fiber-optic cable from its side. With precise movements, he slid the cable into the port, securing the connection before pressing the device flush against the inside of the panel. A recessed switch clicked, and a soft green light pulsed around the edges—confirmation it was now feeding data to the relay.

Satisfied, Noah closed the panel, smoothing it back into place. No outward sign of tampering. Just another silent parasite leeching data from the system.

In his earpiece, Wally's voice crackled in hushed excitement. "Link established. Give me a second to sync up."

Noah eased upright. Katya stood poised near the room's

entrance, shoulders tensed, eyes constantly flicking among the dim corners. The gloom mixed with the pulsing electronics made for an unsettling dance of light and shadow.

"We need to move," Katya muttered. "There's a security patrol scheduled in two minutes."

Wally's channel crackled slightly. "Almost there... and—"

But before he could finish, the entire chamber went dark in a single, deafening moment. The servers' hum died, the overhead lighting vanished, and the crisp hum of air conditioning cut off, leaving a vacuum-like silence.

Noah's heart hammered at the sudden shift—this wasn't part of the plan.

Then, just as abruptly, power surged back into the room. Every screen, every panel, every monitor shimmered to life, bathing the floor in a harsh electric glow. But instead of the usual streams of code or the Council's sealed interface, a single face dominated every display: Allison Peterson.

She stared out from dozens of screens, a faint, triumphant smirk curving her lips. Her voice echoed in the quiet, somehow intimate and mocking all at once.

"Noah Wolf," she said. "Ever the predictable one."

Noah bristled, his jaw clenching. In the reflected light, Katya's hand touched her pistol. She took a half-step toward Noah, as if expecting an ambush to materialize from the shadows.

Allison's voice continued in a calm, cutting tone. "Did you think I wouldn't see this coming? You were always smart, but not that smart. You just walked into the lion's den."

A tense silence followed, broken only by the faint hum of the servers rebooting. In the hush, Noah's earpiece sputtered static—Wally was trying to reconnect, but the system had clearly been hijacked at a higher level.

Noah squared his shoulders, his eyes fixed on Allison's expression across the wall of screens. Adrenaline surged through his veins, a potent mix of dread and determination. Despite the predicament, he felt the old, familiar steel creeping into his spine.

FOURTEEN

Down in the lobby, the mood took a chilling turn the instant the building's glass doors hissed shut and locked automatically. The soft overhead lighting caught on the reinforced glass panes, causing them to glimmer menacingly as the maglocks clamped into place with a resonant click. Every security guard tensed, attention snapping away from Neil's comical antics.

"What's going on?" one guard muttered, stepping away from the desk to inspect the doors.

Neil, feigning a drunken stumble, lifted his gaze to Jenny, whose posture shifted ever so slightly. She sensed trouble even before the heavy thudding of rotor blades reached her ears.

It grew louder, the sound of an approaching helicopter roaring over the street, rattling the glass. A harsh cone of light suddenly blinked on from its underbelly spotlight, casting the rain-soaked streets in a garish glow.

All eyes in the lobby turned to the front entrance as the black tactical helicopter slid into view, hovering just meters above the pavement.

Jenny's stomach lurched. Not good.

Two figures—each clad in matte-black combat gear and

wielding imposing M249 SAW machine guns—fast-roped down with cat-like grace, landing in the drizzle-spattered street.

They raised their weapons.

The nearest security guard gawked. "Who the hell are—"

He never finished. Gunfire ripped through the lobby in a sudden, thunderous eruption. The Elite assassins hammered away with the belt-fed machine guns, unleashing a storm of 5.56mm rounds that chewed through the glass façade with catastrophic force. Shards exploded inward in a glittering wave, slicing through the air and cutting viciously into anything in their path.

Neil and Jenny sprang into action.

Gone was any pretense of drunkenness—survival was the only priority now. As bullets sparked off the marble floor, they dove behind the reception desk. Time slowed to a brutal crawl. The once-distant hum of city traffic was supplanted by the deafening rattle of sustained fire and the splintering shrieks of shattering glass.

Several guards were cut down almost immediately, their bodies riddled with bullets before they could even reach for their sidearms. Blood pooled in widening circles on the polished floor, the stench of cordite and death mingling in the lobby's suddenly stagnant air.

Gasping, Jenny reached out and grabbed a service pistol from one of the fallen guards. Her fingers were slick with the guard's blood, but she yanked the weapon free.

"Well, so much for subtlety!" Neil hissed, pressing himself tight against the desk.

More gunfire. Splinters of marble and glass pelted their cover, scattering like shrapnel.

Jenny wiped blood spatter from her cheek and forehead, clearing it from her eyes. A quick peek over the reception desk confirmed her worst fears: The assassins had fanned out, one maintaining suppressive fire, the other advancing through the blasted remains of the entry. Rain blew in through the shattered doors, whipped into a spray by the helicopter's rotors as it ascended back into the air.

Jenny gripped the pistol. No time to wait—the only path was forward.

"Cover me," she breathed.

In the glow of shattered fluorescents and flickering neon, the first shots of their fightback rang out as the night erupted into thunderous chaos.

FIFTEEN

Noah and Katya sprinted through the server room, weaving between towering racks of hardware. Allison's mocking face still flickered across the screens, a silent taunt they had no time to answer. Their only option was escape.

As they left the server room and entered a corridor running along the outer edge of the building, floor-to-ceiling glass stretched beside them, revealing the vast cityscape beyond.

Noah felt it before he saw it—a faint tremor in the panes, a ripple distorting the city's reflections. He barely had time to process the disturbance before a massive shape lurched into view.

A tactical helicopter rose from the depths of the skyline, climbing fast, its black fuselage slick with rain. It came parallel to them and went into a hover, its nose tilting toward them like a predator locking on to prey.

Searchlights flared to life, flooding them in stark white.

Noah and Katya skidded to a halt, still feet away from their zip-line anchors—close enough to see them, too far to reach before the chopper had them in its sights.

In the open side door, a Council soldier gripped the handles of a mounted M134 Minigun, the six-barreled rotary monster built for sheer, unrelenting firepower. A thin red targeting laser flickered erratically across the windows, swiping over banks of desks and computer servers.

When it settled close to them, their stomachs lurched.

"MOVE!"

The minigun erupted in a deafening roar, barrels spinning with lethal speed. A hail of 7.62mm rounds tore into the building's exterior, shredding glass and steel in a shower of deadly fragments. Sparks flew, and the screech of rounds ricocheting off structural supports rang out in high, grating echoes.

Noah and Katya hurled themselves sideways just in time, rolling across the floor to find a semblance of cover behind a thick concrete pillar. Fragments of shattered glass and bullet-pelted drywall rained down. A relentless stream of bullets continued to gouge out huge chunks of the office floor, shredding the desks and blowing out windows in a cacophony of destruction.

Katya looked at Noah, breathing hard, her face streaked with sweat and rain. "You have a plan?"

Noah inhaled, tasting the tang of concrete dust. "Survive" was his answer. He glanced back at the zip-lines—and at the helicopter that blocked them.

Another barrage hammered the structural pillars, rattling them and sending fine clouds of debris across the floor.

They were pinned down, the exit sealed by an airborne juggernaut. Noah scanned their surroundings with narrowed eyes, searching for a path to reach the protection of the server core or the stairwell—anything to break the pilot's line of sight.

But as bullets whined overhead like metal wasps, Noah silently cursed. There didn't appear to be any exit. And with the minigun's ceaseless barrage, time was fast running out.

SIXTEEN

Gunfire reverberated faintly from above, but here in the main lobby, the battle had narrowed to an enclosed, lethal confrontation.

Neil hunched behind the reception desk, breath ragged, fingers tightening around an empty pistol. Splintered wood and shell casings littered the floor around him. A few feet away, Jenny pressed herself against a concrete pillar, its surface pockmarked with fresh bullet holes.

Both of them were out of ammunition.

Opposite them, the two Elite assassins paused to reload, their machine guns clacking and hissing as empty drum magazines clattered to the ground.

Jenny and Neil exchanged a knowing look—this was their moment.

They burst from cover as one. The assassins dropped into guarded stances, forced to discard their M249 SAW machine guns as they narrowly dodged Jenny's and Neil's opening strikes.

As the four of them circled each other, the assassins unsheathed their blades. One carried a KA-BAR, its clip-point edge designed for deep, lethal cuts—the type that render flesh from bone. The other gripped a Fairbairn-Sykes dagger, its tapered double-edged blade built for quick, precise thrusts.

Jenny exhaled slowly, rolling her shoulders, her karambit flashing in her grip.

"So it's a knife fight, then," she muttered.

Neil had no blade, no weapon of his own. Just the debris-strewn wreckage of the lobby. He'd have to improvise.

The KA-BAR slashed for his midsection, a vicious reverse grip arc meant to open his gut, spill his intestines. Neil twisted side-ways, narrowly avoiding the bite of steel, but the assassin adjusted fast, switching to an icepick grip and stabbing down toward his collarbone.

Neil barely deflected it with a forearm-to-forearm block. Twisting away, he grabbed a half-shattered chair and swung it hard. The impact staggered his opponent, but the assassin recovered quickly, lunging again.

Neil backed away until he hit the half-destroyed reception desk, feeling the solid wood press against his spine.

Nowhere to run.

On the other side of the lobby, Jenny sidestepped her opponent's lunge, his dagger slicing the air where her ribs had been seconds before.

He was fast. Too fast. He fought in tight, brutal arcs, using the dagger like a scalpel.

Jenny shifted to a Filipino grip, flipping her karambit into a reverse curve, ready to counter.

The assassin feinted high, then slashed low. Jenny twisted away but not fast enough. The blade ripped through her sleeve, a shallow line of heat carving across her forearm.

She gritted her teeth. No more playing defensive.

As Neil's opponent charged, KA-BAR glinting under the emergency lights, Neil snatched up a telephone from the desk and hurled it, slamming it into the man's face. The impact threw off the strike, giving Neil just enough time to dart into the open.

They circled each other again, breaths heavy, muscles coiled.

The Elite lowered his stance, blade held in a Pakal grip, shifting his weight from one foot to the other. A close-quarters thrust was coming.

But this time, Neil was ready.

As the assassin came at him, Neil caught his wrist, muscles straining, trying to hold the knife at bay. The assassin punched him across the jaw with his free hand, snapping Neil's head back.

Stars exploded in his vision.

But he didn't let go.

The KA-BAR inched closer, closer—until the fingers of Neil's free hand brushed the assassin's hip holster.

A pistol.

Neil ripped it free, twisting the assassin's wrist with his other hand at the same time. The man grunted in pain—then Neil fired.

The round punched into the assassin's ribs at point-blank range. He stiffened, eyes wide, then collapsed against the desk, sliding to the floor in a heap.

Neil panted, tasting copper in his mouth. But he didn't waste time.

He sent another bullet into the assassin's forehead. Making sure.

One down.

Jenny lunged in, feinting left before hooking her karambit in a tight upward arc, aiming for the assassin's wrist.

He jerked back, twisting the dagger for a thrust—but Jenny trapped his arm, twisting with her entire body.

The Fairbairn-Sykes dagger clattered to the floor.

Jenny didn't waste a second. She yanked his head forward and slammed her knee into his groin. He choked on the impact, stumbling back toward one of the concrete pillars pockmarked with bullet holes.

Jenny followed, ramming his head against the pillar with bone-cracking force. The assassin slumped, dazed.

She snatched up his own fallen blade and—without hesitation —drove it into his throat.

The man stiffened, gagging as blood spilled down his chest and down his windpipe, choking him.

Then he crumpled.

The lobby went still, save for the distant hum of the helicopter's machine guns above them.

Jenny leaned against the bullet-riddled pillar, breathing hard, her forearm slick with blood.

Neil wiped his mouth, wincing at the pain in his jaw. "You good?"

Jenny nudged the Elite's corpse with her boot, grimacing. "I hate these guys."

The building was still shaking from distant impacts, and somewhere above, Noah and Katya were fighting for their lives.

Jenny rolled her shoulder, gripping her karambit tighter. "The night's not over yet."

Neil sighed, tucking the assassin's pistol into his waistband. "Yeah. No kidding."

They moved on, glass crunching underfoot, ready for whatever came next.

SEVENTEEN

BULLETS RICOCHETED OFF STEEL BEAMS, SENDING sparks spiraling into the air of the fortieth floor. Alarms wailed from half-destroyed panels on the walls. Smoke billowed from ruined computer terminals. The once-sterile server room was now unrecognizable, transformed into a war zone of overturned desks, broken glass, and electrical fires sputtering in fits of neon sparks. Outside, the rain-lashed Hong Kong skyline glowed in the distance, a backdrop to the shrieking rotor blades closing in.

Noah and Katya stood back to back in the debris. A short lull had fallen—the pockets of gunfire had paused as their attackers regrouped—but the telltale thump of helicopter rotors grew louder, signaling more danger closing in. Their eyes darted to the shattered row of windows overlooking a thirty-nine-story drop.

Katya flicked a quick, tense glance at Noah. Her hair whipped around her face in the gusts blowing through the broken glass. "We can't hold out here much longer."

Noah nodded curtly. "I won't argue with that."

He raised his eyes to the gaping window and spotted the tactical helicopter floating into view, its spotlight casting a stark beam across the wreckage. The rotor wash blasted through, ruffling documents and sending the sparks from the fires dancing in the wind.

He clenched his jaw. "There's only one thing left to do."

"What?"

"We take the chopper," he stated with certainty, already moving from cover.

Katya blinked. "You're insane."

A thin, wry smile curved Noah's lips. "I know."

The corridor behind them erupted in automatic fire again. Bullets slammed into columns, biting out chunks of concrete.

Noah saw his opening and took off in a sprint.

Time seemed to slow. Bullets whizzed overhead, the crackling discharge echoed. Ribs aching, lungs burning, Noah vaulted a twisted metal beam and flung himself off the ledge.

He was airborne.

Thirty-nine floors below yawned a lethal chasm.

Clank.

His hands found the helicopter's landing skid, gripping the cold metal so hard his knuckles went white.

Inside the cockpit, the door gunner whirled the minigun barrels downward toward Noah. The metallic scream of spinning barrels cut through the roar of the rotors.

But Noah was faster.

Hanging one-handed from the skids, he raised his pistol and fired a single shot into the gunner's chest at near-point-blank range before the first bullet left the spinning barrels. A strangled grunt, and the gunner slumped lifelessly over the minigun.

Behind Noah, Katya emerged at the destroyed window.

She didn't hesitate.

Taking two running steps, she leapt, arms extending in a midair grapple that latched on to the side of the cockpit door. She swung in an arc around the doorframe, hooking her leg onto the skid to pull herself inside.

The pilot—eyes wide—fumbled for a sidearm and shouted muffled threats that drowned in the engine's din.

Katya was on him in seconds.

She seized him by the neck, slamming him back against the seat. As he struggled, she drew a knife and plunged it into his chest, burying the blade to the hilt. His scream caught in his throat, eyes bulging with shock. She yanked the blade free, and his body slumped. With a final shove, she sent him tumbling out the open doorway into the dark void below.

Noah hauled himself up, swinging his legs over the edge and planting his boots firmly on the chopper's floor.

Katya was already sliding into the pilot's seat, hands moving over the controls. The helicopter lurched slightly, stabilizing as she took command.

"Strap yourself in, Jonas," she called over her shoulder. "I need a second to take us out of hover mode."

Noah pulled himself into the co-pilot seat, scanning the cockpit.

The radio panel was dark, no chatter, no signals.

Katya noticed it at the same time. Her eyes flicked toward the comms panel, brow furrowing.

"Jamming device."

She reached under the console, flipping open a secured panel and revealing a small black box with a blinking red LED. Her fingers moved swiftly over the controls, locating the toggle switch embedded on its side. With a quick flick, she shut it off, the LED fading to black.

A faint static crackle burst through their comms, then—

"—the hell is going on up there?! Noah! Katya! Come in!"

It was Jenny.

Noah exhaled, pressing a hand to his earpiece.

"We read you, Jenny," he said. "We have the helicopter."

A brief silence. Then: "You stole their chopper?" Neil's voice, incredulous.

Katya smirked, already working the cyclic stick, angling the nose of the helicopter downward. "We're coming to get you," she said.

Overhead, the stolen helicopter descended, its rotor wash whipping rain and debris into a violent swirl. Jenny and Neil burst from the ruined lobby, boots hammering against the slick pavement. The landing skids barely touched down before the side door slid open.

"Go, go, go!" Noah's voice crackled in their earpieces.

Jenny didn't need to be told twice. She grabbed Neil by the collar and sprinted full-tilt.

At the far end of the street, a black SUV screeched into view, tires screaming on wet pavement as it came to a shuddering stop.

Doors flew open. Gunmen spilled out, weapons raising.

"We got company!" Neil shouted, scrambling up onto the skid.

Jenny vaulted after him, grabbing the frame just as Katya gunned the throttle.

The chopper lurched violently, jerking into an unstable hover as bullets clanged against the undercarriage. Below, more Council operatives fanned out, trying to get a clear shot.

Jenny hauled herself inside, twisting midair to lay down cover fire with the pistol she'd taken off the dead Elite. Her rounds pinged off the SUV's hood, forcing the gunmen to duck for cover.

Neil sprawled onto the floor, panting. "Okay—" he wheezed, "—time to leave."

Noah swiveled in his seat. "Katya—get us clear."

Katya yanked the cyclic control, tilting the nose upward and sending the chopper into a sharp climb over the neon-lit skyline. The skyscrapers blurred past, rain streaking against the glass.

Below them, the gunmen scrambled for heavier weapons—shouldering a rocket launcher.

Noah's eyes narrowed. "RPG!"

A streak of fire and smoke erupted from the street, spiraling up toward them.

Katya jerked the stick left, the chopper banking just in time. The missile screamed past the tail rotor, missing by inches before detonating against the high-rise in a fireball of shattered glass.

Katya leveled out the chopper, fingers white-knuckled on the controls. The explosion from the RPG lit up the storm-choked sky behind them, a fireball swallowing half a floor of glass and steel.

"That was close," Neil muttered.

"Too close," Jenny added.

Noah was already scanning the city below, eyes sweeping the rooftops and intersections—but it wasn't the gunmen on the ground that sent his pulse spiking.

It was the second helicopter, cutting through the storm like a predatory bird.

"We've got another chopper incoming."

Jenny twisted around, catching sight of sleek black rotor blades slicing through the rain, its spotlight flicking on and locking on to them like a sniper's scope.

Then came the muzzle flash.

A blistering hail of machine-gun fire erupted from the second helicopter, streaking toward them.

"Hang on!" Katya barked.

The stolen chopper lurched violently, rotors screaming as tracer rounds tore through the air, punching holes in the fuselage.

A sudden, deafening burst of rounds slammed into the side panel, sending a shower of sparks and shredded metal flying into the cockpit.

Neil instinctively ducked, shielding his head. "Not good! Really not good!"

Noah gritted his teeth. "Jenny, get on the door gun! We need to return fire!"

Without delay, Jenny grabbed the side-mounted M134 mini-gun, yanking it into position. The barrels spun, whining to life, then roared. A storm of lead spewed into the night, bullets slamming toward the enemy chopper.

But their pursuers were fast, skilled, and maneuvering aggressively.

The second helicopter banked hard, dodging the worst of the gunfire while unleashing another vicious burst.

Rounds slammed into the tail boom of their chopper. Warning lights flickered across the console.

Jenny cursed, gripping the side handle. "We need to lose them —fast!"

Katya's fingers tightened on the controls. "Hang on," she muttered.

She threw the helicopter into a sudden dive, weaving between glowing skyscrapers in a near-vertical descent. The city blurred past as they hurtled toward the streets—too fast, too reckless.

For a second, Noah thought she'd lost control.

Then, at the last moment, she wrenched the chopper back up, threading through two glass towers so close that the rotor tips nearly grazed the windows.

The pursuing operatives had no such skill.

Their helicopter, trying to mimic the maneuver, clipped the side of a building—spinning wildly before slamming into an office complex in a fireball of twisted steel and glass.

"Shit," Neil muttered, watching the flaming wreckage spiral downward.

Katya finally leveled out, breathing hard. "We're clear."

Noah exhaled, leaning back against the seat. He shot Jenny a look, then Neil. They were alive. Barely.

Jenny wiped rain from her face, half-laughing, half-scowling. "What the hell happened to our smooth operation?"

Noah steely-faced. "They knew we were coming."

Katya snorted, banking west. "Then let's get the hell out of here."

The city faded behind them, lost in the haze of rain, fire, and sirens.

They weren't safe.

But they were one step ahead.

For now.

EIGHTEEN

THE STOLEN COUNCIL HELICOPTER HURTLED THROUGH the dark Hong Kong skies. Its rotors pounded out a relentless rhythm that matched the frantic pulse in its occupants' veins.

Beyond the cockpit windshield, the sprawling metropolis vanished behind a cloak of cloud and rain, replaced by the vast blackness of the South China Sea. At just before four in the morning, everything felt draped in secrecy, the stars smothered by heavy clouds.

Inside the chopper, the team bore the marks of their narrow escape. Katya's temple was streaked with dried blood, Jenny's jacket torn, Neil's knuckles bruised. Noah, gripping the side rail of the cockpit, tasted copper in his mouth—a reminder of the fierce firefight they'd left behind. Yet each of them clung to the adrenaline still surging through their bodies, fueled by equal parts survival and desperation.

The only real light in the cramped cabin came from a dim overhead panel and the green glow of instrument screens. Katya pushed the controls hard, coaxing every ounce of speed from the stolen bird.

Noah leaned forward, adjusting the comm frequency on his headset. "Wally, do you copy? We're inbound."

Static crackled back through the earpiece. For a beat, the line hissed with nothing but white noise. Then fragments of Wally's voice cut in, distant and distorted.

"...Noah... We're... under att—..."

Noah shot upright, heart thudding. "Repeat that!" he snapped. "Wally, what's happening?"

More static assaulted his ears. Each of them strained to listen but could only make out partial words in the garbled chaos. Suddenly, a new voice broke through—clear, mocking, and painfully familiar.

"Noah, are you there?"

Noah's grip tightened on the side rail. Across the cockpit, Jenny and Neil exchanged sharp glances. Katya's hands flexed over the cyclic stick.

"Allison," Noah said, his voice flat. "I was wondering when you'd show up."

A soft chuckle. "Oh, I've been here, Noah. Watching. Waiting. Letting you think you were outmaneuvering us."

Neil leaned forward, adjusting the comms interface. "How the hell is she on our frequency?"

Allison answered as if she'd heard him. "You didn't really think I'd let you waltz into Olympus' mainframe without consequence, did you?"

Jenny's expression darkened. "Shit."

Noah's jaw clenched. "What have you done?"

"Not me, Noah. You."

A brief silence. Then "You gave us exactly what we needed."

Noah felt his pulse spike. The cockpit was too quiet now, the weight of realization settling in.

"The uplink," Katya murmured.

Allison hummed in mock approval. "Very good, Katya. That little device you so carefully planted? It did exactly what it was designed to do. Only instead of giving you access to Olympus... it gave us access to you."

Neil cursed under his breath. "They traced us."

Noah's stomach dropped.

Jenny exhaled sharply, eyes flicking to Noah. "They know about the *Valkyrie*."

"I know exactly where you are," Allison continued, her tone turning almost playful. "And so does my strike team."

Katya's knuckles whitened on the controls, pushing the stolen gunship toward its limits. Neil's face was grim, a flicker of fear behind his eyes as he tried to wrestle the frequency back to Wally's voice.

But only static replied. Noah could picture Allison's smug expression on the other end, the Council's top enforcer ready to deliver yet another blow. If she truly had found the *Valkyrie*...

"Hang on, Wally," Noah muttered. "We're coming."

The helicopter surged on through the stormy night, slicing through wind and rain, headed for the inky void where the *Valkyrie* waited.

Or so they hoped.

The black horizon became fractured with streaks of orange and red, distant flames licking at the rain-soaked sky.

Jenny's breath hitched. "No..."

Noah squinted through the windshield, his heart hammering. There—just past the curling mist—thick plumes of smoke rose from the *Valkyrie*. A deep crimson glow pulsed beneath the blackness, fire reflecting off the waves like molten glass.

Neil leaned forward, eyes wide. "Tell me that's not what I think it is."

Katya said nothing, jaw tight as she forced the helicopter lower. The ocean churned below them, the wind whipping salt spray against the glass, but there was no mistaking the silhouette of their ship—wounded, burning, fighting to stay afloat.

Noah touched his comms earpiece again. "Wally! Do you copy?"

A high-pitched whine pierced the earpiece, followed by the deep rumble of explosions.

Then Wally's voice—frantic, barely audible over the chaos.

"—HULL BREACHED—FIRE IN ENGINE BAY—HIT US FAST—"

Jenny swallowed hard. "Son of a bitch."

Noah's mind raced. The *Valkyrie* had stealth countermeasures, radar jammers, encrypted comms. It wasn't just a ship; it was a ghost in the water.

Except now it wasn't.

Allison had burned its cloak away.

"How bad?" Noah demanded.

A violent boom cracked through the comms, followed by Wally's strained voice. "Real bad! They're dropping ordnance—fast movers in the air—*CRRRKKK*!"

Katya tightened her grip on the cyclic stick. "Then we get there before they finish the job."

Neil grabbed a pair of binoculars, focusing through the storm. His expression darkened. "I see the attack choppers."

The *Valkyrie* was illuminated by leaping flames and the bright lances of helicopter floodlights. Council gunships hovered overhead, their harsh beams picking out flashes of black-clad operatives moving across the *Valkyrie's* deck.

Then something else.

Lifeless bodies—a mixture of Noah's crew and Council troopers—were strewn amid twisted metal and flaming debris. Now and then, a Council agent would pause, leveling a sidearm at a wounded figure, executing them without mercy.

Neil sucked in a ragged breath. "Oh my God..."

Katya slammed a fist against the side of the cockpit, rage blazing in her eyes.

Near the *Valkyrie's* helipad, Noah glimpsed Dr. Adrian Knox slumped between two grim-looking operatives, being dragged toward a smaller helicopter.

As they loaded the doctor onboard and the craft lifted into the air, Noah felt a jolt of fury—it was almost tangible, like a physical blow to his chest.

Getting up from the copilot's seat, he went into the back,

seizing the mounted minigun at the helicopter's open door. "Take us in—NOW!"

Katya dipped the nose of their stolen chopper, pushing the engines to redline. Noah squeezed the triggers. A blazing stream of 7.62mm rounds tore across the deck, catching Council operatives in the open. Sparks shot up in frantic spirals as the barrage carved into steel plating and flesh alike.

Council troops scattered beneath the hail of bullets, some returning fire with panicked bursts that pinged harmlessly off the helicopter's armored belly. Others ran for cover behind scorched crates or the remains of the ship's superstructure.

"Stay on them!" Noah barked, shifting his aim. The *Valkyrie's* deck shimmered with muzzle flashes, the night lit by a strobing dance of tracer rounds and leaping sparks.

Katya swung the helicopter low, banking into a swift attack run. The smell of salt water and burning fuel flooded the cockpit. But then a new threat emerged: One of the departing Council choppers pivoted aggressively, its nose dipping as a missile streaked out from under its wing.

"Incoming!" Neil shouted.

A rocket trail carved a brilliant line through the night sky, heading straight for the crippled *Valkyrie*. The impact was instantaneous and catastrophic—an explosion ripped through the lower decks, sending fire and twisted debris rocketing into the air. The ship groaned like a wounded animal, tilting sharply as seawater flooded its compartments.

Jenny's face twisted with fury. "They're sinking her!"

Noah ground his teeth, rage boiling in his chest. "Not before we take a few of them with us."

Secondary explosions rattled the air as internal munitions ignited, throwing columns of flame skyward. In a matter of seconds, the *Valkyrie*—once their roving haven—looked like a gravely injured titan, her hull splitting apart under the furious onslaught.

Two Council helicopters peeled away from the retreating

group, banking toward their chopper in a pincer formation. Katya jerked the cyclic, climbing out of easy range, while Noah braced at the door gun, preparing for another torrent of fire.

From the collapsing decks of the *Valkyrie*, black smoke billowed, illuminated by licking flames. It was a final, tragic tableau of what had once been their fortress at sea, now consumed by a war that had only begun.

Noah held fast to the minigun. Rain pelted him as he watched the first gunship swoop into the crosshairs.

Then he squeezed the trigger.

The multi-barreled weapon roared, spitting a fiery stream of 7.62mm rounds that chewed through metal and rotor blades alike. The enemy bird spun wildly, trailing smoke and flames before crashing into the dark ocean below with a muted *whump*.

An instant later, the second chopper filled Noah's sights. He steadied the minigun, exhaled, and fired. The high-powered rounds punched through the cockpit windshield; the pilot jerked, arms going slack at the controls. The helicopter veered sharply, blades carving the air, before it slammed into the twisted wreck of the *Valkyrie*. An explosion of sparks and fire lit up the night as it disintegrated against the burning hull.

Noah gritted his teeth, scanning for more threats. But the surviving Council aircraft retreated, shrinking into the gloom, flames flickering in their slipstream. Through the cockpit window, they could see one last chopper racing away—Dr. Adrian Knox onboard.

"We lost them!" Jenny panted.

Noah stared at the fleeing silhouette, fists clenched in frustration. "Get us down there. Now."

Katya nodded, angling their battered helicopter toward what remained of the *Valkyrie's* deck. The blaze still raged below, flames licking the stormy night, thick plumes of black smoke spiraling into the sky. Their once-mighty stronghold was almost gone. But wherever there were survivors, Noah intended to find them—and God help any Council operatives still on board.

A harrowing scene greeted them as the helicopter touched down on the dangerously tilting deck. Flames roared from ruptured fuel lines, and bodies—some still smoldering—lay scattered across twisted steel plates. The acrid stench of burning metal and flesh clung to the air. Alarm klaxons wailed, cutting in and out as the ship's systems failed.

Jenny hopped out first, pistol at the ready. Noah followed, stepping onto the slick metal.

Suddenly, a faint burst of static cut through their earpieces. A voice—weak, rasping. Wally.

"Noah?... I'm..."

Noah felt a surge of hope and dread in equal measure. "Wally, where?!" he shouted over the roar of flames and collapsing bulkheads.

Static. Then another tortured whisper. "Below deck... In the... operations room... It's... flooding... You need to... find me... I have..."

It cut out.

Jenny met Noah's gaze. "We don't leave without him."

Noah nodded.

NINETEEN

THE *VALKYRIE'S* FINAL MOMENTS TICKED AWAY beneath their feet as they ran headlong into the ship. Below decks, the air was saturated by the brine of seawater pouring through ruptured bulkheads. The flicker of distant flames above cast an eerie glow through vents and stairwells, illuminating a swirling torrent of water that surged at their ankles, then their knees. Every step felt like wading through quicksand as Noah and Jenny pushed deeper into the sinking ship.

The *Valkyrie* groaned around them, metal shrieking with the strain. Lights overhead flickered weakly. Somewhere in the distance, an explosion reverberated, causing the deck to lurch.

They came to an intersection where the corridor dropped sharply, now fully submerged beneath dark, churning water. Noah flicked on a flashlight, its beam cutting through the murky gloom.

He glanced over his shoulder at Jenny, eyes resolute. "We swim from here."

They both inhaled deeply, then plunged into the icy water. Visibility dropped to near zero. The flashlight's cone danced across mangled metal and drifting corpses that bumped against their legs and shoulders. Noah's lungs tightened at the grim sight, but he pressed forward, forcing his body onward through the tangle of wires and steel.

Their path led them toward the *Valkyrie's* operations room— once a hive of activity and data analysis, now a submerged crypt. The door stood open, and inside they spotted a faint glow from an emergency light rig.

Then they spotted Wally.

He was standing on tiptoes on top of a console, trying to reach the last pocket of air, the water lapping at his chin.

Jenny reached him first. Wally offered a shaky grin, then held up a small waterproof bag. Inside was a single hard drive. "We managed to get several terabytes of data," he croaked, each word interrupted by the frantic rise of water. "The uplink worked. They had to let it stay live long enough to trace us—it was just long enough for us to pull some intel."

Noah's mood momentarily lifted. This could be the break- through they'd risked everything for—data that might help dismantle Olympus. But the ship groaned again, this time more violently, and a sudden tilt told them the *Valkyrie* was moments from being swallowed by the sea.

"Hold your breath," Noah warned, voice muffled by the rising water. He and Jenny each took one of Wally's arms, steadying him.

They filled their lungs with air, then pushed off the sinking console and kicked back out into the corridor, swimming with all the strength they had left.

Chaos erupted behind them—a bulkhead collapsed. A twisted metal beam spiraled through the water, nearly pinning Noah's leg. Jenny slammed into him mid-current, using her body as leverage to yank him free from the beam's path. A searing jolt of pain shot up Noah's shin as it brushed past, but he fought through it, lungs burning for air.

At last, they emerged from the flooded corridor, breaking the surface in what remained of an upper walkway. Gasping for oxygen, they clung to a railing that jutted precariously from the angled deck.

Wally wheezed but clung to the bag holding the hard drive. Jenny's eyes flicked to Noah, ensuring he was able to stand. They were soaked, battered, and surrounded by the final throes of the *Valkyrie's* death agonies—but they were alive, and they had the data that just might save them all.

"We all good?" Noah asked.

Jenny and Wally nodded.

"Then let's go."

The ship lurched violently, metal screeching as another section of the *Valkyrie* tore itself apart beneath the waves. Noah pushed off the half-submerged railing, wincing as his leg throbbed from the impact with the beam. No time for that. They had seconds, maybe less, before the ship was fully swallowed by the South China Sea.

A communications room—partially collapsed, but still intact —stood open on their route to the upper deck.

Noah didn't hesitate. He lunged inside, water sloshing against his boots, and snatched up an encrypted SATCOM device from a wall-mounted case.

Jenny threw him a glance. "What the hell are you doing?"

"We need a way to talk that the Council can't listen in on."

Noah shoved the device into his pouch, sealing it tight. "If we get out of here, we'll need to stay dark."

Wally glanced warily at the tilting corridor. "Emphasis on *if.*"

Another explosion rocked the ship, nearly sending them sprawling. The deck pitched again—steeper this time. The *Valkyrie* wasn't just sinking—it was rolling.

"Move!" Noah shouted.

They scrambled forward, gripping on to anything stable. The corridor buckled—pipes ruptured overhead, spraying steaming water, forcing them to duck as they pushed forward.

They burst onto the upper deck.

Wind-driven salt spray lashed the *Valkyrie's* dying deck, the once-majestic warship now reduced to a collapsing hull. Explosions and fire had ripped through her steel heart, leaving only the stern desperately clinging above the waves. Smoke billowed into the overcast sky, mingling with the acrid stench of burning metal and spilled fuel.

With great skill, Katya managed to hover the stolen Council helicopter inches above the pitching deck, its rotor wash whipping flames and debris in every direction. The tilt of the ship made any kind of landing impossible; with every heave, the deck groaned, sliding inch by inch into the hungry sea.

Inside the chopper, Neil hung halfway out the side door, rifle braced against his shoulder. Amid the chaos, a Chinese Coast Guard vessel had appeared on the horizon, its searchlights slicing through the gloom. Whether they came to help or intercept, there was no time to find out. Neil fired a few warning shots in their direction, muzzle flashes strobing against the swirling smoke.

"HURRY, GET ON NOW!" Katya shouted over the comms.

From below, Jenny and Noah raced across what remained of the stern. Between them, Wally staggered forward, still clutching the watertight bag pressed tightly to his chest.

A jagged tear in the hull lurched as the ship's final compartments gave way. The entire deck tilted at a sickening angle, water streaming over railings and gushing through shattered bulkheads. Flames hissed in the spray.

Jenny shoved Wally toward the helicopter's open door. Neil leaned out, grabbing Wally and hauling him up. The moment Wally was safely inside, Jenny scrambled up the skid. She spared a glance over her shoulder to see Noah hesitate—just for a beat—turning his head to look at the *Valkyrie* one last time.

They had lived on this ship, fought for it, bled for it. It had been their sanctuary after the fall of E & E, a place where they'd regrouped and planned their battle against the Council. Now it tilted sharply, the bow disappearing beneath the black water in a roar of churning foam. Fragments of deck plating, supply crates, and debris vanished into the hungry ocean. Bodies of fallen crew and Council invaders alike drifted in the swirling current.

The ship gave one final, tortured groan. Noah's jaw tightened. He stared at the chaos of flames and ruin—then forced himself to turn away.

Jenny grabbed his arm, pulling him aboard. Katya couldn't hold the helicopter any longer; it bucked under the rising tide of heat that came from the burning remains. With everyone in, she yanked on the controls, lifting them away from the doomed vessel.

For a wrenching moment, the old warship stood upright against the sky—then it sank beneath the waves in a cacophony of metal and foam, swallowed by the dark sea.

The *Valkyrie* was gone.

TWENTY

A JAGGED LINE OF DENSE JUNGLE AND PRISTINE WHITE sand stretched out below as the helicopter limped over Vuhus Island. Dawn's early light caught the smoke trailing from its battered tail, rendering it a ghostly plume against a pale sky. Inside the cockpit, warning klaxons blared, red lights flickering in a rapid, anxious rhythm.

Katya's bloodless knuckles gripped the controls. "Brace!" she shouted over the roar of failing engines.

The chopper slammed into the beach with a jarring thud. Sand exploded in all directions, half-burying the landing skids and sending the helicopter lurching forward. For a moment, it threatened to flip nose-first, but the fuselage groaned, the rotors whined, and it settled back with a final, shuddering impact. Alarms died as the engines sputtered their last breath, leaving only the sound of crashing waves.

Neil exhaled a shaky groan from the rear of the cabin. "I think I just lost five years off my life."

Jenny forced the side door open, letting in a rush of salt-laden air. She jumped down onto the sand, rifle at the ready, scanning the immediate area for threats. One by one, the others followed, muscles aching from the crash and the battle just hours before. Noah brought up the rear, helping Wally clamber out. The scientist still clutched the precious hard drive, his face pale with exhaustion.

Behind them, the once-stolen, bullet-riddled helicopter hissed and crackled. Smoke curled from punctured panels. It looked like it might collapse under its own weight at any second—beyond salvage, beyond repair. Another symbol of how much they'd lost in this war.

Noah squinted across the desolate beach, dawn light glinting off rippling surf. Palm trees swayed inland, where thick jungle promised at least some cover. The *Valkyrie* was gone, and now their final mode of escape lay dying in the sand. They were truly stranded.

Still, Noah refused to succumb to despair. "Move," he ordered. "We need to get inland before anyone spots us."

Without another word, they began trudging across the beach, gathering whatever weapons and supplies they could salvage from the crash. The sun climbed higher, the day promising merciless heat. They were alive—for now. But with no ship, no chopper, and half the Council on their trail, survival had just become a far steeper climb.

An hour into their trek, daylight broke through the canopy in streaks of gold, illuminating towering palms and vine-entangled trunks. The dense foliage pressed in from all sides, swallowing the team's footsteps into a hush of insects and distant bird calls.

Noah took point, combat knife in hand, clearing a narrow path through the tangle of branches. Behind him, Katya, Jenny, and Neil trudged on, cautious eyes scanning for any sign of threats. Wally kept pace a few steps behind.

Eventually, the jungle gave way to a small rocky cove, its narrow inlet offering a hidden refuge from prying eyes. Waves lapped gently against the shore, a stark contrast to the chaos they had barely escaped. Tall cliffs curved around the inlet, their jagged faces overgrown with creeping vines, offering natural cover from aerial surveillance.

Noah halted near a cluster of boulders, eyes sweeping the perimeter. The cove was empty. Safe—for now.

Jenny exhaled. "All right. We made it. Now what?"

Noah unslung his pack, kneeling on the damp sand. Without a word, he pulled out the encrypted SATCOM device.

Neil raised an eyebrow. "You planning to call Mom and Dad?"

Noah ignored him, flipping the unit open and booting up the signal relay. The green indicator pulsed to life, and for the first time since their escape, a secure channel flickered onto the screen.

Jenny's gaze hardened. "Who are we calling?"

Noah let out a slow breath. "An old team."

That got everyone's attention.

Katya frowned. "E & E?"

"Yeah." Noah kept his voice even as he continued calibrating the device. "One of the old shadow teams based in East Asia went dark after the collapse. I heard whispers they relocated to Luzon."

Neil let out a low whistle. "And you think they'll help us?"

Noah glanced up. "I think they're our only option."

Jenny folded her arms. "If they're still alive."

"They are." Noah keyed in the frequency, then held the SATCOM speaker closer. A low, rhythmic static hummed over the line as the signal sought a response.

For a long, painful moment, nothing.

Then—a click.

A deep voice crackled through the speaker.

"This is Shadow Three. Identify yourself."

Noah didn't hesitate.

"This is Wolf. I need an extraction."

A sharp pause on the other end. Then a faint chuckle.

"You always find a way to stir up hell, don't you, Noah?"

Noah's grip tightened on the device. "Can you help us or not?"

Another pause. "Where are you?"

"The southeast shore of Vuhus."

"Then you're lucky. We're not far from you—in Sabtang. Keep your signal open. Extraction en route."

"See you soon, Shadow Three," Noah replied. He then turned to the others. "We hold here."

TWENTY-ONE

Through the pale haze of morning, the fishing boat looked more like a ghost gliding across the calm waters. Its hull bore the battered scars of countless clandestine runs, and the single, sputtering engine hummed low enough to be missed by all but the keenest ears. As it pulled up to the rocky shoreline, the boatman—an ex-E & E smuggler with sharp, hawk-like features—eyed Noah and his team with guarded caution.

They wasted no time. The moment the boat nosed up against the makeshift landing spot, Jenny and Katya scrambled aboard. Neil followed, hauling Wally and his precious hard drive. Finally, Noah hopped onto the creaking deck, scanning the horizon for any sign of approaching Council patrols.

"We need to be careful," the boatman warned, voice just loud enough to carry over the water's soft lap against the hull.

"That's our default mode," Jenny returned dryly.

The boatman exhaled through his nose, leaning into the throttle. "Council patrols are in the area," he went on. "They found your abandoned chopper on the other side of the island a few minutes ago. It won't be long before they're here."

Noah shot Jenny a quick look, and with a nod, she untied the mooring line. "Push off. We don't have time to waste."

The little vessel's engine revved in subdued desperation, churning the water behind it. As it glided away from Vuhus Island's shore, the team crouched low, eyes trained on the distant tree line. They all felt it—that thin wire of anxiety winding tighter, knowing the Council might already be converging on their location.

Above, the morning sun broke through gray cloud cover, washing the world in a soft, deceptive warmth. In that fragile light, the boat and its secretive passengers vanished into the wide expanse of the Philippine Sea—fleeing the Council's reach for one more precarious moment.

For eight tense hours, they wove through the azure waters of the Philippine archipelago, threading past coral reefs and skirting the edges of remote islands that rose green and lush from the sea. The boatman—ever vigilant—steered through narrow channels and shallow inlets, ensuring that the small vessel stayed out of sight from coastal radar and curious eyes alike.

At one time, they cut the engine, letting the tide carry them while a Philippines Navy patrol ship churned past in the distance. The team crouched low, exchanging anxious glances as they listened to the thrum of distant engines.

A short while later, a sleek Council patrol boat appeared on the horizon. The boatman cursed under his breath as he killed the motor completely, leaving them drifting aimlessly in the brackish shallows. With guns at the ready, Noah, Katya, and Jenny monitored every shadow that flickered across the water. Their hearts pounded in their chests while the Council boat passed within a mere two hundred meters, its crew scanning the shoreline of a nearby island.

Through careful maneuvering, they slipped away from danger each time, moving ever closer to the main island of Luzon. The sun arced overhead from a clear morning sky to the burnished golds of late afternoon. Hunger and exhaustion gnawed at everyone aboard, but no one dared complain.

Finally, just before dusk, the boatman guided them around a

rocky point that gave way to a long stretch of shoreline. Low mountains framed the horizon inland, lush and remote. Luzon. A cautious sense of relief settled among the group.

Katya exhaled slowly, pulling her rifle strap tighter over her shoulder. Wally, still clutching the hard drive to his chest, managed a weary smile. Neil and Jenny shared a quick nod—small triumphs in a day defined by tension.

They had slipped the Council's net for now, but the war still raged, and the next step remained uncertain.

The boat nosed into the cove's shallows, the keel grinding softly against the wet sand. Jenny and Katya stepped off first, rifles up, scanning the tree line for movement. Neil followed, keeping Wally close, while Noah lingered by the boatman, watching the man reach into his vest and pull out a black, disposable phone.

He offered it to Noah, his expression unreadable.

Noah took it cautiously, lifting it to his ear. Static crackled for half a second before a familiar voice cut through the line—steady, measured, and unmistakably Shadow Three.

"You're late."

Noah's grip tightened around the phone. "We had complications."

Shadow Three snorted. "Yeah, I saw. That wrecked bird of yours made quite the scene. Council's been buzzing like hornets."

Noah ignored the jab. "We need transport."

A pause. "You see it?"

Noah turned, scanning the beach.

There—parked just beyond the tree line—a dark Jeep sat waiting, half-concealed beneath the hanging foliage.

"Got it," Noah said.

Shadow Three's tone remained neutral. "The boatman has the keys."

Before Noah could respond, the hawk-faced smuggler extended his hand—a single key resting in his palm.

Noah took it.

Shadow Three spoke again. "You remember the safehouse we used for the Manilla mission?"

Noah exhaled. "2019."

"That's the one." A faint rustle, like shifting paper, came through the line. "You know how to get there?"

Noah nodded, even though the man couldn't see him. "I do."

A brief silence. "Your prints are still in the system. The security should recognize you."

Jenny arched a brow, watching Noah's face. "Safe?" she asked.

Noah gave a slow nod. "Safe enough."

For now.

Shadow Three's voice dropped slightly. "Clock's ticking, Wolf. Get there fast."

The line went dead.

Noah tossed the phone back to the boatman, who threw it into the water without hesitation.

"Let's go," Noah ordered, heading toward the Jeep.

Jenny slid into the passenger seat, rifle across her lap. Neil, Noah, and Wally took the back, and Katya slid behind the wheel, twisting the key in the ignition.

The engine rumbled to life.

As they sped away from the beach, the jungle swallowed them whole—a path into the unknown and the waiting shadows of the jungle.

TWENTY-TWO

THE JEEP VEERED OFF THE MAIN HIGHWAY AND ONTO A narrow dirt road, its tires jolting over uneven terrain as it snaked through the dense jungle near Mount Pulag. It was night now, pitch-black, the towering trees swallowing what little moonlight remained. Overhanging branches scraped the canvas top, and the headlights revealed thick vines and tangled undergrowth at every twist of the path.

No one spoke.

Tension hung in the humid air, the weariness of the day's ordeals heavy on every face. Finally, the jungle thinned just enough to reveal a barbed wire perimeter fence. A sign at the gate loomed in the headlights:

Department of Science and Technology
Philippine Institute of Volcanology and Seismology
(PHIVOLCS)
SEISMIC MONITORING STATION – NO TRESPASSING

Noah killed the engine. The jungle pressed in from all sides, the dirt road behind them swallowed by darkness.

They had arrived. Finally.

He reached into the glovebox, fingers closing around a small metal key attached to an unmarked tag. Without a word, he stepped out of the Jeep, the night thick with the sweet scent of damp earth and vegetation.

The compound's outer gate loomed ahead—tall, rusted, secured by a heavy chain. No guards. No movement. Just them and the shadows.

Noah unlocked the chain, letting it clatter against the bars. With a firm shove, the gate groaned inward, revealing the shadowy outline of the compound beyond.

Katya took the wheel, driving the Jeep forward, picking Noah up as they passed through the gate.

The PHIVOLCS Seismic Monitoring Station was just as Noah remembered it—minimal lighting, corrugated metal roofs, an outpost forgotten by the world.

They parked near the entrance, then climbed out. The one-story building stuck out of the hillside, partially buried in the mountain. The main door loomed in front of them, a solid slab of reinforced steel with a biometric scanner embedded in the frame.

Noah stepped up, pulse steady, and pressed his thumb against the reader. A soft beep.

Next—the retina scan.

He leaned in, eyes locking on to the scanner's dim green light. Another beep. Then a faint clunk as the locking mechanism disengaged.

The door creaked open.

Inside, the station looked exactly as it had the last time he was here. Flickering fluorescents, a bank of seismographs and satellite monitors, their screens blank. Printouts and old instrument parts littered a battered desk. A single army cot in the corner suggested long nights spent here.

No voices. No allies. No backup. Just them.

Noah stepped inside first, sweeping the space. "Clear."

The others filed in.

"Home sweet home," Neil muttered under his breath, eyeing the dimly lit space.

"It'll do," Katya replied in a clipped tone.

The room felt abandoned, like no one had set foot inside in years. Flickering fluorescents hummed above, casting a cold, sterile light over the old desks and scattered equipment. The air smelled of dust and aging paper, masking the deeper scent of concrete and machine oil.

"It's not all of it," Noah said as he crossed the space.

His boots echoed over the worn tile floor. Against the back wall sat a metal filing cabinet, dented and scratched from years of use.

Jenny raised an eyebrow. "Tell me you didn't bring us here just to look at old paperwork."

Noah ignored her, already reaching for the top drawer.

He pulled it open, letting it rattle on uneven runners. Then, without hesitation, he slid his hand between the rows of manila folders, fingers feeling for the hidden switch.

A faint beep. Followed by a low, mechanical hum.

The entire back wall shuddered, dust shaking loose from the seams. There was a hiss of hidden gears, then a deep groan as the wall eased backward, revealing a narrow corridor lit by recessed LED strips. The air rushed cooler from within, carrying the scent of earth and metal.

Katya's brows lifted slightly.

Jenny took a step forward, peering inside. "Gotta love that government funding," she muttered.

Noah withdrew his hand from the cabinet, glancing at the others. "Let's move."

One by one, they stepped through the opening, leaving

behind the façade of seismographs and satellite monitors. The passage curved downward, leading them into the mountain's core. The cool, underground air wrapped around them, heavy with silence.

Then the space opened up.

A bunker.

Carved from solid rock, reinforced, and hidden beneath layers of jungle and mountain stone. It reminded Noah of the *Valkyrie's* war room—only this one had been here long before them, waiting.

A sanctuary.

Maybe their last one.

Vaulted concrete supports braced the ceiling, while strip lighting along the edges cast the chamber in a stark, utilitarian glow. Along one wall, rows of gun racks displayed an arsenal that ranged from compact submachine guns to long-range sniper rifles and grenade launchers, each neatly secured behind reinforced grates. Nearby shelves offered tactical vests, night-vision goggles, and rows of ammo boxes stacked with exacting precision.

Dominating the center of the space was a command console bristling with equipment: high-performance computers, encrypted radios, and a satellite uplink still humming with a faint white noise.

To the left was a supply station stocked with crates of rations, bottled water, and medical kits—enough to support a small force for weeks. It wasn't the *Valkyrie*, but for now, it was a start.

Wally headed straight for the command console, cradling the waterproof hard drive like a precious artifact. He placed it on a steel work surface and began plugging it into a docking unit. No one spoke while he typed in a quick series of commands, the clack of keys echoing through the still air.

"Let's see what we pulled from Olympus before they nuked our ship," he muttered in a voice thick with weariness.

Katya and Jenny hovered nearby, eyes scanning every corner of the bunker. They were still half-expecting an ambush. Neil sank onto a bench near the armory, massaging his bruised shoulder. Noah remained standing behind Wally, arms folded, watching the computer screen flicker to life with his usual intense focus.

A progress bar appeared, slowly inching forward. Whatever secrets this drive contained might well be the key to continuing their fight—and avenging everyone they'd lost in the *Valkyrie's* sinking. They'd been pushed to the edge, but for the first time since the Council's ambush, hope sparked in the bunker's stale air.

Suddenly, the monitors erupted with a chaotic flood of information: intercepted Council communications, partially encrypted command logs, shifting maps dotted with movement markers. Lines of raw data scrolled by, interspersed with bursts of glitching video feeds.

At first glance, much of it was indecipherable.

"We're looking at everything we scraped in that brief uplink window," Wally explained. "The Council's real-time ops, all jumbled together."

His fingers tapped frantically at the keyboard, each keystroke pulling a new fragment of clarity from the scrambled logs. Small windows popped up, glimpses of Council codenames, disjointed conversations, half-formed directives. Most of it vanished in a haze of encryption. Then a single file blinked open, free of the usual cryptographic distortion.

Wally froze for half a heartbeat. "Oh, hell..."

Neil hovered beside him, tension ratcheting. "That's never good."

Across the screen scrolled a chilling mission statement:

GLOBAL ECONOMIC DESTABILIZATION – LONDON PHASE

TWENTY-THREE

DR. ADRIAN KNOX SHIVERED VIOLENTLY AS HE WAS dragged from the transport plane, the freezing Siberian wind biting through his soaked clothes. He had no memory of the journey, only flashes of the *Valkyrie* flooding, the chaos of the sinking ship, and then—blackness. He had woken up to Council guards, their rifles trained on him, their orders clear.

Now the boots they'd given him crunched against ice-packed gravel, his numb fingers clenching into weak fists as they hauled him toward the compound looming ahead.

A fortress of concrete and steel, half-buried in permafrost, barely distinguishable from the frozen expanse beyond. A black site. Hidden, isolated, inescapable.

The double doors hissed open as he was marched inside. The warmth hit him like a slap—stale, clinical, artificial. His shivers didn't stop as the guards shoved him forward, down a long, dim corridor. The walls smelled of disinfectant and machine oil, the lighting harsh and colorless.

At the end of the hallway, a single figure stood waiting.

Allison Peterson.

She hadn't changed.

Sharp, calculating eyes, her black tactical uniform crisp, her hands folded neatly behind her back. A smile touched her lips, but there was no warmth in it—just the edge of a blade hidden beneath a velvet sheath.

"Dr. Knox." Her voice was smooth, almost amused. "Welcome back."

Knox's breath was shallow, his heart pounding. He had seen what happened to Council prisoners. He had designed some of their methods.

He swallowed. "I—"

"You should be honored," Allison continued, stepping closer. "Few who betray the Council are given a second chance."

Knox flinched at that word—betrayal. As if he had ever had a real choice.

Allison's smile remained. "Don't look so grim, Doctor. We're not here to punish you."

She turned smoothly, motioning to the guards. "Bring him."

They fell in step behind her, Knox stumbling as they led him deeper into the facility, past security checkpoints and through reinforced corridors, the air growing colder despite the artificial heat.

Then the final door slid open.

The computer lab stretched out before them.

Rows of high-end servers hummed, their blinking indicator lights throwing eerie reflections across polished metal countertops. Screens lined the walls, scrolling with encrypted code, intricate network schematics, and—

Olympus.

Knox's blood ran cold.

He knew this system better than anyone. He had built it. Designed its interface, structured its automated learning processes, created its neural framework to think, adapt, destroy.

And now it was here, fully functional, a beast breathing beneath layers of data.

Allison stepped aside, gesturing to the center console.

"Here," she said, her voice a velvet whisper, "you will finish your work on Olympus."

Knox stared at the monitors, at the endless lines of code and chaos, at the weaponized intelligence that had already begun erasing the old world.

He could feel it. Watching him. Waiting.

He swallowed. He had no choice.

For now.

TWENTY-FOUR

THE LOW HUM OF COMPUTERS FILLED THE BUNKER'S subterranean silence, their screens casting a ghostly glow over the exhausted team. For hours, Wally and Neil had been buried in the data, their eyes glazed with fatigue, fingers moving with mechanical precision over the keyboards as they decrypted, dissected, and pieced together the fragments of Olympus's design.

The salvaged hard drive had yielded its secrets slowly, stubbornly. Each file had been layered with encryption, hidden behind firewalls designed to self-destruct on detection. But Wally had anticipated this, and Neil had worked alongside him, running counter-scripts, patching together fragmented logs and scattered transmissions.

Three hours in, the bunker had become a war room of discarded ration wrappers, cold coffee, and a whiteboard smeared with hastily scrawled notes.

Now, at last, the pieces fell into place.

Wally sat back, eyes bloodshot, fingers trembling slightly as he pulled up a new file. "I found it," he said quietly. "I know how they're doing it. How Olympus is being connected to the world's financial systems."

Everyone leaned in.

"It's not brute force. It's not infiltration in the traditional sense. It's being sold to them—as a product."

A few more keystrokes brought up a black-and-white image, a lean-faced man with sunken cheeks and cold eyes. "Victor Brandt," Wally said, pointing at the screen. "German financial mastermind. Born in Munich. By sixteen, he was outmaneuvering entire hedge funds with a custom trading algorithm. The Council recruited him not long after that, and since then, he's been the architect of their economic warfare."

He tapped again, and a cascade of charts, logos, and institutional names appeared.

"You see, Brandt isn't just executing the plan—he's selling it. The Council isn't flipping a switch and calling it a day. They need the banking institutions on board first."

Wally pulled up another screen, replacing the chaotic market projections with a new interface—sleek, corporate, polished. A single word sat at the top in bold, silver letters: ATLAS.

"This," he said, pointing at the display, "is how they're getting in."

Jenny squinted at the screen. "Atlas? What the hell is Atlas?"

"A cover," Wally said. "A Trojan horse. On the surface, it's a financial software package—an advanced AI-driven trading system designed to revolutionize risk management for high-frequency trading firms, hedge funds, and global banks. Brandt has been selling it as a way to predict market fluctuations before they happen, promising nearly infallible accuracy."

Neil let out a low whistle. "And they're actually buying it?"

"Hook, line, and sinker," Wally confirmed. "Atlas is already being installed in every major financial hub—New York, Hong Kong, Tokyo, Frankfurt, and soon, London. Brandt is scheduled to meet with executives at the London Stock Exchange in two days."

Noah's jaw tightened. "Then that's where we go." He hesitated for half a beat before finishing. "London."

The word sat heavily in the air.

The last time they had set foot in London, Noah had lost everything.

"Brandt has convinced them that this is the next evolution of global finance," Wally went on. "They think they're getting an unbeatable edge in trading. What they're actually getting..." He tapped a key, and the screen split in two. On the left was a normal network diagram of a financial trading system, on the right, the hidden backdoor embedded deep within Atlas's code.

"What they're actually getting," Wally repeated, "is a direct pipeline into Olympus."

A heavy silence settled over the room.

Jenny leaned in closer, scanning the tangled web of lines connecting global financial institutions back to a single node labeled *Olympus AI Control Hub*. "So you're telling me that every major bank, stock exchange, and financial regulator on the planet is voluntarily plugging themselves into the Council's system?"

"Exactly," Wally said grimly. His next words came with the finality of a death sentence. "Once it's everywhere, Olympus AI activates. The backdoor hidden inside the Atlas program will allow them to take over the financial system completely—every stock trade, every financial transaction, every government-backed currency. The moment they trigger it, the market won't just crash."

He turned to face them. "It'll become theirs."

They stood in silence for a moment. Then Wally exhaled, rubbing a hand over his tired face before continuing.

"And Brandt isn't in London alone."

Noah's eyes sharpened. "Who's with him?"

Wally tapped a key, and two new profiles appeared on the screen. Side by side, male and female, their athletic physiques were unmistakable even in the grainy security footage.

"This is Leonid and Sofia Petrov," Wally said grimly. "The

Petrovs are Brandt's bodyguards. But they're more than that." He looked to Katya. "You should know what they are."

Katya's fingers curled into fists. She knew exactly what they were.

Jenny squinted at the screen. "Who are they?"

Katya's voice was cold. "They're Elites, like me and Noah."

Jenny's brows furrowed. "Like you?"

Katya nodded once. "Products of the same genetics program."

Jenny's eyes flicked back to the screen, studying the two figures. "So they're just like normal Elites—enhanced?"

"No." Wally's voice was low. Hard. "They're perfected. Top tier Elites."

The room tensed.

Jenny crossed her arms, frowning. "How do we even fight people like that?"

Noah's eyes stayed locked on the screen, his jaw tight. "We get creative."

TWENTY-FIVE

THE GULFSTREAM TOUCHED DOWN, ITS LANDING GEAR screeching against the rain-slicked tarmac, kicking up a fine mist of water as it taxied forward. The aircraft rolled smoothly toward the hangar, its engines rumbling low as it approached the half-rusted structure at the edge of the airfield.

The plane came to a halt, and the fold-down steps descended. At the base, a man with a square face like a brick stood waiting, his coat pulled tight against the bitter wind, his expression unreadable—neither welcoming nor hostile. But the moment Noah emerged from the doorway, the man's brows lifted slightly, surprise flickering across his face.

"I was told never to expect you lot again," he muttered, voice carrying over the rain's steady patter. "I thought Camelot was dead."

Noah flipped his hood over his head, stepping onto the slick metal steps. "Then let's call this a resurrection."

Katya followed, jacket collar turned up against the cold drizzle. Jenny, Neil, and Wally filed out behind them, each carrying minimal baggage.

The man motioned them forward, stepping aside as they descended onto solid ground. The hangar's lights illuminated a nondescript panel van parked near a stack of sealed crates.

"Weapons," the man said simply, flipping one crate lid open. Inside was a modest but effective arsenal—compact carbines, submachine guns, handguns, and extra magazines.

Katya picked up a 9mm pistol, racking the slide with practiced ease. Jenny ran a hand along a carbine's stock, checking its weight. Neil pocketed a handful of burner phones while Wally sorted through forged passports, flipping open each identity.

The man reached into his coat, producing a small ring of keys. He handed one to Noah. "Address is in Whitechapel. Off-grid, low profile. You've got maybe three days before the walls close in. Don't waste them."

Noah slid the key into his pocket. "Appreciate it."

The man's smirk flickered again, but this time it held a hint of warning. "Watch your backs, Wolf. London's not the friendliest place for ghosts like you."

Without another word, they piled into the van, stashing gear and weapons in the back.

Rain drummed against the metal roof as Jenny took the wheel, guiding them out of the hangar. The flickering lights of the airstrip cast them in and out of shadow as the van rumbled onto the wet runway, then veered onto a narrow road cutting through the darkness.

Noah glanced around the cab. Jenny's hands gripped the wheel, steady and certain. Neil checked the gear, Wally clutched the hard drive, and Katya sat in silence, staring out the window.

Beyond the rain-specked glass, the distant glow of London loomed on the horizon.

They had three days. One safe house. And a mission to stop Victor Brandt before the world burned.

The clock was ticking.

The van rumbled down the narrow, rain-slicked road, tires hissing against the wet asphalt as they left the airstrip behind. The countryside blurred into darkness, the occasional glow of street-lights flashing across the windshield as Jenny guided them toward the beating heart of London.

Inside, the team sat in silence, each lost in thought. Katya cleaned one of the 9mm pistols with slow, methodical movements, the only sound the soft clicks of metal against metal. Neil sat checking the burner devices they'd been given. Wally kept the hard drive close, arms wrapped around it as if it were the most precious thing in the world—which, right now, it was.

Noah sat in the passenger seat, staring ahead.

The city was coming. He could feel it.

The air thickened the closer they got, the distant glow of London's skyline breaking through the low-hanging mist. The last time Noah was here, everything had burned down around him.

And now he was back.

Jenny cast a sideways glance at him. "You sure you're ready for this?"

Noah's jaw tightened. "Doesn't matter. We don't have a choice."

The van merged onto a major roadway, the A11 leading them straight into East London. The farther in they drove, the brighter the lights, the denser the traffic. The borough of Tower Hamlets came alive around them, the city still awake despite the late hour.

People walked briskly along rain-dampened streets, hoods up, hands in pockets. Market stalls, long closed for the night, left only skeletal remnants of tarps and wooden stands. Graffiti marked brick walls, remnants of a borough that had seen both gentrification and decay.

Katya peered out the window. "Nothing like blending into a city that never sleeps."

Neil snorted. "You're right. Nothing says stealth like fluorescent chicken shops and drunk students."

Jenny let out a quiet chuckle as she guided the van off the main road and into a labyrinth of narrow residential streets. They passed rows of old terrace houses, most run-down, some abandoned, others still clinging to life.

Finally, she pulled up to their destination—a nondescript terrace nestled between two identical, equally unimpressive properties.

It was perfect.

The kind of place no one looked at twice. The kind of place where neighbors minded their own business.

Noah stepped out first, rain tapping lightly against the hood of his jacket. He scanned the street, noting the old CCTV camera mounted at the far end. A few windows across the road glowed faintly with late-night television or sleepless occupants.

Katya and Neil grabbed the gear, Wally clutching the hard drive like a lifeline.

Noah reached into his pocket, pulling out the key their contact had given him. He slid it into the lock, the door opening with a soft creak. Then he flipped the lights on.

A single bare lightbulb buzzed, casting a weak glow across peeling wallpaper and grimy floorboards. It flickered intermittently, threatening to plunge the cramped flat into darkness without warning. A stale odor of cigarette smoke and mildew hung in the air, tickling the back of Neil's throat as he stepped in behind Jenny.

He wrinkled his nose. "I love what they've done with the place."

"Shut up and check the perimeter," Jenny shot back at her husband. She set down a duffel bag of supplies near a threadbare couch whose cushions were torn at the edges, stuffing spilling out.

Neil offered a half-smile, then nodded and walked off, unholstering his sidearm as he surveyed the shabby rooms. Tattered curtains drooped over grime-streaked windows. The single toilet in the corner stall coughed when he tested the handle.

Across the living area, Wally crouched over a rickety table that threatened to collapse under the weight of his laptop. He started booting it up, pulling out cables and setting up a hasty workstation. Next to him, Katya rummaged through a duffel of weapons, rolling her shoulders to ease knots in her back. She carefully laid out handguns, spare magazines, and boxes of ammunition, readying their arsenal.

By the door, Noah remained largely silent. His coat was still on, the collar turned up against the persistent London chill. One look at his tight jaw and narrowed eyes told Jenny his thoughts were miles away—focused on the war they'd come to wage.

She couldn't help asking, though. "Are you going somewhere?" Her voice was gentle but concerned.

He paused at the threshold, sliding a compact pistol into his waistband. "I won't be long."

It was all he said. No one pressed further. They understood the grim determination that flickered beneath their leader's calm exterior.

Without another word, Noah slipped out into the dark. The old door groaned shut behind him, leaving Jenny, Katya, Neil, and Wally to the faint flicker of light in the dismal apartment.

TWENTY-SIX

CLIVEDEN HOUSE, BERKSHIRE | 01:31 GMT | FEBRUARY 23

CLIVEDEN HOUSE LOOMED LIKE A WOUNDED GIANT IN the pre-dawn darkness, the mansion's once-grand façade marred by gaping holes and hastily erected scaffolding. Floodlights revealed patches of half-rebuilt stonework and bullet-scarred walls, lending the old estate a ghostly outline against the Berkshire countryside. Sections of the mansion remained in darkness, left untouched since the catastrophe that had ravaged this place a year ago.

Noah slipped quietly along the perimeter fence—an improvised barrier of chain-link and wooden planks designed to keep out trespassers during reconstruction. With one practiced motion, he scaled the half-built security fence, boots landing silently on the other side.

The wet grass clung to his pant legs as he made his way toward the mansion, staying at the edges of the floodlit areas.

The sight of the main hall's roof—partially collapsed, open to the starless sky—struck him harder than he'd expected. A massive hole gaped like a wound, testament to the explosion that had ripped this stately home apart. Scaffolding crisscrossed the courtyard, but the real damage was etched into the stone itself: cracks, scorch marks, and a fine dusting of rubble that no amount of sweeping could fully erase.

His breath caught when he reached the grand marble steps leading to the entrance. Even in the dim light, faint streaks of old blood lingered in the crevices. The memories came surging back—chaotic flashes of gunfire, the deafening drone of the nanobot swarms, Sarah's lifeless body dropping to the ground—and Norah, wrenched away in a final, brutal betrayal.

The estate stood as a monument to that horrific night. No matter the reconstruction efforts, it was impossible to hide the scars.

Noah inhaled slowly, steeling himself against the flood of grief and regret that threatened to overwhelm him. His footsteps echoed faintly across the shattered marble floor as he stepped into what remained of the main hall. Floodlight beams danced against splintered columns and sagging rafters. Metal pipes groaned under Noah's grip as he scaled the makeshift scaffolding that wound around the west wing's ruined shell.

Memories assaulted him as he climbed, as vivid and punishing as they'd been on the night it all happened. Sarah's final scream tore through his thoughts, reverberating in the silent corridors of his mind. He could almost see Norah's wide, terrified eyes, hear her voice crying for him.

The ghosts of that night climbed with him, relentless.

He reached the top, emerging onto a skeletal rooftop where broken beams jutted at odd angles beneath tattered sheets of tarpaulin. The structure swayed under his weight, and the wind cut across his cheeks. But he felt none of it, his senses numbed by the knot of grief and rage twisting in his chest.

This was where it had ended—the last stand, the confrontation that left the mansion a wreck of scorched stone and shattered glass.

This was where he'd lost everything.

He placed one hand on a bullet-ruined gargoyle, a lonely

sentinel that offered no comfort. His heart beat heavily in his chest, each thud a reminder of how alive he still was, in spite of it all. He could almost see the moment playing out again—Sarah falling away from him, the look of shock and betrayal on her face as the bullet ripped through her. Norah's small hand slipping from his grasp as Allison tore her away. The rage, the helplessness, the suffocating hollowness that came afterward.

The scaffolding swayed in a sudden gust of wind, but Noah didn't budge. He gripped the metal rail, jaw clenched, heart pounding. This place was haunted by his failures. By the time he left London, he might carry even more ghosts. But there was no escaping the truth—it was the same truth he'd lived with every day since that night:

He hadn't protected them. And now the Council was closer than ever to destroying the world he still knew.

He could hear it as though it were happening now. Norah's scream, filling his ears with a child's desperation.

"Daddy! Daddy, help!"

Hot fury coiled in his chest. The memories would never relent, but he refused to let them drown him. Instead, they lit a fire in him—one that demanded justice, vengeance, and the rescue of the only light left in his world.

His breath turned to steam in the frigid air. "Hold on, Norah," he whispered. "I'm coming."

TWENTY-SEVEN

A GRINDING SCREECH TORE THROUGH THE SILENCE AS the heavy metal door swung open. Norah squinted against the corridor's dim fluorescence, her eyes unused to any kind of brightness after endless hours locked in pitch black isolation. She offered no resistance as rough hands clamped around her arms—fighting back only brought more punishment. Two guards yanked her out of the tiny cell, boots scraping against cold concrete.

Her body screamed at every movement. Days—maybe weeks —spent in a cramped, freezing box had left her muscles stiff and her limbs shaking from exhaustion. Every breath felt like a small victory, though the taste of stale air carried the tang of disinfectant and old blood.

No one spoke. No one ever did. They simply dragged her along a corridor that smelled of damp cement and chemical cleaners. Flickering overhead bulbs threw elongated shadows against the walls, each shape twisting into something monstrous in her peripheral vision.

At the end of the hall, the dormitory doors clicked open— thick slabs of reinforced steel that led into a communal sleeping area. It had been more than a week since she'd last set foot here, back when she still hoped the guards might show mercy.

Now she knew better.

As the rough hands shoved her past the threshold, Norah half expected the relief of a familiar bed, a brief chance to warm herself under a thin blanket. Maybe even some food. But one glance around killed that faint hope.

The dormitory was waiting for her.

Dozens of children, heads shaved like hers, huddled in tense clusters or paced the floor with hollow eyes. Some bore fresh bruises or bandaged limbs; others stared ahead, waiting for the next command.

Norah's stomach twisted. Whatever she'd endured in solitary, whatever pain she'd weathered, it was clear the others had been living through a different kind of hell. The tension in the air felt like an uncoiled wire, ready to snap.

The eight-year-old swallowed back the ache in her throat, keeping her expression neutral. Emotions were dangerous here. *Stay quiet. Stay invisible*, she reminded herself.

When she had first arrived, she had cried endlessly for her lost mother. She had been a child.

That had soon been stripped away.

Now, only a year later, she was something else. Not an adult, but certainly not a child anymore.

As she stared back at the numerous eyes fixed on her, a kernel of defiance still flickered within Norah. She might be battered and starving, but she was not broken.

Stepping inside, the guards released her arms. They stepped back, doors slamming shut behind them, leaving the echo to fade into a suffocating hush. The children looked at Norah with a blend of sympathy and fear—some part of them recognizing she was yet another victim of "Mother's" cruelties, yet all of them knowing one step out of line could mean their own trip to those tiny cells.

Welcome back, the silence seemed to say.

It barely lasted a second.

A figure stepped forward from the huddled clusters, moving with a predator's ease. She was taller than the others, lean with wiry muscle, her posture sharp with unquestioned authority.

Four-Four-Two.

Her cold, calculating gaze locked on to Norah, and a slow smirk crept across her chapped lips. Behind her, her sidekick moved in sync—a girl just as cruel but lacking her leader's control.

Four-Three-Three.

Together, they had ruled this dormitory long before Norah had arrived.

Four-Four-Two tilted her head, her eyes sweeping over Norah's frail form. The slight tremble in her limbs, the bruises on her arms, the sunken look in her face.

A wolf sniffing weakness.

She stopped just feet from Norah, her voice mockingly sweet.

"You know, they haven't let us have pudding the whole time you've been in there."

Norah stayed quiet.

Four-Four-Two's smirk widened. "The only thing I like in this whole stinking place and they took it. Because of you."

Behind her, Four-Three-Three clenched her fists in sneering anticipation.

"Welcome back, bitch!"

Four-Four-Two lunged, a flash of movement—fast, vicious, practiced.

But Norah was ready.

Her body moved on instinct, sidestepping the attack with a fluidity that came not from training but survival. Her breath stayed steady, feet light on the cold floor, never stopping.

Four-Four-Two spun, her face twisting with a flicker of genuine irritation. She had expected Norah to fold immediately.

The others saw it too.

That's when the circle began to form.

Whispers flitted between the gathered children, movement shifting in the dim light. A pack closing in.

Four-Three-Three cackled, circling opposite Four-Four-Two, her voice sharp with excitement. "Get her, Four-Four-Two! Get her!"

The space around Norah grew smaller, the wall of bodies tightening, cutting off escape routes.

She knew this game.

She had seen others beaten senseless, unable to fight off an entire group.

But she wasn't like the others.

Four-Four-Two lunged again, but in the next heartbeat, Norah had seized her fist out of midair. Gasps rippled through the circle. No one had seen Norah move. It was as though her hand simply appeared around the other girl's knuckles.

A flicker of disbelief twisted Four-Four-Two's face. Her fingers flexed in Norah's grip, but Norah gave no ground. At last, Four-Four-Two yanked her hand free. "Lucky grab," she spat, forcing a sneer.

But the circle of onlookers could see it wasn't luck—just like Four-Four-Two could see it in Norah's eyes.

Somewhere in her stillness, Norah carried a fierce awareness, an uncanny ability that told her where every blow would land before it even began.

The next strike came from Four-Three-Three, rushing in with a quick jab aimed at Norah's ribs. Norah shifted her weight, letting the punch slide harmlessly past.

Another girl followed up with a kick, strong enough to bruise if it connected. Norah twisted away—fluid, effortless. The boot whistled past her midsection, missing her by an inch. The attacker nearly stumbled, thrown off balance by the unexpected dodge.

Around them, bunk beds served as a stadium. Broken or battered girls leaned in from their mattresses, eyes flicking from Four-Four-Two to Norah.

The circle tightened, anticipating retaliation. Yet none came.

Norah's hands remained at her sides—she wasn't striking back, only evading. Her head stayed bowed, eyes half-lowered, but her posture radiated calm control.

Four-Four-Two's nostrils flared. She saw it now—the way Norah moved, the way she watched them, reading every twitch before it even started. It wasn't just luck.

It was something else.

Four-Three-Three snarled. "Stop dancing and fight!" She lunged again, swinging with raw frustration rather than skill.

Norah slid back, her movement so quick and seamless that Four-Three-Three overextended, nearly tripping into the girl behind her.

Another girl—a broad-shouldered brute with a freshly healed scar across her temple—rushed in from Norah's left. A kick, wide and sloppy but powerful. Norah ducked, the foot sailing past her head. The girl stumbled into another attacker, sending them both into a tangle of limbs.

The pack was turning on itself.

Four-Four-Two realized it too late. Norah wasn't just dodging —she was using their aggression against them.

A growl of irritation bubbled up in her throat. "Hold her down! Don't let her—"

But Norah was already on the move again.

Another girl grabbed for her wrist. Norah twisted, a seamless pivot, breaking free before the grip could tighten.

Another lunged—Norah dropped low, sliding under the swing of an arm, popping back to her feet just out of reach.

They chased her through the dormitory, tripping over beds, over each other, growing sloppier and angrier with every missed strike.

Norah ducked between bunks, her smaller frame a ghost in the dim light, slipping through gaps too narrow for the others.

A girl vaulted over a mattress to grab her, missed, and landed hard on her knees.

Another nearly collided with a bunk post, barely stopping herself in time.

A frustrated shriek tore from Four-Three-Three. "HOLD STILL!"

Norah didn't listen.

She was fast, too fast. But more than that—she was calm. The others moved like whipped animals, driven by rage, hunger, desperation.

Norah moved like water.

A flicker of a memory surged in her mind—her father's voice, low and steady.

"You don't always need to fight, cub. Sometimes you just need to be faster."

Faster than the enemy. Faster than fear.

Faster than them.

The circle of attackers tightened—more reckless now, more desperate.

Norah breathed evenly, her muscles loose, her mind clear. She wasn't afraid. She was waiting.

The next opening came in a flash.

Four-Four-Two and Four-Three-Three, both seething with frustration, lunged from opposite sides, determined to trap her between them.

Norah's instincts flared.

At the last second, she twisted her weight onto her toes and dropped low—ducking just beneath their wild, vengeful swings.

Time slowed.

Their momentum carried them forward, too fast, too committed. They had no time to stop.

And in a sickening crack, the two slammed into each other.

The impact was brutal.

Forehead to nose.

A muffled cry of pain as Four-Four-Two's skull drove straight into Four-Three-Three's face.

Both girls crumpled.

Four-Four-Two groaned, rolling onto her side, her eyes glazed with shock.

Four-Three-Three was out cold, her arms limp as she slumped onto the dormitory floor.

Silence crashed over the room.

The few remaining attackers staggered back, panting. Sweat dripped from their brows, their limbs shaky with exhaustion. A couple of them clutched bruised elbows and scraped knees, glaring at Norah with equal parts frustration and disbelief.

None of them stepped forward to continue the fight.

The rest of the dormitory—the ones who had chosen not to join in—watched from their bunks, their faces half-lit by the dim overhead lights.

Their expressions were different. Not fear. Not resentment.

Respect.

No one had ever beaten the dormitory's pack before. No one had ever walked away from Four-Four-Two and lived to tell about it.

Until now.

Norah said nothing. She simply turned, walked past the fallen girls, and climbed into her own bunk.

Her limbs ached. Her stomach still felt hollow. But she lay back against the thin mattress, her chest rising and falling with deep, satisfied breaths.

She hadn't won by fighting.

She'd won by being better.

And as her heavy eyelids drifted shut, a single thought flickered in her mind—

I survived today. I'll survive tomorrow, too.

No. Not a child.

Something else.

TWENTY-EIGHT

THE SAFEHOUSE IN WHITECHAPEL WAS MORE neglected hovel than sanctuary—a fading remnant of an older, harsher London. It had been built around the same time as Jack the Ripper had stalked these very streets. A dark, demonic time.

Damp spread like a stain across the walls, and every gust of rainswept wind rattled the windows.

Within the cramped living area, Wally had commandeered the lopsided kitchen table to lay out his laptop, a portable monitor, and two bulky signal scramblers. Tangled cables and blinking LEDs formed a makeshift command center, the hum of processors quietly battling the uneasy silence of the flat.

Nearby, Katya methodically cleaned weapons while Jenny watched the grimy windows for any sign of approach. Neil sat beside Wally, busy helping him hack his way into the London Stock Exchange's security system.

Noah didn't sit. He paced. The restlessness in his eyes was almost electric—a man coiled and ready to spring.

"Okay. I'm in," Wally suddenly said, drawing everyone's attention to him. "Scanning LSE security logs now."

Lines of raw code and encrypted text flickered past. Noah paused mid-step, pivoting toward the table. "What are we looking at?"

"Looks like Brandt just got Level-One clearance at the London Stock Exchange," Wally muttered, reading off the scrawl of data as it cycled across his screen. "That means direct access to their main servers, trade algorithms—full security systems. They've handed him the keys to the kingdom."

Noah leaned forward. "So Atlas isn't just a proposal anymore —it's happening."

A hush settled over the group. Every second they waited meant Victor Brandt had more time to enact Olympus's next deadly phase of global financial collapse.

Wally kept typing, his brow furrowing at a new set of logs. "Hold on. There's a flagged email thread..." He opened it, scanning lines of text. "Someone inside the LSE is concerned about Atlas."

The team crowded nearer as Wally enlarged the text. Subject lines and signatures appeared, followed by paragraphs of anxious warnings.

SUBJECT: RE: Atlas HFT Integration – Security Risks
From: Stephanie Harrington, Senior IT Specialist – London Stock Exchange
To: LSE Cybersecurity Division

STEPHANIE HARRINGTON:
I don't understand why we're integrating an external system with such deep access to our primary trading algorithms.

I've run a sandbox simulation, and there are massive data gaps in Atlas's reporting structure.

It's triggering unauthorized data transfers to an unknown IP outside our network.

I've reported this concern twice now, but I keep getting shut down.

Who approved this? Why isn't anyone talking about it?

NOAH LEANED over Wally's shoulder, eyes scanning each sentence. "They're ignoring her."

"Not just ignoring," Wally corrected, tapping a few keys. "Someone's trying to shut her up. Her access creds are going to be suspended."

Another email popped open on Wally's monitor. It bore a HIGH PRIORITY tag, the text short and ominous.

FROM: *Vincent Draper, LSE Security*
    To: *Victor Brandt*

DRAPER:

Brandt—

We have a problem. One of our IT grunts, Stephanie Harring-ton, is making noise about Atlas.

She's flagged security breaches and is trying to escalate it to compliance.

I've locked her out of the system and she's scheduled for an internal disciplinary meeting tomorrow morning.

Do we need to handle this quietly?

THE ROOM FELL SILENT, every face etched with the same heavy understanding of what 'handle this quietly' meant.

Jenny broke the silence. "She won't make it to that meeting."

Neil snorted grimly. "Nope. The Council'll make sure she disappears first."

Katya exhaled through her nose, setting aside the rag she'd been using to polish a rifle. "So we get to her before they do."

TWENTY-NINE

Canary Wharf bustled with its usual evening energy. Suited city workers hurried to catch the Tube or flagged down black cabs, the tinted glow of skyscraper lights reflecting off the muddy waters of the Thames.

In the crush of rush-hour bodies, a lone Hackney carriage parked beside the curb appeared no different from the rest—except for the driver. Noah Wolf, his flat cap pulled low, sat behind the wheel, hands steady, eyes scanning the crowd with sharp focus.

His gaze flicked to the clock on the dashboard: 7:45 p.m. According to Wally's intel, Stephanie Harrington, Senior IT Specialist at the London Stock Exchange, would be walking out of her office in precisely fifteen minutes.

Having spent the last hour studying recent footage gathered by the CCTV cameras lined up outside her offices, they'd learned her routine. Nine times out of ten, when Stephanie left work she would bypass the usual lines of waiting taxis until she reached the very last one. It seemed like some kind of obsessive compulsion—to always use the very last taxi.

Tonight, the very last taxi would be Noah's.

In the open seat beside him lay a photograph of Stephanie, gleaned from her LSE profile. A bright-eyed woman in her late twenties, hair pulled into a neat bun, looking more focused than fearful. But from the urgent emails she'd sent—and from what the Council had planned—Noah knew she was far from safe.

He pressed a finger to his earpiece. "Wolf here. Everyone in position?"

A crackle of static, then Jenny's voice: "In position. We've got eyes on the entrance. Katya's flanking from the side exit. Neil's got the back alley."

At the safehouse, Wally was glued to half a dozen traffic camera feeds, his software rigged to alert the team if Council operatives or suspicious vehicles were spotted closing in. His eyes flicked to the CCTV watching Canary Wharf's entrance.

Wally's voice came through next, hushed but firm: "All right, she's heading out. Stand by."

Noah's heart rate picked up a notch, adrenaline sharpening every sense. Through the flood of office workers, he spied a woman stepping through the rotating doors of a tall glass tower. Her auburn hair was visible even at a distance. She paused to tuck a stray strand behind her ear, glancing around with the distracted air of someone wanting to go home after a long day.

He recognized her instantly: Stephanie Harrington.

She stepped onto the pavement, her gaze flicking over the line of waiting taxis, her expression tight with unease.

Noah kept his posture relaxed behind the wheel, watching as she bypassed cab after cab, the exact same way she had every other night. A creature of habit.

Right on cue, she reached the very last one.

The one that wasn't supposed to be there.

Noah rolled down the window, tipping his head in a show of casual indifference. "All right, love? Need a lift?" he asked, adopting a thick Cockney accent he'd rehearsed en route.

Stephanie hesitated.

For a second, he thought she might turn away—something in her expression screamed doubt, hesitation, fear. Maybe the accent was a little off. But then she exhaled sharply, shook her head to herself, and pulled open the door.

The second she was inside, Noah pulled smoothly away from the curb.

Jenny's voice came through his earpiece. "She's in. No tails—yet."

Noah glanced up at the rearview mirror. Stephanie was already watching him.

"You're new," she murmured. "I've never seen you before."

"Transferred here from the West End," Noah replied smoothly, keeping his voice even, detached. "You need a ride or not?"

Stephanie chewed her lip, her fingers tightening around the strap of her handbag. "Yeah. Home, please."

She rattled off an address in Notting Hill.

They merged into the flow of traffic as it snaked around glass towers and illuminated corporate logos. Neon and halogen lights shimmered on the wet streets. Stephanie stared blankly at the city passing by, her thoughts somewhere else.

After a moment, she caught Noah's gaze in the rearview mirror. She frowned. His eyes were too sharp, too alert for a typical taxi driver.

"Listen, Stephanie..." he began, his Cockney accent slipping away mid-sentence.

Her posture stiffened. "How do you know my name?"

He met her eyes in the mirror. "It doesn't matter. What does matter is that we need to talk."

Stephanie's grip on her bag tightened. "What the hell is this?"

"An intervention," Noah answered. "You're in danger."

The gearshift clunked as he accelerated, and she realized the doors had automatically locked. Anxiety spiked. Her hand darted into her handbag for her phone. "I'm calling the police."

"Before you do that," Noah interjected, "look behind us.

Dark blue BMW. It was parked opposite your offices and has been tailing us since you left work."

Stephanie froze. Her pulse hammered in her ears as she twisted in her seat, peering through the rear window.

Through the drizzle and the neon reflections, she spotted a dark sedan three cars back. It turned when they turned, slowed when they slowed—an uncanny echo of their every maneuver.

To make it painfully obvious, Noah abruptly turned right at the next intersection without signaling. Tires screeched on wet asphalt as he swerved around a passing bus. In her peripheral vision, Stephanie saw the dark BMW cut sharply across a lane, nearly colliding with a taxi as it scrambled to follow.

A chill seized her.

Everything at work, her concerns about Atlas, the menacing hints that someone was watching her... it all clicked into place.

She was being followed.

Slowly, she set her phone down, heart thudding. When she looked up, Noah was watching her in the mirror again.

"Who are you?" she whispered, glancing at the reflection of the BMW in the rear window. "What do you want from me?"

"We want to keep you alive," Noah informed her.

"Then at least tell me who you are."

Noah's grip on the wheel was steady, but tension darkened his eyes. "My name's Noah Wolf. You flagged something dangerous at the LSE—saw what Victor Brandt's software is really doing. You asked one question too many, and now they plan to make you disappear."

A shaky laugh escaped her. "That's insane. You're lying. I only complained to Draper. That's all."

From the driver's seat, Noah locked eyes with her in the rearview. "Is it insane?" he asked. "Your security clearance is about to be revoked. Your access to the LSE's internal programs was deactivated tonight. You're *scheduled* for a disciplinary meeting tomorrow."

She swallowed, breath catching in her throat. The churning

tension in her gut told her he was right, that she'd stumbled onto something bigger—and far more dangerous—than she'd ever imagined.

"In that meeting," Noah continued, "you'll be fired and, after that, watched. Indefinitely."

Her pulse hammered against her ribcage. "Watched by who?"

Noah lifted his gaze to the mirror again. "Forces with almost unlimited power."

She rolled her eyes reflexively, though panic flickered in them. "Next you'll be telling me it's that bloody Internet hoax the Council."

Since the fall of E & E, the Council's vast propaganda machine had excelled at relegating its existence to the realm of conspiracy theory.

Before Noah could answer, the BMW gunned its engine, appearing in the side mirror. Wally's voice crackled over the earpiece.

"You've got heat inbound! Two more vehicles joining the tail!"

Stephanie caught the clipped urgency in Noah's expression. "Jesus," she whispered, the weight of it slamming into her like a freight train. "This is real."

Noah glanced over his shoulder, just long enough to catch her eye. "As real as it gets. You've been noticed, Stephanie. But if you help me and my friends, we'll keep you safe."

Shallow breaths seized her lungs as she realized she had no other option—no time to question, no time to contact the police or the LSE's HR department. Whatever she was involved in, it was deadly, and the only chance of survival seemed to be trusting this stranger.

Her lips parted in a trembling exhale. "All right. What do you need me to do?"

Noah's features hardened into a determined grin. "First. Hold on tight."

He jerked the wheel, taking a hard right into a narrow alleyway. Tires squealed against the wet pavement, and the cab lurched violently. Stephanie braced herself against the door as they careened off the main road, plunging into dimly lit backstreets. Engines revved in pursuit.

The chase was on.

London's damp streets blurred into a frantic maze of neon-lit signs and weaving headlights as Noah floored the gas. Stephanie clung to the door handle, heart hammering against her ribs. In the side mirror, she glimpsed their pursuers' cars—dark silhouettes with blazing headlights, engines roaring as they swerved through oncoming traffic.

Wally's voice cut through the chaos. "You've got two vehicles closing in from your left, one more swinging around the block."

"Copy that."

Noah spun the wheel, taking a hard left around a corner that scraped the cab's tires against the curb. The engine groaned, but he pushed it harder, slamming the gearshift forward as he threaded the cab through cramped alleyways. The narrow walls of old brick buildings whipped past, the taxi's tires spitting water from the slick pavement. In the mirror, the Council's dark sedans followed relentlessly, their engines snarling as they closed in.

"Neil, you in position?" Noah barked into his comms, weaving between overflowing dumpsters and abandoned pallets.

Neil's voice came back, steady despite the urgency. "Yeah. See you in three... two... one—"

Just as Noah whipped around a tight corner, a hulking truck lurched out of a side street, its headlights bursting into view like twin suns. It screeched to a halt sideways, effectively blocking the alley between Noah and his pursuers. The lead sedan slammed on its brakes almost too late, fishtailing before coming to a jarring stop. The second car couldn't avoid a collision, slamming into the first with a sickening crunch of metal.

Noah didn't slow. "Good work, Neil. Now stall them."

Neil climbed down from the cab of the truck, casually

adjusting his coat as one of the men from the blocked sedans leapt out. "Get that thing out of the way!" the man barked.

Neil rubbed the back of his neck and glanced toward the front of the truck. "All right, mate. Keep your wig on." He climbed back in and cranked the key. The engine whined but didn't turn over. He pushed the clutch, made a show of jamming the gearstick around, and let out a wince as the grinding sound filled the alley.

"You've got to be kidding me!" the agent snapped, shoving a gun into his waistband as he stomped toward the truck's door.

Neil raised a hand helplessly. "It's an old engine, real finicky. Just give me a second."

The agent growled something into his radio and waved for the others to try backing out of the alley. But just as the sedans began shifting into reverse, another truck rumbled into view from the other end—this one driven by Jenny. She flashed her headlights twice before pulling into the narrow passageway, boxing them in.

"Oops," Jenny said into the comms, barely holding back a grin. "Looks like you lads are staying put."

Taking advantage of the moment, Noah gunned the engine and cut hard toward Woolwich industrial estate.

A few minutes after losing the tail, a rusted chain-link fence loomed ahead, barely noticeable in the dark. Stephanie tensed as Noah floored it straight toward the barrier.

"You're insane!"

He didn't argue. Instead, he pressed harder on the accelerator, gripping the wheel as the cab barreled toward the gate at full speed.

The reinforced bumper smashed through the chain-link, snapping the rusted links apart. The gate twisted off its hinges, clattering wildly as the cab surged through, tires kicking up a spray of dirt and debris. Noah kept the throttle open, weaving through the industrial sprawl without slowing.

He swerved the taxi down a dirt path running parallel to the Thames before veering into a railway yard. Old freight containers loomed like rusting sentinels in the dark, their faded company logos barely visible under the sparse glow of security lights. The roar of the city felt a lifetime away.

Noah eased off the throttle, letting the vehicle roll to a slow stop between two derelict train cars. The engine hummed for a few seconds before he killed the lights and turned off the ignition. The silence that followed was deafening.

Stephanie exhaled sharply, her hands still gripping the seat so tightly her knuckles looked bloodless.

Noah turned in his seat to face her. "We're clear—for now."

Stephanie stared at him, her chest rising and falling in sharp, uneven breaths. "You... you just drove through a bloody fence."

He gave a small shrug. "Wasn't exactly my first time."

She released a shaky laugh, but there was no humor in it. "And you expect me to just go along with this? With you?"

Noah studied her, his expression unreadable. "You already have," he said quietly.

Stephanie's lips pressed into a thin line. He was right. Somewhere between the moment she'd hesitated outside the taxi and the moment they'd plowed through that chain-link fence, she had made a choice. Not consciously, perhaps. But a choice nonetheless.

She leaned back against the headrest, rubbing her hands over her face. "All right," she murmured. "Just tell me—what now?"

"Atlas goes live tomorrow," Noah said.

She inhaled slowly, pressing her fingers against her temples. "And you're here to stop it."

He didn't blink. "That's the idea."

Stephanie let out another short, humorless laugh. "Jesus." She shook her head, eyes flicking to the darkened landscape outside. "I don't even know who the hell you are. Noah Wolf doesn't really explain much."

Noah tilted his head slightly. "You already know enough," he said. "You know what Atlas is designed to do. And you know that if Brandt activates it tomorrow, the world as you know it changes forever."

Her stomach twisted. Because she did know. Every buried doubt, every warning sign she had tried to ignore—this man was confirming all of it.

She glanced at him again, taking in the worn edges of his leather jacket, the faint bruising on his knuckles. He looked calm, in control. But beneath that? He carried the weight of a man who had been fighting too long, running too hard.

Stephanie let out a breath. "And if I say no? If I walk away?"

Noah studied her for a long moment before answering. "Then I can't help you. The people behind Atlas will make you disappear."

A shiver ran through her. "Disappear as in..."

"As in, they'll erase you," Noah said bluntly. "The Council doesn't take risks. You flagged something you weren't meant to see. They'll make sure you never see anything again."

Stephanie swallowed hard. The memory of the BMW tailing them, the chase—it all aligned in a way that made her sick.

She rubbed a hand over her face. "This is insane," she muttered. "I'm just an IT specialist."

Noah's voice remained level. "And that's why you're valuable. You have access, knowledge of the system. You know where the back doors are." He leaned slightly closer, his gaze locking on to hers in the rearview mirror. "You can help us stop this."

She hesitated, fingers tightening around the strap of her handbag. There was no good way out of this. Either she ran and got caught or she stayed and became part of something far bigger than herself.

A long silence settled between them. Then, finally, she met his gaze, her voice steadier than she felt. "What do you need?"

A small smirk tugged at the corner of Noah's lips. "A way into Brandt's meeting."

THIRTY

A PALE PREDAWN LIGHT CREPT THROUGH THE GRIMY windows of the Whitechapel safehouse, casting long shadows over the peeling wallpaper.

Noah stood at the rickety table, arms folded, eyes grim. Around him, Katya, Jenny, Neil, Wally, and Stephanie Harrington gathered, the tension curdling in the stale air. A crude floor plan of the London Stock Exchange lay spread out before them, key areas marked in red. Another diagram—more technical—outlined the server architecture, courtesy of Stephanie. She'd spent the last twelve hours pulling every scrap of intel from her stolen credentials, forging passes, and mapping infiltration routes.

"Brandt will arrive to present Atlas at nine," Noah said. "If it installs, the Council takes control—finance, currency, markets. Everything."

"We can't let that happen," Katya said.

Noah tapped the map. "We split into two teams. Neil and Jenny, you're posing as security consultants." He slid over their forged IDs. "You plant an EMP near the server hub. If we can't stop Atlas conventionally, we fry the system."

Jenny smirked at the picture on her fake ID. "Not my best angle."

Noah turned to Katya. "As for us, we go in through maintenance tunnels. Hit the boardroom before Brandt launches Atlas. If we can terminate Brandt, we'll be terminating the Council's lead lieutenant spreading Olympus."

Katya nodded.

Noah shifted to Wally. "The contact has sourced us a surveillance van. That's where you'll be. You're our eyes. Lock down cameras, reroute security—buy us time."

"I'll stay quiet until you're inside," Wally said.

Noah's gaze swept the room. "Primary objective: shut down Atlas. Secondary: eliminate or capture Brandt. Final: get Stephanie out alive."

No one hesitated.

Jenny nudged Neil, exchanging a small nod. Katya checked her watch, silent but ready. Wally triple-checked his scripts. And Stephanie, once just an IT specialist, now prepared to betray her own workplace.

Noah straightened. "We move in two hours. Gear up."

THIRTY-ONE

LONDON STOCK EXCHANGE | 09:00 GMT | FEBRUARY 24

THE MORNING LIGHT IN PATERNOSTER SQUARE CUT through the lingering London fog, glinting off the towering columns and the bronze statue of the Fearless Girl outside the London Stock Exchange. Business-suited men and women hurried past, heads down, focused on the rhythm of their morning routine. They had no idea that in just under an hour, the entire country's financial systems would fall under the control of Olympus.

Inside the LSE, the tension was already thick. A dozen security guards, each armed with handheld scanners, manned the turnstiles. The building's standard security procedures had been tightened for the high-profile unveiling of Atlas, and additional personnel loitered around the entrance, watching the incoming flow of employees with trained, unreadable expressions.

Among the morning crowd, Neil and Jenny approached the main gates, blending in seamlessly. They wore charcoal-gray business suits, but instead of briefcases, each carried a heavy-duty toolbox—the kind used by IT engineers for server maintenance. The forged IDs clipped to their lapels—courtesy of Stephanie—

identified them as external cyber-threat analysts, hired for a last-minute assessment of the LSE's digital infrastructure.

Neil took the lead, stepping up to the security checkpoint. He slid his ID across the scanner, the screen blinking for a brief, heart-stopping second before turning green. The guard, a stocky man with a military-style buzz cut, gave him a quick once-over before gesturing to the toolbox.

"Pop it open."

Neil flicked the metal clasps, lifting the lid to reveal a neatly organized array of tools—network cable testers, insulated pliers, voltage meters, a soldering kit, fiber-optic repair equipment. Everything a tech team might need to work inside the server room.

The second guard waved Jenny forward. She presented her badge, watching as the man unfastened the clasps on her toolbox and flipped open the lid.

Inside, among the rows of neatly arranged tools, sat two pilot chutes, folded tightly.

The guard frowned, reaching in. He held one up. "What's this?"

Jenny didn't flinch. She let out a small, exasperated sigh, as though this was a conversation she'd had a hundred times before.

"Dust sheets," she said flatly.

The guard's brow furrowed. "Dust sheets?"

Jenny gave a patient, mildly irritated smile. "The parachute fabric is non-conductive and doesn't create static buildup. When we have to work on sensitive server racks, we use them to cover exposed components. Last time we didn't, we ended up frying a switchboard, and management was not happy."

The guard gave her a skeptical look, shifting the material between his fingers. "Seems a bit overkill."

Jenny tilted her head, feigning amusement. "Tell that to the risk assessment guys. They love their redundancy measures. We also carry antistatic mats, but the parachute material's better for covering whole workstations when we're pulling cables."

Neil nodded sagely, adding in a dry, matter-of-fact tone, "Plus, it keeps the cleaning staff from moaning when we leave dust everywhere."

The guard exhaled through his nose, clearly bored of the conversation already. He gave the chutes one last glance, then tossed them back into the toolbox.

"Fine. Just don't go jumping off the building," he muttered, latching the case shut.

Jenny smirked. "Wouldn't dream of it."

The first guard waved them through, and Jenny and Neil stepped past the checkpoint.

Beside her, Neil kept his posture relaxed, but she could see the flicker of relief in his eyes.

The first hurdle was passed.

Meanwhile, beneath the city streets, Noah and Katya moved through a damp, claustrophobic tunnel that ran parallel to the London Underground's District and Circle Lines. The walls were slick with condensation, the air thick with the mingled scents of wet concrete, rust, and the faint metallic tang of sewage runoff. Overhead, the distant rumble of passing trains sent tremors through the tunnel walls.

Katya tapped a tablet screen, her gloved fingers scrolling through a digital blueprint of the LSE's underground structure. The map, obtained through a mix of old construction records and Stephanie's internal access, showed a network of tunnels, service corridors, and ventilation shafts.

"You're close." Wally's voice crackled in their earpieces from the surveillance van. "Another ten meters forward. Right at the next junction."

Noah adjusted the weight of his pack and kept moving, the beam of his head-light skimming over the damp brickwork. The sound of another train rumbling overhead vibrated through his bones. He glanced at Katya, who was already stepping ahead, her movements quick and fluid.

They reached a section of the tunnel where the walls

narrowed slightly, the arching ceiling pressing down like a stone throat trying to swallow. Katya checked the tablet screen—this was the spot. The service tunnel leading into the LSE was behind this wall.

She unshouldered her pack and crouched, unzipping it to reveal a set of small, precisely shaped explosive charges. Designed for breaching, not destruction. Noah pulled out a roll of detonation cord, securing it along the edges of the charges while Katya placed them in a careful pattern against the damp stonework.

"Timing's key," Wally reminded them over comms. "Those walls aren't exactly thick. You need cover noise."

Noah checked his watch, counting the seconds. The next train would pass in forty-five.

"Stand by," he murmured. "Katya, get ready."

The ground rumbled. The distant growl of an approaching train built into a full-fledged roar. The vibrations intensified as it neared their position.

"Five seconds," Noah said.

A secondary rumble echoed from the opposite side. A second train—perfect.

"Now," Noah ordered.

Katya triggered the detonation.

A muffled *whumpf* shook the tunnel, but the sound barely registered over the deafening dual thunder of trains speeding past on either side. The carefully placed charges did their job—no fireball, no flying debris, just a controlled breach that sent a spiderweb of cracks through the stonework before a section caved inward with a soft crunch.

The moment the last train thundered past, silence followed. The dust settled in the dim tunnel, revealing a jagged, man-sized hole leading into the LSE's underground service passage.

Noah pulled his scarf over his mouth and stepped through, scanning the dim corridor beyond. The sterile scent of concrete and cleaning chemicals replaced the damp stench of the tunnel behind them. Industrial pipes lined the ceiling, and utility panels blinked softly in the low light. This was the building's underbelly —where maintenance workers and janitorial staff moved unseen.

Katya followed, adjusting her rifle strap. "We're in."

Noah tapped his comm. "Neil, Jenny—status?"

"Through security," Jenny whispered back. "Moving into position now."

"Stephanie?" Noah said next into his comms.

At 9:03 a.m., Stephanie Harrington was stepping out of a black cab, smoothing the creases in her blazer with trembling hands. The cool morning air did little to calm her nerves as she adjusted her earpiece. A sharp burst of static made her wince, and she fumbled with it before Wally's voice crackled through.

"Stephanie, check in."

She exhaled, forcing herself to sound steadier than she felt. "I'm here. Heading inside now."

The cab pulled away behind her as she walked toward the grand glass entrance of the London Stock Exchange. Her heels clicked against the polished stone, her usual confidence buried beneath the weight of what she was about to do.

Her palms felt clammy as she approached the security checkpoint.

"Relax," Wally murmured through the comms. "You belong there. Just walk through like you own the place."

Easy for you to say, Stephanie thought grimly, but she kept moving.

She stepped into the line of employees swiping their ID cards. The guard at the checkpoint barely looked up as she scanned hers. A brief pause. Then the light blinked green.

She let out a slow breath and stepped through.

Inside, the hum of the morning routine washed over her. Conversations layered over the clicking of keyboards, the shuffle of papers, the occasional burst of laughter from an early-morning meeting. It was an ordinary day for everyone else. For her, it felt like walking into the maw of hell.

She adjusted her bag strap and subtly glanced at the security stations. More guards than usual. Olympus wasn't taking any chances.

"All right," she murmured into her earpiece, slipping beyond the barriers into the lobby. "I'm in."

A few streets away, in the back of a nondescript white van labeled *UK Power & Utilities*, Wally sat hunched over a bank of screens, his fingers dancing across a keyboard. A tangle of wires fed into modified hardware, intercepting security camera feeds, building access logs, and communication channels.

The van rocked slightly as a big red double-decker bus passed, but Wally barely noticed. His gaze flicked between different video feeds—Neil and Jenny passing through security, Stephanie blending into the crowd, and the static image of the underground tunnels where Noah and Katya had breached the service entrance.

Wally's fingers drummed against the keyboard as he toggled between cameras—employees shuffling through security, executives making their way toward the upper levels, and then—

"I have eyes on Brandt," Wally muttered into the comms.

9:05 a.m.

The camera feed from the main lobby displayed a tall, silver-haired man striding through the entrance, radiating arrogance with every step of his expensive handcrafted Italian shoes. Victor Brandt, dressed in a perfectly tailored navy suit, adjusted his cufflinks as he approached the security gates. Flanking him were his bodyguards—two lithe figures clad in sleek black suits.

The twins. Leonid and Sofia Petrov.

The genetically superior assassins moved like shadows, their expressions unreadable, their posture honed for combat. No weapons in sight, but that meant nothing.

They were the weapons.

Inside the lobby, Stephanie had already spotted them. She stood near the security desk, watching as Brandt was greeted by one of the LSE's chief executives, a well-fed man in his fifties with thinning hair and a perpetually important air about him. The executive extended his hand, and Brandt clasped it with a confident shake, his easy smile well practiced.

Stephanie took her chance. Moving quickly but not too urgently, she stepped toward them. "Excuse me, sir," she said, addressing the executive.

The man barely glanced at her, distracted by Brandt's presence. "Not now," he muttered, shifting to move past.

She didn't let it go. "Sir, I need to speak with you," she pressed.

The executive turned, finally irritated enough to give her his attention. "Can't it wait until later?" His tone was clipped, dismissive.

Brandt quirked an eyebrow, his bemusement obvious. He glanced at Stephanie, then at his bodyguards, who immediately tensed, their predatory eyes scanning her.

Meanwhile, just behind them, Jenny and Neil moved swiftly through the crowd, their pace natural, unhurried. As they passed Brandt, Jenny's hand flicked out, brushing against the hem of his suit jacket for less than a second. A tiny, near-microscopic GPS tracker adhered to the fabric.

She didn't break stride as she tapped her earpiece. "Target is live."

In the van, Wally's screen blinked as a red dot appeared on the digital map of the LSE. "Confirmed," he whispered.

Stephanie caught Jenny's subtle nod from the corner of her eye. She had what she needed. There was no point pushing further. She sighed, putting on an exasperated face, and stepped back. "Never mind," she muttered, waving a hand in dismissal.

The executive gave her an irritated look before turning back to Brandt. "Shall we?"

Brandt offered her one last, curious glance before moving toward the elevators. The Petrovs followed, their eyes still sweeping the room, hyper-aware of the surroundings.

Stephanie didn't breathe properly until the elevator doors closed behind them.

Then a voice beside her said, "Your data guys are here."

She turned. A security guard, thickset with a buzz cut, jerked his pink chin in the direction of Neil and Jenny.

Stephanie feigned mild surprise, putting on her professional mask. She stepped toward them with the air of someone meeting new hires for the first time. "Right, of course," she said crisply, as if she hadn't spent the last twelve hours plotting with them.

Neil played along, adjusting his tie. "Ms. Harrington," he greeted, polite but neutral.

Jenny offered a small, almost bored nod, as if she'd rather be anywhere else.

"Let's get moving," Stephanie said, leading them toward the elevators.

The guard lost interest almost immediately. He turned back to his post as the three of them reached the next set of lift doors. A ding echoed softly as the doors slid open.

Stephanie stepped in first, followed by Jenny and Neil.

As the elevator ascended, she exhaled softly, gripping the strap of her bag. "That was close."

Neil adjusted his cuff. "It's not over yet."

Jenny glanced up at the floor indicator. "Nope. Just getting started."

The mission was divided into two critical objectives.

One:

Preventing Atlas from going live. Stephanie, Neil, and Jenny were tasked with infiltrating the London Stock Exchange's server infrastructure. Their goal: ensure that Atlas never made it online. Once inside, Stephanie would use her credentials to access the system's administrative framework, while Neil and Jenny worked on physically disabling key hardware components. If necessary, they would detonate an EMP device Neil had hidden on him—an irreversible last resort that would wipe critical segments of the system, delaying Olympus's global rollout indefinitely.

Two:

Exfiltration. Disabling Atlas was a temporary measure. To

shut down Olympus for good, they needed Victor Brandt. The architect of the AI infiltration system—the man whose algorithms could manipulate entire economies—was too valuable to leave in Council hands. Like Adrian Knox, he would be an invaluable prisoner. Noah and Katya would handle the extraction. As soon as Brandt's presentation ended, they would engage, neutralizing his personal security and dragging him into the LSE's service tunnels before anyone could react. Once underground, they would move through the maintenance corridors beneath the building, using the same breach point they had entered through. If all went well, they would have Brandt in their custody before security even understood what was happening.

That was the plan.

But plans rarely survive first contact.

THIRTY-TWO

9:07 A.M. THE ELEVATOR HUMMED SOFTLY AS Stephanie, Jenny, and Neil ascended toward the server operations floor. The ride was quiet, tension humming beneath their measured breaths. The mission was live. No turning back now.

The elevator dinged.

They stepped out onto the 28th floor—home to the LSE's IT and server operations center. The floor was sleek and ultra-modern with glass partitions and rows of cubicles occupied by busy technicians. Screens flickered with streams of financial data, numbers shifting in real-time, a constant pulse of the world's economic heartbeat.

A receptionist glanced up from her desk as they approached. "Can I help you?"

Stephanie didn't hesitate. "I have the consultants here for the cyber-risk audit," she said, nodding toward Neil and Jenny. "They'll need access to the infrastructure reports."

The receptionist tapped a few keys. "I don't see an appointment for today."

Stephanie sighed, already prepared for this. "Because the Board rushed this through after last week's penetration test failed.

If we're not in there before the transition, the regulators will have a fit. Check again—there should be a priority flag."

She leaned forward, her ID badge flashing just enough to emphasize her authority. The receptionist hesitated, then checked the system again. A moment later, her shoulders relaxed. "All right, I see it now." Of course, because Wally had only just placed it there. She handed over three visitor badges. "Sign in here. You'll be granted floor access for the next two hours."

Stephanie signed quickly, then led Jenny and Neil down the hall without another glance.

Wally's voice buzzed in their earpieces. "No alerts so far."

9:10 a.m.

Stephanie, Neil, and Jenny moved through the open-plan server operations floor, their footsteps muffled against the thick carpet. Rows of sleek workstations were occupied by IT specialists monitoring the Atlas transition process. Flat-panel screens flickered with lines of code, diagnostic readouts, and system logs. The entire floor pulsed with activity, but no one paid them much attention.

Stephanie led them toward a restricted-access door at the far end marked *Server Control*. Swiping her ID badge, she glanced at the small camera above the panel, hoping Wally had done his job.

The lock clicked open.

"You're good," Wally confirmed in her earpiece. "You're in their system, but they'll notice any major changes. Keep it subtle."

Stephanie pushed open the door. Inside, the temperature dropped significantly. The air hummed with the quiet power of server racks lining the walls, blinking LEDs casting faint blue glows in the dim lighting. Thick fiber-optic cables snaked across the floor, running into a central hub that controlled the Stock Exchange's core functions.

Neil stepped up to a workstation and pulled a USB drive from his pocket, plugging it in. Code scrolled down the screen, his custom script burrowing its way into the security systems. "I'm spoofing the monitoring logs," he muttered. "That way they won't see us messing with the core."

Jenny moved to the hardware panel on the wall, unscrewing a metal plate. Behind it, neatly organized cables connected to power regulators and backup systems. She glanced at Stephanie. "How much time do we need?"

Stephanie pulled out a second USB drive, loading her own program. "Five minutes to inject the script, then another five for it to spread through their servers."

"Too long," Neil muttered. "We'll be flagged before then."

"Not if we keep their system busy." Stephanie nodded toward Jenny. "Cause a small issue. Nothing major, just enough to get their IT guys distracted."

Jenny grinned, pulled out a pair of insulated wire clippers, and sliced through two secondary power leads.

The effect was instant. Overhead, some lights flickered. Across the floor, an error message flashed on a few workstations, followed by the sound of confused murmuring.

Stephanie smirked. "That should buy us time."

9:12 a.m.

Noah and Katya moved with electric precision through the dimly lit maintenance corridors, their steps careful on the concrete flooring. The walls were lined with old electrical panels, the air thick with the sterile tang of industrial cleaners and the faint mustiness of old ventilation ducts.

"Next left," Wally's voice crackled in their earpieces. "Then up two flights. Brandt's just started his presentation."

Noah reached the turn, but Wally's voice cut in sharply. "Wait. Halt."

He stopped mid-step, pressing his back against the wall. Katya mirrored him, both their bodies perfectly still. A second later, a faint scuff of shoes echoed from around the corner. A janitor appeared, pushing a mop along the corridor, the wet mop slapping against the tiles in lazy strokes.

Wally's voice came again, barely a whisper. "He's taking his time. You need to move in three... two... go."

Noah pushed off the wall and swept around the corner. Katya followed, their footsteps silent. They passed behind the janitor as he bent to wring out his mop, moving swiftly before he could glance over his shoulder.

At the next junction, Wally's voice guided them again. "Step back. Now!"

Noah yanked Katya into a shallow alcove as two LSE employees passed by, deep in conversation. One gestured animatedly, the other nodding, oblivious to the two figures pressed into the shadows just feet away.

Katya exhaled through her nose as they waited for Wally's next cue.

"Clear. Move."

They reached a heavy metal service door—the access point to the executive stairwell. Noah tried the handle. Locked.

Katya swung her pack off her shoulder and pulled out a small cylindrical device no larger than a soda can. She twisted the top, activating the timer, and carefully affixed it to the lock.

"Micro thermite charge," she murmured, pressing it flush against the latch. "Minimal noise, concentrated burn."

Noah nodded. It was the right tool for the job. The charge didn't rely on concussive force like C4. Instead, it used a controlled reaction of iron oxide and aluminum powder, generating heat upwards of 2,500 degrees Fahrenheit. The reaction was rapid but localized, burning through the metal like a hot knife through butter without sending a shockwave or loud bang to alert security.

"Five seconds," Katya muttered, stepping back.

The charge ignited with a soft hiss, a pinpoint-bright flare momentarily illuminating the metal before fading just as quickly. The lock deformed under the intense heat, sagging and warping. Katya tapped it lightly with the butt of her knife, and the mechanism crumbled inward, leaving the door free to push open.

Noah led the way into the stairwell. The narrow industrial staircase ran alongside the main executive lifts, its concrete steps flanked by steel railings.

Noah pressed a hand to his earpiece. "Wally?"

"Brandt just pulled up the Atlas interface," Wally said. "Security's watching the boardroom, but they don't expect anyone coming from your side."

"Perfect," Noah murmured.

They reached the top landing. A final door separated them from the executive level. Beyond it, a long hallway led to the glass-paneled boardroom where Victor Brandt was unveiling the most dangerous piece of software ever created.

Katya checked her pistol. "Let's finish this."

9:14 a.m.

Victor Brandt stood at the head of a long, polished conference table, his fingers resting lightly on the glass surface. The room was packed—executives, government liaisons, and high-ranking economists all listening intently as the screens along the walls displayed scrolling lines of code.

"Atlas represents the future," Brandt declared smoothly, his rich voice filling the space. "An economic ecosystem that doesn't react to human errors but anticipates them. The system is predictive, proactive, and most importantly—untouchable."

A few murmurs of approval rippled through the room.

Brandt gestured to the screen, where a global map flickered to life. Red and green indicators pulsed over major financial hubs.

"Right now, Atlas is running in shadow mode. Watching. Learning," Brandt said. "But in exactly two minutes, it will go live, integrating itself into every major financial institution across the UK. And from there... the world."

The room fell silent. The weight of what he was saying settled over them.

One of the executives leaned forward. "And what about external threats? Interference?"

Brandt smiled. "Impossible. Atlas is decentralized, quantum-protected, and self-adaptive. Even if someone attempted to compromise it, the system would rewrite itself before they could touch the core."

He glanced at the countdown on the screen.

One minute, thirty seconds.

Brandt adjusted his cufflinks, exuding confidence. "We are standing at the precipice of a new era. An era where—"

The lights cut out.

Instantly, emergency LEDs flickered on. Red alarms flashed along the ceiling.

"What the hell—" Brandt snapped, turning sharply.

The large display screen behind him distorted, lines of code glitching. Atlas's interface flickered erratically, error messages flooding the screen.

On the 28th floor, Neil yanked the USB drive from the workstation. "They know something's wrong," he muttered.

Stephanie cursed. "Security's responding. We need to move."

Back in the boardroom, a voice crackled over the internal security comms. "Sir, we have an intrusion in the IT sector. Multiple breaches—"

Brandt's expression darkened.

And then, before he could react, the boardroom doors exploded inward.

A flashbang detonated, blinding white light and a concussive blast sending executives sprawling. Smoke filled the space, fire alarms screaming in protest.

Noah and Katya stepped through the haze. Weapons raised.

Brandt's bodyguards, the Petrov twins, moved instantly, sleek as panthers, their bodies flicking into fighting stances.

For the first time, Brandt's confidence wavered.

Noah glared at him. "Meeting's over."

THIRTY-THREE

9:15 A.M. THE BOARDROOM ERUPTED INTO CHAOS. Executives and high-ranking officials scrambled for cover, knocking over chairs, spilling glasses of water, and shoving each other in blind panic. The high-tech screens along the walls flickered wildly, displaying distorted error messages as Atlas's launch sequence faltered.

Noah and Katya raised their weapons, but before they could fire, the Petrovs moved like bolts of lightning, weaving through the confusion with impossible speed.

Using the screaming executives as human shields, the twins twisted and spun, their movements impossibly fluid, positioning themselves in a way that blocked any clear shots.

Noah adjusted his aim, but in that split second, Leonid kicked a chair into his legs. It clipped his knee, throwing his stance off. Sofia lunged low, grabbing a fleeing executive and hurling him forward. The man crashed into Noah, sending them both sprawling into the conference table.

Katya fired twice, but Sofia was already rolling over the back of a chair, dodging each shot by millimeters. Katya adjusted her aim—too late. A black boot snapped up, kicking the silenced

Glock from her grip. The weapon spun through the air, clattering across the polished floor.

Noah shoved the executive off him, but before he could recover, Leonid was already on him. A hand locked around his wrist, twisting his SIG Sauer out of his grip with an effortless motion.

In the same breath, Sofia spun into Katya, delivering a lightning-fast spinning back kick to her chest. The impact sent her skidding backward, slamming into the wall.

Both Noah and Katya were disarmed in under five seconds.

The twins straightened, eerily synchronized, stepping toward them with deliberate menace. They cracked their knuckles in perfect unison.

Then they attacked.

9:16 a.m.

Neil barely had time to react before the building's security systems locked down.

Across the server room, steel shutters slammed down over windows, security doors sealed shut, and alarms blared through the entire LSE. Red warning lights strobed along the walls. Panic erupted. Employees shrieked, hammering at doors that refused to budge.

Stephanie paled. "They've initiated a full lockdown."

Neil swore under his breath, yanking the USB drive from the terminal. "That means reinforcements are coming."

Stephanie turned to him. "How are we going to stop Atlas now?"

Neil's jaw tightened. "We go to plan B."

He yanked open his pack and pulled out the EMP charge Wally had given him as a contingency. The fail-safe.

Jenny's eyes flicked to it, realization dawning.

"Neil—"

He was already moving. He ripped off the safety clip, armed the device, and slammed it against the wall.

The EMP detonated.

A pulse of raw energy surged outward.

The red emergency lights flickered—then died. The alarms fell silent. The steel shutters juddered, some freezing mid-motion, others slamming open. The server racks exploded with static, monitors flashing garbled code before going dark.

For a split second, the entire London Stock Exchange fell into a black void of silence.

Then—

The building began to wake up.

Backup power flickered to life, but it was sluggish, incomplete. Security systems lagged. The locks on the doors released.

Jenny was already moving. She grabbed their packs, the ones with the chutes, and bolted toward the emergency stairwell. "We go. Now!" she snapped.

They barely made it into the corridor before the server room doors slammed shut behind them.

No turning back. No more chances.

They forced their way past panicked employees, weaving through the chaos. Arriving at the stairwell first, Neil peeked down over the banister—

Security swarmed up the stairs from below. There was no going down.

"Rooftop," Jenny said. "We get to the roof, signal Wally, and extract. Move!"

They ran up the stairwell.

9:17 a.m.

Outside, the streets of Paternoster Square were flooded with sudden, ominous movement. Black armored vans screeched to a halt along every access point to the London Stock Exchange, tires smoking as reinforced doors were flung open.

Dozens of Council operatives poured out, clad in full tactical gear—sleek, black armor plating over their chests and shoulders, visors covering their faces. Their rifles were raised and their movements were sharp as they surged toward the entrance in perfect formation.

Overhead, drones buzzed to life, hovering high above the building, their cameras locking on to every exit, every possible escape route.

Through the crackling comms of the assault team, a voice spoke—cold and methodical.

"The LSE is secure. All external exits locked. Ground teams, move in. Overwatch, establish aerial containment. Basement teams, clear the tunnels. No one gets out."

The first wave of Council operatives stormed the main lobby, boots thundering against the marble floors. Employees screamed and dropped to the ground, hands raised as the heavily armed men fanned out with brutal efficiency, taking control of the space in seconds.

"Alpha team, stairwells secured. Bravo, take the elevators offline. Charlie, move to the IT sector—our intruders are still inside."

Deep inside the building, elevator doors slid open, and another wave of black-clad soldiers stepped out, their rifles sweeping the corridors.

The lead officer's voice crackled through every operative's earpiece.

"Find them. Now."

The hunt was on.

9:18 a.m.

Noah barely dodged the first strike.

Leonid exploded forward with blinding speed, throwing a precise leaping knee strike aimed at his ribs. Noah twisted, absorbing most of the impact on his forearm. The force rattled his bones, but he was still standing.

Before he could counter, the twin pivoted smoothly, spinning into a reverse elbow strike aimed at Noah's temple.

Noah ducked, but the twin's other hand lashed out, fingers grabbing his collar. In a flash, Noah was airborne—hip-thrown over Leonid's shoulder. He slammed onto the glass conference table, which cracked beneath him.

Katya, meanwhile, was fighting her own battle.

Sofia was a ghost, floating between her attacks, slipping past her punches with razor-thin margins.

Katya lashed out with a low roundhouse kick, but Sofia leapt over her leg, twisting in mid-air before landing smoothly. Then she countered with a brutal axe kick, her heel dropping straight toward Katya's face.

Katya barely rolled away in time. The impact shook the floor beneath them. It would have crushed her skull.

She had never fought anyone this fast before.

Before Katya could recover, Sofia flipped into a back handspring, vaulting onto the conference table, then springboarding off it—delivering a devastating flying knee to Katya's chest.

She crashed into the wall, gasping for air with burning lungs.

As Noah rose from the table, he scanned the room. Brandt was already on the move. The executive had slipped through the chaos, making his way toward the room's exit.

The Petrovs moved to cover his retreat.

"Stop him!" Noah growled, but the twins closed in again.

Brandt disappeared through the side door, vanishing into the executive hallway.

9:19 a.m.

Inside the surveillance van, Wally's fingers flew over the keyboard, scrambling to keep the team's access online.

The Council's digital strike team was already inside the LSE's systems, countering him in real-time. Firewalls slammed shut, cutting off his remote access. Surveillance feeds blinked out one by one, sealing him in darkness.

His screen flashed with red alerts.

System Breach Detected.

Location Exposed.

His stomach dropped.

9:20 a.m.

Neil, Jenny, and Stephanie burst onto the rooftop, wind whipping against them as they stumbled into the open. The city stretched out before them, a sprawling maze of glass, steel, and stone, but there was no escape below—the entire block was crawling with Council operatives.

More black armored vans screeched to a halt outside the LSE. The back doors slammed open, and wave after wave of Council troops flooded out—black-clad, rifles raised, moving with mechanical precision. The air hummed with the distant drone of surveillance UAVs, circling the building like vultures.

Stephanie's breath hitched. "Is that for us?"

Jenny's reply was instant. "Yes."

Neil tapped his earpiece. "Wally, we need immediate evac! Now!"

Static.

Then—Wally's voice, strained. "Guys, we have a big problem—"

A muffled thud. Then silence.

Neil and Jenny exchanged a look.

9:21 a.m.

A black SUV screeched to a halt outside the alleyway, engine growling as its doors swung open. Inside the van, Wally snatched his laptop, shoving it into his backpack, already reaching for the van's side door.

Too late.

A flashbang bounced off the pavement, detonating in a blinding explosion of white light and concussive force.

Wally threw up his arms, staggering back, his ears ringing. Before he knew what was happening, Council troops had surrounded him, boots hammering against the pavement.

Through the haze, Wally saw six black-clad figures moving fast, rifles locked on to him.

One of them spoke, voice calm and precise.

"Hands where we can see them."

Wally hesitated.

The rifles cocked in unison.

So Wally dropped the laptop and slowly raised his hands.

A black hood was yanked over his head, the world vanishing into darkness. The last thing he heard before he was dragged into the SUV was the operatives' voice talking into his radio.

"We have the asset."

9:22 a.m.

On the roof, Jenny tried again. "Wally?"

Nothing.

Neil swore, his stomach twisting. "They've got him."

They had no time to dwell on it.

A helicopter roared in, its rotors slicing the air as it wheeled around, banking hard toward them. The side door slid open, revealing a black-clad Council gunner standing in the open doorway, rifle raised, the barrel tracking them like a predator locking on to its prey.

A flash—then the crack of a rifle shot.

The bullet slammed into the concrete, inches from Jenny's foot, spraying debris.

Jenny flinched back, her heart hammering against her ribs. The gunman adjusted his aim, preparing for a second shot.

She didn't wait to see what happened next.

The three of them took cover behind the stairwell bulkhead, using it as a shield while the helicopter circled, angling for a clear shot. Jenny then tore open her pack, yanking out the pilot chute —a compact base-jumping rig designed for fast, desperate exits.

Neil did the same. No hesitation. No wasted movements.

"Strap in," Neil ordered, tightening his harness.

Jenny tossed Stephanie a harness, urgency in her voice. "Put it on. Now."

Stephanie stared at the chute in disbelief, her chest rising and falling too fast. "You—you want me to jump?"

Jenny grabbed her by the shoulders, forcing her to meet her gaze. "It's our only way out!"

Stephanie's hands trembled violently as she fumbled with the straps. The thought of throwing herself off the side of a skyscraper froze her in place. "I can't—"

Another shot rang out.

The bullet whipped past Stephanie's shoulder, so close she gasped and stumbled back.

Jenny snapped. "You don't have a choice!"

She grabbed Stephanie's harness, yanking it into place, strapping her in with brutal efficiency. No more time. No more arguments.

Neil peered over the edge. It was a long way down. The narrow alley below was nothing but scaffolding, dumpsters, and steel beams. Not ideal. But survivable.

"Thirty seconds," he muttered.

The helicopter swung around again, the gunman repositioning.

Jenny clipped herself into Stephanie's harness, pulling the straps tight, securing the two of them together. "Hold on to me and don't let go."

Stephanie shook her head, terror raw in her eyes. "Jenny, please—"

Jenny gripped her tighter. "We'll make it. Trust me."

The rooftop doors exploded outward.

Council operatives poured out, rifles raised.

Jenny had no more time.

"Go!" Neil shouted.

Jenny grabbed Stephanie—and jumped.

The wind tore past them, a deafening roar as they plummeted into the open air. The ground rushed up to meet them, a dizzying blur of concrete and steel. Jenny yanked the pilot chute. The canopy burst open, snapping them backward, their descent slowing sharply as they glided downward.

Neil was right behind them, his own chute deploying smoothly, the wind whipping at his face.

Above them, the Council troops rushed to the edge, aiming their rifles—desperately trying to get a clear shot.

For a moment, Jenny thought they'd made it.

They landed hard, their feet slamming into the pavement in

the alleyway behind the LSE. Jenny skidded to her knees, unfastening the harness as quickly as she could.

She turned to Stephanie. "We're clear. Come on."

Neil was already stripping off his chute, scanning the street. They needed an exit, fast.

Then came the gunshot.

A sharp, hollow crack that split the air.

Stephanie gasped, her body jolting.

Jenny froze.

A single, dark red bloom spread across Stephanie's chest. Her knees buckled. She fell against Jenny, her weight slumping forward.

Jenny caught her, lowering her to the ground. "No, no, no—stay with me!"

Stephanie's lips parted, but no words came. Her eyes were glassy, her breath shallow, fading.

Neil spun around—but there was no clear shooter. The shot had come from above, from the rooftops, one of the Council snipers taking their final shot before moving out.

Jenny pressed her hands over Stephanie's wound, but it was useless. Stephanie's fingers grasped weakly at Jenny's sleeve, trying to say something—but then she went still.

Jenny's breath hitched.

Stephanie was gone.

"Jenny!" Neil yanked her back to reality. "We have to move!"

Jenny stared down at Stephanie, her mind screaming at her to do something—but there was nothing left to do.

More Council troops were coming.

Jenny's hands clenched into fists, but she stood, forcing herself to turn away.

Turn away and run.

THIRTY-FOUR

9:25 A.M. NOAH AND KATYA BURST AWAY FROM THE wreckage of the boardroom. The hallway stretched ahead, and at the far end—Victor Brandt, running for his life.

"He's getting away," Katya snarled.

Noah sprinted beside her, boots pounding against the carpeted floor as they pursued him down the corridor. Brandt was fast for a man in his fifties—but then, panic was a hell of a motivator. His perfectly tailored suit was disheveled, his silver hair out of place, but he ran like a man who knew the price of failure.

The twins flanked Brandt at a distance. Shepherding him.

The stairwell loomed ahead.

Brandt lunged for the door and threw it open.

As he vanished through it, the twins stopped in perfect sync, pivoting to face the corridor.

Noah pushed harder, his legs moving like pistons—but now Leonid and Sofia stood between them and the exit, motionless and poised like statues waiting to spring.

Silent. Deadly. Unyielding.

Noah jerked back just in time to dodge a palm strike aimed at his throat. Leonid followed up with a spinning back kick that clipped Noah's ribs, sending him stumbling into the wall.

Katya swung for Sofia, but the twin was already inside her guard, snapping a leg up for a vicious side kick to her stomach. The impact sent Katya slamming backward into a glass partition, cracking it.

On the other side of the corridor, Noah barely blocked a knife-hand strike aimed at his carotid, countering with a brutal elbow to the ribs. Leonid absorbed the hit, his expression eerily placid, before he spun, using the wall as leverage to twist into a downward hammer fist.

Noah dodged, but the narrow hallway left no room to maneuver.

Katya lashed out with a rising knee, but Sofia caught her leg mid-air, flipping her with a sharp whip motion. She hit the ground hard, gritting her teeth as she rolled away from a stomping kick that struck the floor in an almighty crack.

Noah knew they couldn't win this fight—not here.

"Down the stairs!" he barked.

Katya twisted away from a second kick and lunged for the stairwell door, throwing her full weight against it. It burst open.

Noah threw a blind punch to disrupt Leonid's rhythm, then spun, yanking Katya inside before slamming the door shut behind them.

They raced downward.

9:27 a.m.

Neil flagged down the nearest vehicle—a black cab, the driver staring wide-eyed at the chaos unfolding in the street.

"Out!" Neil barked, yanking the door open.

The driver didn't argue—he scrambled out, hands raised.

Jenny threw herself into the passenger seat, her chest heaving, her hands still sticky with Stephanie's blood.

Neil slid behind the wheel, shifting into gear with a sharp jerk. The engine roared as he slammed his foot on the accelerator, sending the cab lurching forward.

Tires screeched against the wet pavement as they shot into the London streets, merging into the chaotic flow of traffic.

Jenny pressed two fingers to her earpiece, urgency rising in her voice. "Noah, come in," she said into her comms. "Noah—do you read?"

Static.

She tried again.

"Katya? Wally?"

Nothing.

Neil swung the wheel hard, taking a corner too fast. The cab skidded slightly, its tires fighting for grip on the rain-slick asphalt.

Jenny's breath was ragged, her hands shaking as she switched frequencies.

"Noah, dammit, answer me!"

The line hissed with static, the kind that meant one of two things—either they were out of range... or the Council was jamming communications.

Neil's jaw tightened, his knuckles white against the steering wheel.

"Wally's down," he muttered. "Stephanie's dead. We have no idea if Noah and Katya even made it."

Jenny gritted her teeth.

"They made it," she snapped. "They have to."

She tried one last time.

"Noah, come in! Are you there?"

9:28 a.m.

The stairwell was cold concrete and steel, the echo of their boots bouncing down the empty shaft. Flickering fluorescent lights cast harsh shadows, turning the space into a cage of angles and motion.

Below, Victor Brandt's head bobbed into view as he hurtled down the stairs, taking them two at a time.

Two flights above, the Petrovs were closing in. Fast.

Noah and Katya glanced up sharply, but they had only a second to react.

Leonid vaulted onto the railing, using it like a gymnast's bar, swinging his entire body over the drop. He flipped downward, twisting mid-air, landing with catlike grace on the steps just below them, blocking their path.

Sofia didn't bother with the stairs—she vaulted straight onto the concrete wall, using the momentum to kick off it at an angle, launching herself directly at Katya.

She'd barely turned before Sofia smashed into her, slamming her spine-first into the metal railing with a force that sent pain ricocheting through her entire skeleton.

Noah had no time to help her—Leonid was already attacking, striking low with a sweeping kick aimed to take him off his feet.

Noah leapt backward, but Leonid wasn't done—he used the momentum to pivot into a spinning backfist, forcing Noah to throw up his arms in a desperate block.

Twisting away, he used the wall to spring back at the twin, throwing a hook punch, but the man leaned just out of range, countering with a rapid-fire series of palm strikes to Noah's ribs.

Noah absorbed the hits, knowing he couldn't block them all. He took the impact, then used his size and strength to tackle Leonid outright, driving him backward into the steel railing. The metal groaned under their combined weight.

The twin grappled on to Noah's shoulders, twisting his body, and suddenly they were falling.

Noah crashed onto the next landing, rolling to absorb the impact. The twin landed gracefully, already snapping into a low fighting stance.

Meanwhile, Katya was inches from getting thrown off the side of the stairwell. Sofia had her in a brutal wrist lock, forcing her dangerously over the railing. Her back arched, her balance compromised, Sofia's grip tightening like a vise.

Noah moved fast.

He grabbed a loose metal conduit box from the wall, yanked it free, and hurled it like a fastball.

The heavy metal casing smashed into Sofia's shoulder, forcing her to release Katya just in time.

She rolled away, gasping, before planting a boot on the railing and vaulting over it to the next landing down.

They had to keep moving.

Noah and Katya scrambled down the stairs, taking them three at a time. The twins recovered fast, but it didn't matter.

The bottom was in sight.

9:30 a.m.

As Neil weaved the stolen black cab through the congested London streets, Jenny sat beside him, tablet balanced on her lap, fingers flying across the screen as she tracked their surroundings.

Then—something ominous in the mirror.

A matte-black SUV tore through traffic behind them, moving with rapid intent, slicing between vehicles like a predator zeroing in on its kill. Its tinted windows gave nothing away, but Neil didn't need to see inside to know who was driving it—Council enforcers, armed and relentless.

Jenny's voice was clipped and urgent. "They're tagging us with traffic cameras. They'll cut off every route ahead if we don't shake them fast."

Neil swung the wheel hard, taking the cab onto Bishopsgate. The tires squealed, the rear kicking out slightly before gripping again.

A red light loomed ahead.

Neil didn't slow down.

The cab shot through the intersection, missing a double-decker bus by inches. Horns blared. Pedestrians stumbled back onto the curb. There was no time for caution now.

Jenny scanned the map. "Turn left—no, wait—shit!"

Neil cursed. "Make up your mind!"

"Right! Now!" Jenny shouted.

Neil yanked the wheel. The cab lurched, nearly clipping a parked van as it shot down a narrow side street, barely wide enough for a single vehicle.

The SUV didn't hesitate—it followed.

Neil's grip tightened.

Jenny zoomed out on the map, searching for anything they could use. She found something—

"Spitalfields!" she snapped. "Take the next right—cut through the market!"

Neil didn't argue.

He slammed the cab into a hard right, mounting the curb and plowing through a set of bollards, smashing them down as the cab barreled straight into Spitalfields Market.

9:32 a.m.

At the bottom of the stairwell, Noah and Katya burst through the final door—

And stopped dead in their tracks.

The lobby was a wall of black-clad troops.

Dozens of armed Council operatives stood in formation, rifles raised, ready. The moment Noah and Katya appeared, the air tensed, fingers hovering over triggers.

And there, in the center of it all—Victor Brandt.

He wasn't running anymore.

He was perfectly composed, standing in front of his men as he smoothed back his hair with practiced elegance. His suit was rumpled but intact, his face sheened with sweat, but his hands were steady as he pulled a pristine white handkerchief from his pocket and dabbed his forehead.

Noah and Katya stood frozen, their chests rising and falling from exertion. They had no weapons. No cover. No way out.

Brandt straightened his cuffs, adjusting them with an easy, unhurried grace.

Then he looked directly at Noah. "I'll be seeing you around, Noah Wolf."

A smug smile curled at the edges of his lips. Behind them, his twin bodyguards emerged from the stairwell. They cautiously moved around Noah and Katya before joining their boss.

They gave a small, synchronized bow—a taunting farewell. Then, like a king disappearing into his court, Brandt turned and strolled toward the doors, the Petrovs falling into step behind him, the Council troops closing in their wake.

For a single second after they left the building, there was silence.

Then—

"MOVE!" Noah shouted.

He and Katya spun on their heels, sprinting back into the stairwell as the lobby erupted in gunfire. Bullets tore through the air, punching holes into the concrete walls, shattering glass partitions.

Slamming the door shut behind them, Katya grabbed the nearest metal storage cabinet, yanking it down. It crashed in front of the door, buying them some precious time.

"Basement!" Noah barked.

Katya was already moving. They took the stairs two at a time, heading downward—toward the tunnels.

Behind them, the Council troops slammed into the barricade.

9:34 a.m.

Spitalfields Market was packed, rows of stalls selling everything from fresh produce to antiques, pedestrians meandering under the glass-and-iron canopy, sipping coffee, haggling over vintage records, unaware that a high-speed pursuit was about to rip through their morning.

Until it did.

The black cab roared in, tearing between fruit stalls and makeshift kiosks, sending crates of oranges exploding across the pavement.

Shouts of confusion and panic rippled through the market as vendors and shoppers threw themselves out of the way, dodging the barreling taxi.

The SUV followed without hesitation, smashing through a stand selling handmade pottery, sending ceramic shrapnel raining onto the cobblestones.

Jenny's breath was tight. "Neil, we can't—"

"No choice!" he growled.

A hot food stall loomed ahead, its heavy metal frame directly in their path.

Neil made a split-second decision.

He spun the wheel hard, throwing the cab into a sideways skid, barely squeezing between two vendor tents, the fabric ripping apart as they tore through.

Behind them, the SUV wasn't as lucky.

It slammed into the food stall, crashing into boiling vats of oil and burning coals. Flames burst up the side of the vehicle, market-goers screaming as fire erupted.

But the SUV didn't stop.

The doors burst open, and black-clad Council operatives spilled out, moving fast, weapons raised.

Neil didn't wait around. He punched the accelerator.

The cab screeched onto Commercial Street, leaving the burning wreckage of Spitalfields behind.

Jenny's eyes flicked to the tablet, heart hammering.

"Take the next left," she said. "The rendezvous is twenty-three minutes away."

"That's if they even make it," Neil added.

"They'll make it. It's Noah."

9:37 a.m.

Noah and Katya raced through the tunnel, their footsteps bouncing sharply off the tight space as gunfire erupted behind them.

Bullets pinged off the damp brick walls, ricocheting off overhead piping, sending sparks cascading into the darkness.

Katya ducked instinctively as a round zipped past her head, splitting open a steam pipe. A hissing cloud of white vapor burst out, momentarily obscuring their pursuers.

"Ladder's ahead!" Noah shouted.

They pushed forward, their lungs burning, the air thick with the stench of rust. The hole loomed ahead, the jagged, man-sized opening they had blasted through earlier. Beyond it—the ladder. Their only way out.

Katya vaulted through first, gripping the rough, rusted rungs and hauling herself up fast. Noah was right behind her, but the Council troops were too close now—shapes moving through the steam.

More gunfire erupted.

A round slammed into the ladder just as Noah grabbed it, rattling the metal.

"MOVE!" Katya yelled from above, already throwing open the manhole cover with her shoulder.

Noah gritted his teeth and climbed fast.

9:38 a.m.

Neil gripped the wheel as the taxi hurtled through the city. Jenny sat beside him, her eyes locked on the tablet in her lap, guiding him toward the extraction point.

"It should be right up ahead," she said, scanning the streets.

Neil nodded, his focus locked on the road—

The manhole cover ahead suddenly popped open.

Neil's eyes widened. "Shit—!"

He slammed the brakes, the taxi screeching to a stop, its rear fishtailing slightly. Katya emerged from the hole, gun raised, her expression hard and focused.

Neil barely missed plowing into her.

Noah was right behind, panting, his face streaked with sweat and grime. His gaze snapped to the taxi, then to Neil and Jenny inside. Recognition clicked.

"Get in!" Jenny yelled.

Noah and Katya wasted no time. They ripped open the back doors and threw themselves inside.

Neil punched the accelerator.

The taxi roared forward, tires spinning before catching grip, launching them away from the alley just as shouts erupted behind them. Council troops—pushing up into the street from the manhole, too late to stop them.

Noah slumped back, catching his breath. He turned to Jenny.

"Stephanie?"

Jenny's expression darkened instantly. She swallowed, jaw tight. "She's gone."

Noah exhaled sharply, staring forward, his expression unreadable.

Katya watched him carefully but said nothing.

A long beat of silence.

Then Jenny looked back.

"Brandt?"

Noah didn't answer at first. His fingers tightened against his thigh. Then, finally, he spoke.

"He got away."

THIRTY-FIVE

COUNCIL FACILITY, SIBERIA | 18:08 KRAT | FEBRUARY 24

THE AIR WAS FRIGID AND STERILE, LACED WITH THE scent of damp concrete, sweat, and antiseptic. Beyond the frost-coated windows of the training compound, a dozen child recruits moved in perfect synchronization, their thin, sinewed bodies pushing through exhaustion as they ran drills under the watchful gaze of white-coated scientists and armed guards.

They were barefoot in the cold, their breath misting in the freezing air, clad only in thin gray uniforms that did little to shield them from the elements. Their movements were meticulous—calculated, controlled. Their faces devoid of emotion.

Those same twins that protected Victor Brandt had been forged here. First inside its laboratories. Then inside this curse of a training base.

Allison Peterson stood at the edge of the observation platform, her arms crossed, watching with the cold detachment of an investor surveying assets.

Below, children sparred in pairs, their bodies moving in perfect fluidity—not wild, not frantic, but in practiced, deliberate motions designed to inflict maximum damage. Not one of them flinched or hesitated. This was not only training. This was conditioning.

To the left, another group performed gymnastic drills, flipping through the air with inhuman precision. Their bodies were being molded into weapons, flexible and strong. This wasn't about grace—it was about how fast they could climb, evade, kill.

Farther inside the compound, in side rooms, more lessons were taking place.

One classroom was dedicated to firearms training. Children sat at long steel tables, blindfolded, dismantling weapons by touch alone. Tiny fingers worked with mechanical precision, stripping handguns, cleaning the components, and reassembling them in under a minute.

In another room, anatomy lessons were in progress. Not biology. Not medicine. No.

This was anatomy for killers.

The children were being taught the weak points of the human body—where to strike for instant death, how to snap a neck with minimal force, where to slide a knife between ribs to avoid resistance.

And they weren't just taught how to inflict death. No. They were also taught how to survive.

Here they learned how to pull a bullet from their own bodies, how to seal a wound on the battlefield, how to keep themselves alive long enough to kill again.

They weren't being taught human biology so they could become doctors. They were being taught it so they could survive in a world of death.

Allison let her gaze drift back to the main yard.

One of the boys, his frame wiry but strong, stumbled mid-sprint.

Seven-Eight-O.

He hit the ice-packed ground hard, his thin arms shaking as he struggled to push himself back up.

The other children didn't stop.

Neither did the guards.

One of them stepped forward, grabbing the boy by the collar and yanking him up like discarded trash. His legs buckled, but it didn't matter. He was dragged off the training ground, his fate already decided.

A scientist in a lab coat turned to Allison. He adjusted his round glasses, unbothered by the sight of the boy being hauled away.

"This is the third time in the last month Seven-Eight-O has collapsed during extended exercise," he said.

Allison didn't look away from the remaining recruits, who continued their brutal endurance drills without a single break.

"Then he won't make the cut," she said simply. "And you know what that means."

The scientist nodded, his expression utterly devoid of anything even remotely touching sympathy. "I shall organize the termination myself."

Allison merely inclined her head.

She had long since stopped seeing them as children. To her, they were only numbers—and only the strong were useful.

A guard approached, his boots crunching against the ice. He saluted stiffly.

"Ma'am, you have a call waiting."

Allison glanced at him, then turned away from the training floor.

"I'll take it in my office," she said, striding toward the steel doors.

A short while later, Allison stepped into the dim confines of her office, the heat from the old radiator barely keeping the Siberian chill at bay. She removed her gloves, smoothing the cuffs of her tailored jacket as she approached the secure comm terminal on her desk.

The screen flickered, then stabilized, revealing the sharp, lined face of Victor Brandt. He was in a well-lit office, likely somewhere warm, a stark contrast to her icy surroundings.

His smirk was faintly annoying.

"Number Eleven," he greeted smoothly.

Allison leaned back in her chair. "Number Seventeen."

Brandt sighed, rolling his neck. "It was just as you said. Wolf and his band showed up right as we were about to go live."

A small, satisfied smile curled at Allison's lips. "Of course they did."

Brandt poured himself a large crystal glass of brandy, swirling the amber liquid. "They stopped nothing, though," he continued. "Only delayed it by a few days. Atlas will still go live. Nevertheless, once again, the Wolf has escaped the snare."

He exhaled sharply, swirling his glass again before downing the drink in one smooth motion.

Then his expression shifted. A flicker of triumph.

"But we did get something else."

Allison's fingers paused against the desk. "Oh?"

Brandt leaned forward slightly, the smirk returning. "We secured Wally Lawson."

For the first time in the conversation, Allison's smile widened.

"Then we have Noah's brain."

Brandt nodded. "Exactly."

Allison's gaze drifted slightly, her mind already working through the implications.

"Where is he now?"

Brandt refilled his glass but didn't drink this time. He simply watched the amber liquid swirl.

"En route to you. As we speak."

Allison gave a slow nod, the flickering light from her desk screen reflecting in her cold eyes.

"Good."

She let the weight of that hang between them before shifting gears.

"This is good, Number Seventeen. Wolf will home in on you now."

Brandt arched an eyebrow. "Oh? And why is that a good thing?"

"Because it'll allow us to use you as a decoy," Allison said, voice even.

Brandt let out a dry, humorless snuff. He set the glass down with a soft clink and leaned back.

"Great," he muttered. "I do so love being chased around Europe by murderous assassins."

Allison went to speak, but before she could, her private comm terminal flashed red. A priority transmission. Personal.

Number One.

Her breath hitched for just a second—but only a second. She had only ever received one such call before from the supreme leader of the Council. That one had been very important. This one would be too.

Certainly more important than Brandt.

She straightened, her fingers gliding across the screen as she severed the link to Seventeen. Brandt's image vanished. Then she opened the new line.

The screen remained dark, the video feed showing only the suggestion of a shape, blurred and featureless. A shadow, hidden behind layers of encryption.

The voice was altered as well.

When Number One spoke, it wasn't a single voice, but a seamless cascade of many voices blended together, shifting in tone, accent, and cadence with every word—a deliberate distortion that made it impossible to identify who they truly were.

As it went, only a select few knew their identity. Allison hoped—no, intended—that one day, she would be among them.

"Number Eleven," the inter-changing, amorphous voice said.

Allison sat straighter, her heart rate rising ever so slightly. "Number One."

"Congratulations on your progress with the Elite Assassins program." The voices morphed constantly, an unsettling symphony of command and control. "You have taken it to new heights. It has become our sharpest blade, our silent hand."

Allison dipped her head, accepting the praise without speaking.

"And," Number One continued, "your fight against Noah Wolf has not gone unnoticed. Olympus' future is all but guaranteed because of your work in predicting his movements."

A slow, thrumming sense of satisfaction built in Allison's chest. The assassins, Olympus, Noah Wolf—all pieces on her board, all moving exactly where she wanted them to.

But Number One wasn't done.

"The Inner Council has recently lost one of its longest-serving members."

Allison's fingers curled slightly on the desk.

"A position has opened."

Her breathing remained even, but something tightened deep inside her.

"Your name has been put forward."

She almost let herself smile. Almost.

Instead, she said the only thing she could: "I only wish to serve."

A slight pause. Then the ever-shifting voices replied, "And you have served well."

There was a finality to the words. A promise.

"Once Wolf is in our hands and Olympus is live, a seat in the Inner Council will be yours."

The transmission ended abruptly. No farewell. No discussion.

Just a statement of fact.

Allison sat back in her chair, exhaling slowly.

For the first time in years, she allowed herself a moment of true satisfaction.

This was it.

All these years. The battles. The politics. The sacrifices. The bodies she had buried—some figuratively, a lot more not. And now she was on the precipice of something greater than she had ever imagined.

The Inner Council.

The true rulers of the Council—not the bureaucrats, not the handlers, not the outer ring of schemers and operators. The Ten. The Ones Who Knew.

She knew exactly how it would happen. Her entrance into the inner sanctum of this vast reaching organization.

She would be summoned to the Grand Chamber—a place so secret that only a handful of people in the entire world knew its location. Upon arrival, she would be taken into a side chamber, where she would be introduced to the other nine members in their truest form. No distorted images on a video feed. The real people pulling the strings.

Then she would be masked and robed, as they were. Only then would she step into the vast main hall of the Grand Chamber, where the next 150 members of the Council—the elite minds behind the global machine—would be gathered.

Every thinking part of the Council in one room.

To celebrate her.

The idea sent a thrill through her, though she kept her expression calm.

And she would make a speech.

A speech they would never forget.

A speech that would define her legacy.

She could already hear it.

Noah Wolf was just another stepping stone to something greater. Another battle in a war she had already won.

Except... she had lost before.

The thought came out of nowhere, slicing through her moment of satisfaction like a dull blade, tearing at the edges of her carefully constructed certainty.

Allison closed her eyes, the two-year-old memory pressing in like a whisper at the back of her mind. A smell—blood, burning wood, gunpowder. A sound—screams and the crackle of fire.

Then the faces.

Areola Singh, frozen in terror. Her bodyguard Curtis, defiant to the last. Roger Connelly, gasping for breath as blood bubbled from his lips. The ghosts she had tried to forget.

The night the dragon fell.

The gunfire had stopped. That was the worst part. Not the pain burning in her side where the bullet had ripped through. Not the acrid smoke curling into the basement, slithering along the ceiling like a living thing. Not even the bodies around her, their eyes vacant, their blood cooling against the cold tile floor.

It was the silence.

Silence meant it was over.

That the next part was coming.

Two years ago, Allison Peterson sat slumped against the safe room door in the basement of her Long Island home, pressing a bloodied hand to her wound. The pistol in her other hand was empty—she had felt the slide lock back on the last shot. She didn't remember firing it. Didn't remember the last time she'd breathed without tasting blood.

Across the room, Curtis was on his knees, swaying, a deep red stain spreading across his chest. His gun was still in his hand, but he had no strength left to raise it.

"Stay with me," Allison whispered.

Curtis' head lolled forward, his lips moving, but no sound came. A second later, his body slumped, dead before he hit the floor.

Allison closed her eyes.

The others were already gone.

Areola was crumpled in the corner, her designer blouse drenched in blood. Roger had lasted the longest—he'd still been gasping when she'd tried to drag him to cover. That was minutes ago. A lifetime ago.

Allison was the only one left.

But she wouldn't give them the satisfaction.

She let out a slow breath, shifting her grip on the pistol. Even empty, it was still a weapon.

The stairwell creaked.

A shadow moved in the thick smoke. A figure emerged, rifle raised, his movements controlled and precise. Not sloppy, not hesitant. A professional.

Allison gritted her teeth and lifted her empty gun, her muscles screaming from exhaustion. If she could just make him hesitate—just for a second—maybe she could—

A boot slammed into her wrist, knocking the pistol from her grasp. The pain shot through her arm like lightning, but she refused to make a sound.

A second figure stepped into the light.

Henrik Schultz.

His eyes swept over the room, taking in the dead without a flicker of emotion. He didn't gloat. Didn't smirk.

That would have made this easier.

Instead, he crouched in front of her, studying her like a man examining a relic—something broken, something once powerful that no longer mattered.

"Dragon Lady," he said.

She spat blood at his feet.

Schultz sighed. "You always did have spirit."

"I'm not going to beg," she rasped.

"Of course not." He sounded almost amused. "You're a fighter. That's why we're having this conversation."

From his pocket, he pulled a slim black device—an iPad. With a swipe of his fingers, he made a call.

A new voice crackled through the speaker.

"Show me."

Jacques Monnet.

Allison kept her face blank as Schultz turned the iPad toward her. She met the old man's gaze through the screen. His sharp blue eyes studied her the way a butcher studies a cut of meat.

"The Dragon Lady," Monnet mused. "Look at you now."

Allison held his stare. "Still breathing, Frenchie."

Schultz chuckled, shaking his head.

Monnet's lip curled. "Not for long, I imagine."

The operative beside Schultz raised his rifle, the barrel leveling at her head.

Allison took a slow breath, letting the tension drain from her body.

She had lost. But she would not break.

The finger on the trigger tightened—

Darkness...

Allison's eyes snapped open. The taste of blood was gone. The heat of the burning safe house—gone. The pain in her side —gone.

She was sitting in the high-backed leather chair of her office. Her hands were clean. The wound in her side was nothing more than a ghost of an ache, a scar buried beneath layers of cotton and silk.

Her heart was still hammering.

The past had clawed its way into the present, dragging her back down, back into the moment she had died.

Except she hadn't.

She had woken up somewhere else. Somewhere worse.

Allison exhaled, pressing her palms against the armrests to steady herself. The past was dead. She had buried the Dragon Lady the moment she accepted the truth.

The truth that had led her here. To the precipice of something greater than she had ever imagined. To the Inner Council.

She forced herself to smile, to push the ghosts back into their graves.

Noah Wolf was just another stepping stone.

Nothing more.

THIRTY-SIX

THE BLACK CAB ROLLED TO A STOP DEEP IN EPPING Forest, the soft crunch of gravel beneath the tires the only sound beyond the whisper of the wind through the trees.

Neil killed the engine. They sat for a second, the weight of exhaustion pressing down on them. Then, without a word, Jenny and Noah opened their doors, stepping out into the frigid air.

They had to disappear. The Whitechapel safehouse was no longer safe—London itself was no longer safe. The Council had moved too fast, too precisely. It was clear they knew they were coming. London was locked down. They would have eyes everywhere.

The four of them left the cab behind, disappearing into the trees, moving on foot to the rendezvous. A lone van waited in a clearing, its engine idling softly.

Their contact—the same man who had met them when they first arrived in England—stood outside, leaning against the van, smoking. In his fifties, he was built like someone who had once been military but had long since let the years soften him just enough to blend in with the world. He took a final drag of his cigarette, flicked it into the dirt, and exhaled through his nose as they approached.

"Nice morning for a drive," he remarked dryly, glancing at the blood spatter on Jenny's coat.

Noah ignored the small talk. "You have what we need?"

The man just jerked a thumb toward the back of the van. "Fresh clothes, burner phones, and a little breakfast. Thought you'd be hungry."

Neil opened the van's rear doors, and the smell of McDonald's hash browns and coffee drifted out. Jenny didn't even hesitate—she grabbed a paper bag and tore it open, shoving a still-hot sausage muffin into her mouth like it was the first food she'd seen in days.

"Where to?" the contact asked.

Noah climbed in, rubbing grime and sweat from his face with the edge of his jacket. "You know the Cotswolds place?"

The man nodded, got behind the wheel, and they rolled out.

THIRTY-SEVEN

COUNCIL FACILITY, SIBERIA | 20:27 KRAT | FEBRUARY 24

THE SIBERIAN WIND HOWLED OUTSIDE, RATTLING THE frosted windows of the underground compound. Inside, the Council Training Facility thrived in its cold, merciless routine. Children did not grow here; they were shaped, hardened, broken, and reforged.

Allison Peterson stood in the observation room, watching the monitors lining the walls.

Each screen showed live feeds from the dormitories, training areas, and medical bays. Her gaze flicked across them dispassionately—one cell of recruits performing brutal endurance drills, another group being evaluated in hand-to-hand combat, their faces bloodied but silent.

A knock at the door.

She didn't turn. "Enter."

The door hissed open.

A uniformed officer stepped in, his stance rigid. Captain Lysenko, head of dormitory security.

He saluted sharply. "Mother."

Allison finally turned. "What is it?"

Lysenko's voice was calm, clinical. "We have intercepted whispers among the trainees in Dormitory 113. A planned attack."

Allison folded her arms. "On whom?"

Lysenko did not hesitate. "Three-O-Two."

The name piqued her interest.

Norah Wolf.

"Tell me," she said, pacing to the side, "is this an organized act of dominance or desperation?"

Lysenko checked his tablet, scrolling through the compiled reports from surveillance and informants.

"Dominance, ma'am," he confirmed. "The dormitory leader, Four-Four-Two, has orchestrated it. The others will follow. Their objective is elimination. They plan to kill her."

Allison nodded, her mind already moving through the implications.

Four-Four-Two was older, stronger, and had maintained control over Dormitory 113 for months. The other girls followed her because they feared her.

And yet Three-O-Two had disrupted something.

She had not submitted. Not yielded.

This had bred resentment. And resentment, in the right conditions, became action.

Allison turned to face Lysenko fully.

"Have the guards provide them with weapons."

Lysenko didn't blink. "Yes, ma'am."

She smiled—a small, deliberate curve of the lips.

"Make sure Three-O-Two is unaware of it."

Lysenko nodded once. "Any preferences?"

"Something crude. Bats, knuckledusters, short blades. Nothing they wouldn't find in the real world."

He made a note on his tablet, not questioning the order. "Understood."

Allison turned back to the monitors.

One of the feeds showed Dormitory 113—dimly lit, the children sitting on or standing about their bunks.

She could already see the tension in their posture, the way they whispered in hushed tones. They were waiting. Planning. Preparing to kill.

And Three-O-Two?

She was curled in her bunk, appearing asleep—but Allison knew better.

Norah had already sensed the threat.

The real test was coming.

Allison exhaled softly, watching the screen as if it were the only thing in the world that mattered.

Then, without looking at Lysenko, she spoke again.

"We shall soon see if Three-O-Two will fight in order to live."

THIRTY-EIGHT

ALMOST THREE HOURS LATER, THE DORMITORY WAS pitch black. The only sound came from the night wind howling against the thin walls. The twelve girls moved as one, slipping from their bunks without hesitation. Bare feet on cold concrete. Silent. Precise.

They gathered in a loose circle around Norah Wolf's bed.

She lay still under the blanket, breathing steadily, but she wasn't asleep. She had been waiting for this. She felt them before she saw them, sensed the weight of their presence in the room, the shift in the air.

A whisper passed between the girls.

Under their mattresses, small weapons lay hidden. Knuckledusters. Short bats. Knives. The guards had secretly handed them out two hours before when the girls had returned from the shower block.

It was a test. A culling.

Four-Four-Two stepped forward, giving a single nod.

Two girls grabbed a heavy blanket and threw it over Norah,

pinning her beneath it. Hands pressed down, tightening the fabric, sealing her inside.

They expected panic. Thrashing. Screams.

But Norah didn't fight blindly. She had a weapon of her own.

A tiny screw she had found days ago, sharp and jagged, hidden in her palm. As they held her down, she worked it against the blanket's fibers, slicing them apart, inch by inch.

The moment the fabric weakened enough, she struck.

With a sudden, violent twist, she tore through the last threads and exploded from the bed.

Chaos erupted in a pitch-black blur of violence.

A bat swung toward her skull in a vicious arc, and she ducked low, feeling the rush of air as it missed by inches.

A knife lunged at her from the side. She twisted, grabbing the bed frame and vaulting over it, landing lightly on the other side as the blade sliced open the thin mattress.

The dorm was drenched in darkness, but Norah's eyes, finely tuned to the void, adjusted instantly to the lack of light.

She moved without sound, slipping between their attacks as the others stumbled and collided in the blindness.

Two girls charged her at the same time.

Norah ducked.

They crashed into each other, the impact sending them sprawling.

Another girl swung with knuckledusters. Norah dropped into a roll, coming up fast. A sharp kick to the knee. A second to the ribs. The girl collapsed.

More hands grabbed for her.

Too many.

She struggled, feet kicking, arms twisting—pinned.

Then her hand moved on instinct.

She drove the sharp edge of the screw into the nearest attacker.

A gurgled cry. Warm blood. A body collapsing.

The others froze.

Then—

A click.

The overhead lights flickered on.

The guards burst in, weapons raised, expressions taut.

The dormitory was a wreck. Beds overturned. Blankets scattered. The scent of blood in the air.

In the center, Four-Four-Two clutched her throat, blood pouring through her fingers.

She tried to speak. Only a wet, choking sound came out. Then she dropped.

Dead.

Norah stood over her, small, unshaken, her tiny hand still gripping the bloodied screw.

The guards watched. They didn't move. Didn't speak.

They had been waiting for this.

At eight years old, Norah Wolf had taken her first life.

She lifted her chin. Met their eyes.

And she did not look away.

THIRTY-NINE

THE COTSWOLDS, SOUTHERN ENGLAND | 22:10 GMT | FEBRUARY 24

THE DRIVE WAS LONG, THE TWISTING ROADS TAKING them deeper into the countryside. Rolling fields stretched into the mist, gray and endless, broken only by scattered trees and the occasional stone-walled farmstead.

They passed through sleepy villages basking in the midday sun, the streets quiet except for a few locals strolling after lunch, shopkeepers chatting outside their storefronts, and children cycling lazily along the pavement—all oblivious to the fact that four fugitives in the back of a van were plotting against the most powerful organization in the world.

At one point, the road narrowed into a single lane. The van slowed to a crawl.

Sheep.

A full flock of stupid, fat sheep were blocking the road.

Jenny sighed, rubbing her forehead. "Great."

Neil glared at the animals like they had personally offended him. "Shouldn't you honk?"

The contact in the driver's seat scoffed. "You honk at 'em, they'll just look at you."

They sat there for a full minute, the sheep milling around, chewing grass, utterly indifferent to the world's problems.

Finally, a farmer appeared, a weathered-looking man with a crook in hand, and whistled for his sheepdog. The animal shot forward, barking orders at the flock, and just like that, the sheep cleared the way.

As they drove on, Jenny muttered, "Highly trained killers, fleeing an international conspiracy, held up by a freakin' petting zoo."

The safehouse was a small stone cottage nestled at the edge of a dense forest, miles from the nearest town. Cold, isolated, and barely furnished.

Inside, it smelled of old wood and dust, the air damp and stale. The wind howled faintly through the thin gaps in the window frames. There was no Internet, no signal, just a crackling wood-burning stove and a table covered in maps and burner phones left by their contact.

They wasted no time. The team got straight to work.

Neil set up his laptops, working off battery power and a mobile data link. Katya checked the weapons stash while Jenny stood by the window, watching for anything out of place.

Noah leaned over Neil's shoulder as the screens filled with data—snippets of decrypted transmissions, intercepted chatter from Council operatives still swarming London.

Then the breakthrough came.

An hour into it, a new transmission came through—fresh. Just a few minutes old.

Neil's fingers flew over the keyboard, decrypting the text. His face darkened.

"I've got something."

The others immediately gathered around as he enlarged the message on his screen.

. . .

INITIATION OF ATLAS *Phase Three confirmed. Core node secured. Mission will proceed under the planned cover.*

NOAH'S BROW FURROWED. "PLANNED COVER?"
   Neil kept reading, scrolling further.

PRIMARY OBJECTIVE REMAINS UNCHANGED. *Coordinate the deployment of Phase Three. Link Atlas to the Banque de France and key regulatory networks—integrating the AI into the economic bedrock of the EU.*

NOAH'S JAW TIGHTENED.
   "They're expanding Atlas," he said, voice sharp, deadly. "They're going to anchor it into the French economy—and they're using Olympus to do it."
   The room went silent.
   Through Olympus' infiltration of critical infrastructure and financial systems, the Council would be able to manipulate a market crash, a false cyberattack, or a corrupted update—essentially rewire the French economy to serve Olympus.
   "Who's running the operation?" Noah asked.
   Neil cross-referenced movement patterns, timestamps, secured digital signatures—then froze as the name appeared.
   Victor Brandt.
   The room stilled.
   Jenny stared at the screen, then at Noah. "Brandt."
   Noah's expression didn't change.

Neil's voice was low, tense. "It looks like he's already in Paris."

Jenny leaned against the table, dragging a hand down her face. "This guy again."

"And his bodyguards," Noah added.

Katya remained silent, but her knuckles turned white as she gripped the back of a chair.

Victor Brandt.

The man who had set the trap for them in London. The man who had smirked as he walked away. And now, he was about to lock the French economy into the Council's machine.

Noah exhaled through his nose. His eyes were cold, hard.

"How long?"

Neil ran the final calculations, then looked up.

"Less than seventy-two hours."

The room felt colder.

No one spoke.

Then Noah straightened.

"We're going to Paris."

FORTY

THE COUNCIL DETENTION FACILITY'S MEDICAL WING was a place of cold precision, stripped of anything resembling life. No windows. No warmth. Just a reinforced bed where Wally Lawson lay, strapped down tight, leather restraints biting into his wrists, ankles, and chest.

The overhead surgical lights were blinding. The walls were seamless concrete, sterile, smooth, trapping him in a bubble of silence. The only sound was the soft hum of medical machines.

He didn't know where they had taken him—he'd been drugged most of the journey—but something told him he was far underground.

A hiss of hydraulics.

The door slid open, and Allison Peterson stepped inside. Heels clicking. Composed. Cold.

Wally let out a breath. Smirked. "Nice place, Dragon Lady. Is this your lair?"

Allison didn't bite. She just rolled in a medical cart and positioned a large monitor directly in front of his face.

The screen flickered to life.

At first, just static—then the image sharpened.

Footage.

A patient on an operating table, their skull partially exposed. Neurosurgeons in pristine white coats moved around them, working with eerie precision.

Wally's smirk faded.

Allison's voice was smooth. Clinical. Detached.

"We've come a long way in intelligence extraction, Wally. Torture is inefficient. Chemical methods unreliable. But this? This is pure science."

The screen zoomed in. The procedure was already in progress. Thin electrodes were being inserted directly into the exposed brain tissue—wires snaking from the patient's skull to a massive supercomputer nearby.

Allison folded her arms, stepping aside as a figure in surgical scrubs approached the table. The surgeon—Dr. Vasilyev, head of the Council's neural extraction program—adjusted his gloves, his expression clinical, detached.

"Tell him, Doctor," Allison instructed smoothly. "Let him understand exactly what is about to happen."

Dr. Vasilyev gave a small, professional nod before turning his attention to Wally, who could only lie there, strapped to a reinforced medical bed. His restraints were tight, his arms immobile, but his mind raced.

The surgeon's voice was calm, methodical, as he relayed the process without emotion.

"We are about to begin a cognitive extraction procedure, Mr. Lawson."

Wally said nothing, but his pulse monitor betrayed him—a slight increase, a flicker of unease.

Dr. Vasilyev continued. "You will undergo a precise craniotomy, exposing the key memory centers in your brain—the prefrontal cortex, hippocampus, and temporal lobe."

The display screen flickered, showing an animated cross-section of a human skull, the top portion removed.

"Mild sedation will be administered," the doctor went on, his tone unchanging. "You will remain semi-conscious, able to feel and recall, but too weak to resist."

Wally's jaw tightened, but he refused to speak.

Allison's expression didn't change, her eyes locked on him, watching every micro-reaction.

Dr. Vasilyev continued. "Microelectrodes, thinner than a human hair, will be inserted into your memory-processing regions."

The screen displayed the procedure, a network of tiny wires piercing into exposed brain tissue, data streams lighting up as synapses fired.

"The AI-powered algorithm will decode your thoughts—reconstructing your memories in real-time. Everything you've ever seen, heard, or known will be revealed to us."

Wally's breathing slowed, controlled, but his muscles remained taut. He understood exactly what this meant. There would be no lies. No deception. If they got far enough, they would see everything.

The doctor's voice remained steady. "By stimulating specific regions, we will force involuntary memory recall—pulling forward information you do not consciously remember."

The screen displayed a test subject, their eyes darting wildly, mouth moving soundlessly as memories were ripped from their mind and displayed on an external monitor.

"The procedure isn't perfect," Dr. Vasilyev continued. "In some cases, patients never wake up."

A brief pause. "In others, they wake up... wrong."

The monitor played on.

The patient on screen convulsed, their eyes fluttering, mouth moving as if trying to scream—but there was no sound. The AI was extracting everything, even their fear.

Then the images on screen shifted—their thoughts made visible, memories flashing like a decrypted file. A conversation appeared, painstakingly reconstructed, word by word.

Wally's stomach tightened.

Allison leaned in slightly, watching him. Amused.

"It's remarkable, really. A direct window into the mind. No lies. No misdirection. Just... raw thought." Her tone darkened. "Of course, it isn't always perfect."

The screen shifted again—now showing a different patient.

A man sitting upright in a chair, his eyes vacant, empty. He wasn't dead, but he wasn't alive either. A broken husk of what he had been.

Allison turned back to Wally.

"You can make this easier, Wally." Her voice was smooth. Almost inviting. "Give me what I need. Willingly."

Wally let out a short, dry laugh, shaking his head.

"Would you even believe me if I did?" he said.

Their eyes locked. Allison's faint smile confirmed nothing.

"No."

The silence stretched. Then Allison checked her watch. "They'll begin prepping you in fifteen minutes."

She turned to leave. But before she reached the door, Wally spoke.

"What happened to you, Allison?"

She stopped.

Wally tilted his head slightly. "What made you sell out your friends?"

For just a second—the smallest flicker of hesitation.

He pressed on. "Is this 'subterranean concrete pit' your home now?" His voice lowered. "Is this where you keep Norah?"

That got a reaction.

Just a flicker, a small shift in her shoulders, but it was there.

That was all Wally needed.

Noah's daughter was here. Somewhere.

Allison didn't answer. Didn't acknowledge it. She just walked out, the door hissing shut behind her.

Wally's mind raced. His hands were strapped tight, but it didn't matter.

In the inside of his cheek, tucked between gum and molars, was a biological nano-tracker.

A failsafe.

Undetectable by standard scans, coated in a polymer that wouldn't trigger metal detectors or X-rays. It would only activate once swallowed.

One signal. Twenty minutes before it burned out.

One shot.

He shifted his tongue, dislodging the capsule, and swallowed.

A faint warmth spread through his stomach. The tracker was going live.

If Noah was out there, if the team was monitoring any signals, this was it. His only chance. His only way out.

Wally exhaled slowly.

They were coming.

And when they did, he'd be ready.

FORTY-ONE

THE FIRST LIGHT OF DAWN BARELY TOUCHED THE frost-laced fields outside the isolated cottage. The place was cold, damp, and far from safe, but it was the only place left to regroup.

Inside, the team moved with quiet urgency, gathering their gear, making their final preparations. Weapons were checked. Passports inspected. Plans finalized. Their next destination was Paris—ground zero for the Council's digital infiltration of the French economy. The weight of the mission thickened the air around them. There was no margin for error.

Katya flipped through the forged documents, double-checking details, her fingers tight around the edges. Across the room, Neil zipped a duffel bag shut, his movements efficient despite the tension coiling in his shoulders. Jenny, silent but sharp, slid a fresh magazine into her pistol, her hands steady.

Then—a ping.

The sharp sound cut through the air, freezing them in place.

Neil's laptop screen flashed red.

The room shifted, all movement stilled as they gathered

behind him. Neil's fingers moved quickly, pulling up the data, his breath hitching as he focused in.

A signal. A GPS marker. A small blinking dot.

Its location? Deep in Siberia.

Neil leaned closer, refining the coordinates.

His voice came out low, urgent.

"It's him. It's Wally."

For the first time in days, a pulse of hope ran through them.

Noah was already moving, strapping on his gear, his eyes locked on the screen. Then his voice dropped—sharper now.

"That's not just Wally." He pointed at the signal. "That's Norah."

A ripple of disbelief passed through the room.

Jenny was the first to speak. "Noah, we don't know that."

Noah's conviction was ironclad. "I do."

His words hung in the air, heavy, undeniable.

Then he exhaled, gaze never leaving the screen.

"A month ago, I met someone. A contact who claimed he'd been inside one of the Council's hidden training facilities. He told me that Norah was there. Alive. That she was being trained—shaped into one of their own."

Jenny's breath caught, but she said nothing.

Noah pressed on.

"Wally and I tried to pinpoint the location. Spent weeks chasing leads, analyzing satellite data—but it never turned up. Too well-hidden. Too deep in the wilderness. It was a dead end."

He gestured to the blinking GPS marker on the screen.

"Until now."

The team absorbed the weight of his words.

The Council's elite assassin program. A secret training ground buried in the heart of Siberia.

And Norah was in it.

The team's focus split in two. On one side—Paris, where the only chance to stop Olympus lay ahead. On the other—Siberia, where Wally and Norah could already be lost.

Noah made the call.

"We split up."

Katya stepped forward, her blue eyes unyielding.

"I'll go with you."

Noah shook his head. "No. Norah's my daughter. You're better off in Paris. Olympus is bigger. If you don't stop it—"

She already knew. If they failed, civilization would fall.

Katya's fists clenched. She hated this. Hated leaving Noah to face Siberia alone.

But she nodded.

"Then you better not die, Jonas."

Noah smirked, brief and sharp. "I'll do my best."

The air between them was thick with unspoken things, but there was no time to dwell on them. Decisions were made.

They moved out.

FORTY-TWO

THE ISOLATION CELL WAS A VOID—CONCRETE WALLS, cold steel beams, and a silence thick enough to smother you. Norah sat on the bare floor, knees pulled to her chest, the stench of metal and dried blood clinging to her like a second skin.

She hadn't slept. Couldn't. Not when she knew they were watching.

Then—light.

The overhead bulb flickered to life, its sterile glow blinding after hours of darkness. The door unlocked with a soft clunk, and Allison Peterson stepped inside.

Her heels clicked deliberately on the cold floor as she approached.

Norah didn't move. Didn't react.

Allison stopped in front of her, head tilting slightly.

"So you're a killer now, Norah."

Norah didn't look up. Her hands curled into small, defiant fists.

"I don't care," she said in a frail whisper. "I still won't fight."

Allison's lips curled into a faint smirk, amusement dancing in her cold blue eyes. "They'll kill you, you know."

Norah's gaze flickered—barely a reaction, but it was there.

"I don't care." She said it again, even quieter this time.

The air between them stretched, heavy with unspoken things. Allison crouched, meeting Norah at eye level. Her voice softened —just enough to pull her in.

"You want my advice?"

Norah said nothing.

Alison went on, "If you ever want to see your father again, then fight."

Norah's entire body went still. Her breath hitched.

"My father?" The words felt foreign in her mouth.

Allison leaned in. "Yes. Noah Wolf. You remember him, don't you?"

A memory rushed back—warm arms lifting her up, bedtime stories whispered in the dark, the sharp crack of gunfire, the screams of her mother tearing through the night.

She swallowed hard, staring at the floor.

He had promised to keep her safe.

But he hadn't found her.

Not yet.

Allison stood slowly, watching her carefully. "He's out there, Norah. And he is fighting for you."

Norah's hands dug into her arms, her breathing tightening.

"If he was coming... he would have found me already."

Allison let the silence sit for a beat before speaking again. "He is coming. But will you be alive when he gets here?"

The words hit harder than Norah wanted them to.

Allison pulled her phone out and swiped a finger across the screen. A moment later, it flickered to life, the old Sony camcorder footage grainy and dim, as though time itself had been captured in static.

"Here, take it," Allison said, handing her the phone.

Norah tentatively reached up and took it. Her brows knitted together as she began watching the screen.

The image was of the same domed room they trained in. But the boy standing in the center of the frame wasn't her or any of the other children she knew from this place.

It was someone else.

The footage shook slightly as the cameraman adjusted the zoom. The image cleared, and she saw him.

A boy—lean, sharp-eyed, and eerily familiar.

Her father. Noah Wolf.

Except he was just a child—her age. Eight years old.

Norah's breath caught as she watched.

The Noah on screen moved like a ghost, slipping between opponents twice his size, his body a perfect machine of instinct and control. His small fists struck with precision, his attacks methodical, deadly, his movements honed into something beyond natural ability.

He fought multiple enemies, the other boys desperately trying to bring him down.

Without exception, each one of them failed.

One lunged. Noah sidestepped, caught the wrist, and snapped it.

Another came from behind. Noah turned, ducked, drove an elbow into the ribs, then twisted into a takedown.

By the end, he was the only one standing, the floor littered with injured fighters.

The screen flickered off.

Norah's chest felt tight.

Allison stepped forward, her voice soft but firm.

"Your father was the Council's greatest creation."

Norah blinked at her. "What?"

Allison's gaze held hers. "What do you know about your grandparents, Norah? Your father's mother and father."

"They're in heaven."

"No," Allison said softly. "They are not. Your father wasn't born, Norah. He was designed."

The words felt wrong but undeniable.

Allison continued. "Like your companions here, he was made in the Council's genetic program. Made to be better than ordinary people. Stronger. Smarter. More capable."

She crouched beside Norah again, voice low.

"And you, Norah? You are the same. You have his genes."

Norah's hands tightened into fists, her nails digging into her palms.

Allison's voice was gentle but absolute. "You are not normal. You were never meant to be."

Norah's breath came sharp and fast.

The phone's screen stayed black, but the image of her father as a child burned into her mind.

Noah Wolf. A boy trained in this very facility. A boy engineered to be something else.

And her?

Norah's throat tightened.

Allison watched her carefully, then whispered, "Show them what you can do, Norah."

A long silence.

Norah's pulse pounded in her ears.

Finally, she lifted her head.

And for the first time, she wasn't sure who she was anymore.

FORTY-THREE

THE COTTAGE STOOD SILENT BEHIND THEM, swallowed by mist. No trace of them remained—only the faint imprint of tires in the damp grass, the lingering scent of gun oil and adrenaline in the cold air.

They didn't look back.

The road to the airstrip was quiet, desolate—a ribbon of asphalt stretching through the sleeping countryside. The van's headlights cut through the dense fog, illuminating empty fields, skeletal trees, and lonely farmhouses where the world still slept in ignorance of what was coming.

Paris. Siberia. Two fronts. Two impossible fights.

At the end of the road, on a quiet tarmac, two aircraft waited, engines humming in the frigid night.

One bound for Paris. Jenny, Katya, and Neil, heading straight into the heart of the Council's Olympus plot.

One bound for Siberia. Noah—alone, stepping into the frozen unknown, chasing the faintest signal of hope.

The moment felt suspended in time, each breath visible in the biting air. There was nothing left to say, but they said it anyway.

Jenny turned first, her grip tightening on Noah's shoulder, her voice urgent, raw.

"Find her. Bring them both back."

Noah held her gaze—steady, unshaken.

"Count on it."

Katya was next.

For a second, she hesitated.

Then her fingers fisted in his jacket, pulling him close, her voice low and sharp, edged with something she refused to name.

"If you die, Jonas, I'll hunt you down in hell and kill you a second time."

A short chuckle left him, too quiet, too fleeting.

He stepped back. No more words.

The team boarded their planes, the doors sealed shut, and in the next breath—

They were gone.

Splitting into the night, racing toward fate itself.

FORTY-FOUR

THE AIR HUNG THICK WITH COLD, SWEAT, AND BLOOD. The floor beneath them was hard-packed dirt, its surface marred by the stains of previous battles—faint but ever-present, a lingering testament to those who had fought and lost before.

A tight circle of trainees stood around the pit, their eyes sharp, their expressions hungry for violence. Guards stood at the edges, their posture rigid. Above, weak Siberian afternoon light filtered through the iron grates, carving fractured beams into the pit below, as though even the sun itself was imprisoned here.

Norah stood in the center of the pit, her small form a picture of controlled stillness. Across from her loomed Four-Three-Three —a girl older, larger, fueled by a singular need for retribution.

Four-Three-Three had bunked with Four-Four-Two—the girl Norah killed. Trained with her. Ate with her. Now she was alone, and in her mind, there was only one way to settle that debt.

High above, watching from an elevated platform, Allison Peterson stood motionless. Her expression revealed nothing, but her gaze never wavered. She was waiting.

A guard stepped forward into the circle, his heavy boots pressing into the dirt. He raised a gloved hand.

"Fight."

The word fell like a hammer. The hand dropped. The fight began.

Four-Three-Three charged like a bull, fists raised, her body coiled with raw aggression. She was bigger. Stronger. She knew it. Norah knew it. Everyone watching knew it.

Her first punch was wild but powerful, aimed with the force of grief and fury.

Norah didn't meet her head-on. She moved.

With a careful sidestep, she slipped just outside the strike, her small frame gliding past the danger. Four-Three-Three's momentum sent her barreling forward, skidding across the dirt. But she was quick—too quick for hesitation. With a furious snarl, she twisted, using her planted foot to pivot, driving her elbow toward Norah's head.

Norah ducked again. Smooth. Effortless. Instinctive.

The drills. The reflex training. The starvation that had forced her to adapt, to endure. It was all part of her now, woven into her very being.

Four-Three-Three fought with rage.

Norah fought with composure.

Yet there was still a level of skill in her opponent.

Four-Three-Three feinted left, drawing Norah's attention, then snapped her leg out in a vicious kick that slammed into Norah's ribs.

Pain detonated through her small frame like a firecracker. The impact sent her stumbling back, breath hitching as she fought to stay upright.

Around the pit, the trainees erupted in shouts, their voices blending into a frenzied roar, urging Four-Three-Three to finish it.

Norah barely had a moment to reset before another strike came—this time, a brutal punch aimed at her jaw. She got her arm up just in time, absorbing the blow, but the sheer force of it rattled through her bones.

Then another.

She twisted with the momentum, rolling away before the next strike could land. The pain pulsed through her body, but she ignored it. She had to.

Four-Three-Three grinned. She thought she had her now.

She was wrong.

Norah moved suddenly, closing the distance in a blur.

Before Four-Three-Three could react, Norah drove her elbow hard into the bigger girl's stomach. The impact was solid—precise —forcing a sharp gasp from Four-Three-Three's lips as she staggered back, winded.

Norah didn't wait for her to regain her balance.

She struck low—a sharp kick to the knee. Four-Three-Three buckled.

Then high—a palm strike under the chin. Her head snapped back.

The shift in the fight was instant.

For the first time, Four-Three-Three's confidence wavered. Her stance faltered. The certainty in her eyes flickered, replaced by something dangerously close to fear.

Norah wasn't just fast.

She was skilled.

She might not have fought before, but she had trained. She had been drilled, punished, forged through suffering. Every strike, every evasion, was a lesson beaten into her over months of endurance.

She knew exactly how to break someone.

And now she did.

Four-Three-Three roared in frustration, her breath ragged. She lunged forward for a final, desperate attack. It was a wild swing, a reckless punch aimed at Norah's head—one last attempt to end the fight.

Norah didn't back away.

She moved forward.

In a swift, accurate motion, she dropped low, sweeping Four-Three-Three's legs out from under her. The larger girl crashed onto her back, the impact slamming the air from her lungs.

Before Four-Three-Three could recover, Norah pounced.

She straddled Four-Three-Three's chest, her knees pinning the girl's arms to the dirt. Four-Three-Three thrashed, twisting, trying to break free—but Norah's grip was iron.

Silence fell over the arena.

Even the trainees, who moments ago had been jeering and cheering for blood, went still.

Norah's fist hovered above Four-Three-Three's face, her knuckles bruised and ready. She could end it right now. She could do what was expected of her.

Four-Three-Three lay beneath her, breathing hard, glaring up, but the rage in her eyes was diluted now—poisoned by something else.

Fear.

"Finish it," Four-Three-Three spat up at her, her voice half-snarl, half-dare.

Norah hesitated.

She had already killed once.

And she knew what would happen if she did it again.

She would change. She would become something else—something she might never come back from.

And above them, watching with that sharp, calculating gaze, stood Allison Peterson.

The moment stretched, taut and suffocating.

Norah lowered her fist.

She stood up. Turned away. Walked out of the pit without a single word.

Up on the Observation Deck, Allison leaned against the railing, her expression unreadable as she watched the crowd part for Norah.

The trainees had expected brutality. They had expected a bloodbath.

Instead, Norah had shown something far more dangerous.

Control. Precision. Mastery.

She could have killed. She didn't need to.

A slow, knowing smile curled at the corner of Allison's lips.

"Good girl," she murmured to herself.

The child would make a very good assassin.

FORTY-FIVE

NORILSK, SIBERIA | 16:09 KRAT | FEBRUARY 26

Norilsk Airport sat like a scar on the frozen tundra, surrounded by endless stretches of snow and soot-darkened ice. The terminal was a squat, gray structure—more industrial bunker than welcoming gateway—its windows rimed with frost, its runway cracked and dusted with permafrost. Smoke stacks loomed in the distance, spewing a permanent haze that blurred the horizon and stained the sky a dirty gray.

Once upon a time, this desolate, frozen place had been a launching pad for Cold War annihilation. Built to accommodate Soviet bombers, Norilsk Airport was designed as a strategic staging base for attacks on the United States. Its runways, long and hardened against the brutal Siberian cold, were meant to withstand the weight of nuclear-laden aircraft, such as the Tupolev Tu-95 "Bear"—the plane used to drop the Tsar Bomba (RDS-220) in 1961, the largest nuclear bomb ever detonated. For decades, pilots stationed here trained under the assumption that one day, they might never return.

That war had ended. The bombers were gone. But the cold remained.

As Noah stepped inside the small, single-terminal airport, the chill bit into him, cutting through layers of fabric like a knife. Even indoors, the air carried an unforgiving edge, the heating system weak, rattling away and struggling. The space was dimly lit, the flickering bulbs doing little to combat the gloom.

Beyond the glass doors, a frozen landscape stretched endlessly —flat, white, empty. The kind of place where bodies could disappear forever.

A handful of passengers shuffled through the terminal, bundled in thick coats and fur hats, their faces reddened by the cold. They moved with the quiet efficiency of people accustomed to Siberia's brutality.

Among them, Noah walked unnoticed, speaking good Russian to the men checking his forged documents. A ghost in plain sight.

Mikhail Leonov.

That was his name now. A traveling geologist contracted by a private Russian mining firm. His thick brown parka and heavy fur hat concealed most of his features, while steel-toed boots crunched softly against the icy tile floor. A rugged canvas duffel hung over his shoulder—not filled with weapons but with survival gear. In his coat pocket sat a fake Russian passport, carefully worn and stamped with the right amount of fading to make it look real.

His Russian was good. Not perfect, but good enough— accented in a way that suggested a native speaker who had spent too much time abroad. In a place like Norilsk, where people minded their own business, it was the kind of cover that didn't raise questions.

Except for the two men standing near the exit.

Noah didn't look directly at them. He didn't need to. He knew the look.

The first man was in his late forties, built like a dock worker, his frame thick with muscle. A simple wool coat hung over his broad shoulders, and though his posture was relaxed, his eyes weren't. They kept darting toward Noah.

The second man was younger, lean, wearing a black turtleneck beneath his jacket—standard ex-FSB attire. He was sure that they were now working for the Council.

They didn't approach. But they didn't look away.

It was clear they suspected him.

Noah adjusted the strap of his bag and stepped outside, bracing against the bitter cold. He didn't turn to see what the two men were doing. He didn't need confirmation.

They would follow.

Noah slid into the backseat of an old Soviet-era taxi, a Lada. Its cracked leather seats reeked of stale cigarettes. The air inside was thick, suffocating, as if the decades of unfiltered tobacco had soaked into the upholstery.

The driver barely looked up, his voice gruff and uninterested.

"Where to?" he asked in Russian.

Noah gave him the name of a village—something small, isolated, the kind of place where strangers weren't welcome and questions weren't asked.

As the taxi rattled forward, Noah caught a glimpse of the agents through the smudged rearview mirror. The two men were climbing into a black SUV.

They weren't even trying to be subtle.

The taxi pulled onto the icy road, tires crunching over compacted snow. The SUV followed at a careful distance, never too close, never too far.

Noah watched the landscape pass—bare trees standing like skeletal sentries, old Soviet apartment blocks crumbling under the weight of time. He counted every turn, mapped every street in his head.

He was already deciding where they would die.

A short while later, the taxi rolled to a stop on the outskirts of the village. Noah stepped out, thanking the driver in Russian before pulling his gloves snug over his fingers.

As the taxi pulled away, his pace remained steady, unhurried.

Behind him, the black SUV parked half a block away. The agents moved quickly, stepping out and flanking him with quiet efficiency.

Noah didn't run.

Instead, he turned down a narrow alleyway, moving between two old buildings where the wind howled through the gaps in their rotting wood fences.

He was letting them believe they had him cornered.

The sound of boots crunching in the snow followed. A shift in the icy air. A breath exhaled too loudly.

They made their move.

But Noah moved faster.

The first agent reached for him. Noah spun, his knife flashing in the dim light. One deep, decisive slice across the throat—clean, efficient. The man's eyes widened in shock as blood sprayed into the pristine snow. He dropped to his knees, clawing at his neck, as though he could gather the blood back in.

Soon he would be dead.

The second agent yanked a pistol free, his instincts good but not good enough.

Noah closed the distance in a blink, wrenching the weapon from the man's grip. Without hesitation, he slammed the barrel into the agent's nose with a sickening crunch. Cartilage shattered, blood splattering across the man's face.

He staggered back, dazed.

Noah didn't wait.

He shoved the pistol under the man's chin and pulled the trigger.

A muffled crack. A spray of blood and skull.

The agent collapsed, his body crumpling into the snow, steam rising from the wound as the cold stole his last breath.

For a moment, only the wind remained.

Noah exhaled, wiped the blood from his knife, and tucked the stolen pistol into his coat.

Without another glance at the bodies, he turned and disappeared into the buildings of the village.

FORTY-SIX

THE SMALL JET TOUCHED DOWN ON THE RAIN-SLICKED tarmac of Paris-Le Bourget Airport, its tires skimming the ground with a whisper of friction.

This was the perfect place for discretion.

Once the primary airport for Paris, Le Bourget now served private fliers, government officials, and those who preferred to avoid prying eyes. Tonight, that made it ideal.

A thick blanket of fog curled across the runway, swallowing the lights in swirling tendrils of white. Beyond the perimeter, the glow of Paris flickered against the low clouds—a city unaware of the catastrophe ticking closer by the second.

The jet's door hissed open, releasing a breath of warm air.

Jenny, first to step down, moved with urgency, her eyes scanning the mist-laden darkness. Katya followed, pulling her jacket tighter, the Parisian night heavy with moisture, clinging to skin and fabric alike. Neil brought up the rear, a tablet tucked under his arm, his mind already racing through possible next moves.

At the edge of the runway, a black sedan idled, its engine a low, steady hum in the mist.

Inside, their contact waited. No pleasantries. No wasted moments. The countdown had already begun. And they were running out of time.

The black sedan cut through the quiet pre-dawn roads, its tires humming softly against the wet pavement. Inside, the contact—Mathieu Roux—drove with the ease of a man who had long since abandoned nerves.

Roux was in his late fifties, his graying hair unkempt, his eyes heavy with the weight of too many years in the shadows. A cigarette dangled lazily from his lips, the smoke curling around him like an old companion.

Once, he had been one of the best operatives in France's counterterrorism units—a name spoken with respect in the halls of the DGSI and whispered in fear among the enemies of the Republic.

He had spent years dismantling terrorist cells, tracking high-value targets, and eliminating threats before they ever reached the public eye. His work had taken him from the backstreets of Algiers to the underground bunkers of Eastern Europe, always one step ahead, always in pursuit of the next mission.

Then he had been recruited into E & E—a place where his talents were not just valued but perfected. Under Camelot's banner, he had learned that the game was bigger than borders, that the world of intelligence was not about loyalty to a flag but to the mission itself.

And now?

Now Camelot was gone.

The fall of E & E had scattered its agents to the wind. Some had vanished entirely, disappearing into new identities. Others had been hunted down by the very governments they once served. And then there were those like Roux—adrift, surviving in the murky depths of the intelligence underworld, selling information to whoever had the means to pay the right price.

But he never strayed too far.

Like the rest of E & E's former agents, Roux was clinging on, watching the world from the sidelines, waiting.

Waiting for a call from Noah Wolf or one of the other remaining vestiges of Camelot.

Because in the end, the mission was never truly over.

Roux glanced up at the rearview mirror, his gaze landing on Katya as he took a slow drag from his cigarette.

"The famous Wolf team," he said, his voice gruff, amused. "I thought you were all dead."

Jenny ignored him.

Neil stayed focused, fingers flying over his tablet.

Katya, however, leaned forward, her eyes sharp and unamused. "We didn't come here for pleasantries. What do you have for us?"

Roux exhaled, the smoke lingering in the confined space of the car. His lips curled slightly—not quite a smile, not quite a smirk.

"Victor Brandt arrived in Paris two days ago," he said. "He's staying in a private penthouse under a false name, but I have no doubt it's him."

The temperature inside the car seemed to drop.

Neil looked up from the tablet. Jenny's posture stiffened. Katya's fingers curled into a fist.

The mission was truly underway.

FORTY-SEVEN

THE HOUSE SAT AT THE EDGE OF VALOK, A FROZEN village nestled along the banks of the Noril'skaya River—a remote outpost in the vast, merciless expanse of Siberia.

It was old but sturdy, a relic of another time, built long before the nickel mines of Norilsk turned this land into an industrial wasteland. The air carried the faint metallic bite of industry from the distant city, but here, in Valok, time moved slowly, frozen in the grip of endless winter.

Thick logs formed the walls, their surfaces scarred and darkened by decades of Siberian storms. The windows were small, built to trap what little heat they could, and the roof sagged slightly under the weight of the latest snowfall.

A thin wisp of smoke curled from the chimney, rising into the gray sky, disappearing into the low, heavy clouds that threatened more snow.

Noah approached the door and knocked once.

He stepped back. Waited.

The door creaked open.

The man standing in the doorway looked like he had been

carved from the same unforgiving land that surrounded them. Sergei Markov—a name whispered in old GRU circles, spoken with both reverence and caution.

He was in his late sixties, stocky and built like a tank. Even in old age, he had kept his formidable athleticism. A thick gray beard framed his face, though it did little to soften the sharpness of his eyes. A deep scar ran from his temple down to his jaw, a silent testament to the wars he had fought and survived.

A pistol rested under his belt. A formality, not a necessity.

"You are late," Markov said, his voice like gravel grinding against steel.

His gaze flicked to the blood staining Noah's sleeve. He said nothing about it. He didn't need to. Instead, he simply nodded and stepped back from the door.

"Inside," he said. "We have limited time."

Noah crossed the threshold, and the warmth hit him instantly. The scent of wood smoke filled the air, wrapping around the room like an old embrace. The furniture was simple—functional. A heavy wooden table sat near the fireplace, its surface worn from years of use. A hunting rifle rested against the far wall, next to a set of maps and a radio that had seen better days.

Markov moved to the table and poured two glasses of local vodka. He sat, gesturing for Noah to do the same.

"The Council already knows you are here," he said. "But it is not the agents that worry me."

Noah lifted an eyebrow.

Markov tilted his head toward the window. Outside, the sky had begun to shift, thick clouds rolling in from the Arctic north. The wind whistled through the house's infirm structure, carrying with it a silent warning.

"It is the weather," Markov finished.

Noah followed his gaze.

"There's a storm coming tonight," Markov continued, his voice calm but certain. "We must make camp before sundown, or we won't last until morning."

The words settled between them, heavy with unspoken urgency. It was clear: They had to leave as soon as possible.

Markov stood, moving toward the back of the house. Noah followed without question.

Behind the house, partially covered in frost, sat two snowmobiles. Their engines were silent, but the scent of fuel and cold metal filled the air.

No words needed to be spoken.

They both knew time was running out.

Without hesitation, they began loading gear—food, weapons, fuel. Once they left, there would be no turning back.

FORTY-EIGHT

THE RENTED APARTMENT IN THE 11TH ARRONDISSEMENT was small, unassuming—just another quiet space above a café, indistinguishable from the thousands of others scattered along the River Seine. That was what made it perfect.

Inside, the team worked in near silence, each member focused on their role.

Jenny positioned herself near the window. From this vantage point, she had a clear view of the cobbled street below—watching for anything out of place, any sign that they weren't the only ones hunting tonight.

A series of laptops hummed on a small wooden table, screens flickering as Neil ran continuous Council communication intercepts, searching for signals, patterns—anything that would give them an edge before it was too late.

Across the room, Katya sat at a coffee table, silently assembling a sniper rifle with practiced efficiency. Every movement was smooth, deliberate. The weapon was an extension of herself, a tool that required no hesitation, no second thoughts.

Near the kitchen, Roux leaned back against the refrigerator, cigarette dangling from his lips. Smoke curled lazily toward the ceiling, his tired eyes flicking between them, as if weighing just how much trouble they were about to walk into.

"Brandt is not alone," Roux finally said, exhaling smoke through his nose. "His bodyguards are with him. The same assassins that gave you all so much trouble in London."

That got Jenny's attention. She turned from the window, her expression tightening.

"The gymnasts?" she asked.

Roux nodded. "The twins. Leonid and Sofia Petrov. They don't leave his side. Even sleep in the penthouse with him. If you're planning on getting close, you'll have to deal with them first."

Katya smirked as she checked the slide of her sidearm, the soft metallic snick filling the quiet room. "So it's to be a rematch, then."

Before anyone could respond, Neil interrupted.

His screen flashed. New intel.

And just like that, the game shifted again.

Neil's fingers flew across the keyboard, decrypting the latest Council communication. Lines of coded text filled the screen—shipments, manifests, schedules. Pieces of a puzzle that, once assembled, could reveal how the enemy planned to expand Olympus.

"We need to figure out how they plan to deploy it," Neil said, eyes scanning the data. "It's not just software. Olympus needs infrastructure—servers, core modules, physical integration points."

He pulled up an encrypted email chain, the language cold and clinical.

COUNCIL COMMUNICATION INTERCEPT
   Origin: Unknown
   Recipient: Paris Ground Team

Timestamp: 14 Hours Ago

MESSAGE:
Phase Two complete. Core components secured. Arrival scheduled for 48 hours. Integration site to be confirmed by Brandt's team prior to install.

SILENCE FILLED THE SAFEHOUSE.

Jenny processed it first. "They're still setting up," she said.

Roux exhaled, tapping his cigarette against the table. The ash fell in lazy spirals. "That means they're waiting for their gear to turn up."

Neil scrolled further, lines of data flashing past until—

He found it.

A cargo manifest, buried within the Council's shell company records. A single shipment flagged for restricted access, its listed contents vague and deliberately misleading.

SHIPPING CONTAINER – *Port of Le Havre*
   Manifest: Data center cooling systems & power regulation units
   Handling Restrictions: Level 5 – Authorized Personnel Only
   Approval Signature: Victor Brandt

"THERE'S OUR DELIVERY METHOD," Katya said coldly.

The core hardware needed to anchor Olympus inside the French financial system was arriving by sea. It hadn't been physically set up yet. They still had time.

But not much.

Jenny stood from the windowsill, rolling her shoulders as if shaking off the weight of what was coming.

"We need eyes on that shipment," she said. "If we can track it before it disappears into the city, we can stop the install before it starts."

Roux shook his head, letting out a slow breath as he flicked his cigarette into a half-empty coffee cup. The ember hissed out in the dark liquid.

"That won't be easy," he muttered. "The Port of Le Havre is one of the most secure in Europe. You can't just walk in and check a container."

Neil smirked. "We won't walk in. We'll hack in."

Katya, unfazed, loaded a magazine into the rifle, the sharp click of the round chambering punctuating the silence.

"And if that doesn't work?" she asked.

Jenny grabbed her pistol, tucking it smoothly into her belt as she met Katya's gaze.

"Then we do it the old-fashioned way."

"There's more," Neil said, his eyes lit by the cold glow of the monitor.

All eyes turned to him.

Something else had come through in the communique. An attachment.

A video file.

Neil opened it.

The screen flickered to life, revealing a slick corporate-style presentation. Logos of various international tech contractors flashed across the top corner—Euratek Systems, Novus Core, Helion Infrastructure—all Council shell companies.

The footage cut to surveillance images: data centers, government facilities, and hardened military bunkers. Each location was marked with a timestamp and GPS coordinates. Then came the overlays—schematics of power grids, floodgate control networks, metro rail systems, and missile command interfaces. All converging into a central node.

The node was labeled: OLYMPUS INTEGRATION POINT – PHASE FOUR

Neil's eyes narrowed. "This isn't just about the economy."

The video continued, showing predictive models. A simulated cyberattack rippled across the screen—power grids going dark across Paris, traffic systems collapsing, water treatment plants dumping raw sewage into rivers. Then another simulation: air defense networks hijacked. Dams opened. Civilian panic.

And finally—one last sequence.

A nuclear missile launch interface. French military command structure. Access granted. System override: Olympus AI.

Neil's eyes bulged.

"They're building a system that doesn't just control the economy," he said quietly. "It controls the entire country."

FORTY-NINE

COUNCIL FACILITY, SIBERIA | 00:11 KRAT | FEBRUARY 26

THE ROOM WAS A COLD, STERILE VOID FILLED WITH nothing more than the low hum of high-tech medical equipment. Bright surgical lights glared down from overhead, their unforgiving glow reflecting off polished steel surfaces. The air smelled of antiseptic, sharp and clinical, devoid of anything human.

In the center of the room, Wally lay strapped to an operating table, his wrists and ankles bound with reinforced leather restraints. A thick belt secured his chest, pressing him against the cold steel beneath him.

To his left, a sleek medical cart was arranged with unsettling precision—scalpels, syringes, and surgical instruments gleaming under the harsh light. No wasted space. No unnecessary tools. Everything here had a purpose.

At the head of the table, an advanced neural interface device sat idle, waiting to be connected. Wires coiled neatly around its base like a nest of vipers, silent and waiting to sink into his mind.

In the background, a masked anesthesiologist moved with quiet efficiency, adjusting the intravenous fluids, preparing the sedative that would blur the line between consciousness and nightmare.

The door hissed open. Allison Peterson stepped inside.

Wally glanced at her as she approached, her arms folded across her chest, her expression unreadable.

No words. No pretense. Just the cold inevitability of what came next.

The anesthesiologist held the syringe steady, tapping the glass lightly to remove any lingering air bubbles. The clear liquid inside shimmered under the cold surgical lights—a silent promise of what was to come.

Wally watched the needle for a moment, but his attention shifted to Allison.

"You don't have to do this, Allison," he said, his voice calm, measured.

She didn't react.

Wally pressed forward, his tone soft but insistent. "This isn't you. You were one of us once. You fought alongside Noah. Alongside Jenny, Neil, Marco, Reneé—"

Allison finally turned to face him. Her expression was cold, detached.

"They're all dead, Wally."

The words hit like a hammer, sharp and unforgiving.

But Wally didn't break.

Instead, he leaned forward against his restraints, his voice dropping lower. "Not yet. Not all of them. Noah. Jenny. Neil. They're still out there. They're still fighting."

For the first time, something flickered in her eyes. A crack in the ice. A moment of hesitation.

But then, just as quickly, it was gone.

The anesthesiologist stepped forward. The IV line was connected. The sedative began to drip, slow and deliberate, its effects creeping through Wally's veins like a tide pulling him under.

He had nothing more than seconds, so he used them.

"You can still stop this," Wally said, his voice steady despite the weight pressing against him.

Allison didn't move. She didn't flinch.

Wally's stare hardened, his voice sharp. "If you do this, there's no going back. This—this right here—is the moment that defines you."

Silence.

Allison remained still. A statue. A ghost.

Then, without warning, she leaned in close, her breath warm against his ear. When she spoke, her voice was barely above a whisper.

"I crossed that line a long time ago, Wally. I think I'm pretty much fully defined now."

And with that, she straightened. Turned away.

Wally's vision blurred, the drug dragging him down. His limbs became heavier, his breath slowing as his body surrendered to the drugs.

Allison walked away without looking back.

The cold sterility of the operating room faded behind her as the door hissed shut, cutting off the rhythmic beeping of the monitors, the hum of machines, and the quiet, efficient movements of the surgeon preparing to break into Wally Lawson's mind.

She told herself she wouldn't feel it this time.

But she did.

She had hurt someone she'd once called a friend. Again.

It wasn't the first time, and it wouldn't be the last. She had learned long ago that loyalty was nothing more than an illusion —a fleeting construct that dissolved under the weight of necessity.

And yet.

A shadow of something unwelcome curled in the back of her mind. Guilt. Disgust. A flicker of regret.

She crushed it down.

It had no place here. No place in the world she had chosen.

But as the door hissed shut behind her, sealing Wally's fate, she could still hear his voice.

"This—this right here—is the moment that defines you."

No.

That moment had come long before.

In the dark. In the silence. In the place where she ceased to exist.

Two years ago, Allison had awoken to nothing. No light. No sound. No warmth. Just the weight of concrete pressing in from all sides. Her breath came fast, shallow. She reached out, fingers skimming the floor. Cold. Rough. Unforgiving. She moved slowly, blindly, tracing her prison. Twelve steps across. Eight steps deep. A ceiling just high enough to stand.

No window. No door handle. No bed.

Just darkness.

She had no idea how long she had been here.

Time didn't exist.

In those early days off her imprisonment, she had counted meals, but they were sporadic—sometimes twice a day, sometimes once, sometimes not at all. The water came in a metal cup, left at irregular intervals. The food was bland, textureless, just enough to keep her alive.

She learned quickly: hunger was a weapon. So was thirst.

And the worst of it wasn't the deprivation. It was the silence.

The cell was soundproof. She had screamed once—just once—and the sound had died against the walls, swallowed whole.

So she learned to stop.

They didn't come every day. Sometimes, they left her alone for what felt like weeks. Other times, they came back-to-back, dragging her from the black nothing of her cell into the blinding fluorescence of interrogation.

Shultz was dead, they told her—killed by Noah Wolf not long after she'd been pulled from the burning ruins of her home.

The fire had wiped everything out. E & E was convinced of her death. No one was coming.

The only thing coming was a merry-go-round of Council interrogators. And each time she was dragged into that brightly lit room, the game changed.

Some tried kindness.

A soft-voiced woman who brought warm broth, who called her Allison instead of Prisoner 48, spoke of past E & E operatives who had been through the same thing. She said the same thing every time, gentle and patient: "You don't have to do this alone."

Allison simply didn't answer.

Some tried brutality.

A man with thick hands and cold eyes held her under ice water until her lungs burned and her body seized.

A younger man smiled as he shocked her with a cattle prod, taking his time, learning her thresholds.

A doctor who injected her with something that made her veins feel like they were on fire.

Still, she did not break. Not openly.

Not when they left her to rot in the dark for what felt like weeks. Not when they starved her until she could barely lift her arms. Not when they showed her names, dossiers, lists of E & E operatives "confirmed dead."

She held on.

Until Number Four.

Not another interrogator but a member of the Inner Council itself.

He did not come with needles or electrodes or lies.

He did not bring a gun.

He did not threaten her at all.

He just sat.

A composed, articulate man in an expensive charcoal suit. Polished shoes. No rings, no watch. Clean. Precise.

His voice was smooth, patient. Like silk. Like a scalpel.

"You're strong, Allison," he said. "Stronger than most. That's why you're still alive. But even strong people break against inevitability."

Allison said nothing.

Number Four leaned forward. "Your resistance is impressive. But it's also... expected. I don't need you to betray your morals. I just need you to realize you never had a choice."

She let out a slow breath. "That's where you're wrong."

He smiled, not unkindly. "Am I?"

He extended a hand toward the guard at the door. Without a word, the guard stepped forward and placed a tablet in his palm. Number Four swiped the screen.

And then... history. The Council's history. Not myths. Not speculation. The truth.

Allison watched as names and dates scrolled across the screen. Not just world leaders but their handlers. Their financiers. Their makers. Wars that hadn't started over ideology or land or resources but because the Council willed it. Revolutions controlled from the shadows. Presidents. Prime ministers. Generals. All puppets, all playing a part they didn't even know was scripted.

"You thought E & E was a power player," Number Four mused. "But E & E was always a tool. One of many. Disposable."

He swiped again. A different file.

E & E's founding.

Names. Dates.

Allison stared, the air in her lungs turning to ice.

It had been Council-funded from the beginning.

"You see," Number Four said, "you've never been outside our grasp. You just believed you were."

She forced herself to meet his eyes. "You're lying."

He tilted his head. "Am I?"

The evidence was right there. Dossiers. Financial records. Declassified communiqués from the early '90s. Every mission she had ever orchestrated. Every assassination she had signed off on. All connected.

"Control is an illusion, Allison." Number Four's voice was almost gentle. "You were always part of the machine. The only question is whether you want to be a cog... or something greater."

She looked at the files again. And for the first time, doubt wasn't the enemy.

It was the truth.

Two years later, Allison stood motionless in the corridor, her reflection staring back at her from the glass of a window. Beyond it, the Siberian tundra stretched endlessly, a world of ice and silence, swallowed by the raging storm outside.

The blizzard howled against the facility, flinging sheets of snow against the reinforced glass, obscuring the world beyond in a swirling white void. Wind shrieked through the frozen wasteland, rattling the metal fixtures along the exterior, making the building feel like it was under siege from the elements themselves.

She barely saw it. Her mind was elsewhere, caught in the tangle of a past she had long since buried.

E & E had never been real.

She had spent her life believing she was fighting in the shadows, an unseen force battling the darkness. But in the end, she had only been a piece on the board, moved at the Council's whim. She had resisted. She had fought. And she had lost. Because there had never been a war. Just the Council.

She inhaled slowly, forcing the memories down, sealing them away. This was her life now. She had made peace with that.

...Hadn't she?

FIFTY

THE WIND HOWLED LIKE A LIVING THING, SHRIEKING against the canvas walls of their reinforced tent, its fury unrelenting. Outside, the world had been consumed—a vast, featureless expanse of white where the blizzard erased everything in its path.

Inside, the air remained frigid, but it was at least survivable. The small compact heating unit flickered with dull, mechanical persistence, barely enough to stave off the deep cold. Even so, their breath hung in the air, swirling in slow, ghostly tendrils.

A small red LED light blinked near the tent's entrance—a silent beacon marking their coordinates, ensuring they didn't become lost to the storm.

Noah sat against the side of the tent, his M4A1 carbine resting across his lap. He methodically checked the barrel, running his gloved fingers along the steel, ensuring no frost or ice had crept in. Out here, a jammed weapon meant death.

Across from him, Sergei Markov crouched near the heater, his weathered hands wrapped around a small handheld device, its screen casting a faint blue glow across his scarred face. The ex-

GRU commander barely seemed to notice the cold, his focus locked on whatever data scrolled across the screen.

Neither man spoke. Outside, the storm raged on.

Markov was holding a Kestrel 5500 Weather Meter. The device measured wind speed, temperature, barometric pressure, and altitude. Equipped with a digital compass and weather trend analysis, it could detect approaching shifts in storm intensity.

He studied the data, his expression turning grim.

"Bad news," he muttered, shaking his head. "Storm won't clear completely, but it will weaken. We'll get maybe four hours before it builds again."

Noah exhaled slowly, rubbing his gloved hands together, the chill gnawing at his bones despite the heating unit.

"Enough time to get close?" he asked.

Markov nodded, though he didn't look pleased about it. "If we push hard. But forget the snowmobiles. This terrain is too rough, too deep." He glanced toward the tent entrance, where the wind howled against the fabric. "We'll use skis."

Not ideal. But nothing about this mission was.

Markov stowed the weather meter, then locked eyes with Noah. His gaze was sharp, unyielding.

"We have our window," he said. "We either move when it opens or we don't move at all."

Noah pulled out a rugged, military-grade watch, its illuminated dial cutting through the dim interior of the tent. 1:42 a.m.

The clock was ticking.

By 5:00 a.m., they needed to be in position, ready to breach.

Markov's hacker—a trusted ghost buried deep in the digital underground—had agreed to launch a cyberattack against the base's security grid at that time. It was a favor Markov had called in, one that came with no guarantees.

A test run a day ago had confirmed a brutal reality. The hacker could infiltrate the system, but only for 15 to 20 minutes. After that, the base's security AI would adapt and purge him from the network.

That was their window. Five a.m. Fifteen, twenty minutes.

And once inside, communication would be impossible. The storm's interference would block all signals, cutting them off from the outside world.

The hack was pre-programmed to begin at exactly 5:00 a.m. No delays. No second chances.

Markov reached into his pack and pulled out the last essential tools for their journey—two sets of Asnes Combat NATO Cross-Country Skis.

Designed for Arctic military operations, they were built for endurance in extreme conditions. Plus, they were equipped with full-length metal edges, providing stability on uneven terrain.

Noah took his pair, running his fingers over the bindings, checking for any weakness.

"We move at first light," he said.

Markov fastened his own skis to his pack, then nodded toward Noah's M4A1, his tone matter-of-fact.

"Make sure you keep it warm," he said. "In this cold, your firing pin will freeze if you let it."

Noah nodded, wrapping his weapon in an insulated cover, ensuring it wouldn't turn into dead weight when he needed it most.

They would travel light. No unnecessary gear. Only what they could carry, what they could trust.

Everything was prepped. Now all that remained was the storm's brief mercy. When the gap came, they would move.

FIFTY-ONE

THE WIND CUT ACROSS THE ROOFTOP, CARRYING THE scent of salt, oil, and diesel. Below, the dock bustled with mechanical precision—floodlights casting harsh cones of white over a forest of shipping containers and looming cranes.

Neil lay prone behind a rusted ventilation unit, binoculars pressed to his eyes. "There," he said. "Brandt. And the twins."

Katya shifted beside him, eyes locking on to the familiar silhouettes through the scope of her suppressed SR-25. Victor Brandt stood near the central loading bay in a black overcoat, calm and in control. Leonid and Sofia Petrov flanked him—still, watchful, coiled like predators.

Jenny peered through her scope. "They brought the entire Council circus."

She wasn't exaggerating. Dozens of armed guards patrolled the perimeter—body armor, suppressed rifles, earpieces. These weren't dockworkers. They were trained. Disciplined. Council muscle.

Forklifts rolled between transport trucks, offloading sleek, matte-black crates from the shipping containers. Neil zoomed in on the markings.

"Fiber-linked quantum nodes," he muttered. "Thermal-regulated server racks. Next-gen cooling arrays. All the ingredients of a bleeding-edge AI server farm."

Katya scanned the operation. Three trucks stood lined up at the dock, trailers yawning open, swallowing crate after crate. Each container was marked with innocuous branding—Euratek Systems, Helion Dynamics—harmless tech firms on paper. But the cargo was anything but harmless.

"This is the backbone," Neil whispered. "This is Olympus Phase Three."

Jenny's voice was flat. "Paris goes dark once all this is installed."

They watched in silence as Brandt nodded to a logistics officer, then checked something on a tablet. The operation moved with surgical efficiency. No wasted motion. No room for error.

Katya tracked the Petrovs with her scope. "If we try anything here, we're dead before we hit the ground."

Jenny agreed. "We don't destroy the parts here. We track them."

Neil lowered his binoculars, already reaching into his gear and pulling out a set of compact GPS trackers—small, adhesive-backed devices designed for high-risk operations.

"We tag the trucks," he said. "Then we take them down when they're vulnerable. Away from these troops."

It wasn't ideal. But it was the best option they had.

One by one, the team moved into position.

The guards were watching the main entrances, focused on potential outside threats. They weren't paying attention to the side access routes, where the containers and stacked cargo created a maze of shadowed pathways.

Perfect cover.

Still. One mistake, and it was over.

They had to be quick. Methodical. Precise.

The team left the rooftop, then split up.

Neil moved first.

Keeping low, he slipped behind a parked forklift, staying in its blind spot. The hum of engines and machinery masked his footsteps, allowing him to inch forward without drawing attention.

In his fingers he held the small magnetic tracker—compact, discreet, pre-synced to their own system.

With a smooth motion, he reached beneath the first transport truck and slapped it onto the undercarriage. It stuck into place with a faint metallic click.

One down. Two to go.

Jenny moved carefully, staying in the shadows as she crept toward the second truck. The steel crates around her provided cover, but not much. One wrong step, one miscalculation, and they were all dead.

She ducked behind a stack of cargo, her breath steady as two guards passed by, their assault rifles slung across their chests.

Just twenty feet away, Victor Brandt stood, speaking in low, clipped tones to one of his lieutenants. His posture was relaxed, but his eyes never stopped scanning—always calculating, always in control.

Jenny waited, watched. Timed their movements.

The moment their backs were turned, she slid under the truck, moving fast but silently. Her hands worked quickly, pulling the tracker from her vest. She reached up, placing it firmly against the truck's axle, when—

A voice. Too close.

"Did you hear something?"

Jenny froze, her pulse spiking as the sound of boots crunching over gravel moved closer. She pressed herself against the vehicle's undercarriage, making herself small, willing herself invisible. The guard's feet stopped inches away.

A long, dangerous silence stretched between them.

Jenny kept her breathing slow, steady, waiting—

Another voice. Low, irritated.

"It's nothing. Keep moving."

The footsteps receded. Jenny exhaled silently, waiting another ten seconds before slipping back into the shadows.

Two trucks tagged. One left.

Katya moved next, staying low, a ghost in the dark.

The dock was alive with movement—forklifts buzzing, workers shouting, security teams pacing the perimeter. Every step had to be measured, exact, invisible.

Up ahead, a group of workers unloaded crates near the transport trucks, their backs turned to her. Too much open space. She needed a distraction.

Katya's fingers curled around a metal bolt left abandoned near a stack of shipping pallets. A flick of her wrist, and it sailed through the air, clanking loudly against a steel container a dozen meters away.

A guard spun toward the noise, his partner following.

That was her window.

Katya moved quickly, silently, weaving behind their backs, using the hulking shadows of stacked cargo to mask her advance.

The third truck loomed ahead, its trailer half-loaded with the marked crates. This was it.

She dropped to a crouch, pressing herself against the cold metal, her breathing steady. Quick, efficient hands slid the tracker into place, securing it beneath the chassis with a single, practiced motion.

Done. But she didn't relax.

Footsteps. Close.

Katya flattened against the truck's undercarriage, her heartbeat steady as a pair of boots crunched toward her position.

She didn't breathe. Didn't move. A second's hesitation could mean death.

The guard's boots stopped just feet from her position, the crunch of gravel shifting as he adjusted his stance. She could feel the moment stretch—seconds dragging like slow-moving steel gears.

A radio crackled.

"Status check—Sector Four. Report."

The guard exhaled, shifting his weight.

"All clear," he muttered into his comm.

Then with a bored grunt, he turned away.

Katya didn't move. Not yet. Let him walk away first. Let the moment breathe.

Only when his footsteps faded into the din of the port did she slide out from her cover, keeping low, controlled.

Three.

But her work wasn't finished yet.

Not far from the loading zone, Brandt's sleek black Mercedes idled near the dock's exit. Standing right next to it were Leonid and Sofia.

Katya caught sight of them through a gap between stacked crates—Leonid leaning against the hood, scanning the area with slow, deliberate movements, his sharp eyes cutting through the shifting shadows.

Sofia stood nearby, arms crossed, her posture casual but deceptive. She was listening, sensing, her head tilting slightly as if she could hear Katya's very breath.

Bloodhounds on the prowl.

Katya's gaze locked on to the car's undercarriage. That was her final mark.

She needed a distraction.

Her fingers brushed the inside of her vest, plucking a coin from her pocket—a one Euro piece. With a flick of her wrist, she sent it skittering across the pavement toward a pile of discarded crates behind them.

Clink.

Leonid's head snapped in that direction. His body followed instinctively, muscles tensing. Sofia turned at the same time, her sharp gaze narrowing.

Katya moved.

She kept low, slipping through the narrow gap between

stacked pallets and crouching just behind the car. The metal was still warm from the engine.

She dropped to her stomach and rolled under it.

The ground was cold, the underside of the chassis slick with oil residue. She reached into her gear, fingers finding the compact magnetic tracker. It took less than two seconds to secure it, pressing it firmly against the frame, the faintest click barely audible over the ambient noise of the port.

Above her, Sofia sniffed—actually sniffed the air.

Katya's pulse remained steady.

Sofia's eyes flicked toward the car.

Katya clenched her jaw. If she had to kill them now, it would set off every alarm in the port.

Don't breathe. Don't even think.

Then, like fate intervening, a gust of wind rattled a loose tarp on a nearby pallet—making a whipping crack.

Sofia's gaze flicked toward the sound. She made a small, dismissive noise in her throat and turned away.

Leonid followed.

Katya didn't waste another second.

She slid out from beneath the car, staying low, her body moving like liquid through the shadows. She weaved through the maze of cargo, forklifts, and moving workers, retracing her route with the same surgical precision she had used to get in. No sudden movements. No hesitation. No sound.

When she finally reached the warehouse edge, she spotted Jenny and Neil waiting in the shadows of the loading bay, their eyes scanning for her.

She slipped beside them—mission complete.

Jenny whispered, "You got it?"

Katya gave a small nod.

Neil checked his watch. "Then let's get the hell out of here."

Without another word, they melted back into the night.

FIFTY-TWO

COUNCIL BASE—OUTER PERIMETER | 04:57 KRAT | FEBRUARY 27

THE BLIZZARD HAD BECOME THEIR ALLY.

The wind howled like a living beast, whipping across the snow-covered landscape in furious, biting waves. Thick sheets of snow fell relentlessly, reducing visibility to just a few feet.

At the perimeter fence, cameras were coated in frost, their lenses blurred, struggling against the storm. Nearby patrols moved much slower than normal, hunched against the wind, their faces half-buried in scarves and balaclavas.

From a ridge above, Markov raised his thermal binoculars, scanning the shifting red silhouettes of the guards below.

"Three minutes until the hacker's window," he muttered. "You better go."

Noah moved.

Dressed in full white camouflage, he was a ghost within the storm, blending seamlessly into the snow-swept terrain. No wasted motion. No sound.

He slid down a snowbank, landing near the perimeter fence in a controlled crouch. Just ahead, a lone guard stood watch in front of a door, his back slightly turned, shielding his face from the relentless wind.

Noah didn't hesitate.

He lunged forward. Fast. Precise. Silent.

His arm locked around the guard's throat, cutting off his breath before he could react.

The man struggled, his gloved hands clawing at Noah's grip, but the cold had already drained his strength. Within seconds, his movements weakened, his gasps turning into muffled chokes.

Finally, he went limp.

Noah eased him down into the snow, ensuring no sound escaped. Then, without missing a beat, he checked the door. It was unlocked. The hack had worked.

He opened it and was inside.

The corridors of the base were cold, concrete, sterile. The gray walls stretched endlessly, sharp angles and unmarked doors forming a labyrinth of concrete and steel.

The base was massive, a sprawling underground fortress, its scale almost incomprehensible. Thousands of rooms. Hundreds of hallways. A city beneath the ice.

Noah kept close to the walls, ears sharp. The occasional footstep echoed through the corridors—patrols, moving in careful, disciplined routes. He waited each time, let them pass, then slipped forward again.

Within a side room, he found a security terminal. Kneeling, he pulled a data device from his gear, inserted it into the port, and watched as the screen flickered, the device loading into the system's restricted files.

He worked fast. No time to waste.

Then—his breath caught.

RECRUIT DATABASE → Batch 302
Status: Active | Location: Block C

. . .

302. That's the number the contact had told him they'd given to his daughter.

It was Norah. She was here.

Noah clenched his jaw, his pulse hammering. She was alive.

Then another thought cut through the noise.

Wally.

His fingers moved swiftly over the keyboard, pulling up another file.

WALLY LAWSON → *STATUS: Detained*
  Location: Medical Wing

NOAH'S EYES NARROWED. The Medical Wing was close.

He could save them both.

FIFTY-THREE

THE TEAM'S VAN SAT IN DARKNESS, PARKED NEAR A quiet intersection, the city eerily silent at this hour. Streetlights flickered faintly, casting long shadows across the empty sidewalks.

Inside, the three of them worked in tense silence.

Neil hunched over his laptop. Three red blips moved steadily on the screen—tracking the three trucks they had tagged back in Le Havre.

A fourth red blip—Victor Brandt's Mercedes—was currently stationary within the city. They would deal with him and his bodyguards in due course. First came the trucks.

Katya sat across from Neil, loading bullets into magazines with cold, methodical movements. Her expression was tight, controlled, but her green eyes burned with focus.

Jenny sat behind the wheel, her fingers gripping it tightly. She hated waiting.

Neil scanned the map, watching as the trucks diverged, their routes splitting into different sections of the city.

His jaw tightened.

"They're splitting up," he said. "Three different drop points."

Katya exhaled sharply, snapping a loaded mag into place.

"Then we split too," she said. "We take them all down at once."

They moved out, ready to stop the next phase of Olympus before it began. The van's sliding door whispered open, cold Parisian air rushing in as Neil and Katya stepped out into the quiet street. The distant hum of the city droned on, but this part of town was still. The trucks had disappeared into the arteries of Paris, and now they had to chase them down before it was too late.

Parked along the curb, two black Citroën sedans waited for them—supplied by Mathieu Roux, their contact. Roux stood beside the driver's door of one, a cigarette dangling from his lips. His eyes watching them through the wisps of smoke with the wary patience of a man who had seen too much but still couldn't walk away from the game.

Neil nodded at him. "Appreciate the wheels."

Roux smirked, lifting the cigarette from his mouth. "It would be nice if you brought them back in one piece."

Katya scoffed, tossing her bag into the backseat of one of the cars. "Not making any promises."

Jenny stayed behind the wheel of the van, her engine already idling, her gaze flicking between them. "We each follow our own red dot," she reminded them.

Neil pulled up the tracker again, watching the three blinking markers moving through the city. The trucks had spread wide—one heading deeper into the financial district, another weaving toward Montmartre, and the last crawling through the southern outskirts of the city.

"We stay in contact," Neil said as he climbed into the driver's seat of his sedan. "If something goes wrong, call in immediately."

"Or kill them first and call later," Katya muttered as she slid behind the wheel of her Citroën.

Jenny exhaled, gripping the wheel. "We end this here."

No more words.

Engines rumbled to life.

Neil peeled off first, his taillights glowing red as he surged into the streets. Katya followed a second later, her car cutting through the night like a predator on the hunt. Jenny remained in the van, her jaw tight as she turned onto a different route, heading after her own target.

Three vehicles. Three trucks.

One mission.

They disappeared into the Parisian night, each racing toward their own red dot—toward the unknown.

FIFTY-FOUR

NOAH SLIPPED THROUGH THE STERILE DOUBLE DOORS of the Medical Wing, carbine raised, breath controlled.

Then he froze.

Wally lay on a surgical table, his skull partially open, a thin layer of blood pooled along the edges of the incision. A dozen thin wires snaked into his exposed brain, feeding directly into a glowing neural interface.

Noah's stomach tightened.

The screens flickered, displaying fractured images—memories being forcibly extracted. The process was still active, the machines pulling Wally apart thought by thought.

Three figures stood over him.

A surgeon and two assistants, adjusting the inputs, monitoring the twitching vitals on the screens.

Noah whistled, drawing attention to his M4A1.

"Step away from him," he growled.

The surgeon, Dr. Vasilyev, looked up, his face eerily calm.

"If we stop now," he said, voice cold, professional, unfazed, "the damage to his brain will be irreversible."

The words hung heavy in the air.

Wally's eyes were open, barely blinking, but unfocused—his pupils sluggish, his breath shallow. He was barely there.

Noah's grip tightened on the carbine. Every fiber of him screamed to shoot them all, to tear the wires from Wally's skull, to end this now. But if the surgeon was telling the truth, if he ripped him away too soon—

Wally might never come back.

Noah swallowed the rage burning in his chest. His jaw clenched. His fingers curled around the stock of the carbine. Then, without a word, he turned and disappeared back into the halls.

He would come back for Wally.

But first, Norah.

FIFTY-FIVE

GROUPE CAISSE DES DÉPÔTS DATA CENTRE IN NANTERRE, PARIS | 02:02 CMT

THE GROUPE CAISSE DES DÉPÔTS DATA CENTRE IN Nanterre was nondescript from the outside—concrete, window-less, tucked behind layers of industrial parks and government buildings. But inside, it housed the financial nerve center for billions in French public assets: pensions, infrastructure funds, and municipal accounts. Linking Olympus into this site would give the Council deep access to the lifeblood of France's economy.

Jenny's truck was the first to arrive at its destination.

Her hands tightened on the wheel as she caught up with it, its taillights glowing red in the night ahead of her. The vehicle rumbled down a quiet industrial road, its path steady, deliberate.

Then its turn signal blinked.

She watched as it pulled off the main road, swinging through the security gate of the data center. The facility was stark—rein-forced walls, electric fencing, and low-mounted surveillance cameras. A quiet giant in the city's financial machinery, normally unnoticed. Tonight, it was the delivery point for something far more dangerous.

Jenny slowed the van, letting it drift into the shadow of a nearby loading dock. She killed the engine. Waited.

The truck rolled through the gates.

She expected tight security. That's not what she got.

Instead, a single night watchman sat slumped inside the gatehouse, eyes glued to the flickering glow of a television. Feet up. Ignoring the bank of security monitors behind him. Not even looking up as the truck passed.

Jenny smirked. Too easy.

She slipped out of the car, keeping low, her movements fluid as she crept toward the fence line. She tracked along its edge, staying in the shadows, approaching the gatehouse.

Inside, the night watchman remained glued to his television, the faint glow flickering across his face. He didn't even glance toward the yard.

Jenny barely had to crouch as she slid beneath the window, her footsteps silent against the damp ground.

Pathetic.

Moving swiftly, she eased her body beneath the barriers, slipping inside the yard.

She froze.

There was movement.

A second guard stood near a stack of crates, leaning lazily against a server rack still wrapped in plastic sheeting. A vape pen hung from his lips, blue smoke curling into the cold air. His gaze was locked on his phone screen, thumb scrolling idly.

Jenny's brow twitched.

He didn't look up. Didn't even shift his position. She was barely more than a couple of meters away. She could have tapped him on the shoulder.

As she passed by, barely bothering to slink deeper into the shadows, she exhaled a quiet snuff of disbelief.

"Really?"

The guard kept scrolling.

Jenny kept moving.

Through the loading bay doors, she saw the workers inside. Clean uniforms. Gloves. Headsets. A sterile tech operation.

They began unloading crates—hundreds of them. Each stamped with dry, meaningless acronyms: NTX NODE, Q-CELL POWER ARRAY, OL-CORE INTERLINK.

Jenny's jaw clenched. She knew what they were.

Server cores. Quantum processors. The central nervous system of Olympus.

A group of men in suits stood near the truck, watching the operation closely. Their posture too stiff. Their expressions too sharp.

Not technicians. Council operatives.

Jenny moved fast. She slipped between the pallets, pressing against a stack of crates. Close enough to hear them talking in hushed tones.

"...integration begins tonight."

"Node goes live by morning."

Jenny's stomach tightened. They weren't just staging equipment. They were activating it. Right here. Now.

This place wasn't just a delivery point—it was the upload site.

No hesitation.

Jenny crept along the truck's undercarriage, reaching its fuel tank. She retrieved a small, circular explosive from her belt and pressed it against the metal.

A faint beep. A red LED.

Thirty seconds.

She slipped back into the shadows, drawing her silenced pistol. Raised it. Took aim.

Two quick, clean shots.

The first Council operative crumpled before he even knew what hit him. The second spun, his hand jerking for his weapon—

Jenny fired again.

Another body down.

The workers froze, their hands trembling over the crates they'd been unloading.

Jenny stepped into the light, her gun lowered but firm.

"Beat it. Now."

They didn't hesitate.

Dropping everything, they ran, darting toward the exit, boots slapping against the concrete.

Jenny followed, moving fast.

Then—

BOOM.

The truck exploded, the blast ripping through the loading bay. Fire consumed the cargo, incinerating the Atlas components before they could ever be linked to France's economic systems.

At the gatehouse, the two security guards snapped to attention for the first time that night—one jerking away from his television, the other looking up from his phone, his vape slipping from his lips.

Jenny didn't look back as she strolled across the yard, her silhouette framed by the inferno as the entire operation went up in flames.

One down.

FIFTY-SIX

Noah stormed into the dormitory, his boots silent against the cold concrete floor. Rows of bunk beds stretched into the dim light, small figures curled beneath thin blankets. Some barely moved. Others stirred in restless sleep. Girls of different ages, made in laboratories.

Created. Engineered. Designed for obedience.

Noah moved quickly, scanning each tiny face, his pulse hammering in his chest.

No sign of her. The desperation grew, tightening like a vise around his ribs. But before he could go on—

A voice from the doorway. Calm. Familiar.

"She left an hour ago."

Noah spun, his M4A1 snapping up—

And came face to face with Allison Peterson.

She stood in the doorway, unshaken, calm, two Council assassins flanking her, their hands resting on weapons—but not drawn.

She made a quick gesture.

The girls—all of them—rose without hesitation, filing out in perfect obedient silence. Not a single one looked back.

Now it was just Noah, Allison, and the two assassins.

When Allison spoke, her tone was mocking.

"You didn't think I wouldn't know Wally had a tracker hidden in his teeth, did you?"

Noah stared at her, silent.

"I was there four years ago when he first demonstrated his Nomad Capsule. I let him trigger it, knowing you'd come."

Noah kept the rifle trained on her, his breath steady but his mind racing. Allison didn't move, didn't so much as flinch at the sight of the barrel aimed at her chest.

"You should have stayed dead," Noah said, his voice low, lethal.

A small smirk touched the corner of her lips. "I could say the same for you."

Noah's grip tightened on the weapon. He should put a bullet right through her skull. End this now.

Instead, he said it. "I should shoot you right where you stand."

Allison's smirk didn't waver.

"Go on, then."

Noah fired.

The shot cracked through the air—a clean, precise round aimed straight for her heart.

But before the bullet could hit, a swarm of nanobots rose from her like a living shadow, forming a protective metallic mist around her. The bullet never reached its intended target, deflecting harmlessly into the floor.

Noah's jaw tightened.

He fired again.

And again.

Each shot met the same impossible resistance—the nanobots shifting, intercepting the bullets in mid-air, dispersing them like dust in the wind.

There wasn't a scratch on her.

Amusement flickered in Allison's cold, calculating eyes.

"There was at least something that we managed to keep of Nakamura's work," she said smoothly.

She took a step forward. Unshaken. Unstoppable.

"Now put the gun down. Fight me properly."

Noah exhaled sharply, his jaw clenching as he lowered the rifle and set it on the nearest bunk. Then without breaking eye contact, he rolled his shoulders back, hands coming up into a fighter's stance.

Allison mirrored him, stepping lightly onto the balls of her feet as they began circling each other.

"You can't hope to beat me," Noah told her, his eyes locked on hers, watching every shift of her stance, every flicker of movement.

Allison's lips curled into something resembling a smile.

"You think I'm just a trainer," she murmured. "But once, I was a fighter. The best."

She stopped circling, lowering her chin, shoulders loose but poised for an attack.

Her voice dropped. "I still am."

Then she moved.

A blistering fast strike—a high feint, meant to draw his guard up, immediately followed by a brutal elbow toward his temple.

Noah barely dodged, twisting his head just out of range. The wind of the strike brushed over his skin.

He countered instantly—stepping in and driving a sharp Muay Thai knee into her ribs.

The impact should have knocked the wind out of her.

It didn't.

Allison absorbed the blow, pivoting on her back foot. Before Noah could reset, she torqued her hips and sent a roundhouse kick slamming into his side.

Noah grunted, pain radiating through his ribs as he staggered back.

She was fast. Ridiculously fast.

He barely had time to adjust before the assassins moved in.

Now it was three against one.

FIFTY-SEVEN

MINISTÈRE DE L'ÉCONOMIE ET DES FINANCES AUXILIARY DATA FACILITY—BERCY, PARIS | 02:11 CMT

THE MINISTÈRE DE L'ÉCONOMIE ET DES FINANCES Auxiliary Data Facility in Bercy didn't look like much—just another anonymous government annex surrounded by concrete and glass. But it handled a staggering volume of real-time data: tax flows, national debt tracking, currency stabilization algorithms. If Olympus was embedded here, it wouldn't just observe the French economy—it would control it.

Neil's target arrived at the rear of the facility, pulling into a secured loading zone usually reserved for hardware upgrades and IT support shipments.

This was the most dangerous site yet—too many civil contractors working inside, too many layers of state infrastructure tied to the location. A wrong move here meant national panic, not just collateral damage.

Neil didn't have the luxury of brute force. He had to be smart.

From a nearby rooftop, laptop balanced on his knees, Neil hacked into the facility's internal security system.

First step: Trigger the fire alarms.

A high-pitched wail filled the air, flashing red lights blinking across the receiving bay. Workers panicked, following emergency protocols as automated announcements ordered them to evacuate. Within seconds, the data hub was empty—except for security and the Council operatives stationed near the truck.

Second step: Kill the truck.

Neil moved fast, using the confusion to his advantage. With the alarms blaring and personnel funneling toward the exits, he descended from his rooftop perch, slipping through a side gate unnoticed. The security guards were too busy shouting into radios, unsure whether this was a test or a breach. The Council operatives remained by the truck, eyes sharp, hands twitching near their weapons.

Neil crept along the loading docks, keeping low behind storage cases marked with "Data Terminal Backups" and "Encrypted Node Arrays." He spotted the truck, parked in a secured bay, its trailer filled with crates stenciled ATLAS CORE HARDWARE and FR-DATA LINK MODULES.

Neil reached into his pack, pulling out a C4 charge. No time for finesse. It had to be quick and clean.

He slipped beneath the trailer, staying low as the strobing emergency lights painted the space in frantic pulses of red and white. He found the perfect spot—up against the truck's fuel tank. Pressed the explosive into place. Armed it, watching as a small red LED blinked to life.

Neil backed away, cutting across the yard's perimeter, swift and silent. The guards were still distracted, waving at hesitant staff and arguing about protocol.

He slipped back through the side gate, retracing his path to the rooftop where his laptop waited.

Final step: Detonate.

From his vantage point, Neil scanned the scene below. Clusters of workers loitered just outside the fence, waiting for the all-clear to return. The truck sat exposed, Council operatives unaware that it had already become their funeral pyre.

Neil pressed the trigger.

A deafening explosion ripped through the facility. The truck went up in a fireball, its fuel tank igniting instantly, sending a shockwave through the loading docks. A plume of black smoke erupted into the night sky, silhouetting the crumpled remains of the vehicle as fire consumed its contents.

The Atlas infrastructure was gone. None of the normal workers harmed.

Neil let out a slow breath, watching the chaos unfold below. Security scrambled, shouting into radios, but the job was already done.

Two down.

FIFTY-EIGHT

COUNCIL BASE, SIBERIA | 05:18 KRAT | FEBRUARY 27

THE ASSASSIN LUNGED—A TALL, WIRY MAN, HIS movements fluid, almost serpentine. He threw a jab to Noah's face, a feint for the knife-hand strike aiming for his throat.

Noah parried the jab, twisting just enough to let the knife-hand graze past his neck. He caught the assassin's wrist, yanked it into a brutal wrist lock, and drove a side kick into his knee joint.

A sharp pop.

The assassin collapsed, but the second one—a shorter, stockier fighter—was already on him.

Noah barely turned before the man slammed into him with a brutal shoulder check, sending him crashing into a bunk bed with a hollow metal clang. The impact rattled through his spine.

Allison was already moving.

She closed the gap in a heartbeat, twisting into a spinning back kick aimed at his chest.

Noah dodged at the last second, the kick grazing his ribs. But before he could recover, the stocky assassin struck—an elbow driving into his spine.

Pain exploded through Noah's back. Electricity snapped through his nervous system. His limbs went involuntarily loose.

He had no time to process it—the wiry assassin was already back up, despite his wrecked knee. Snarling with pain, he plucked a knife from his belt and slashed at Noah as he evaded Allison and the other assassin.

Noah saw it late. He twisted—but not fast enough.

The blade ripped through his side in a diagonal arc of searing agony.

Noah gasped, his breath catching, pain tearing through his nerves. The cut was deep—too deep, slicing dangerously close to the inside of his hip bone.

For a split second, his vision wavered.

The stocky assassin took the chance—kicking at his legs, forcing him down onto one knee.

The knife-wielding assassin lunged for another strike—going for Noah's throat.

Noah moved on instinct.

He grabbed the attacker's wrist, plucking it from midair, twisted hard, and snapped the bone with a sharp crack. The knife clattered to the floor as the man crumpled, howling in pain.

Noah didn't wait. He chopped down with the edge of his hand, striking hard and precisely against the assassin's throat. The man's eyes bulged, a strangled gurgle escaping his lips as he clutched at his crushed windpipe.

He collapsed onto the cold concrete floor, his body convulsing as he desperately tried to suck in breath, hands scrabbling at his throat, legs kicking weakly. The only sound was the wet, choking struggle of a man drowning in open air.

One down.

Noah was already up and moving.

But Allison was already on him. She grabbed his collar, pivoting into a hip throw. Noah barely countered in time, hooking his leg inside hers to block the technique. Instead of being thrown, he twisted in midair, dragging her down with him.

They crashed onto the cold floor, grappling for control—the pain tearing through Noah's side. It felt like he would split apart.

As they scrambled to their feet, Allison's fist drove into his ribs—a short, vicious body shot that made his stomach lurch.

Noah shifted his weight, twisting away from her just as the stocky assassin came down with a hammer fist aimed at his skull.

Noah countered mid-strike, catching the assassin's forearm as he pivoted underneath, twisting the arm into a joint lock before driving a palm strike into his nose—sending bone fragments into the frontal lobe.

Blood spurted from the impact. The assassin went limp.

Two down.

Noah spun back to Allison.

She standing there. Breathing hard. Smirking.

She wiped blood from the corner of her mouth, then shifted back into her stance, shoulders loose, balanced, ready.

"This is fun," she said.

Noah stood in the wreckage of the fight, his body screaming in pain. Blood poured from his side, soaking into his tactical gear, each breath a sharp, serrated agony. His muscles shook from exhaustion, his mind fighting to stay sharp despite the rapid blood loss.

Across from him, Allison was barely standing, clutching her ribs, her fingers slick with blood. Sweat dripped down her face, but her eyes still burned with defiance.

That was when things escalated.

Outside the dormitory, alarms began blaring, their mechanical wails bouncing off the concrete corridors.

The hack was over. The window had closed.

It was followed by the sound of marching boots.

Noah stiffened.

The hallways outside filled with movement, a low, rhythmic thunder of troops pouring into the facility.

He and Allison locked eyes, both aware of the same truth.

If he stayed here, he would die here.

Allison exhaled, her smirk finally fading.

"Don't be dumb, Noah," she said, her voice edged with exhaustion. She took a shaky step back, pressing her hand tighter against her wounded ribs.

Her voice dropped, quieter now.

"Stay alive," she murmured.

Then softer still—"For your daughter."

The words hit like a bullet.

Noah's fingers twitched, still primed to fight—but he knew.

No time.

Not now.

Not yet.

With one last glare, he turned and ran.

FIFTY-NINE

SFR TELECOM INFRASTRUCTURE HUB – SAINT-DENIS, PARIS | 02:15 CMT

THE SFR TELECOM INFRASTRUCTURE HUB IN SAINT-Denis wasn't just a relay station—it was a gateway. From here, SFR managed critical fiber-optic nodes and data routing systems that serviced millions of users across France. If the Council integrated Olympus into this site, they'd have a direct line into the country's communication backbone—emails, financial transactions, surveillance feeds. Every signal compromised.

Katya tracked her target to the rear loading zone, where a truck had just pulled into the receiving bay. The facility sprawled across several blocks—concrete, fencing, razor wire. Unmarked but unmistakably important.

Inside, workers in red SFR vests moved efficiently, unloading crates from the truck. They had no idea what they were handling.

But the guards watching them did.

Heavily armed. Alert. Too many to take head-on.

Katya exhaled slowly, adjusting her gloves. Precision over force.

She cut through the shadows like a scalpel, weaving between stacks of cabling spools and server crates, her movements silent.

Once she reached the truck's undercarriage, she slid underneath, working quickly.

A small pack of C-4—military-grade, perfectly placed.

A timer set—one minute.

With the charge armed, she slipped toward the server racks being prepped for indoor installation. Workers were scanning barcodes, logging equipment. Red LED strips lined the casing of the crates: ATLAS NODE - SERIAL 114B.

Katya reached into her gear pouch, pulling out a thermal charge—a compact but powerful incendiary device designed to burn hot enough to destroy circuitry, casings, and cooling systems beyond repair.

She placed it behind a stack of quantum interface modules, activated the trigger, and slipped back into the shadows.

The timer hit zero—

A deafening explosion ripped through the rear lot.

The truck detonated first, its undercarriage blowing apart, sending a fireball into the ceiling.

Then the thermal charge ignited.

A chain reaction of fires erupted across the staging area, consuming the Atlas components, reducing next-gen processors and quantum nodes to slag within seconds.

Alarms blared. Sirens screamed. Chaos erupted.

Katya slipped into the night, her breath steady, her pulse calm. Three down.

SIXTY

NOAH'S FEET POUNDED AGAINST THE COLD FLOOR, each step burning agony as he pushed forward. The pain in his side was a raw, gaping wound, bleeding too fast, weakening him with every second.

Down the corridor. Through the steel halls.

Guards were already searching. Already following the blood trail he was leaving behind.

Noah burst into the open tundra, the freezing air burning his lungs as he stumbled forward. The storm howled, snow slashing across his vision, but he kept running.

Behind him, troops poured out of the base, their dark silhouettes emerging from the whiteout, rifles raised, voices shouting through the wind.

He couldn't stop.

He pushed through the pain, his body failing, but he kept moving—into the storm, into the unknown.

Because he wasn't done yet.

He reached the tree line, his legs finally giving out beneath him.

Markov appeared from the storm, grabbing him before he hit the snow.

"Where's the girl?" Markov's voice was urgent, demanding.

Noah gasped, struggling to stay conscious.

"I don't... know..." he choked out.

Then—movement in the blizzard.

Troops emerged, rifles raised, forming a loose perimeter around them.

Markov's jaw tightened. He didn't hesitate—he glanced at his watch, then fired a flare into the sky.

The red glow burned against the storm, illuminating the swirling snow as it drifted above them. The guards hesitated, speaking into their radios, eyeing the red glow floating above their heads.

A reply crackled through the static.

"Take Wolf alive. Shoot his accomplice."

Markov cursed under his breath, his grip on Noah tightening.

The nearest guard stepped forward, raising his rifle.

Then—

A sound. A deep, thunderous roar cutting through the howling wind. The whine of rotors slicing the air.

A Mi-24 Hind gunship burst from the storm, its massive frame ripping through the whiteout, side cannons whirring to life.

Gunfire rained down.

The world exploded into chaos.

The troops scattered, diving for cover as heavy rounds tore through the snow, kicking up ice and debris. A winch line dropped from the chopper, swinging wildly in the storm.

Markov grabbed it, looping it around Noah's harness, securing him in place as bullets ripped into the ground nearby.

Through the radio, a voice cut through the static.

"Where's the girl?"

Markov gritted his teeth, pulling himself onto the winch.

"I don't know," he admitted as it began lifting him and Noah into the air. Then, scanning the chaos below, he muttered, "But if we don't get out now, we're all dead."

The Mi-24 gunship banked hard, engines roaring as it climbed into the storm—disappearing into the white void.

But they weren't alone.

From the darkness behind them, two more helicopters emerged—sleek, black Council attack craft, their silhouettes barely visible against the storm.

Their spotlights cut through the snow, hunting, chasing.

Inside the Mi-24, Markov braced against the cold wind whipping through the open doors. He glanced at Noah, lying in the back of the chopper's cargo bay, his body limp, his wounds leaking blood onto the metal floor.

Noah's eyes fluttered, his vision swimming. The sounds of gunfire and alarms faded in and out as his body struggled to hold on.

The pilot shouted something, but Markov barely heard it over the storm. Ahead, jagged ice cliffs loomed from the whiteout, forming a narrow canyon of frozen rock and sheer drops. The Council choppers followed, their engines screaming, closing the distance.

Markov gritted his teeth, grabbing the side-mounted PKT machine gun, swiveling it toward their pursuers.

A burst of tracer rounds cut through the air, forcing one of the choppers to pull back—but not enough.

Missile lock warnings screamed in the cockpit.

Noah's vision blurred, his body too weak to move.

The last thing he was aware of before the darkness finally pulled him under was a sudden impact.

The chopper lurched violently, metal screeching, alarms blaring, Markov shouting something—but Noah was already gone, his body succumbing to unconsciousness.

SIXTY-ONE

ABANDONED TRAIN YARD, PARIS | 03:42 CMT | FEBRUARY 27

WHILE THE INFRASTRUCTURE FOR ATLAS BURNED, Victor Brandt was hiding inside a heavily fortified penthouse. The moment his Mercedes emerged from its gateway, the team was moving.

Jenny gripped the steering wheel tightly as she guided the van through the late-night Parisian streets. Ahead of them, the sleek black Mercedes sped away from the building's underground garage, weaving through the dimly lit avenues.

As always, Sofia and Leonid Petrov were guarding Brandt like the sentinels they were. Sofia was driving, while her brother sat in the passenger seat beside her, Brandt in the back.

"Looks like they're heading north," Neil muttered, his eyes locked on his laptop screen, tracking the blinking dot of their target. "There's a private airstrip a few kilometers out."

The team had regrouped and were now all back inside the van.

"They're trying to leave the country," Katya said. "We can't let that happen."

Jenny's foot pressed harder against the accelerator. The van groaned as it shot forward, tires screeching against the wet pavement.

"We won't," she said.

The chase exploded into the streets of Paris.

It wasn't long before the twins spotted the van in their side mirrors and began accelerating.

Sofia had skill, but Jenny had experience. She kept the van tight to the Mercedes' tail, threading through the sparse traffic with cold-steel precision. Streetlights blurred past as they tore through intersections, their headlights flashing like ghosts in the darkness.

Katya leaned out of the window, her AK-105 braced against the door, its compact frame perfect for the tight confines of the speeding van.

She flipped the selector to full-auto.

"Hold us steady!"

Jenny swerved around a slow-moving sedan, expertly bringing the van level with the Mercedes. The city lights flashed across Katya's face as she took aim—

And fired.

She went for the tires first—short, controlled bursts aimed low. The rounds struck with precision, but the reinforced wheels held. Armor-plated. Run-flats.

Katya shifted her aim, raking the side of the vehicle with suppressive fire. 7.62mm rounds sparked off the Mercedes' reinforced frame. One shot punched through the rear windshield, sending glass shattering into the cabin. Brandt ducked into the footwell, shielding his head.

A flash of movement—Leonid twisting in his seat, yanking a pistol from his holster.

He hung out of the window, firing back. Hard, fast shots.

The bullets whizzed past Katya, one punching a hole in the van's hood. Jenny cursed and yanked the wheel, narrowly avoiding a collision as they barreled through the night.

"Watch it!" Neil shouted.

Leonid fired off more shots, shattering the windshield of a civilian car. The driver panicked, swerving hard—right into another vehicle.

A chain reaction.

Tires screeched. Metal crunched. A delivery truck jackknifed, blocking the lane. The Mercedes swerved violently to avoid the pile-up, narrowly missing an oncoming taxi.

Neil's fingers flew across his keyboard. "I can slow them down, but I need a minute—"

"You've got ten seconds," Jenny snapped, wrenching the wheel to avoid the wreckage, the Mercedes rapidly increasing the distance between them.

Muzzle flash from the passenger window.

The bullet slammed into the van's side mirror, blasting it apart.

Katya turned her aim to Leonid. He was still hanging out the window, trying to get a clear shot.

She fired.

But the twin was too quick.

Leonid ducked back inside a split-second before the side mirror of the Mercedes exploded. Glass rained onto the street.

"Jenny, punch it!" Katya cried out.

Jenny floored the gas, closing the distance as Neil finally got control.

"Diverting traffic now," he muttered, fingers blurring over the keys.

A block ahead, every traffic light in the area suddenly shifted —red in all directions. Cars screeched to a stop. Horns blared.

Sofia had no choice but to swerve the Mercedes onto a side street, losing momentum.

Jenny took the opening, closing the distance.

Katya exhaled, raising her rifle. "Now we hit them."

But before she could line up a shot, their earpieces crackled.

It was Mathieu Roux.

"How's it going?" the Frenchman asked.

Jenny scoffed. "We're still on them."

"Yeah?" Roux's tone was casual, but there was an edge beneath it. "And how's that going?"

Neil's eyes narrowed. "Are you in a car?"

"*Oui*. I am," Roux replied.

Neil's fingers froze mid-keystroke. His head snapped up. "Where exactly?"

Roux's voice was amused. "Driving south along the Rue de Marseille."

Neil's eyes widened as he brought up his map. His breath hitched.

The Mercedes was seconds away from crossing Rue de Marseille.

"Roux," Neil said, urgency creeping into his voice. "You're about to intersect them. Stay on course."

Roux's voice turned sharp. "What are you planning?"

Neil was already hacking into the CCTV, jumping between traffic cameras until—there.

Roux's car. A dark SUV. Moving at a steady clip.

Neil's hands blurred over the keyboard. "I'm clearing your lane."

Jenny, catching on, smirked. "Oh, this is gonna be good."

Katya leaned forward, gripping the dashboard.

Neil killed the red lights on Roux's side of the intersection. Green.

At the same time, he flipped the signals for the Mercedes, funneling cars into its path—trapping them into a single route.

They were headed straight for the intersection.

Neil's voice was tight. "Roux, when I say now—floor it!"

Through the earpiece, they heard Roux chuckle. "Copy that."

Jenny pushed the van forward, hanging back just enough to watch it unfold.

The Mercedes barreled toward the intersection at full speed, no time to adjust.

Neil's eyes locked onto the CCTV feed.

"Roux—NOW!"

Roux pressed his foot all the way down on the gas pedal.

The dark SUV burst into the intersection, its engine roaring angrily. The timing was perfect. It smashed into the Mercedes' side with brutal force—T-boning it.

The armored car spun out, tires screeching, metal crumpling, then—

CRASH.

It plowed through a chain-link fence, careening into derelict land until its front end smashed into the skeletal remains of an old industrial lot. The brickwork crumbled as the car finally came to a stop, half-buried in the overgrowth of an abandoned structure.

Dust and debris filled the air.

Jenny yanked the wheel, skidding the van to a stop outside the fence. The back doors flew open, and the team moved fast.

Weapons up. Eyes scanning.

The wrecked Mercedes sat tilted against the ruins, steam hissing from its twisted hood. From where they stood, they couldn't see enough through the smoke and dust to know if anyone was still inside.

Roux climbed out of his SUV, dusting himself off. "You're welcome," he groaned.

Jenny barely spared him a glance. Her focus was on the wreckage. She signaled for the team to spread out as they cautiously advanced through the derelict land. The area was a graveyard of industry, long-abandoned and reclaimed by nature. Rusting scaffolding, crumbling brick walls, and skeletal remains of buildings jutted out of the overgrowth, casting jagged shadows under the dim glow of streetlights.

No movement. No sound—except for the slow hiss of steam escaping from the wrecked Mercedes.

Katya moved ahead, AK-105 raised, steps silent against the cracked asphalt. Neil stayed close, his sidearm drawn, scanning the dark corners of the lot. Roux kept a distance, his own Glock 17 at the ready.

Jenny reached the car first. Gun trained. Finger steady on the trigger. She kept her breath even as she took in the damage. Glass littered the ground. The frame was twisted, the passenger side caved in from the impact.

She crept closer. Katya mirrored her, moving along the opposite side.

Jenny reached for the driver's door—yanked it open.

Empty.

Her stomach tightened.

She stepped back, scanning the ground.

Katya pointed. "Blood."

A faint trail of red droplets led away from the wreckage—disappearing into the thick weeds and collapsed stonework beyond.

"They got out," Katya muttered, stepping back from the car, her rifle sweeping the lot. "Fast."

Jenny's mind raced. They had hit them hard—hard enough that at least one of them had to be injured.

But no bodies. No movement. Where the hell were they?

Roux followed the blood for a short distance. His expression darkened. "Of course."

Jenny turned to him. "What is it?"

Roux exhaled, gesturing toward an ancient stone entrance disappearing into pitch-black depths. Its rusted metal gate had recently been broken open.

"One of many entrances," he murmured.

"To what?" Jenny asked.

"To the catacombs."

Neil frowned. "The real catacombs? The underground labyrinth?"

Roux nodded grimly. "Sixty feet below Paris. Hundreds of kilometers of tunnels. Most of it uncharted. Wouldn't be the first time someone disappeared down there."

Jenny exhaled sharply. Of course. The Paris catacombs—miles and miles of underground tunnels, unmapped sections, twisting paths where people got lost forever. The perfect escape route.

Katya tilted her head, studying the entrance. "You think they planned this?"

Roux's jaw tightened. "Maybe. Maybe not. Either way, if they go too deep, they might never come out."

Jenny checked her rifle. "Then we'd better find them first."

Katya smirked. "And not get lost ourselves."

Roux hesitated. "I'd be careful. Many people don't return."

Katya tightened the strap on her rifle, stepping forward. "Then we'd better not get lost."

Jenny flicked her flashlight on. The beam disappeared into the abyss.

Roux gave them one last look, then nodded. "Good luck," he muttered.

Jenny took the first step inside.

Then Neil.

Then Katya.

The black swallowed them whole.

SIXTY-TWO

THE AIR WAS THICK WITH THE SCENT OF ANCIENT bones and damp stone. The deeper they went, the more oppressive the catacombs became. Walls of centuries-old skulls and femurs watched them with hollow eyes, stacked neatly in endless corridors—a grotesque reminder of the countless dead provided by the city above.

Water pooled at their feet in some sections—cold, ankle-deep, stagnant. The tunnel ceilings were so low in places that they were forced to duck, the space tightening around them like a living tomb.

Jenny flicked her flashlight across the narrowing tunnels. Shadows danced over the bones, stretching and twisting, making them look like they were writhing in the dim light.

"Keep moving," she murmured.

Neil's breathing was steady, but she could feel the tension rolling off him. Katya stayed at the rear, eyes sharp, AK-105 raised.

They had been following the blood trail for what felt like forever. It led deeper, snaking through the catacombs, dragging them farther into the city of the dead.

Then—a sound.

A scrape of movement, somewhere in the tunnels ahead.

They all froze.

Jenny swung her rifle toward the noise, her pulse pounding.

Silence.

Then—gunfire.

The echoes made it impossible to pinpoint the exact direction, but the bullets slammed into the walls, sending chips of bone and rock flying.

They were here.

Sofia. Leonid. The twins had been waiting.

A flash of movement.

More gunfire—louder now, closer.

A burst of bullets shattered the skulls stacked to Jenny's right, sending fragments flying into her face. She ducked, rolling behind a pillar of bones, taking cover. Neil did the same.

Katya dropped into a knee-slide behind a half-collapsed archway, raising her rifle—just as Sofia fired.

A round clipped Katya's shoulder, sending her staggering back. She barely had time to hiss in pain before Sofia was on her, moving with the speed and grace of a trained predator.

The fight broke into chaos.

Leonid came straight through the bones, crashing into Jenny with brutal force. The two of them hit the ground hard, bones scattering beneath them. She barely managed to roll away before his boot stomped down where her head had been.

Neil fired—but Leonid was too fast.

He twisted, grabbed a loose femur from the pile beside him, and swung it like a club. The thick bone smashed across Neil's ribs, sending him crashing into a mound of skulls and femurs.

Jenny lunged, tackling Leonid before he could follow up. They hit the stagnant water of a partially flooded section, her grip locking around his wrist as he tried to bring a knife to her throat.

He was stronger. Much stronger.

Jenny gritted her teeth, muscles straining as he pushed her down, his knee pinning her arm. She tried to reach for her pistol —too late.

Leonid wrenched himself free and—

CRACK.

Neil had swung the femur like a bat, breaking Leonid's wrist mid-strike.

The blade clattered into the water, and Jenny rolled free, grabbing a skull from the floor and smashing it into Leonid's face.

He staggered back, blood trickling from his nose—but still standing. Still ready.

But not ready for this—Neil raised his pistol. Fired.

The bullet hit Leonid in the chest.

He stumbled, eyes wide, but still didn't go down. Another step forward—Jenny fired, too.

He took the second shot in the face, and finally collapsed into the water, sinking beneath the surface.

Neil and Jenny stood over the body, listening.

Somewhere farther into the catacombs, the sounds of Katya and Sofia fighting echoed through the tunnels.

Sofia was made for this. She moved like a ghost—too fast, too fluid for Katya to pin down. Every time she tried to line up a shot with the AK-105, Sofia was already gone, her movements a blur of gymnastic agility.

Katya lost her behind a pile of bones, moving cautiously around the edge of it—

A flash of motion.

Sofia's leg snapped out in a lightning-fast kick, striking the rifle clean from Katya's grip before she could react.

The AK clattered against the stone floor, skidding across a pile of bones.

Katya adjusted instantly, shifting her stance just in time to duck a high kick, the air whipping past her face as Sofia's boot missed her by inches.

Katya countered—a sharp elbow to the ribs, landing solid.

Sofia barely reacted.

She flowed with the impact, pivoting like a dancer before driving a knee into Katya's stomach.

The blow slammed into her core, knocking the breath from her lungs. Pain flared, but Katya stayed standing.

Sofia smirked. "Slower than I remember, One-Sixty-Two."

One-Sixty-Two had been Katya's number back in Siberia.

You were a number until you finished training. That's when they gave you a name.

Katya wiped blood from her lip, eyes narrowing. "Try me again."

Sofia lunged. Katya ducked low, twisting to grab the AK from the ground.

She didn't shoot it, though. Didn't have time.

She swung it instead—fast, brutal.

Sofia dodged the first strike but not the second. The butt of the heavy assault rifle smashed across her ribs, forcing a sharp gasp of pain.

Staggering back, Sofia grabbed a skull from the wall and hurled it at Katya. The skull broke apart as it smashed into her.

The distraction was enough. Sofia tackled her, knocking the rifle from her hands a second time.

They crashed into a section of water, the impact sending ripples through the flooded chamber. Jagged bones littered the floor beneath them—skulls, femurs, ribs—ancient remnants of the dead.

The fight didn't slow.

They rolled through the murky water, bones shifting and snapping beneath them, hands clawing for purchase, knees slamming into ribs, fingers grasping for throats.

Katya barely had time to react before Sofia's elbow snapped into her jaw, the crack echoing off the damp stone walls. Stars burst behind Katya's eyes as she staggered, but she refused to fall.

Sofia lunged.

Katya caught her.

They crashed again, sending water spraying up in violent arcs. Sofia thrashed like a wild animal beneath Katya, her strength monstrous, her limbs twisting with an unnatural grace. She threw an upward strike, the heel of her hand colliding with Katya's nose. Pain exploded, blood mixing with the stagnant water.

But Katya wouldn't be deterred. She too was made for this.

She saw her opening.

She slammed Sofia back, forcing her down beneath the surface. Sofia's body bucked, her hands latching on to Katya's arms, nails digging deep, legs kicking violently, trying to push free.

Katya held firm.

Sofia's face contorted with rage, then desperation. Bubbles erupted to the surface as she thrashed harder, her body writhing beneath Katya's weight.

Katya didn't let go.

She forced Sofia's head deeper.

The struggle went on—seconds stretching into eternity.

Sofia's fingers clawed at Katya's wrists, scraping, tearing, fighting for air, her body arching off the ground, twisting like a serpent.

Then—slowing.

Her movements became sluggish.

Her fingers loosened.

Katya's grip remained like iron.

She held her down.

And held her down.

Until Sofia finally stopped moving.

Silence settled in the catacombs, broken only by Katya's ragged breathing as she continued to hold her.

A hand landed on her shoulder.

She spun, her pulse still hammering, body primed for the next attack.

Jenny stood behind her, her face grim. She glanced down at Sofia's motionless form, then back up at Katya.

"I think she's dead," Jenny said quietly.

Katya released a slow breath as her hands let go.

They ached. Her arms burned from exertion. She took one last look at Sofia's body, then pushed herself to her feet.

"She should've been... faster," Katya murmured, exhausted.

Neil approached, a fresh gash across his brow, blood smearing his cheek. He and Jenny had barely won their fight against Leonid. They didn't need to say it—the struggle was written all over them.

"We need to move," Neil said, voice rough from exertion. "Brandt's still down here."

As if on cue, a faint noise echoed through the catacombs.

A stumble. A scraping of boots against stone. Labored, panicked breathing.

The three of them exchanged glances.

Jenny reloaded her pistol. Katya retrieved her AK-105 from the murky water. Neil adjusted his grip on his own weapon.

Then, as one, they followed the sound.

The deeper they went, the narrower the passageways became. The air thickened, damp and stale. The ground sloped downward, uneven with ancient bones stacked against the walls. Some had collapsed into the pathways, creating grotesque obstacles they had to step over.

The water deepened in sections, sloshing around their boots. Cold. Unforgiving.

Ahead, Brandt's stumbling continued. He was getting slower.

He was running out of places to run.

Roux's words rang in their ears. *Many have become lost in these tunnels.*

Finally, the passage widened into a chamber.

The bones here were untouched, stacked high, forming crude walls of the dead. The ceiling stretched up into blackness, disappearing beyond the reach of their flashlights.

And in the center of the chamber, slumped against the skeletal remains—Victor Brandt.

He was crouched in the center of a small chamber, shaking, his expensive suit streaked with blood and dirt. His eyes were wild and unfocused.

But he wasn't afraid.

He smirked as he took in the team surrounding him—Jenny with her pistol trained on his head, Neil clenching his fists, Katya looking down the barrel of her AK.

Jenny kept her pistol leveled at his head. "End of the road."

Brandt... smiled.

"You think you've won?" His voice was hoarse, ragged, but still laced with that insufferable mockery.

Jenny's grip tightened. "We stopped you deploying Atlas," she said. "Stopped Olympus from hijacking France's systems."

Brandt chuckled—a dry, humorless sound. He shook his head slowly, his teeth flashing through the dim light.

"Did you?"

A vibration cut through the tense silence.

Neil's phone.

One buzz. Then another. Then a cascade of them, a growing wave of frantic notifications.

Brandt's smile grew. Like he knew what was coming.

"I'd check that if I were you," he said smugly.

Frowning, Neil glanced down at the phone. The blood drained from his face.

Live news alerts flooded the screen.

—*Berlin: Market collapse triggers mass bank run. Rioting begins outside several branches.*

—*Brussels: Automated systems fail across stock exchange. Euro in freefall.*

—*Madrid: Telecom blackout spreads across financial districts. Government servers offline.*

—*Rome: Energy grid down. ATM networks failing. Mass panic reported.*

Jenny sucked in a sharp breath.

It wasn't a weapon of mass destruction. It wasn't a bomb.

It was collapse. Controlled, calculated economic destruction.

A slow, satisfied exhale left Brandt's lips. He leaned back against the bones, his expression one of pure, undiluted satisfaction.

"You were too eager to get me," he whispered. "All I ever was… was a distraction. Something to chase while we plugged Olympus into the rest of Europe."

Jenny's hands shook. Her finger hovered on the trigger.

Her vision narrowed to that smirking face, that smug, victorious expression. She wanted to pull it. Wanted to wipe that look from his face forever.

Brandt kept talking. "You've done no more than—"

BANG.

The shot cracked through the chamber, deafening in the enclosed space.

Jenny flinched.

Neil jerked his head sideways.

Katya stood beside them, arm extended, AK smoking.

Brandt's head snapped back, his expression freezing in shock. A small, clean bullet hole sat perfectly between his eyes. His body stiffened.

Then he collapsed into the bones, his corpse tangled in the skeletal remains of the long dead.

The only sound left was the faint dripping of water in the distance.

Neil was the first to break the silence.

"Jesus, Katya." His voice was hollow, strained. He gestured at the body. "We needed him. He could have helped us stop Olympus—"

Katya didn't even glance at Brandt's lifeless form. She kept her eyes forward, lips pressed into a thin, unshaken line.

"He would have never helped us," she said simply.

The three of them were silent for a moment.

Then, finally, Katya turned to them, her gaze sharp, unyielding.

"We need to find Jonas."

SIXTY-THREE

THE VERKHOYANSK RANGE, SIBERIA | TIME UNKNOWN

Noah woke to pain.

A deep, searing agony that laced every breath, turning his ribs into iron bands of fire. His body felt like it had been dragged through hell, stiff and frozen, his limbs barely responsive.

Something heavy and rough was draped over him—a thick military coat. The fabric scratched against his skin as he shifted slightly.

Then the cold hit.

It wasn't just cold. It was Siberian cold—the kind that sank into bone, burrowed into muscle, and threatened to never leave you.

He blinked, trying to force his vision to focus.

The cave around him was dim, shadows flickering from a small fire, its flames barely pushing back the darkness. The entrance was little more than a jagged opening, through which the howling wind sent blasts of freezing air spiraling inside.

A shape moved nearby.

Markov.

The grizzled ex-GRU commander sat on a rock, his rifle across his lap, carefully wiping frost from the chamber with a scrap of cloth. His movements were methodical, steady, the soft sound of metal brushing fabric the only thing breaking the silence.

Without looking up, he muttered, "Good. You're awake."

Noah tried to sit up—and instantly regretted it.

A white-hot spike of pain tore through his abdomen, making his vision blur, his breath catch in his throat.

Markov watched, unimpressed.

He set the rifle aside, moving closer, eyes scanning Noah's bandaged torso with a practiced gaze.

"I stitched you up as best I could," Markov said gruffly. "No broken bones, but I don't know about internal bleeding."

Noah gritted his teeth, nodding slowly.

A gust of wind howled through the cave entrance, sending a spray of ice and snow swirling inside.

Markov's gaze snapped toward the cave mouth, his jaw tightening.

"We've got big problems, Yankee."

Markov gestured toward the cave entrance, where the storm raged in full force.

Beyond the howling wind and churning snow, visibility was almost nonexistent. The sky was a dark, endless gray, and the bitter cold gnawed at everything, creeping in through the rock and ice.

"After the RPG hit," Markov muttered, "the chopper couldn't hold altitude. We had to put her down hard."

They must've dragged him here, Noah thought, through the snow and wreckage, keeping him from freezing to death.

Markov continued, his expression unreadable.

"The pilot and crewman went out to scout. If we're lucky, the Council hasn't—"

A sudden movement at the entrance.

Markov's hand shot to his pistol, and Noah tensed despite the pain.

Two dark figures emerged from the storm: the pilot and crewman, wrapped in heavy coats, their faces nearly hidden beneath scarves dusted in ice.

Their expressions were grim.

The pilot pulled down his scarf, his breath coming in sharp white puffs as he spoke.

"We've got a new problem."

Markov's eyes narrowed. "One more. Excellent. What kind of problem?"

The crewman shook off snow, his voice low and urgent. "We spotted a large search party."

Noah pushed himself upright, pain ripping through his body, his hip burning, bones screaming, but he forced it down.

Markov was scowling. "How many?"

The pilot exhaled, shaking his head. "Too many. We spotted helicopters sweeping the valley. They've already found the wreckage."

That meant one thing. They knew they'd survived.

The crewman's voice dropped lower, his next words filled with certainty. "More than that. There's a ground team heading this way. Dozens of them. With dogs."

The cave fell silent, save for the distant roar of the wind.

Noah inhaled slowly, letting the reality sink in with the pain. His jaw clenched. His fingers curled into fists.

"So we're out of time."

Markov reached into his jacket, pulling out a folded map. The paper was worn, its edges creased and frayed, but it was detailed—military issue, printed long before satellites made maps obsolete.

He spread it across a flat rock, smoothing it out with callused fingers.

Noah leaned forward, his ribs protesting every movement, but he ignored them.

The cave sat high in the mountains, but several paths led downward. Most of them were exposed—open trails where snipers, drones, or aerial patrols would cut them down in seconds.

Markov tapped a particular route on the map.

"Here," he said. "It leads to an old gulag town. Soviet-era prison colony. Still has structures standing." He looked at Noah. "If we can make it there, we can disappear. Hide amongst the buildings. At least we wouldn't be out in the open."

The pilot frowned, adjusting his gloves. "How far?"

Markov didn't hesitate. "Six, maybe seven kilometers."

The crewman swore, shaking his head.

"Through this storm?"

They all glanced toward the cave entrance.

The wind howled even harder, carrying blinding sheets of snow that lashed against the rocks, burying the landscape in white chaos. It was going to be hell.

But it was their only chance.

Markov turned to Noah, his sharp eyes scanning him for any sign of weakness.

"You up for this?"

Noah barely managed a nod. His wound was raw, his body wrecked, every muscle stiff and burning from the crash, the cold, and the haphazardly stitched-up cut. But it didn't matter.

He had no choice.

Gritting his teeth against the searing pain, he forced himself upright. His vision swam for a moment, but he steadied himself.

"Let's move," he muttered, his voice rough.

Markov watched him carefully, weighing his condition. Then, with a short nod, he turned back to the pilot and crewman.

"You're staying here," he said.

The pilot blinked. "What?"

Markov pointed at the map. "You know where you are now. The storm will cover your heat signatures. If you stay inside this cave, you'll be fine. The two of you aren't fighters. You're not built for this. He and I are."

The crewman's jaw tightened. "You're just gonna leave us here?"

Markov nodded. "We'll draw them away. Give them something to chase."

The pilot looked at Noah, as if waiting for him to argue. But Noah just met his gaze evenly.

"This isn't your fight," Noah said.

The pilot hesitated, then gave a slow nod. He knew they were right. He and his crewman were ex-military, but they weren't operatives. They weren't killers. They were just pilots, flying for an old contact.

Markov handed the pilot his compass. "You wait the storm out. Once it clears, follow the valley south. That'll lead you to a road. From there, you find your own way back."

The pilot exhaled sharply but nodded.

The crewman shook his head, muttering something in Russian before collapsing onto a rock. "Madmen," he muttered.

SIXTY-FOUR

COUNCIL FACILITY, SIBERIA | 15:57 KRAT | FEBRUARY 27

Allison sat motionless inside her office, her hands steepled, her expression unreadable. Beside her keyboard, an untouched glass of whiskey reflected the faint glow of the monitor.

She was about to pick the drink up and take a sip when the monitor flickered to life.

A shadowed figure appeared, their form barely distinguishable beyond the layers of encryption and distortion.

But Allison didn't need to see the face.

She knew who it was.

It was Number One. Their voice was masked, altered just enough to scramble recognition.

"Number Eleven."

Allison kept her face neutral.

"Number One."

Number One's silhouette shifted.

"You've done well. The plan to split Wolf and his team, and divert their attention, worked. The integration of Atlas into Europe has been a success. Olympus is online. The world is tearing itself apart—just as planned."

Allison remained silent.

She knew.

Congratulations weren't the real reason Number One was calling. A pause stretched between them. Then Number One's tone turned casual but pointed.

"And the girl?"

"Norah is safe. Hidden away. Out of the reach of her father."

Number One's head tilted ever so slightly, a predatory shift—as if they could hear the hesitation in Allison's voice.

"Good," they said in their constantly changing voice. "She is valuable, after all. The only surviving blood of Noah Wolf."

Allison forced herself to remain still. Her fingertips pressed together, her posture unwavering. But inside—a cold, unshakable weight settled in her gut.

Number One's tone shifted. "But we must begin cleaning up loose ends."

A pause.

Allison felt it before it came.

"Kill them both," Number One announced. "The girl and Wally Lawson."

The room felt colder. The screen flickered slightly, an imperceptible shift in the feed's encryption, but Allison barely noticed.

She'd expected Wally's termination order.

But Norah?

That was unexpected.

She kept her voice carefully neutral. "That's not necessary. We could use the girl. I've only just broken through to her. She will become an asset to us."

Number One's voice didn't change. Still calm. Still absolute.

"It is necessary." A slow, deliberate pause. "Noah Wolf is relentless. You know him better than anyone."

Her words felt calculated, like a move in a game Allison hadn't realized she was playing.

"With them alive, he will never stop."

A long silence stretched between them.

Allison's mind raced, calculating, weighing options, considering her next words carefully. But before she could muster a response, Number One delivered the final blow.

"Kill them both, Number Eleven. Today."

Allison inhaled slowly, her fingers still steepled, her expression unreadable. She could not refuse outright. Not without consequences. This was a test.

Number One watched her, waiting to see if she hesitated. If she flinched, she would never reach the Inner Council. And that meant she would never control what happened next.

So she made her move.

Her voice remained controlled, professional. "Understood."

She waited for Number One's reaction.

For just a fraction of a second, approval flickered in the shadows. Then Number One spoke.

"You are so close to the Inner Council, Eleven. Do not disappoint me."

The screen went dark. The room fell silent.

Allison sat motionless, staring at her own reflection in the blank monitor.

She had a decision to make.

This was a test. A final threshold before she ascended to the Inner Council. She had played every move flawlessly. Calculated. Precise. Everything had led to this moment. So why did it feel like something was tightening around her throat?

She exhaled slowly, pressing her palms against the desk. She had made her choice long ago. She had seen the truth.

The past clawed at the edges of her mind, dragging her back into the moment when everything changed. The moment when Number Four showed her the world.

The real one.

Two years ago, Allison walked in silence, her boots echoing softly against polished concrete as she was escorted into the depths of the Archive of Truth.

The walls stretched far beyond her sight. Row upon row of classified intelligence—each aisle meticulously organized, bound in leather, sealed in glass, or preserved in digital vaults that pulsed softly with electric life.

She had seen government archives before. The CIA. The NSA. MI6.

But this was something else.

This was every government. Every empire. Every war.

She stopped walking. She couldn't help it.

How far back did this go?

Number Four walked beside her, hands clasped behind his back, the very picture of a patient teacher. He watched her pause, then spoke in that smooth, composed voice that could slice through steel.

"We have existed longer than your government. We have survived every war, every regime, every system."

Allison turned her head slightly, her eyes narrowing.

Number Four continued, unbothered. "Your resistance? It's nothing but an ant kicking against a tidal wave."

He gestured to the rows upon rows of files, servers, and recorded histories.

"You want to understand power, Allison? You must understand that power is not won. It is preserved."

He turned sharply, leading her deeper into the chamber. The lights overhead flickered, revealing ancient parchment alongside cutting-edge AI systems—ink-stained treaties stacked beside monitors projecting live financial markets.

This wasn't just history. It was reality.

And then the screens lining the walls flickered to life.

Allison saw everything then.

Live feeds from world leaders' private meetings. The president of the United States receiving orders from a nameless operative. The prime minister of the UK signing documents he hadn't read. The chancellor of Germany, a puppet in a marionette theater she never realized she was part of.

Bank transactions rerouting entire economies. She watched billions shift across accounts with a keystroke. A minor adjustment in a stock algorithm that would send entire nations into a recession—not because of market forces but because it had been decided. By the Council.

Wars, rebellions, political assassinations. All preordained. Orchestrated. Controlled.

Number Four let her absorb it for a moment. And then he changed the feed. New images.

The planet was dying.

Not just because of war but because of humanity itself.

Satellite footage showed sprawling cities collapsing under their own greed. Deforestation carving through the lungs of the world like an infection. Famine spreading in places that had once flourished. Nations choking on pollution while politicians swore nothing was wrong.

And then there were the people.

Endless footage of riots, violence, sickness.

A man beating another to death in an alleyway over a stolen phone. A mother abandoning her child because she could no longer afford to keep her alive. Corrupt leaders selling their own people for power.

Humanity was rotting.

And then... the vision shifted.

The screens cleared.

A world without poverty.

Without pollution.

Without war.

Towering cities, clean and efficient, gleaming with innovation. Children in classrooms, taught not by outdated ideology but by pure logic. Society functioning without corruption. Without chaos.

A utopia.

One species. One future.

Number Four stepped closer, lowering his voice as if he were letting her in on a secret. "Do you know what stands in the way of all of this, Allison?"

The screens shifted again, filling with a blueprint.

It was the nanobot purge. A controlled extinction.

Not random. Not reckless. Engineered.

The weak. The corrupt. The diseased. The useless.

Gone.

Leaving behind only the strongest, the most intelligent, the most capable. A world without parasites. Without burden. Without failure.

A perfect world.

Number Four turned to her. His voice softened. "It is the people who stand in the way of perfection. That is why they must perish. Now you could die screaming, Allison, or you could do something useful with your life. The choice is yours."

Back in the present, Allison's hands curled into fists.

She was no fool. She knew what Number One was really asking. Norah and Wally weren't just loose ends. They were the last vestiges of who she once was. Norah was her godchild, after all. Wally one of her oldest friends. They were weaknesses.

In the world the Council was building, weakness had no place.

She exhaled slowly, forcing herself to relax.

She had seen the truth. And the truth was inevitable. This wasn't about good or evil. It was about order or chaos.

And she had already made her choice.

She reached for the whiskey glass beside her keyboard, her fingers closing around the cool crystal. Then without hesitation, she tipped it over.

The amber liquid spilled across the desk, spreading like blood. A quiet answer to a question she hadn't realized she'd been asking.

She realized then that there was still one line she refused to cross.

SIXTY-FIVE

THE VERKHOYANSK RANGE, SIBERIA | 16:12 KRAT

THE COLD WAS A LIVING THING, AND IT WAS HUNGRY—biting, gnawing, relentless.

Snow fell in thick waves, reducing visibility to only a few meters, turning the world into a blinding white void. The wind howled, a razor-edged scream that cut through layers of thermal gear, sinking deep into their bones.

Every step was a battle, boots crunching through ice-crusted snow, bodies fighting against the elements, exhaustion pressing down with every stride.

But they kept moving.

They had to.

Noah gritted his teeth, his breath coming in sharp bursts, his body burning and freezing all at once. Pain pulsed through his side, a deep, raw throbbing ache, spreading like fire beneath his ribs, through his hip, and down his leg.

He could feel the blood—the warmth leaking out of him, seeping through his coat, staining the fabric dark red.

Markov watched him carefully, his breath visible in the

freezing air. His voice was gruff, edged with a concern he wouldn't outright admit. "You're bleeding again."

Noah barely glanced down, his vision blurred from fatigue, his focus on the narrow path ahead. He didn't slow down. Didn't acknowledge it. Just kept moving.

His jaw tightened, his voice a low growl through the cold.

"I'll live."

But they both knew the truth.

He was running on borrowed time.

The storm howled, masking the world in an endless white abyss. But behind them, shadows moved.

Dark figures, silent, methodical—a well-trained strike team, cutting through the blizzard like wraiths. Their movements were precise, their footsteps swallowed by the snow, their weapons held steady.

They weren't just following. They were herding them.

Thermal optics flared in the whiteout, scanning for heat signatures. The storm should have been their cover, but these men knew what they were doing. They were closing in, pressing Noah and Markov toward a choke point—a narrow stretch of terrain where the snowdrifts rose high on either side.

A perfect kill box.

Markov glanced back, his sharp eyes picking out movement in the storm. His teeth clenched tighter than they already were.

"They're moving to cut us off."

Noah exhaled slowly, his mind calculating, shifting through options. They couldn't outrun them. Not in this terrain. Not in his condition.

That meant one thing. They had to fight.

Noah signaled to Markov with a subtle flick of his fingers, his voice low, controlled. "We set a trap."

Markov's eyes flicked toward him, understanding immediately. They'd discussed it back at the cave. What to do once they got the hunters close enough.

Noah glanced into the storm, watching the snow swirl and dance in chaotic currents.

They would use it.

Disappear into it.

He pulled his M4A1 from his back, his breath steady.

"We become ghosts."

They split up, their movements swallowed by the blinding storm. The wind roared and howled, thick snow whirling in violent gusts, making shadows dance, turning everything into a white void.

To the Council strike team, the world was a shifting nightmare—the terrain unclear, their enemies invisible, the thermal imaging erratic at best. They advanced cautiously, battle rifles raised, scanning for movement.

One by one, their tracking lasers flicked through the fog.

They saw nothing but distortion until—

Noah emerged from nowhere, stepping from the storm like a phantom.

Fast. Fluid. His blade flashing in the cold light.

Before the soldier could react, Noah's knife slashed cleanly across his throat. A choked gurgle, eyes wide with shock—then nothing.

Noah caught the man's rifle mid-fall, his grip steady, lowering the body soundlessly into the snow.

The first kill.

The storm swallowed it, leaving only whispers of blood on white.

The second soldier fared no better. He too never saw it coming.

Markov dropped soundlessly from a low overhang of rock. Coming in from behind, his combat knife drove deep into the soldier's spine, severing nerve and bone.

A sharp inhale of pain—then silence.

Markov lowered the body gently, already shifting into new cover.

The second kill.

Still, the enemy did not realize they were being hunted. Snow whipped around them, visibility shrinking to near zero. The Council team adjusted, uneasy now, sensing something was wrong. For one, they'd lost sight of the targets.

Noah and Markov struck hard and fast, vanishing into the white abyss before the enemy could react. A third soldier stepped into a small clearing, his rifle sweeping left and right, his breath fast, uncertain.

Noah emerged from the storm, creeping up behind him, his blade glinting under the pale light.

Silent. Precise.

He closed the distance before the soldier even sensed him, wrapping a hand around his mouth from behind. A quick step, a sharp motion—Noah's blade drove deep into the man's side, slipping between the ribs. The soldier barely had time to gasp before Noah wrenched the knife upward, severing flesh, muscle, lung.

A choked exhale. The body went limp.

Noah lowered him silently into the snow.

Three kills.

A fourth soldier stumbled slightly, his movements uncertain. The whiteout had disoriented him, the storm's screaming winds playing tricks on his ears. He turned—too late.

Markov was already there.

A hand clamped over his mouth.

A blade whispered across his throat—fast, surgical.

The soldier's body twitched, then went still, blood steaming as it pooled into the snow.

Four kills.

The remaining soldiers hesitated. Their leader's voice crackled over the radio, static-laced, tense.

"We're losing men! Fall back to regroup—"

Too late. Noah and Markov already had them in their sights.

Gunfire erupted, sharp cracks tearing through the blizzard.

The storm lit up with the asterisks of muzzle flashes. It wasn't a battle. It was an execution. A kill zone in the whiteout. The storm howled, a wall of white and wind—and red.

The bodies lay still in the snow, their blood freezing almost instantly upon contact with the ice. The storm consumed everything—the tracks, the struggle, the echoes of dying breaths. Soon, it would be as if nothing had ever happened here.

A burst of static interrupted the storm. A faint, crackling transmission from one of the dead men's radios, the voice distorted by the wind.

"Squad Four, this is Squad Five leader. Do you copy?"

Noah picked up the fallen soldier's comm unit, lifting it from his ear. He didn't answer. He just listened. A few seconds of silence stretched before the voice came again, more urgent.

"Squad Four, respond. What's your status?"

Noah turned to Markov, his breath visible in the frigid air. "More are on the way."

Markov exhaled slowly, his fingers clenching around his rifle. He gave the surrounding terrain a sharp glance, already calculating. "Then we need to move."

He pulled out his map again, unfolding the worn paper against the stiff wind. With a gloved hand, he tapped a point not far from where they stood.

"The old prison colony isn't far," Markov shouted over the storm. "If we can reach it before dark, we'll have cover. Ruins, old buildings—plenty of places to lose them."

Noah studied the map, his exhaustion dragging at him, but he knew Markov was right. They couldn't fight another wave. Not in the open. Not against reinforcements that would be better prepared.

Noah adjusted the strap of his rifle, feeling the wet warmth of blood still seeping through his coat. He forced himself to push forward, ignoring the pain. "Let's go."

Markov gave him a quick nod, then turned into the storm.

Together, the two of them disappeared into the white abyss, leaving the dead behind.

For the next hours, the storm raged all around them, a howling white abyss that drove them forward. Noah staggered along, his body swaying, his legs heavy. His bandages were soaked through, fresh blood seeping from his wound, the warmth spreading beneath his coat.

His body screamed in protest. But he didn't stop. Couldn't.

Markov walked beside him, silent, his sharp eyes scanning the distance. Every movement was measured, every breath controlled. The enemy had been dealt with—for now. But they weren't safe yet.

Then through the shifting fog, through the gaps in the swirling snow, it came into view.

The village.

A dark, abandoned skeleton of a place. Buildings half-collapsed, roofs bowed under decades of ice, shattered windows staring like hollow eyes.

Once, it had been a prison colony, a gulag buried in the frozen wasteland. Now it was a graveyard of the past.

Soon, it would be their battleground.

Markov's gaze flicked toward Noah. His voice was low, blunt. "Can you make it?"

Noah was cold, bleeding, exhausted. His body was on the verge of collapse. But his voice was steady. His jaw set like iron.

"I don't have a choice."

Markov nodded once.

Then, without another word, they vanished into the ruins.

SIXTY-SIX

COUNCIL FACILITY, SIBERIA | 21:15 KRAT | FEBRUARY 27

THE MEDICAL WING WAS QUIET.

No voices. No movement. Just the soft beeping of a heart monitor, the faint hum of medical machinery. The lighting was harsh, clinical, exposing the sterility of the space. No windows. No warmth. Just walls, equipment, and a single bed.

Wally Lawson lay propped up, head wrapped in thick bandages, his skin pale, his breath slow. The forced neural extraction had done its damage. It had drained him, hollowed him out, left his body frail and his mind raw.

But despite his condition, despite the pain, the exhaustion, the haze pressing in on his skull, the moment the door hissed open, his eyes sharpened.

Allison Peterson stepped in.

The door sealed behind her, locking them in together.

She moved with deliberate ease, her hands folded behind her back, her expression a mask. Her tailored suit was pristine, her hair pulled back into a severe knot.

No hesitation. No pity. Only purpose.

For a long moment, neither of them spoke. The tension thickened, stretching between the pair like a wire pulled taut.

It was Allison who broke the silence.

"We got what we needed from you," she said.

Wally's voice came out hoarse, weak, but the sarcasm still cut through. "Congratulations. I hope you found my deep love for eighties synthwave and bad takeout food."

Allison didn't react. Didn't blink. Didn't smile.

She simply watched him, cool, composed, completely unaffected.

Then she spoke.

"We found exactly what we expected."

Her tone was even, clinical, as if reading from a sterile report.

"We now know that since we destroyed your ship, you have virtually nothing. A few safehouses. Some weapons caches scattered here and there. A handful of contacts spread across the globe."

Her voice dropped.

"What we didn't find, however, was a clear purpose. No long-term strategy. No real infrastructure."

She leaned in slightly, her voice soft but lethal. "Without the *Valkyrie*, without the rest of your team, you have nothing."

Wally's throat tightened, the words hitting harder than he wanted to admit. He already knew this. Knew that without their tech, their resources, their intelligence networks, Noah's team was fighting with nothing more than a pocket knife against a fleet of tanks.

But hearing it from her—hearing it so matter-of-factly, so final—made it feel like a knife twisting in his ribs.

He swallowed hard, his throat dry, raw.

"Noah will still come," he said.

Allison's lips curved slightly, something that wasn't quite a smile—but wasn't far from it either. Something knowing. Something dangerous.

Quietly, like a whisper meant to cut deep, she said, "He already has."

"Has what?"

"Come for you."

Wally's breath stilled. His pulse slowed, his body rigid, his mind racing. He watched her carefully, reading every tiny shift in her expression, every measured movement.

His voice came, low, edged with quiet tension. "What did you do?"

Allison tilted her head slightly. "Nothing," she said. "He failed all on his own."

"He came for me?"

"Yes. Noah came for you. He made it inside the base. He fought, he killed, he bled."

She paused, letting the words sink in, letting Wally feel every ounce of it. Then—soft, almost cruelly gentle—she added, "And now, he's out there in the snow, half-dead, running for his life. All alone."

The room felt smaller. The hum of the machines faded. Wally's fingers curled against the sheets, his jaw tightening, his breathing controlled but shallow.

His voice came, low, gritted, unshaken. "Then he's not dead yet."

Allison shrugged—just a small movement, casual, dismissive. "Yet."

Her eyes flickered down at him, her presence towering, suffocating. Then as if discussing something trivial, she continued, "As for your friends in Paris, they've accomplished nothing."

She gestured vaguely, a flick of her fingers, like brushing aside a meaningless distraction.

"Olympus is live. The old world is already burning. And you?" She leaned in slightly. Her voice quiet, certain, final. "You'll soon be dead."

The words hung in the air, thick, inescapable. Suffocating.

Wally exhaled slowly. But then something unexpected happened.

He chuckled. A quiet, shaky breath of laughter, escaping past his lips.

Allison's expression flickered—just for a second. A blink. A hesitation. A brief, almost imperceptible tilt of her head.

"Something funny?"

Wally shook his head slightly, his breath still unsteady, but his eyes steady.

"I just... I just feel bad for you, Allison."

She raised a single perfectly shaped eyebrow, unimpressed, waiting. Wally's voice dropped softer now, but no less firm.

"You think you're winning. You think you're safe. But the thing is..."

He took in a shallow, uneven breath.

"...you're just another pawn. Another number to the Council."

Something darkened in her gaze. Not anger. Not amusement. Something else.

But she didn't speak.

So Wally did—his voice weak, but unwavering. "And when it all comes crashing down, you'll realize that you were nothing but a tool to them. Just like the rest of us. Once you've finished serving your purpose, you'll see."

The silence stretched, heavy, weighted. And for the briefest of moments, something flickered in her eyes.

Doubt? Regret? Something else?

Then—just as fast—it was gone.

She reached into her coat and brought out a small injector—a matte black autopen with a capped needle.

She uncapped it and stepped forward.

Her voice was quiet, emotionless.

"Goodbye, Wally."

She pressed the injector against his neck and pulled the trigger.

There was a soft hiss. The chemical entered his bloodstream in a single, cold pulse.

Wally jerked against the restraints, his breath catching in his throat. His chest seized, lungs burning, vision blurring. The world tilted. Cold seeped in.

His fingers twitched, grasping at nothing.

The room felt distant now.

His eyes stayed on hers.

And for the first time in a long time, Wally Lawson looked tired.

His voice was barely a whisper now. "...I hope you see it before it's too late."

Then his body slumped.

The beeping of the monitors slowed.

The hum of the room faded.

Allison stared down at him, the injector still clasped in her hand. Then without a word, without a flicker of hesitation, she turned and walked away, leaving Wally alone as the darkness took him.

SIXTY-SEVEN

THE WIND HOWLED THROUGH THE SKELETAL REMAINS of the gulag. Snow flurries whipped through shattered windows. The ruined compound stretched beyond sight, buried beneath layers of ice and time, swallowed by the storm.

For the two days since they got here, the blizzard had held its grip over the land, turning the abandoned colony into a frozen tomb. The Council troops had found the remains of Squad Four on the second morning—frozen where they stood, their bodies locked in stiff, contorted shapes, faces twisted in silent agony.

Since then, the enemy had chosen to remain at the edges of the village. Waiting. Preparing.

Inside, a fire flickered weakly in the corner of what had once been an administrative building or barracks. The room stank of damp rot and old stone, the heat from the flames barely pushing back against the relentless cold. The wind forced itself through cracks in the walls, threading its way between broken beams and rusted steel.

Noah stirred, his body a slow protest of pain. His ribs felt like they were bound in razor wire. His hip had been numb for a day now.

The exhaustion, lack of warmth, and constant pain tugged at the frayed edges of his psyche. The firelight played tricks on his sight, warping the edges of the room into something more distant, more hollow.

Across from him, Markov crouched near the fire, his hands extended toward the weak warmth. His breath came in soft, visible plumes, dissipating into the frigid air. He was bundled in layers of scavenged clothing, his face set in its usual mask of quiet calculation.

Noah swallowed against the dryness in his throat and forced his voice to work. "Anything?"

Markov shook his head, tapping the side of the radio with two fingers. A static hiss answered, unchanging and indifferent.

Noah exhaled and peeled himself up from the floor, every muscle screaming in protest. His joints felt stiff, his movements sluggish from the cold and from the days of tension locked into his frame.

He dragged himself toward the radio and took it from Markov's hands, steadying it in his grip before pressing down the transmitter.

His voice was low and controlled. "This is Wolf. If anyone's out there... Neil, Jenny, Katya... we need exfil... Do you copy?"

The radio answered with more static. A hollow void of silence.

He let out a slow breath, the condensation curling in the air between them. His fingers tightened around the radio before he set it aside. "We're on our own."

Markov gave a short nod, his eyes unreadable. He turned back toward the fire, watching the embers pulse.

"They're still out there waiting," he said.

"And there was me thinking they might leave," Noah snuffed dryly.

"We should be ready before they decide to move."

Noah glanced toward the boarded-up window, toward the swirling white beyond it. The Council was out there, just beyond sight. And when the storm finally broke, they'd come.

The two men pulled themselves up from the frozen floor, tightening their ragged clothes around them. They gathered their gear, bracing against the cold, then stepped outside.

There, the blizzard raged on.

As they had since the first morning of their arrival, they worked in silence, moving methodically through the ruins and setting boobytraps.

The cold had settled deep into their bones, but they had no choice—before their pursuers came, they had to make this place into a death trap.

Knowing the old Soviet equipment better than anyone, Markov had early on during their first day found a storeroom. Prying open the rusted door, he'd pulled out what remained of the gulag's security measures—bear traps, their teeth corroded but still sharp enough to snap bone.

Markov now went about setting them in the narrow corridors and alleyways, disguising them under thin layers of snow and debris.

Noah, slower-moving, gathered shattered glass from broken windows, scattering it across entry points. Any footfall would give away an intruder before they reached the heart of the building.

His ribs screamed out in protest as he lifted a broken chair, shoving it against a collapsed doorway to create a choke point. Markov did the same with fallen beams, reinforcing their position.

Farther into the structure, they had found the remnants of an old heating system. The gas lines were corroded, but some pressure remained in the pipes. Markov had rigged a crude detonation trap in one of the buildings—one spark, and the place would turn into an inferno.

Having finished with the bear traps, Markov headed toward the highest vantage point—an old guard tower, its roof half collapsed but still providing the best sightline over the ruins. He placed his sniper rifle against the broken ledge.

On the next street, Noah stepped outside for a moment, pulling his coat tight against the biting wind. The cold sliced through him like a blade, seeping into the spaces between layers. His breath came in slow, controlled puffs.

Then—a whistle.

Sharp. Piercing. Cutting through the storm.

Markov froze at the base of the guard tower. His muscles tensed, every nerve screaming to listen.

A second later, the sky exploded in red.

A flare arced up from beyond the ruins, inside the trees, painting the frozen wasteland in a crimson glow. The snow reflected the eerie light, shifting the landscape into something surreal—deep shadows stretching between skeletal structures, the ice glowing blood-red.

Noah grabbed his binoculars, ignoring the fresh jolt of pain as the lenses pressed against his bruised face. He scanned the distance, his breath shallow, his pulse steady.

At the edge of the ruined village, dark figures emerged. A line of them. Moving in perfect unison. Disciplined. Methodical.

Noah tracked their advance. Through the swirling snow, their shapes became clearer—tall, broad-shouldered figures clad in heavy black gear, their faces obscured by hoods and masks, their weapons held at their sides.

Noah watched them come, feeling the weight of inevitability settle in his chest.

At that moment, Markov came beside him.

The Russian exhaled, calm, resigned. "They're coming."

Noah tightened his grip on the binoculars.

He didn't say anything.

Just watched.

The hunt was about to begin.

SIXTY-EIGHT

PUTORANA PLATEAU, SIBERIA | 13:00 KRAT | MARCH 1

THE COUNCIL COMPOUND LAY BURIED DEEP IN THE Putorana Plateau, a vast, frozen expanse in northern Siberia, hidden beneath layers of snow and ice. No roads reached this place, and only the occasional helicopter shattered the endless silence.

The landscape stretched out in an unbroken white sheet, the jagged basalt mountains rising like ancient guardians, their cliffs and valleys carved by time and glacial winds. The trees, sparse and skeletal, stood motionless, their branches heavy with frost. It was the kind of stillness that felt eternal, untouched—a place where the world forgot to look.

A low thump-thump-thump cut through the quiet, distant at first, then growing louder. Snow stirred into a blinding swirl as a chopper descended onto the mountainside helipad.

The craft settled, the engine winding down. The side door slid open.

Allison Peterson stepped out.

She moved with quiet purpose, seemingly unaffected by the cold. She wore black gloves, her coat drawn tightly around her frame. The wind pulled at her hair as she walked, but she didn't hurry.

At the entrance, she pulled off her gloves, one finger at a time, methodically. Pressing her palm to the scanner, she waited. A soft beep. Next, the retinal scan. She lifted her face to the reader.

The metal door slid open, and she stepped inside.

The concrete walls swallowed her as she left the storm behind. A guard waited just beyond the threshold. He was tall, his presence impassive, eyes sharp beneath the dim lights.

"She's inside," he said.

Allison nodded once and walked forward.

The room was small and sparse. A single wooden table sat at its center, unadorned except for the jigsaw puzzle being carefully assembled atop it.

Norah sat there, her small hands methodically fitting the pieces together. She didn't rush. She didn't fumble. Each piece found its place with quiet precision.

She didn't look up when the door opened. Didn't startle when Allison entered.

There was no fear in her face.

She was calm but watchful.

Allison took the seat across from her, her movements measured. The silence stretched between them, thick but unspoken.

A moment later, the door opened again.

An attendant stepped inside, carrying a tray. An elegant tea set rested on its polished surface—porcelain cups, a delicate pot, a small plate of sugar cubes. The tray was set down between them.

Allison poured. The soft clink of ceramic against ceramic was the only sound in the room. She slid one of the cups toward Norah, then took her own.

Norah didn't move at first. She just stared at the steaming tea, her expression unreadable. Finally, she reached out and lifted the cup, cradling the warmth in her small hands.

They sipped in silence.

For a brief moment, it felt almost domestic. The quiet ritual of tea. The rhythmic placement of puzzle pieces.

The tea was followed by another arrival.

A different tray, this one bearing something else entirely.

Cake. Scones. Strawberries and cream.

The sight of them made Norah blink. A hesitation, a flicker of something unguarded.

She had not seen a dessert in a year. The hunger broke through her caution. She forgot herself, reaching forward. She grabbed a scone, sinking her teeth into it.

She didn't stop.

For a moment, she was just a child again.

A few minutes later, Norah had eaten her fill. The plate was nearly empty now, only a few crumbs left in the wake of her hunger. She sat back in her chair, eyes lowered, her small fingers idly tracing the wooden grain of the table.

Allison watched her, then sipped her tea.

"You used to call me Aunty," she said softly. "Do you remember that?"

Norah didn't react at first. She reached for her cup, lifting it carefully.

Finally, without emotion, she replied, "That was before."

Allison nodded, as if she had expected the answer.

She set her cup down gently. "I remember when I first met your father. He was much younger then. So was I."

Norah didn't respond, but she was listening.

Allison continued. "Back then, your father was on death row."

Norah's fingers stilled against the wood. Her gaze lifted, eyes meeting Allison's for the first time since the conversation had started.

"That's not true," she said, though there was no conviction in her voice.

"It is." Allison tilted her head slightly. "He didn't tell you?"

Norah didn't answer.

Allison studied her for a moment before taking another sip of tea. "Your father was sentenced to die because he killed six men."

Norah's hands curled into small fists in her lap. "Why did he kill them?"

Allison exhaled, setting her cup down again. "Because he caught them attacking a woman. An Afghan woman. Your father walked in on it, and he made a choice."

Norah blinked. "Attacking?" she asked. "Attacking her how?"

For the first time, Allison hesitated.

She winced, her lips pressing together slightly. "It doesn't matter."

"It does." Norah's voice was quiet but firm.

Allison studied her, then exhaled through her nose. "They were hurting her in a way she could never come back from," she said finally. "Your father stopped them. But to do that, he had to kill six US soldiers. One of them was his own commanding officer—the son of a congressman, no less."

Norah's face was unreadable.

Allison continued, her voice smooth, almost gentle. "For that, they shipped him back to America and gave him the death penalty. Six lives. And it would have been seven, if they had gone through with the sentence."

She reached for her tea again, her fingers resting lightly on the handle. "Six lives," she murmured. "All for one ruined Afghan woman."

Norah looked down at her lap. Her small hands clenched tighter. "It's because he believed it was the right thing to do," the girl said.

"But was it? Your father and his moral compass. It would have gotten him killed—and for nothing."

Norah looked up from her hands. "Nothing?"

"Yes. Nothing. The woman they attacked was subsequently disowned by her family," Allison added, almost idly. "I know that personally. It's in the intelligence files. She brought them shame, even though it wasn't her fault." She stirred her tea once, watching the liquid swirl. "She committed suicide not long after. Was already dead by the time your father was being sentenced."

Norah didn't move.

The silence stretched between them again, heavy but not uncomfortable.

Allison took another sip of tea.

Norah did the same.

Allison lowered her cup. The delicate porcelain clicked softly against the saucer, but she barely noticed.

For the first time, she really looked at Norah.

Not as a mission. Not as leverage. Just as a child.

Her voice, when she spoke, was softer than it had ever been.

"I'm sorry I killed your mother."

Norah didn't react. She simply watched her, her face unreadable.

Allison exhaled, a long, slow breath. "I'm sorry for all of it."

The words drifted into the quiet. No response came.

Then Norah blinked.

A subtle change. A faint, unnatural blur in her vision.

She shifted slightly in her chair. A small, almost imperceptible movement—restless, unfocused.

Her breathing slowed.

The teacup trembled in her grip.

She tried to stand, but her legs gave out beneath her.

The chair scraped against the floorboards, then tipped over as she slumped forward. The teacup slipped from her hand, falling in slow motion—spinning, tumbling—before shattering against the wooden floor.

Dark liquid spread across the surface, seeping outward, staining the grain.

Irreversible.

Norah gasped, her lips parting as if to speak—but no sound came. Her fingers twitched weakly. Her vision narrowed. The edges of the room tilted, warping as if the world itself was folding inward.

Allison remained seated. Watching.

No expression. No movement. Just quiet observation.

Norah's small body stilled. It was over. No fight left.

Allison lifted her gaze and called for the guards.

The door opened, and two men entered without a word. One carried a folded black body bag.

Neither hesitated.

They lifted Norah's limp frame with ease, handling her like just another task—one of a hundred they had done before.

Allison didn't move. Didn't help. Didn't interfere.

The zipper hissed as it closed.

Loud in the silence.

Final.

Allison watched but said nothing.

When it was done, she stood, smoothing the front of her coat with practiced ease. Her fingers adjusted the collar, straightened the fabric. No rush. No wasted motion.

Her gaze flicked to the floor.

The spilled tea had seeped into the wood, dark and permanent. A stain that would never fully fade.

SIXTY-NINE

KATORGA-17, SIBERIA | 13:41 KRAT | MARCH 1

THE WIND HOWLED THROUGH THE ABANDONED PRISON colony, a relentless force that shrieked between the crumbling walls and whistled through rusted bars. Snow lashed against the ruins, thick and blinding, reducing visibility to mere feet. The old gulag was little more than a decayed skeleton, its walls broken, its tunnels filled with detritus.

Noah and Markov lay motionless beneath a thick layer of snow, their bodies pressed into the frozen ground. They barely breathed, their weapons gripped tightly, their eyes sharp as they scanned the ruins.

Nothing yet.

Markov lifted his binoculars, sweeping the storm.

He tensed. Movement.

Figures glided through the snow, barely visible—white shapes against white. Silent. Ghostly.

Markov's grip tightened. He muttered, "They don't see us yet."

Noah remained still, watching.

Through the binoculars, the figures resolved into something more defined—disciplined strike teams in all-white tactical gear, moving with a deadly efficiency. Their weapons were held low but ready, their footfalls careful but confident.

The first wave entered the ruins.

They moved cautiously, their heads on swivels. They knew this place was dangerous. What they didn't know was just how dangerous.

Two of them split off, entering one of the larger buildings—an old dormitory, the rusted frames of bunkbeds pushed to the edges. Their boots crunched over the ice-crusted floor, their breath visible in the cold air.

In the middle of the room lay an old, worn-down carpet.

Both men stepped onto it.

DROP!

The ground vanished beneath them. A hole in the concrete floor—a deep, unseen pit that swallowed both men whole.

Their screams tore through the storm, sharp and brief—then silence, broken only by the wet, sickening sound of bodies slamming into jagged rebar far below.

A nearby squad turned toward the sound, their movements quick and controlled. They rushed to help—

SNAP!

A rusted bear trap sprang shut, its metal jaws crushing a soldier's ankle with a bone-snapping crunch.

His cry of agony was lost in the wind.

Markov exhaled, watching the chaos unfold. His voice was low, edged with grim satisfaction. "Let them bleed."

Noah said nothing.

They waited. Patient. Hidden.

Like wolves among the ruins.

The storm howled. More soldiers advanced, pushing deeper into the broken buildings. Their discipline remained intact—for now. They moved in coordinated formations, covering angles, sweeping through the crumbling hallways with the efficiency of professionals. But efficiency meant nothing against an enemy they couldn't see.

One soldier took a careful step forward, his boot brushing against something thin, nearly invisible—

A tripwire.

There was a brief second of nothing. Then a rush of air, followed by a deep, wet thud.

From the rafters above, a rigged mechanism swung down on the end of rope—a line of breeze blocks, reinforced with rusted metal spikes at their ends. It impaled two men mid-step, driving straight through their bodies. The force pinned them to the wall behind them, leaving them twitching as their lifeblood darkened the snow-covered floor.

The others fared no better. They were caught inside a trap.

Near the central courtyard, a squad advanced toward a clearing, their boots crunching through ice. As they moved beneath the shadow of a water tower, Noah watched from the edges of the courtyard, hidden in the snow and ruins. He waited, breath steady, muscles coiled.

The moment they were close enough, he pulled a chain.

It snapped taut, emerging from the snow, linked to one of the tower's rusted legs—one that had already been half-severed.

The structure groaned.

Metal screamed as the weakened support gave out.

CRACK.

As the tower began to collapse, Noah was already moving, sprinting away toward his next hiding spot.

The tower went down in an avalanche of metal and ice, crashing down with the weight of a freight train. Soldiers screamed, trying to dive clear, but they were too slow. A wall of iron and debris crushed them where they stood, leaving only mangled limbs protruding from the wreckage.

Panic spread.

Shouts filled the air as the enemy tried to regroup, their cohesion beginning to crack.

Markov smirked from the shadows, exhaling a slow breath into the cold. He muttered, almost amused, "We're just getting started."

From the edge of a rooftop, Noah watched a group of soldiers enter the building below. He reached into his vest, pulled a flare, and struck it against the frozen tiles.

The bright red phosphorescent glow cut through the storm, sending harsh shadows dancing across the ruins.

Noah ran to an opening in the roof, tossing the flare down into a narrow corridor soaked in engine oil.

The fire ignited instantly.

A whoosh of flames erupted, tendrils of fire slithering through the entire building like living serpents. The blaze raced along the ground, cutting off the enemy's escape routes, forcing them into a death trap of their own making.

The squad caught in the inferno screamed as the fire engulfed them. Flames licked at their tactical gear, melting synthetic fabric into their flesh. Some flailed, trying to pat the fire out. Others simply collapsed where they stood, their bodies still burning.

The rest began breaking formation, some sprinting away, others trying to retreat—but that only made them easier to hunt.

Noah picked them off one by one.

A soldier turned, trying to make for cover—Noah put a round through his neck.

Another dove behind a collapsed wall—Noah waited until they peeked out, then drilled a shot clean through their visor.

Markov moved like a phantom, his form barely visible through the haze of fire and snow. He waited in the shadows, then emerged from a ruined hallway, raised his weapon, and dropped a squad leader with two quick shots before vanishing again.

On the rooftops, Noah unhooked a grenade, pulled the pin, and let it drop.

The unsuspecting team below barely had time to register the clink before—*BOOM!*

A concussive blast shredded them in an instant, their bodies torn apart by the explosion.

The enemy started turning on each other in the confusion. The flames, the traps, the sudden, brutal strikes—it all pushed them to the edge. Commands were shouted. Some soldiers pivoted, firing wildly at shadows that weren't even there.

But, still, they were capable of adapting.

The Council's soldiers weren't just well-trained—they were intelligent. Specially picked.

The survivors began modifying their tactics.

Noah saw the shift almost immediately.

One soldier knelt, tapping his helmet—infrared engaged.

The red glow of thermal vision flickered across their visors.

A soldier snapped his weapon upward, spotting Noah instantly through the smoke.

"CONTACT!"

A burst of gunfire shredded the stone where Noah had been a second earlier. He dove behind cover, rolling hard onto the frozen ground. Bullets ricocheted off the walls, sending up bursts of shattered ice and concrete.

Noah's breath came fast, his ribs, hip, protesting with sharp, brutal pain.

A voice cut through the smoke. Markov, grinning as he reloaded. "I think they're catching on."

For a moment, there was nothing.

No more gunfire. No more screams.

Only the storm.

The wind howled through the ruins, carrying the scent of fire and blood. The snow churned, swirling in eerie silence over the bodies littering the ground. Flames flickered in pools of oil, reflecting in shattered ice.

Noah and Markov stayed low, watching.

The surviving soldiers had stopped firing. Their movements changed—no longer advancing, no longer pushing forward.

Instead, they were retreating.

Noah saw them fall back, methodically shifting toward the outer edges of the ruins. Their weapons were still raised, but their focus had shifted.

Something had changed. A radio call must've come in.

Markov's eyes narrowed. "Surely they're not retreating," he murmured.

Noah's gut tightened.

"No," he said. "They're making room."

From the storm, new figures emerged.

These ones moved without hesitation—tall, armored, fast.

The Council's elite assassins.

Noah felt it immediately—the shift in presence, the sheer force of them. They weren't just soldiers. They weren't even human in the way normal men were.

Exoskeletons clung to their bodies, enhancing every movement. Their gear was sleek, reinforced, designed for brute power and inhuman speed. Their faces were hidden behind smooth, black featureless helmets—no visors, no exposed flesh, no weakness.

They didn't even acknowledge the soldiers retreating past them.

They only moved. Forward.

Markov barely whispered, "This is bad."

Noah raised his rifle, leveling the sights on one of them.

BANG!

A perfect shot—center mass. The kind that should have dropped a man where he stood.

The assassin barely flinched as the bullet sparked off the chest-plating of his exoskeleton. It slowed him down for a fraction of a second—then he just kept coming.

The Elites swept through the ruins with surgical efficiency. Unlike the soldiers before them, they didn't hesitate. They didn't waste time moving cautiously like blind rats feeling their way to the traps.

They knew.

They sensed the traps before they could trigger them.

One of them moved toward an old corridor, the only viable path forward. Inside, Noah and Markov had set tripwires—thin, nearly invisible, leading to a fragmentation device rigged to the wall.

Any normal soldier would have walked straight into it.

The Elite paused.

Without looking, he reached down, picked up a piece of brick, and tossed it forward.

The brick bounced once—then click.

BOOM!

The fragmentation charge detonated instantly, sending shards of broken brickwork in all directions.

The Elite never moved. He had already calculated the blast radius, stepping just outside of it before the explosion ripped through the space.

The smoke cleared. The corridor was gone—but so was the trap.

The assassin turned his head slightly, as if assessing the damage. Then he kept walking, unfazed.

Watching from the sidelines, Noah exhaled slow and steady, lining up a shot. His M4A1 was braced against his shoulder, the crosshairs hovering over the black, featureless helmet of one of the assassins moving through the ruins below.

A clean shot.

His finger tightened on the trigger.

Then—

A shadow moved to his left.

Too late.

A hand wrenched him backward, his carbine clattering against the stone as he was ripped from his position.

Noah barely had time to register the shape—a towering black-armored figure, inhumanly fast, impossibly strong. He twisted just in time to avoid a crushing fist, but the force of the attack still sent him staggering.

He recovered, snapping his pistol up from its holster, but the Elite was already on him.

A gloved hand snatched his wrist, twisting brutally. The gun fired into the sky before being ripped from his grip.

Noah pivoted, throwing a sharp elbow into the assassin's ribs. It was like hitting steel. The impact jolted up his arm, numbing it instantly.

A counterstrike.

The assassin's knee smashed into Noah's stomach, lifting him off the ground. Pain exploded through his ribs, his already fractured bones screaming. He barely landed before a fist whipped across his jaw, sending him reeling sideways into a rusted support beam.

Noah shook off the pain. Instinct took over. He had to move.

He reached for anything, his fingers finding a rusted length of pipe half-buried in the snow.

He flung it with everything he had.

The pipe whistled through the air only to stop, dead, mid-motion.

The assassin had caught it. One hand. Effortless.

Noah barely had a second to process before the assassin jerked forward, sending the pipe back at him.

Noah deflected it with his forearm as the assassin came at him —a headbutt.

Noah's skull cracked against reinforced armor. His vision exploded in white-hot pain as he was sent sprawling backward into the snow.

His ears rang, and the world tilted.

A black shadow loomed over him, the Elite closing in. Noah tried to push himself up, but his muscles refused to respond. His ears were ringing, his vision swimming. He blinked rapidly, trying to force his body to move—

A thunderous crack.

A figure crashed into the assassin, slamming him sideways like a battering ram. Snow and ice erupted in a spray as both men went down in a violent tangle of limbs.

Markov.

Noah blinked, forcing his eyes to focus. Markov had driven into the Elite with full force, shoulder-first, sending both of them skidding across the frozen ground. The Russian moved fast, faster than any man his size should, his rifle already swinging up—

A gunshot.

Markov fired at point-blank range, the round sparking off the reinforced exoskeleton armor.

It did nothing.

The assassin retaliated.

A heavy backhand caught Markov across the face, sending him staggering. The assassin pressed the advantage, closing the distance—

Noah pushed himself upright, his body protesting every movement. His vision doubled, his balance unsteady.

Through the haze, he heard Markov snarl in pain.

Noah's blurry vision snapped toward the fight.

Markov was pinned against a stone wall, his feet barely touching the ground. The Elite held him by the throat, lifting him like he weighed nothing.

The assassin slammed Markov into the wall with enough force to crack the stone.

Markov coughed blood.

The Elite did it again, and Markov went limp, sliding down the wall into the snow, his breath shallow.

Noah tried to push himself up—too slow.

A black boot planted onto his chest, pinning him down.

His vision blurred as the assassin raised his weapon, preparing the final strike.

Both of them, sprawled in the snow.

Helpless.

The storm roared, swallowing sound, but a distant gunshot cut through it like a crack of lightning.

BANG!

The Elite looming over Noah jerked violently, a single .50 Browning machine gun round tearing straight through helmet, then skull, a perfect shot. The black-helmeted figure collapsed instantly, hitting the snow in a motionless heap, a hole for a head.

Another shot rang out—

Another assassin who was moving in on their portion convulsed as an armor-piercing bullet ripped through his head, his body stiffening before crumpling lifelessly to the frozen ground.

The remaining Elites froze.

Noah could almost feel them recalculating, reassessing.

Markov saw their chance.

"Go! NOW!" he barked.

Noah hesitated. He didn't want to leave him.

He reached for Markov's arm, ready to haul him up—

Markov shoved him away. "GO!"

There was blood on his lips, and you could hear his crushed lungs in every breath. A small, tired smile crossed his lips.

"I'm just glad... I got to die in battle," he said. "Now I beg you. Go."

Noah nodded, turned, and hauled himself out of there.

Markov lifted his head, just barely catching Noah's retreating form through the snowstorm.

His voice was weak—a whisper against the wind.

"It was nice knowing you, Noah W..."

The name was never finished.

His breath left him for the last time.

His body slumped forward.

Markov was gone.

Noah didn't stop. Didn't turn around. Didn't let himself feel the loss.

He just ran.

His breath burned in his throat, his legs aching with every step through the deep snow. The ruins blurred past him, shapes distorted by the storm and the glow of fire. His boots slipped on ice, his body numb, but he forced himself forward.

Gunfire cracked behind him, but he didn't look back.

All that mattered now was survival.

Ahead, the silhouette of the guard tower loomed at the edge of the compound, its skeletal remains barely holding against the wind.

A flash of movement.

Noah didn't hesitate. He climbed, hands slipping against the icy metal, pulling himself up rung by rung. The wind slammed against him, trying to rip him down. His ribs screamed, his muscles burned, but he didn't stop.

He reached the top, half-dragging himself over the ledge onto the narrow, unstable platform.

A figure turned toward him.

Noah froze.

The sniper lowered their rifle, then their scarf.

Katya.

She smirked, her breath curling in the cold.

"Took you long enough," Noah muttered, chest heaving.

Katya gave a small shrug, casually chambering another round into her Barrett M107. "You weren't exactly easy to find, Jonas."

Noah exhaled, steadying himself against the rusted railing. Below them, the ruins burned, flames licking at the remains of the gulag. Thick smoke curled into the storm.

Markov was gone.

The gulag was lost.

But Noah was still alive.

And now he had Katya.

SEVENTY

The ruins burned behind them, thick smoke twisting into the storm. The glow of the distant fires flickered through the heavy snow, casting long, eerie shadows across the wasteland.

Katya half-carried Noah forward, her grip firm around his arm. He was barely on his feet, his body swaying with every step. Blood streaked his side, seeping through his coat. His breaths were ragged, uneven.

"Stay with me," Katya muttered, pulling him through the snow.

Noah's boots dragged, his strength waning. The world tilted around him, his vision narrowing to a tunnel of white and red.

They reached a rusted hatch, half-buried under layers of ice. Katya yanked it open, revealing a dark void beneath—an old Soviet service tunnel, hidden beneath the gulag.

Without waiting, she hauled him inside.

The cold hit them instantly—a different kind of cold. Not the biting wind above, but something deeper, ancient. The air was heavy with frost, the walls slick with ice.

Noah staggered along, the pitch black tunnel narrowing.

Katya glanced at him, her tone steady. "We heard the chatter," she said. "That's how we found you."

Noah tried to focus, his mind sluggish, fading. "Chatter?"

"We've been in the area for a day now, intercepting Council radio traffic." She shifted his weight, keeping him moving. "An hour ago, they started talking about the gulag. We came straight here."

Noah's head lolled slightly, his body barely holding up. The edges of his vision were darkening.

He forced himself to ask, his voice rough. "How'd Paris go?"

Katya's expression darkened.

She shook her head, eyes flicking away.

"You don't want to know."

Noah didn't press.

They kept walking, the tunnel stretching ahead—dark, endless. The only sound was the slow, steady crunch of their boots against the ice.

Then Katya stopped.

She froze mid-step, her entire body going still.

Noah barely noticed at first, his mind fogged with exhaustion, but then he saw it too.

A shift.

The air moved unnaturally, like a breath where there shouldn't be one.

Shadows detached from the darkness.

Two Elite assassins emerged, their exoskeletons humming softly, the faint mechanical whirr of artificial muscles flexing beneath armor.

One of them struck a flare and tossed it to the ground. It hissed to life, flooding the frozen tunnel with crimson light, painting the air in shifting red shadows.

They moved like phantoms—silent, precise, predators in the dark.

Katya's knife flashed into her hand as she turned.

Noah barely had time to lift his fists before they were on them. No time for guns. This was close-quarters combat.

The first assassin lunged—fast. A piston-powered strike shot toward Katya's ribs. She twisted at the last second, letting the fist barely skim her jacket.

She stepped inside the attack, elbowing him hard in the throat before hooking her leg behind his and slamming him backward onto the ice.

The Elite's exosuit compensated instantly, rolling him back to his feet.

Noah barely had time to react to his own opponent before a fist slammed into his ribs, pain exploding through his fractured bones. He staggered, blood on his pale lips, but anger and sheer determination kept him upright.

The Elite advanced, throwing a brutal knee strike toward Noah's gut.

Noah caught it mid-air, twisting his body and using the momentum to drive the Elite into the tunnel wall, the assassin's helmet slamming hard against the frozen concrete.

Katya ducked low, avoiding a brutal spinning backfist aimed at her head. She countered with a sharp upward palm strike, catching the assassin's helmet under the chin—the impact sent a crack through the visor.

He stumbled back.

Katya followed up instantly, throwing herself into a rising Muay Thai kick—knee up, shin slicing toward the side of the Elite's head.

He caught her mid-air.

His hand clamped around her leg like a vise, armor groaning with the force of his grip. Then with a roar of mechanical power, he swung her like a weapon, slamming her into the tunnel wall.

Stone cracked. Dust rained down.

Before she could rise, her knife already halfway drawn, he stomped forward and kicked the blade from her hand. It skittered down the tunnel, lost in the red flare's trembling glow.

He grabbed her by the hair, lifted her again, and hurled her down the corridor like a rag doll.

Her body struck the ground hard—shoulder, ribs, hip. The air left her lungs in a single, brutal gasp as she bounced once, then slid to a stop.

Noah came inside his opponent's guard, aiming a jab at his throat. But the Elite parried it with his forearm, then countered.

Pivoting off his back foot, he grabbed ahold of Noah by the neck.

The Elite's exosuit whirred as he lifted Noah clean off the ground, one massive hand clamped tightly around his throat. The red flare on the tunnel floor cast flickering shadows across the walls, turning the narrow space into a blood-lit cage. The heels of Noah's boots scraped against the cracked concrete wall, struggling for purchase.

The Elite's free hand moved toward his hip, slow and deliberate, and prodded the already torn wound.

Pain exploded through Noah's side as the fingers dug in, peeling at the raw edge of the wound. Stitches tore. Blood ran hot down his leg.

The Elite tilted his helmeted head, watching him squirm like an insect.

Katya hit the ground hard. The impact was brutal.

She groaned, pain blooming in her side.

She could hear the Elite marching toward her—preparing to throw her again and again until there was nothing left to throw.

With the last of her strength, she pressed her hands to the cold ground and tried to lift herself.

Her hand landed on something brittle.

Bone.

She blinked, disoriented, and looked down. A skeletal body lay half-buried in the gravel—its ribcage shattered, its Soviet uniform rotted to threads.

But in its chest, gripped tight in a long-dead fist, was a knife.

Old. Iron. Serrated.

She snatched it without thinking.

Noah choked, vision blurring, muscles screaming. He braced both hands on the arm holding him and drove his knees up—hard—twisting just enough to kick the inside of the exosuit's thigh, where the plating met a control joint at the hip.

The result was immediate. The suit convulsed, servos stuttering with a high-pitched whine. The Elite stumbled back, grip loosening just enough for Noah to drop to the floor like dead weight.

He hit hard.

The cold rock stole his breath, the pain from his hip radiating like fire through his abdomen. He rolled, half-blind, heart hammering, body barely obeying commands.

But he was moving. Alive.

And for now, that was enough.

The Elite was almost on Katya, one foot pounding after the other.

As he reached for her, she rolled under his arm, twisted, and drove the Soviet blade up into the exposed mechanics behind his knee joint—right into the actuator.

The Elite spasmed. The suit screamed—metal grinding against metal—as the joint locked up mid-step.

He pitched forward, the weight of the armor dragging him down.

Katya staggered upright, breath ragged.

But she had to move.

Before the Elite could react, she spun behind him and drove the Soviet knife upward—straight through his chin and into his skull.

The rusted blade punched through bone with a wet crunch. His body convulsed once, then dropped like a stone. Dead before he hit the ground.

Farther down the tunnel, the other Elite lashed out at Noah, trying to grab his leg.

Noah moved fast, pushing the pain and the injuries ravishing his body far, far away.

He snatched a frozen, rusted piece of metal from the tunnel floor—twisted rebar—and drove it hard into the elbow joint of the Elite's exosuit. A targeted strike just beneath the armor plating.

The servos in the limb spasmed, locking up as a sharp mechanical whine cut through the cold air.

Noah didn't wait around.

He yanked the jagged metal free, reversed it in his grip—then with a swift, brutal motion, drove it straight through the assassin's neck.

The exoskeleton seized, servos locking as the body went rigid. The Elite shuddered once—then collapsed, motionless.

The tunnel fell silent.

Noah stood there, chest heaving, his breath misting in the freezing air.

Katya was walking up to him, wiping the blade against her thigh.

She met Noah's gaze.

"Not bad, Jonas."

Noah nudged one of the bodies with his boot, making sure they were truly dead.

"Not bad yourself, Kat."

Katya grinned.

They turned toward the darkness beyond the shimmering red light of the flare, leaving the dead where they lay.

Noah staggered, his body betraying him. Every muscle screamed, every breath was fire in his ribs. He no longer felt his hip, but he knew it would need fresh stitches. His vision blurred at the edges, the tunnel tilting slightly. The cold bit into his wounds, but exhaustion was the real enemy now.

And they weren't done yet.

They came around a corner to find four more Elite assassins, untouched, unshaken—cutting off any chance of escape.

"Oh, you gotta be kidding me," Noah groaned.

He let go of Katya and forced himself upright, raising his fists, his knuckles split and bleeding. He could barely stand, but he would keep fighting until he couldn't.

Beside him, Katya gripped the rusted knife, her breaths coming hard and fast. She knew it too—this was it.

The Elites closed in.

No hesitation. No mercy. The end was coming.

It was plain to see that neither Katya nor Noah had much more fight left in them.

But as they closed in, something happened.

Gunfire.

A deep, punishing roar filled the tunnel, drowning out the storm outside. Not the sharp cracks of standard rifles but something heavier, deeper. A barrage of .338 Norma Magnum rounds tore through the passage, the sheer force hammering into the Elites like sledgehammers.

Their exoskeletons sparked and buckled. They staggered back as reinforced plating was punctured, high-velocity rounds chewing through armor like paper. They tried to move, but another brutal burst of fire punched through them.

The Elites collapsed onto the ice, motionless.

Noah barely had time to react.

Footsteps. Fast. Controlled.

Two figures emerged from the darkness, rifles smoking.

Jenny. Eyes cold, shoulders squared, the SIG MG 338—a belt-fed and relentless machine that fired .338 Norma Magnum rounds—braced tightly against her shoulder.

Neil. Carrying another MG 338, eyes locked on the downed Elites, tracking for movement.

Katya's voice cut through the settling dust.

"You both took your time."

Jenny's lips pulled into a dry smirk. "Yeah, well, we had a little problem."

Katya arched a brow.

Jenny nodded toward the bodies. "When we first spotted them, we were still packing MAC-10s." She let out a short breath, shaking her head. "Figured a pair of glorified submachine guns wouldn't even scratch them, so we doubled back to grab the heavy firepower." She patted the MG 338. "This beauty, on the other hand, gets the job done."

Neil let out a small chuckle, slapping the MG 338's receiver. "Yeah, and if you think we were slow, imagine how embarrassing it would've been if we showed up slinging nine-mil rounds at these things."

Katya exhaled, shaking her head. "Fine. You're here now." She turned to Noah. "And he's still standing."

Jenny followed her gaze, and for the first time since stepping into the tunnel, her hardened expression cracked. The adrenaline was fading, and now she really saw him—blood seeping from his side, his face pale beneath the frost, his stance just barely holding.

Her voice softened. "Jesus, Noah."

He waved a hand, already turning away. "I'm fine."

Jenny wasn't having it.

She caught his wrist before he could take another step. "Like hell you are. Sit down."

Noah sighed but knew better than to fight her. His legs were barely holding him up anyway. He sank onto a slab of ice and exhaled sharply as the movement jarred his side.

Jenny crouched beside him, already pulling her med kit from her belt. She tore off a packet of gauze, pressing it against his hip before peeling back his coat to inspect the wound. The stitches had torn. Badly.

"You need patching up." Her voice was calm, but he could see the tension in her jaw.

Noah smirked faintly. "Gotta keep you busy somehow."

Jenny didn't laugh. Instead, she grabbed her needle, threading it with quick, precise motions. "This is gonna hurt."

"What else is new?" Noah muttered.

She didn't hesitate. The needle pierced his skin, and the familiar, sharp burn shot through him. Noah clenched his jaw but stayed still. Jenny worked fast, her fingers sure and steady despite the freezing air. Neil hovered nearby, shifting his weight restlessly as he kept watch.

There were still possibly more Elites out there.

Katya crouched beside them, arms resting on her knees, watching the repetitive motion of the needle sliding in and out of Noah's skin. "He's lost too much blood."

Jenny didn't look up. "He's had worse."

Katya arched a brow. "And that's supposed to be reassuring?"

Jenny tied off the last stitch and cut the thread with a quick flick of her knife. "It means he'll live."

She pressed fresh gauze over the wound and wrapped it tightly, her touch firm but careful. She was about to say something else—maybe another remark about him pushing too hard—when she caught the gaze of Neil.

His face was dead serious.

Something unspoken passed between them.

Jenny's smile faded. Her body tensed.

Noah's breath slowed. He'd noticed. His instincts screamed.

Something was wrong.

Jenny hesitated, swallowing hard. Then with the same steady hands she'd just used to stitch him up, she reached out, placing a gentle hand on his arm. Her grip was firm but uncertain. Her voice barely rose above a whisper.

"Noah... before we got here, we intercepted Council chatter."

Neil looked away. Jaw tight.

Katya's expression darkened, her hands curling into fists.

Noah's heart hammered against his ribs. His pulse roared in his ears.

Jenny hesitated—then forced herself to say it.

"Norah is dead."

Noah stared at her.

"They killed her."

The world stopped.

The air vanished from his lungs.

The cold rushed in, sharper than any blade.

His body swayed, his hands clenching instinctively at his sides.

For a moment, his mind refused to process the words.

Jenny's face blurred. Neil's voice was distant. Katya's silhouette was a shadow against the ice.

Then—reality crashed down.

The exhaustion. The blood loss. The pain.

It all came at once.

Noah tried to stand, but his legs buckled.

Jenny and Katya moved to catch him—but it was too late.

He hit the ice, his body giving in, his mind slipping into darkness.

The last thought in Noah's mind wasn't pain.

It was the unbearable, suffocating weight of loss.

SEVENTY-ONE

THE SCREEN FLICKERED TO LIFE.

Allison Peterson straightened in her chair, smoothing the sharp lapels of her blazer.

Number One's shadowed figure filled the screen. The image distorted, features obscured in shifting blackness. The voice, when it spoke, altered—mechanical, cold, devoid of gender or emotion.

"Number Eleven."

Allison kept her expression composed. "I'm listening."

There was a pause, a slight crackle in the transmission. Then the voice returned, as precise as a scalpel.

"The Inner Council has convened. The decision is final."

Allison's fingers curled against the edge of her desk. Her heartbeat remained steady, but she could feel the slight shift—the weight of something monumental pressing into the air between them.

"You have proven yourself indispensable," the voice continued. "Your execution of the Kirtland operation, your neutralization of E & E, your unwavering commitment to the Council's vision. These past two years, you have been tested. And you have not failed."

A pause.

Then the words she had waited for.

"You have been accepted into the Inner Council."

The faintest flicker of something passed through Allison's chest. Anticipation. Triumph.

She did not move. Did not blink.

Her voice remained measured, controlled.

"My designation?"

"You will be Number Three."

A title. A rank. A seat at the highest table among the architects of the new world.

The voice pressed on, devoid of anything but command. "An aircraft will arrive for you in one hour. You will be taken to the Grand Chamber, where your induction will take place. Be prepared."

Allison exhaled slowly, deliberately. She had known this moment would come. She had worked for it, sacrificed for it. But now that it was here, it felt even greater than she had imagined.

The final step. The culmination of years of careful moves, betrayals, and bloodshed.

She had won.

She inclined her head. "Understood."

The screen blinked out, leaving only darkness in its wake.

Allison sat still for a moment. Then she rose.

She crossed the room, stepping toward the window. Outside, the blizzard still raged, wind battering against the glass. The world below was crumbling—just as it was meant to. And she was no longer merely a participant in its destruction.

She was among the ones who would reshape it.

Allison Peterson was Number Three now.

And everything was about to change.

Her mind cast back to the last days of her captivity. The genesis of her plans.

The underground chamber had been cold. Not in temperature but in presence. The air held a weight. A pressure that settled into the bones.

Allison sat across from Number Four.

No chains. No restraints.

She wasn't a prisoner anymore.

She was something else.

Number Four regarded her with quiet patience, his posture poised, his hands folded neatly on the table between them. He had said nothing for the last few minutes, allowing the silence to sink in.

Because silence had a way of revealing truths.

And the truth was simple.

She had lost.

Noah Wolf would never stop the Council. E & E had never been real. Camelot had been a desperate whisper against a hurricane. There was no force on this earth strong enough to destroy the Council.

Not from the outside.

The realization had broken something in her.

Not in a way that shattered. Not in a way that could be seen. But in the way tectonic plates shifted beneath the surface. In the way mountains crumbled over centuries.

She had resisted, fought, endured. She had faced torture, starvation, psychological warfare. And yet she was still here.

Not because she had won.

Because they had let her.

Number Four finally spoke.

"There it is."

His voice was soft. Pleased.

"You understand now, don't you?"

Allison didn't answer.

"You see it. The scale of it. The weight of it. You finally understand what you are up against."

She clenched her jaw.

"It's not a war, Allison. Wars can be lost. Regimes can be toppled. But this..." He gestured around them. "This is inevitable."

She wanted to fight.

Even now, some part of her wanted to spit in his face, tell him to go to hell.

But hell was already here.

And it had won.

The past bled back into the present.

Allison blinked, her reflection caught in the snow-slicked window before her. She let out a slow breath, rolling her shoulders back, pushing the memory of that cold underground chamber aside. That was then. That was before.

She was Number Three now.

The weight of the designation settled on her like a second skin —unshakable, permanent.

Her comm unit crackled.

She pressed a finger to her earpiece. "Go ahead."

A voice—low, urgent—cut through the line. "We're closing in on the target."

Allison's lips curled into the faintest ghost of a smile.

"Remember," she said, "I want him alive."

There was a pause. A flicker of hesitation on the other end.

"Understood."

The line cut out.

Allison let the silence settle around her, then exhaled, eyes narrowing against the storm.

It was almost time.

SEVENTY-TWO

THE VERKHOYANSK RANGE, SIBERIA | 14:37 KRAT | MARCH 1

Noah stood outside his home in Kirtland, the crisp mountain air filling his lungs.

The water shimmered before him, reflecting the towering Colorado Rockies like a perfect mirror. Lake Temple was still, the sky above an endless stretch of blue. A breeze stirred the trees, rustling leaves in the distance.

He exhaled slowly.

Sarah was there.

Norah too.

The girl laughed—a sound so pure it made his chest ache. She sat by the edge of the water, tossing pebbles, watching them ripple across the surface. Sarah stood nearby, smiling, her hair catching the morning sunlight.

For the first time in a long time, he felt whole again.

He turned and walked toward the house.

Inside, warmth enveloped him—the smell of home-cooked food, fresh coffee, the faint trace of woodsmoke from the old fireplace. The light was golden, soft, the kind of light that only existed in memories.

Sarah turned to him, a knowing smile on her lips.

"You're safe now, Noah."

His throat tightened.

He sat with them at the kitchen table, the three of them together, just like before.

They ate breakfast.

Norah chattered between bites of toast, swinging her legs beneath the table. Sarah reached across, her fingers brushing against his, warmth radiating from her touch.

For a moment, it was real.

But only for a moment.

A cold wind swept through the house.

The air shifted, unnatural, sharp.

The lake outside turned to ice in an instant, its smooth, glassy surface stretching toward the horizon. The sky darkened, black clouds swallowing the sun.

The golden glow of the kitchen flickered.

Sarah's smile faded. Her face distorted, the warmth in her eyes vanishing, replaced with something empty.

Noah's breath caught.

He turned to Norah—

She was gone.

Only a humanoid pile of ash remained—before a gust of wind whisked it away, out of the house, into the void.

Noah lunged for her—but there was nothing.

The air grew colder. The warmth bled from his skin.

He reached for Sarah, his fingers brushing her wrist—

She too was ash, fading. Dissolving like smoke, her body vanishing into the blackness.

"Sarah—"

The house collapsed inward—the walls, the warmth, the light —all swallowed by the dark.

Noah jolted awake with a painful gasp.

His head slammed against cold metal, the jolt sending fresh

agony ripping through his body. His vision swam, the world lurching around him.

No Lake Temple. No warmth. No Sarah. No Norah.

Only the frozen wasteland of Siberia.

The low rumble of an engine vibrated beneath him. The metal walls around him shook with every bump and jolt. A vehicle.

He tried to move, but a firm hand pressed him back down.

Katya.

Her sharp green eyes met his, steadying him. "Easy," she murmured. "The wound's opened again."

Noah blinked, his breath still uneven. The Snowcat trundled forward, its caterpillar tracks crunching through the endless tundra. The interior was dimly lit, every surface lined with metal, gear, and emergency supplies.

Jenny was at the wheel, her hands gripping it tightly, eyes locked on the frozen horizon.

Neil sat beside her, navigating, checking the map, adjusting their course.

In the back, Katya stayed with Noah, her expression a mix of concern and frustration.

Noah gritted his teeth, trying to sit up. Pain lanced through his body, sharp and unforgiving.

Katya pushed him back down.

"Don't be stupid," she snapped. "You'll make it worse."

Noah's hand drifted to his side, feeling the warm stickiness of blood soaking through his layers.

"Shit," he muttered.

Katya nodded grimly. "We've got supplies at a safe house. We can fix you up better there."

Noah let out a slow breath. "And then what?"

Katya blinked, taken off guard. "What do you mean?"

Noah's jaw clenched. He shifted slightly, wincing as he stared at her. "Then what will we do?"

Katya hesitated. "We regroup. Rethink."

Noah scoffed, shaking his head.

"Regroup? We already have regrouped." His voice was low, sharp, edged with something raw. He gestured vaguely at the cramped cabin around them. "This is the group. We are it now. All there is left."

The words hung in the air, heavy and final.

Katya stiffened but refused to look away.

"Then we—" she started, defiant.

Noah cut her off, his voice as cold as the tundra outside.

"Then we fail again."

A silence settled.

Noah's gaze was distant, staring past her.

"Chase our tails. All the way up until it's our own turn to die."

Katya's fingers tightened into fists. Her jaw clenched.

She wasn't having it.

"No." Her voice was steel. "We are all we need. We will rise again. We will—"

BOOM!

The explosion ripped through the night. The Snowcat lurched violently, metal screaming.

Noah's world turned upside down.

BOOM!

The second RPG slammed into the frozen ground just ahead of them, detonating on impact. The shockwave hit first, a wall of fire, ice, and concussive force that lifted the Snowcat's front end like a toy.

Jenny fought the wheel, teeth clenched, trying to wrestle the skidding vehicle back under control.

"Hold on!" Neil shouted, his hands bracing against the dashboard.

In the back, Katya threw herself over Noah, shielding him as the Snowcat lurched sideways.

The world turned into a violent blur.

The Snowcat spun, tracks kicking up ice, metal groaning under the strain.

The vehicle tipped—flipped—slammed onto its side.

Skidding.

Sparks erupted as the armored body scraped across frozen ground, the deafening grind of steel on ice filling the air. Noah's head snapped back, pain ripping through his already battered body. Glass shattered. The world spun. For a moment, it was nothing but chaos.

Then, as suddenly as it had happened, silence.

Everything stopped.

The Snowcat lay still, half-buried in the ice. Smoke curled from the wreckage.

No one moved for several stretched seconds.

Jenny was the first to crawl out, coughing against the cold, dragging their MG 338s free. Her hands moved instinctively, loading, checking, bracing.

Neil followed, slower. Blood ran down the side of his face, and his left arm hung at an awkward angle. He cradled it as he moved, his jaw tight with pain.

"I think it's broken," he gritted out, trying to lift the rifle with one hand. Jenny caught him before he stumbled.

Katya followed, pulling Noah out, her grip firm.

But the moment his boots hit the ice, his body failed him.

He collapsed against the upturned Snowcat, his breath ragged. His mind screamed at him to move. But his body refused.

It got worse.

Footsteps were approaching. The rhythmic crunch of boots moving through the snow. Precise. Methodical. Unstoppable.

A Council strike team had arrived.

At least fifteen Elite assassins.

They emerged from the storm like ghosts, weapons raised, moving with perfect synchronization.

Noah tried to lift his rifle, but his arms felt like lead, the pain in his side burning deep. He could barely keep his head up.

They weren't going to win this.

Not here.

Not now.

Jenny took cover behind the Snowcat, rifle up, ready to fight. Neil dropped beside her, teeth clenched in pain as he braced the barrel of his MG 338 with one hand. The broken arm hung awkwardly against his body.

He used the wreckage to steady the weapon, gritting out each breath as he locked into position.

Katya's breath steamed in the cold, eyes flicking between Noah and the incoming enemy.

Noah saw the truth before they did.

If they stayed, they would die. This wasn't a battle. It was a trap. And he was the bait. His mind made the choice before his body did.

He turned to Katya. "Run."

She shook her head instantly, defiance flashing in her eyes. "Jonas—"

He grabbed her arm, his grip stronger than it should have been for how broken he felt. His voice was sharp. Final.

"Run. Get them out of here."

Katya stared at him, eyes burning. She knew what he was doing.

Jenny hesitated, torn between orders and instinct.

She looked to Neil. He nodded once, pale from blood loss but focused.

Noah took a shallow breath, then forced himself up.

His body screamed, but he ignored it. With the last of his strength, he pushed off the wreckage and took a slow, deliberate step forward. Exposing himself. Making himself the target.

Katya's face twisted with fury, but she knew.

There was no other choice.

Jenny grabbed Neil's good arm, pulling him toward the tree line. He stumbled, swore under his breath, then pushed forward —using his own rifle like a crutch as much as a weapon. The snow soaked into his clothes as he half-limped beside her, shoulder slumped but pace steady.

Katya hesitated for only a second longer—then she too turned and ran.

Noah didn't look back.

The Council soldiers raised their rifles. But they didn't fire.

The leader stepped forward, his expression unreadable. His posture calm. Cold. Calculating.

Noah smirked, blood on his teeth.

The leader tilted his head. "On your knees."

Noah didn't move.

The leader's grip tightened on his rifle. "I said—"

Noah's grin widened, his voice rough, jagged.

"It's best you kill me now."

He spat blood onto the ice, his eyes locked on the leader. "Because if you don't, I'll burn your world to the ground."

The rifle butt swung fast, slamming into Noah's skull. Pain exploded. His body crumpled. Darkness took him.

SEVENTY-THREE

SAKTENG WILDLIFE SANCTUARY, BHUTAN/TIBET BORDER | 17:59 BTT | MARCH 1

THE HELICOPTER SLICED THROUGH THE STORM, ITS rotors screaming against the howling wind. Snow lashed against the cockpit glass, a relentless barrage of white and shadow.

Beneath them, the Himalayas loomed—a vast, ancient spine of rock and ice, untouched by time. Sheer cliffs rose like fortresses of the forgotten, their jagged edges lost beneath shifting clouds.

Then—a glow.

A thin seam of golden light appeared, almost imperceptible against the dark mountain face. A fracture in the stone, so precise it could not have been natural. Hidden from satellites. Absent from every map. A place that did not exist.

The helicopter angled downward, its trajectory calculated, as if drawn by gravity itself toward the invisible threshold. The landing zone was unseen until the last moment—a flat, reinforced platform jutting from the mountainside, nestled within a narrow gorge where no uninvited eye could ever find it.

Allison sat perfectly still as they descended. Her expression remained calm. Measured. But inside, her pulse quickened.

This was the moment.

Everything—every betrayal, every kill, every sacrifice—had led to this. Her reward.

The landing was flawless. Smooth. Controlled.

As the rotors powered down, the security team emerged. A line of black-clad enforcers, faces obscured by tinted visors, waited at the edge of the pad. Their movements were as precise as the mountain itself.

Allison stepped out.

The wind cut like a blade. The thin, high-altitude air bit at her lungs. But she didn't flinch.

A figure stepped forward—a woman with sharp, severe features. No rank insignia. No name. Just authority.

"Bag, please."

Allison handed her handbag over without hesitation.

The guards moved with silent efficiency, searching it with clinical precision. One of them extracted a large can of hairspray, holding it up to the dim light.

The lead guard's eyes flicked to Allison. A moment of hesitation.

Allison smiled faintly, her voice smooth. "I'm old school. As you can see."

Another pause. A decision calculated.

In the end, the guard returned the hairspray. A shrug. A silent acknowledgment. A gesture that said *You belong here now.*

They returned her bag, and the doors ahead groaned open, their sheer size alone a declaration of power.

Carved directly into the mountainside, the entrance stood over sixty feet high, its metal reinforced with ancient symbols— Bhutanese, Tibetan, Sanskrit—etched in gold, their meaning known only to those who had stood here before.

A message, silent yet absolute: Power is eternal.

And Allison Peterson had finally stepped into its heart.

Beyond the doors, the corridor was pristine, stretching endlessly into the mountain's heart.

The floor was polished obsidian, a mirror of black glass, reflecting the faint glow of recessed lights. Along the walls, massive gold-trimmed banners hung in perfect symmetry, bearing the Council's insignia—a black and gold eye, bordered by eagle's wings, crowned in silent dominion.

Lined along the hall, guards in ceremonial uniforms stood at rigid attention, their faces emotionless, their black rifles gleaming under the light.

Allison walked forward, her footsteps silent on the flawless stone. Her gaze didn't flicker. She had waited for this moment for years. Every betrayal, every kill, every sacrifice—this was the reward.

At the end of the hall, the doors to the Grand Chamber stood before her. Beyond them, the Inner Council waited.

SEVENTY-FOUR

COUNCIL FACILITY, SIBERIA | 18:31 KRAT | MARCH 1

NOAH DRIFTED IN AND OUT OF CONSCIOUSNESS, THE world slipping in like fragments of a shattered mirror. Light. Too bright. A rhythmic beeping, steady and mechanical. The sharp, sterile scent of disinfectant.

He tried to move. Nothing.

Cold metal pressed against his wrists and ankles, the bite of restraints locking him down. His breath was slow, sluggish, his chest rising and falling under an unseen weight. His mind felt distant, as if he were floating outside his own body, watching himself from somewhere far away.

A figure moved in his periphery.

Noah's vision swam, blurring at the edges before snapping into place. A man stood over him—middle-aged, dressed in surgical scrubs, his face lined but emotionless. His sharp, calculating eyes studied Noah like a scientist observing a test subject.

The doctor gave a small, satisfied nod.

"Ah. You're awake," Dr. Vasilyev said, his voice calm, detached. "Right on schedule."

A mechanical whirring filled the room as an arm-mounted

telescreen adjusted overhead, lowering until it hovered directly above Noah's restrained form. The screen flickered, static crackling across its surface before an image coalesced.

Noah exhaled slowly.

Allison Peterson's face filled the screen, her expression composed, unreadable—triumphant.

The glow of candlelight flickered behind her, reflecting off marble and gold. She wasn't in a cell, a bunker, or even an office. No, this was opulence. She was somewhere important. Somewhere untouchable.

"Noah," she said, smooth and almost warm. "It's good to see you. I was afraid you wouldn't wake up before the ceremony began."

His body was leaden, but his mind fought through the haze. He licked his lips, throat dry as sandpaper.

"What the hell is this?" His voice was slow, thick with drugs.

Allison tilted her head slightly, a faint smile curving her lips.

"This is the final step," she said. "For both of us."

The camera shifted slightly, allowing Noah to see more of the room she was in—tall, arched ceilings, polished marble, golden candlelight flickering against pristine walls. It reeked of power.

"I wish you could see it, Noah," she murmured. "The grandeur of it all. The Inner Council, gathered for my induction. The most powerful people in the world, watching as I take my place among them." Her voice was almost wistful, like someone describing a long-anticipated homecoming.

Then her gaze flicked back to him, a satisfied gleam in her eyes.

"And you, well... you made this possible."

Noah's fingers twitched against the restraints, his body still too weak, too sluggish. He forced his jaw to tighten, ignoring the way his vision swayed.

"Go to hell," he gritted out.

Allison sighed, shaking her head in amusement.

"Now, now. We both know that if such a place existed, we'd both have seats waiting for us."

Her voice softened, like a mother explaining a hard truth to a child.

"You've always been a problem, Noah," she continued. "A loose end. A force of chaos in a world that needs order. We tried to control you through E & E, but you refused to stay in line. We tried to kill you, and you wouldn't die."

She paused, letting that truth settle between them.

"So," she said at last, "we've chosen a different route."

A cold weight settled in Noah's chest.

Allison's expression remained poised, her tone gentle, almost comforting.

"We're going to fix you."

Noah's breath slowed.

Dr. Vasilyev stepped back into view, adjusting a surgical instrument, its polished edge gleaming under the sterile lights.

"A weapon is most effective when it doesn't question its purpose," he murmured, his voice as clinical as a scalpel.

Noah's chest rose and fell, his body frozen, but inside, his mind screamed.

Allison's voice turned soft, almost affectionate.

"Don't fight it, Noah," she said. "When this is over, you'll be free."

A pause.

"Free from doubt. Free from hesitation."

Her eyes darkened, the final words coming like a slow, deadly whisper.

"Free from yourself."

The screen flickered once.

Then—blackness.

Noah Wolf was going to be lobotomized.

SEVENTY-FIVE

VERKHOYANSK RANGE, SIBERIA | 18:42 KRAT | MARCH 1

THE BLIZZARD HOWLED, A VIOLENT, UNRELENTING force that tore through the night. The wind lashed against them, cutting through their clothes, sinking into their bones.

Katya pushed forward, eyes narrowed against the storm, leading the way through the white void. Snow swirled like ghosts around them, obscuring everything beyond a few feet.

Behind her, Jenny staggered, one arm braced under Neil's good shoulder, the other gripping his broken one carefully.

His arm was limp and useless, cradled awkwardly against his chest with makeshift support.

He collapsed into the snow, his breath coming in weak, ragged gasps.

"No," Jenny gritted out, hooking her around his torso and hauling him up. "Not here. Keep moving."

Neil let out a low groan, his head lolling against her shoulder, but his legs moved, just barely.

Katya's gaze swept ahead, searching, scanning—there.

Through the churning white, she spotted the dark outline of a rock face.

"Come on!" she called, shouting over the wind.

They forced themselves forward, every step a battle.

Finally, they reached the mouth of a cave, a black hollow in the mountainside, hidden beneath layers of snow and ice.

Katya ducked inside first, her boots crunching over frozen stone. Jenny dragged Neil in, and they collapsed against the cold, damp walls, gasping for air.

Neil curled forward slightly, shielding his broken arm as his back thudded against the rock. He winced hard, jaw clenched.

Jenny knelt beside him. "Let me see it."

He nodded, teeth gritted, as she gently unhooked the sling she'd improvised. His arm was already swelling, bent wrong at the elbow.

She tore another strip from her shirt and used a pine branch they'd broken off earlier as a splint. Wrapping it tightly, she kept the joint firmly immobilized.

Neil didn't cry out, but his breathing hitched as she pulled the last knot tight.

Inside the cave, gnarled tree roots snaked along the rock, half-exposed, dried gray from years of exposure.

Katya pulled her survival knife free and scraped at the bark, peeling away thin, fibrous strips. The shavings drifted to the ground like paper-thin curls, dry enough to burn.

Neil stirred weakly, muttering something under his breath. His voice was slurred, barely above a whisper.

"...bullets..."

Katya turned, glancing at him.

"...bullets..." he repeated.

Then, without a word, she pulled a single rifle round from her vest. With practiced efficiency, she cracked it open, sprinkling a pinch of gunpowder onto the tinder pile.

She grabbed a flat rock, pressed the edge of her knife against it, and struck.

A single spark jumped.

Then another.

Finally—a flicker of flame.

Jenny leaned close, cupping her hands around the tiny ember. She blew gently, coaxing it, feeding it with breath and patience. The flames grew, crawling hungrily across the tinder, curling into a small, flickering beacon of warmth.

Jenny exhaled. "Let's hope the storm hides the smoke."

The dim glow filled the cave, pushing back the shadows. The heat was weak, but it was something.

Neil let out a shaky groan, his body limp, his breathing shallow. Jenny pressed two fingers to his neck, checking his pulse.

"...Shit," she muttered under her breath, her jaw tightening.

Katya moved to the entrance.

She listened, head tilting slightly.

For a moment, it was just the wind.

But before long it was—something else.

A rhythmic crunching.

Boots in the snow.

And farther away—the low, guttural bark of a dog.

Her stomach tightened.

The Council's search teams.

She turned back to Jenny, her voice barely above a whisper. "They're close."

SEVENTY-SIX

THE GRAND CHAMBER | 18:01 BTT | MARCH 1

The corridors of the Grand Chamber were a labyrinth of gilded marble, towering archways, and silent whispers woven into the very stone. Symbols, patterns, runes, and ancient images were all carved into it.

Allison was led through a towering set of golden double doors, but instead of entering the Grand Chamber itself, she was guided into a side room—a space even more magnificent, more intimate, more terrifying.

The room was a sanctuary of excess, its walls carved from pure white marble, streaked with gold and silver veins, the ceiling adorned with a fresco of gods and kings watching from above. Art wasn't merely framed here—it was embedded into the structure itself, scenes of conquest and empire etched into the very walls.

At the center stood nine figures, robed in black and gold, their faces concealed behind elaborate masks, each more ornate than the last.

This was the Inner Council. The true heirs to mankind. The pilots of its fate.

The doors shut behind her with a final, echoing thud.

No guards. No cameras. No witnesses.

Just them.

One by one, they spoke, their voices distorted by the intricate voice-warping mechanisms embedded in their masks. It rendered them inhuman, as if she were standing before nine phantoms rather than nine people.

And yet she would soon know them.

A beat of silence filled the room, the air thick with expectation. Then, one by one, they reached for their masks.

The first to remove his was the man directly before her. He lifted the gold-trimmed mask from his face with slow, deliberate grace, revealing a high forehead, deep-set gray eyes, and skin lined with the passage of time but untouched by the burdens of labor. His thin lips remained pressed into something that wasn't quite a smile—more an expression of knowing amusement, of quiet supremacy.

She recognized him immediately.

Grand Duke Alistair IX of Luxembourg.

A monarch in name alone, his nation was nothing more than a ceremonial relic, but his influence stretched beyond what most world leaders could fathom. Though his parliament made laws, though his people believed him a passive figurehead, it was he who whispered into the ears of presidents, prime ministers, and ministers of finance. Generations of power had not faded—it had only gone unseen.

He set the mask down upon a black marble pedestal beside him and gave Allison a slow nod, as if acknowledging a new player stepping onto the board.

The second moved next.

The Middle Eastern man beside the grand duke removed his mask in a single, fluid motion. His face was weathered, lined by both age and the desert sun, though his eyes were as sharp as polished glass. His perfectly trimmed beard, streaked with white, gave him the air of a scholar, but the gleaming emerald signet ring on his hand spoke of something far more dangerous—the power to dictate the movement of wealth itself.

This one she also knew.

Suleiman Al-Farsi.

The Oil King. The invisible hand that turned pipelines into war zones, that dictated the price of energy and, by extension, the fate of entire economies. He did not simply own oil fields—he owned leaders, governments, the very air of the Middle East itself.

His voice, now unaltered by the mask, came like rolling thunder. "You've earned your place here, Number Three."

Then came the third.

A younger man—or at least younger than the others. He pulled his mask free with an eager kind of arrogance, revealing a face too perfect, too chiseled—a face the world knew. His cold blue eyes sparkled with something dangerous, predatory. His smile was a calculation, not an expression.

Matthias Kessler.

The Tech Prophet. A billionaire before he was twenty-five, a trillionaire by thirty. His companies had rewritten the very fabric of society, weaving his technology into every device, every transaction, every connection the world made.

People thought they owned their devices. They didn't.

Matthias Kessler owned them.

He winked at Allison, his teeth gleaming beneath the golden light. "You already know me, of course," he said with the arrogance of a man who had never been told no.

The fourth followed.

He removed his mask with a soldier's efficiency, revealing a square jaw, high cheekbones, and eyes that had seen too many wars. His short-cropped hair was graying, but his posture was unyielding, unbroken.

General Hayden Locke.

The General Without a Nation. Once, he had been a three-star general, the man who led the largest army in history—until he had abandoned nations entirely. Now he answered only to the Council.

His voice was measured, clinical, as if assessing her like a battlefield. "You've fought well to be here."

The fifth lifted slowly, revealing a face that had once been known to every home in the Western world. His graying hair, his piercing blue eyes, his familiar jawline—his face was etched into the history books, into presidential portraits, into the memories of a nation.

Sebastian Monroe.

The Kingmaker. A former US president—the man who had once been the most powerful figure on Earth. And yet, his true power had only grown since leaving office. He had installed leaders, buried others, ensured the world bent to the will of the Council.

He gave Allison a single nod, as though anointing her with a silent blessing.

The sixth followed without hesitation.

He removed his mask with a quiet, almost dismissive motion, revealing a face that no one knew yet everyone obeyed. His dark eyes held no warmth.

Gabriel Duvall.

The Market Phantom. His fortune was untraceable, his presence erased from all but the most hidden ledgers. Stocks, currencies, entire economies trembled at his will.

His voice was smooth, detached. "I always expected you to make it this far," he murmured.

The seventh lifted her mask.

A raven-haired woman, strikingly beautiful in the way that danger often was. Her sharp cheekbones, her cold, predatory eyes, the faint smirk on her lips—this was a woman who owned entire industries, entire empires.

Irina Volkov.

The Black Widow. Russian oligarch, financier, puppet master.

She had outlived kings, presidents, and revolutions, carving her power into the bones of the world itself.

She met Allison's gaze, her lips curling at the corners. "I do so love seeing new blood."

The eighth removed his mask.

His robe gleamed with white and gold, his face serene, untouched by the weight of human suffering. His gray eyes held billions of souls in their depths.

Cardinal Rafael Ortega.

The White Cardinal. A religious leader whose devotion was not to God but to power. His words could ignite crusades, topple rulers, silence entire nations.

His voice was gentle, dangerous. "Faith is nothing without action."

And then came the last.

Number One.

The unknown man at the center of it all.

He reached up with deliberate slowness, unfastened his mask, and removed it.

His face was utterly unremarkable. Not famous. Not tied to any known power structure. Just a man. A man who should not have held such immense presence and yet commanded it completely.

His voice, now unaltered, was calm, absolute.

"Only these eight people know my identity," he said. "Now you make it nine."

The others stepped back, their black robes shifting as they formed a perfect circle around Allison.

One of them extended a set of folded robes. Another held out a mask of black and gold, identical to theirs.

Allison took them without hesitation.

Her face remained unreadable, her body poised, but as she turned away to change, she kept one hand tightly gripping her handbag.

She lifted the Council robes, slipping them over her shoulders. The fabric settled onto her like a mantle. She reached for the mask, smooth and cold beneath her fingers.

And as she did, her hand slid discreetly into her bag.

Her fingers curled around the hairspray bottle.

A quiet, precise motion. A practiced sleight of hand.

She tucked it beneath the folds of her robe, securing it against her body.

Then she straightened, lifted the mask, and placed it over her face.

When she turned back, she was one of them.

Each of them placed their mask back on, and then, in his distorted voice, Number One announced, "The Grand Chamber awaits."

The doors opened once more.

The ten of them moved as one, stepping through the towering entrance and into the vast expanse of the Grand Chamber.

Golden chandeliers bathed the room in regal glow, their light reflecting off gilded arches and flawless obsidian floors. Towering banners of the Council's insignia—the black-and-gold eye, crowned, with eagle's wings—hung like declarations of sovereignty.

And beyond them, filling the space like disciples awaiting their gods, sat the ninety members of the Greater Council.

The true administrators of the world.

They rose as one.

A thunderous applause filled the air, a sound that wasn't celebration, but affirmation. The masked elite of the world's inner circle stood in reverence, their eyes locked on the ten figures entering the chamber.

The Inner Council moved forward in perfect synchrony, their robes flowing behind them like banners in a silent war, their black-and-gold masks gleaming under the grand chandeliers. Allison walked at their center, the newest piece in a game centuries in the making.

The applause continued to thunder through the colossal chamber, filling every inch of space like an avalanche of devotion.

The ten figures ascended the dais at the head of the room, where an immense obsidian table rested at the center, carved into a perfect black circle. Each chair, identical in design, sat at equal distance around it—save for the seat at the very front, which stood slightly raised.

The seat of Number One.

The members of the Inner Council took their seats—except Allison, who remained standing at the center.

Number One raised a single hand, and the chamber obeyed.

The applause faded into silence.

The stillness that followed was almost deafening.

Then he spoke. His voice—distorted, inhuman, unreadable— filled the vast space, not loud but inescapable. A presence, a force beyond the man beneath the mask.

"We stand here today, not as rulers of nations, nor as leaders of governments, but as something greater."

Every figure at the obsidian table remained motionless, listening. Statues in devotion.

"We are the unseen architects. The hand behind the throne. The mind behind the war. The whisper that turns the course of history."

A pause.

A slow, deliberate scan of the room.

"The people of the world believe they are free. They believe their choices matter. But it is we who set the choices before them. It is we who shape the flow of their lives, as a sculptor shapes stone."

Allison stood motionless, absorbing every word.

Number One continued.

"This world has known chaos, rebellion, war—but none of it has threatened us. The rise and fall of nations is nothing but a game we play, a theater we control."

Then, slowly, his masked face turned toward Allison.

"And now we welcome into our fold a person who has proven their devotion beyond question."

A ripple of silent agreement passed through the chamber.

"A person who helped burn down an empire to build a better one."

The words hung in the air, deliberate, final.

"A person who understands that the future does not belong to the weak, the lost, the unworthy—it belongs to those who have the will to shape it."

He extended a gloved hand, palm up.

A gesture of invitation. Of power.

"Come forward, Number Eleven."

His voice did not ask. It commanded.

The moment stretched, like a blade hovering above flesh.

Then, slowly, Allison stepped forward.

The applause returned—slow, deliberate, measured.

Not approval. Not celebration.

Coronation.

She ascended the steps to the center of the chamber and stood where so few had before—where true power was cemented.

With a quiet incline of her head, she bowed—not deeply, not submissively, but in acknowledgment. A gesture of humility, of deference—the final step before ascension.

As she kept her head lowered, the weight of the moment settled over her. Years of betrayal. The endless bodies left in her wake. Every choice. Every sacrifice. Every deception. All leading to this.

"You entered this chamber as Number Eleven," Number One went on.

A pause.

A ripple of stillness through the Inner Council.

"Now you rise as Number Three."

SEVENTY-SEVEN

COUNCIL FACILITY, SIBERIA | 18:57 KRAT | MARCH 1

THE OPERATING ROOM WAS ALL WHITE WALLS, stainless steel, and cold fluorescence humming softly overhead.

Noah lay strapped to the table as a robotic arm lowered toward his temple, its laser tracing a thin red line against his skin —the incision point. The spot where they would break him.

Dr. Vasilyev stood over him, observing Noah with the cold detachment of a sculptor studying raw marble.

On the table beside him, a tablet glowed softly, lines of code scrolling across the screen as he adjusted settings with silent precision.

The machine shifted, responding to his touch. The scalpel on the end of its arm gleamed, perfectly aligned.

"We will keep your intelligence," the surgeon said in a clinical tone. "Your instincts. But your will?" His eyes glinted with something unreadable. "That will belong to us."

Noah's jaw tightened, his breathing ragged.

He forced the words through clenched teeth.

"Go to hell."

The doctor's expression didn't change. If anything, he looked amused.

"Oh, but you misunderstand, Mr. Wolf." He adjusted a control on the tablet, and the robotic arm whirred softly, calibrating. "We are saving you from hell. From chaos. From the burden of choice."

The machine hummed louder. The scalpel lowered, positioning itself just above the skin. A thin red dot painted the side of Noah's temple.

Dr. Vaselyev's voice was gentle, almost reassuring.

"It will be painless. You will wake up with the same mind, the same hands, the same skills."

A slight pause.

Then, with certainty, "But your thoughts will be clean. Your emotions balanced. You will obey without hesitation."

His gaze flickered to Noah's, almost admiringly.

"A perfect weapon. A perfect soldier."

When he spoke, Noah's voice was a rasp, barely more than a growl.

"I will kill you," he stated.

The surgeon tilted his head, as if genuinely considering the possibility. Then he smiled faintly, his voice light, mocking.

"Perhaps."

A slow blink.

"But only if we tell you to."

SEVENTY-EIGHT

VERKHOYANSK RANGE, SIBERIA | 19:12 KRAT | MARCH 1

THE WIND HOWLED THROUGH THE MOUNTAIN PASS, A long, mournful wail that slipped into the cave like a ghost, threading between the jagged stone walls.

The fire burned low, its flickering light casting twisting shadows against the damp rock.

Jenny sat near the flames, her arms wrapped tightly around Neil, trying to keep him warm. His breathing was shallow, his skin cold as the stone beneath them.

Katya sat near the entrance, the rusted Soviet knife resting lightly in her grip, eyes scanning the black void beyond the cave's mouth.

She listened. Her breath held.

Then she spotted something—flashlight beams moving.

She heard it, too.

The slow crunch of boots on snow. The distant panting of dogs, their breath misting in the freezing air.

A voice, low and deliberate, cut through the storm.

"They can't have gone far."

Katya's grip on the knife tightened.

A flashlight beam swept across the snow outside, the glow cutting through the storm, searching.

Katya stayed perfectly still in her hidden spot, her muscles coiled like a spring held too tightly.

The footsteps paused.

One of the hunters knelt at the base of the hill near the entrance, his gloved fingers brushing the ground.

Katya watched him, her breath shallow, controlled.

One mistake. One noise. And they were dead.

Inside the cave, Jenny's fingers trembled, her knuckles white from the bitter cold. Neil let out a faint, unintentional sound—a sharp, ragged breath, barely more than a whisper.

Katya's stomach clenched.

One of the hunters stopped. His head tilted slightly, listening.

The silence stretched thin.

But as Katya held her breath, the tracker rose, brushing snow from his gloves.

"Move forward," he said. "We'll sweep the next ridge."

The men resumed the search, their flashlight beams disappearing into the storm.

Katya didn't move. Didn't breathe.

Not until the last beam had been swallowed by the wind.

Then at last, she let out a slow, quiet exhale.

Behind her, Jenny shuddered, the relief mixing with exhaustion.

They were still alive.

But for how much longer?

SEVENTY-NINE

THE GRAND CHAMBER | 18:22 BTT | MARCH 1

THE CHAMBER WAS SILENT.

Not the polite quiet of a crowd waiting its turn, nor the passive stillness of an audience merely observing.

This was absolute silence. A silence of power, of focus, of attention sharpened to a knife's edge.

At the center of it stood Allison Peterson.

It was time for her to make her speech.

All around her, the world's true elite listened. Some with rapt admiration, some with calculated indifference, some swirling crystal glasses of aged wine, savoring both her words and the momentous shift they represented.

"Every empire is built by hands that hold power," she said, following it with a slow, deliberate pause.

"It does not matter how large the system, how vast the network—true authority always distills itself to the few. The many may serve, they may follow, they may fight, but they do not rule.

"Only a hundred hands ever truly shape the course of the world."

The room remained motionless. No one shifted, no one whispered. She let them absorb it. Then she continued.

"That is the lesson I learned two years ago, in a cold room with no windows in an underground facility run by the very people inside this room."

Her voice did not waver.

"In that underground room, I was remade. Not just through words. Not just through ideology. But through pain. Through loss. Through the slow, surgical stripping of everything I once was."

Her gaze swept across the chamber, taking in the presidents, the kings, the moguls, the warlords.

"And when there was nothing left of me, I saw it."

Another pause. A moment for the weight to settle.

"The truth is simple. If you sever the hands that hold the world, the body collapses. The empire crumbles. Remove those hundred hands, and the structure of control fails. It does not adapt. It does not recover. It dies."

She let the words linger, watching as they settled into the minds of those before her. She could see it in some of their faces. Some nodded, understanding. Others sipped their wine, unbothered, because they believed themselves untouchable.

She smiled slightly. They always believed that, she thought.

"It took time to get here," she continued. "Time, blood, sacrifice, and betrayal. You know this better than anyone. The road to power is paved in corpses. We cut away the weak. We burn the useless. We shape the world to our will, and we do not hesitate."

Her eyes found Number One's, locking on his masked face with unwavering steadiness.

"I did not hesitate when I dismantled E & E."

She let that sit. A ripple of interest flickered through the gathered Council members.

"When I killed my colleagues. My friends. My family."

Her voice did not soften.

"When I chased Noah Wolf harder than anyone has ever chased him."

Another shift in the room. Satisfaction. Approval.

"When I took Sarah Wolf's life and left a child without a mother."

That moment landed heavier. The weight of it sat in the air, lingering like the smoke from an extinguished flame.

Allison lifted her chin, unshaken.

"I did not hesitate because I knew what had to be done."

EIGHTY

NOAH STARED UP AT THE CEILING, HIS BREATH SLOW, his body useless against the restraints.

The mask lowered over his face, the rubber pressing tightly against his skin.

Above him, Dr. Vasilyev watched impassively, his expression detached, clinical.

This was routine. Just another procedure.

"Now," the surgeon said, voice calm. "Begin counting backward from one hundred."

The gas hissed, cold against his lips. Noah exhaled shakily, his mind racing. He knew the second his body gave in, it was over. His thoughts would stop being his own. His will would vanish into the abyss.

He gritted his teeth, forcing himself to fight—to hold on, to resist, to think.

But the gas seeped into his lungs, heavy and thick.

His vision blurred, the lights above him stretching into soft, distorted shapes. His limbs felt heavier. His mind was slipping, drowning in a chemical fog. He tried to hold on. Tried to stay in the fight. Tried to think of anything that would tether him to himself.

But the darkness was closing in.

EIGHTY-ONE

THE WIND HOWLED, A RELENTLESS FORCE THAT TORE through the mountains, shaking the trees and churning the snow into a swirling haze. But it did nothing to mask the sound of boots.

The hunters had returned.

The dogs had led them back, panting heavy, noses pressed to the frozen ground as they followed an invisible scent trail.

The crunch of boots on ice was deafening in the silence of the cave.

Jenny pressed herself closer to Neil, feeling the frailty in his trembling body, his breath fevered and shallow against her shoulder.

He was getting worse.

Katya crouched near the cave entrance, the knife held low, her eyes locked on to the storm beyond.

She listened. Watched.

A voice carried through the wind, muffled but unmistakable.

"The dogs keep bringing us back here. They're close. I can feel it."

Katya's pulse slammed against her ribs.

A flashlight beam swept across the entrance of the cave.

It stopped. Lingered.

Jenny held her breath, her fingers tightening around Neil, as if she could will him into silence.

Outside, the tracker knelt, pressing gloved fingers into the snow, his breath coming out in sharp, thoughtful exhales.

"I got something," he muttered. "Two sets of footprints. A third, heavier—one of them is injured."

The hunter straightened, his hand settling on his rifle.

"Then let's check this ridge out."

The footsteps moved.

Closer.

Katya's grip on the knife continued to tighten.

EIGHTY-TWO

THE GRAND CHAMBER | 18:26 BTT | MARCH 1

ALLISON'S VOICE LOWERED, EACH WORD SLIPPING through the grand chamber like a knife in the dark.

The first flickers of confusion had just started to ripple through the gathered elite. This wasn't a speech like the ones they'd witnessed before.

At the head of the room, Number One shifted slightly. Not enough for most to notice, but Allison saw it—the faint stiffening of his spine, the tilt of his head, his unseen eyes watching her with something close to fear.

Something was wrong.

He could feel it.

Allison took a measured step forward, her gaze sweeping across the Council—over the men and women who had shaped empires, dictated wars, crushed nations beneath their boots.

"But here's the thing about sacrifices," she said, her voice quieter now, each syllable razor-edged, slicing through the charged silence. "They are only worth something if they serve a greater purpose. And I have always served a greater purpose."

The air shifted. A murmur. A whisper of something felt but not yet understood.

Number One's masked face remained still, but she knew he was listening now. Really listening.

Allison slid her hand beneath the folds of her robe, her fingers brushing against the can of hairspray. They quickly found the base of the can.

She twisted it anticlockwise until it clicked.

The canister activated. A fine, invisible vapor hissed out from her, its dispersal soundless, weightless, slipping from her like an exhaled breath, spreading through the air, carried instantly by the chamber's vast ventilation system.

A mist. Silent. Unseen. Death, blooming from her.

Allison watched them, the most powerful people on Earth, as they failed to notice their own demise.

"You see, I never belonged to you." She smiled. "Not really."

She stepped forward, dropping the canister onto the marble as it emptied its contents.

"Instead, I belonged to an idea."

Her gaze locked on to Number One.

"And that idea is simple: You will not live to see the world you want to create."

A hush fell over the chamber.

Somewhere, a well-known billionaire set down his glass of wine, his fingers tightening around the stem as if suddenly uncertain.

Across from him, a senator's brow furrowed. A flicker of concern.

Not fear. Not yet.

But the first seed of it.

Allison continued, "For years, I have fought to reach this moment. For years, I have burned everything that stood in my way—including those I once loved. And now, the path is clear."

She saw it then—the first shifting of bodies, the subtle tightening of shoulders.

"You sit here, believing yourselves untouchable. But you are wrong."

Someone inhaled sharply. The first few flickers of discomfort rippled through the chamber.

It was beginning to do its work.

Allison smiled. Her voice remained steady. "You are all flesh and bone, just like the billions you have ordered to die. Just like the governments you have crushed. Just like the families you have torn apart."

The smile faded. Something else replaced it. Something final.

"And just like them, you are mortal."

There was a breath of silence. Then—

A single cough.

Soft. Barely audible.

Followed by another.

And another.

And another.

Someone pressed a hand to their throat, a flicker of discomfort tightening their jaw.

A French industrialist at the far end of the room let out a sharp breath, his fingers trembling slightly as he reached for his silk handkerchief.

Blood.

A single drop, rolling from his nostril.

Number One sat utterly still.

Allison knew he saw it now.

The room was changing.

A low murmur turned into something else.

Panic.

Allison tilted on her feet slightly, almost falling. A bead of blood fell from the corner of her mouth.

"This is the price I must pay," she murmured. "The price for bringing the Council to its end."

Someone stood too quickly, their chair clattering against the floor. A gasp. A choked breath. A hand gripping a throat, fingers clawing at nothing.

The panic erupted.

Bodies stumbled. Some collapsed where they sat, others lurched toward the sealed doors.

But there was nowhere to go.

The air had already taken them.

A man fell to his knees, blood leaking from his mouth, his eyes, his nose.

Number One stared at Allison, realization settling like a cold weight in his chest. He got up from his chair and took one step forward, his hand outstretched, reaching—

Allison simply smiled.

"You built your world on control," she said softly. "On obedience. On the unshakable belief that you were the architects of humanity's future."

Number One's lips parted, as if to speak—

But blood bubbled up instead.

Allison took a slow breath.

"But architects can be replaced."

She exhaled.

"And your time is over."

The sounds of choking filled the air—desperate, clawing gasps, bodies slumping onto polished marble.

Allison closed her eyes, breathing it in.

The sound of an empire dying.

Her voice was barely above a whisper.

"Goodbye."

EIGHTY-THREE

THE GAS SANK DEEP INTO NOAH'S LUNGS, THICK AND numbing, dragging him down into the abyss.

But still he fought it.

His mind spiraled, the darkness pulling at him, smothering his thoughts, erasing the edges of reality.

Above him, Dr. Vasilyev watched his vitals, methodical, unhurried. The robotic arm lowered, its movements precise, laser-guided. The scalpel gleamed, poised over Noah's skull.

Then an alarm blared.

A deep, echoing klaxon shook the room, rattling equipment, bouncing off sterile walls. Red emergency lights flashed, their flickering glow turning the pristine white into pulses of crimson.

The surgeon hesitated. His fingers hovered over the tablet controls, a flicker of confusion breaking through his detached focus. The program had frozen.

At that moment, Noah began realizing something. The gas had stopped.

There was a metallic click.

Noah's restraints snapped open.

He didn't waste a second. The moment his arms were free, he moved.

The scalpel glinted under the flashing red lights.

Noah snapped it off the arm and drove it into Dr. Vasilyev's throat.

A wet, gurgling scream filled the air. Blood sprayed against the pristine walls, stark red against the sterile white.

Noah yanked the mask from his face, his voice cold, a rasp of steel through his teeth.

"See," he said breathlessly. "Told you I was going to kill you."

EIGHTY-FOUR

THE CAVE WAS FREEZING.

Jenny held Neil close, his body a dead weight in her arms. His breath was shallow, his skin cold. Too cold. He was barely conscious, slipping further into the darkness with every passing second.

Katya crouched near the cave entrance, Jenny's SIG MG 338 having replaced the knife. She held the machine gun tightly to her shoulder, frost clinging to the worn fabric of her gloves. Despite the exhaustion in her limbs, her eyes remained sharp, unyielding.

Outside, the hunters were closing in.

Footsteps crunched through the snow, slow, deliberate, making their way up the embankment that lead to the cave.

Dogs barked and snarled, their handlers keeping them on tight leashes, holding them back just enough—restrained but ready. Flashlight beams cut through the swirling snow, sweeping across the cave entrance in steady arcs.

Someone spoke. "I think we found them."

The words hung in the air, thick with finality.

There was a pause. Then someone added, almost mocking, "Nowhere left to run."

Jenny's grip tightened around Neil. Her breath fogged the air as she tried to lift him, but her limbs were weak, stiffened by cold and fatigue.

Neil stirred slightly, his head lolling against her shoulder. His lips moved, but the words were barely audible.

Jenny leaned in, desperate to catch them.

His voice was weak, but there was still a flicker of amusement in it.

"Didn't think it'd end like this."

Jenny swallowed hard, her throat tight. Her eyes stung, the cold masking the burn of something deeper. But she forced a small, fierce smile anyway. "It hasn't ended yet."

Katya exhaled slowly, her breath a thin mist in the freezing air.

She raised the machine gun, steady despite the shaking in her fingers.

She had one clip left.

No chance of winning.

No chance of escape.

But that didn't matter.

She was prepared to die fighting.

To Valhalla.

EIGHTY-FIVE

NOAH STAGGERED THROUGH THE EMPTY CORRIDORS OF the base, one hand clutching his wounded hip, the other pressed against the wall for support. His breath came in ragged bursts, his vision swimming as he pushed forward.

The halls were eerily silent, abandoned in the chaos. No soldiers. No guards. Nothing but emptiness.

Suddenly, the wall monitors flickered to life.

Noah stopped, his pulse hammering in his ears as Allison's face filled the screens.

She was dying.

Her skin was pale, her lips tinged with blood, her breath ragged. The bioweapon was tearing through her, devouring her from the inside.

But still she spoke. "I've cleared that section of the base for you." Her voice was weak but steady. "The doors are unlocked. If you—if you keep moving down the corridor you're on, you'll reach the western helipad. There's a helicopter waiting. I've already uploaded the coordinates of the others into the nav system. Just start it up, and you... you'll make it."

Noah didn't stop moving.

He pushed forward, forcing one foot in front of the other.

As he did, more monitors flickered on, Allison's face following him down the corridor.

"Noah."

He hesitated.

Allison's breath hitched, her fingers trembling as she pressed a weak hand against her chest. "I don't have much time. But I need you to listen."

She swallowed hard, trying to keep her voice steady. She didn't beg for forgiveness. She didn't expect it.

"I did what I had to do." A weak, bitter laugh escaped her lips. "I know that doesn't mean a damn thing to you. But it's the truth. I needed to get here. I needed them all in one place. I needed to burn them down to the foundation."

She coughed, a wet, guttural sound. Blood seeped through her fingers, dark against her pale skin.

"You were right about me. I betrayed everything we believed in."

Her expression flickered—something unreadable, something human. Then the words that stopped him in his tracks.

"I killed Sarah."

Noah's grip tightened on the wall. His vision blurred. His breath came in slow, uneven bursts.

"I killed your people. *Our* people. I hunted you all like animals. And I would do it all again. Because it was the only way."

She leaned forward, her body wracked with pain.

"You don't have to understand, Noah. I don't need you to. But I need you to know this—I never forgot who I was. Not really. I just buried her. Deep enough that no one could see. Not even you."

Noah forced himself to move, pushing forward, his muscles screaming in protest.

The screens continued to follow him, her voice following him through the corridors.

"This war was never going to be won with bullets and good intentions. You tried. You fought. And they crushed you. Every time. Because they were bigger than you, stronger than you, older than you."

A deep, labored breath.

"The Council doesn't die. It evolves. It adapts. The only way to kill something that refuses to die... is to cut out its heart."

A weak smile ghosted her lips. "That's what I did today. I severed the monster's heart. They are gone, Noah. The top one hundred. The ones who pulled the strings. The ones who helped build and perpetuate this nightmare. Their empire is dying, and there's no one left to hold it up."

She winced, her head swaying slightly.

Her voice softened, but still held steady.

"I didn't want to do it alone. But I had to."

For the first time, her gaze softened, her voice quieter, almost hesitant.

"There's something else. I know you think you lost everything. But you didn't. I made sure of that."

Noah's breath caught. He stopped, turning to the nearest monitor.

Allison hesitated. The weight of what she was about to say was immense.

"Norah and Wally. They're alive."

For the first time, Noah reacted. A flicker of something between disbelief and something deeper.

"I faked their deaths," Allison continued. "It was the only way to keep them out of the Council's reach. The helicopter has their coordinates loaded into its navigation."

She exhaled, a faint, broken smile ghosting across her lips.

"You can hate me for everything else. You should. But not for this."

She leaned back, her strength fading, her breath coming shallow now.

"Go get them, Noah. They need you."

A long pause.

Her eyelids drooped, her fingers loosening at her sides.

She knew. This was it. "I would say I'm sorry," she murmured, "but that's not what you need to hear. And I don't deserve to say it."

She looked down. Her body sagged.

And then—barely a whisper.

"Goodbye, Noah."

The screen flickered.

Then—black.

Noah stood there for a long moment, watching as the screen faded to nothing. For a split second, he almost felt something close to grief. Then his mind cleared.

He had work to do.

Noah shoved through the heavy metal doors, stepping into the icy night. Snow slammed against his face, the wind biting through his clothes, but he barely felt it. He blinked against the storm, then saw it.

The helicopter. Fully fueled. Ready to fly.

The cockpit glass was frosted over, the rotors still, but it was there. His way out. His way to them.

Noah moved toward it, gripping the handle and hauling himself inside. His fingers trembled as he flipped switches, the engine groaning to life. His breath was uneven, his chest tight, but his hands were steady. Through the windshield, the storm raged, but he barely noticed. His grip tightened on the controls.

A whisper escaped his lips. "Hold on," he rasped, voice hoarse but unbreakable. "I'm coming."

The helicopter lifted off, the rotors slicing through the blizzard—

Straight toward the last of his people.

EIGHTY-SIX

VERKHOYANSK RANGE, SIBERIA | 19:58 KRAT | MARCH 1

THE CAVE WAS SUFFOCATING IN ITS SILENCE.

The only sounds were the faint, ragged breaths of the three inside, the distant howl of the wind, and the low, predatory hum of footsteps in the snow outside.

Katya held the MG 338 up, her grip tight, her pulse steady despite the odds.

Jenny crouched beside Neil, pressing her fingers against his freezing skin. Too cold. Too still. His breathing was shallow, but he was alive. For now.

Outside, the hunters were close. Really close.

Boots crunched on the ice-crusted ground, slow, measured. A rifle clicked, a round being chambered. A dog barked once, then twice, then was silenced by a sharp command.

Jenny's eyes squeezed shut. Bracing. This was it. They were out of time. Then—a crackle.

The static hum of a comm channel opening. A voice. Unmistakable. Calm. Commanding.

"All units, fall back. Return to base immediately."

It was Allison Peterson.

The hunters froze. One of them touched their earpiece, their posture shifting. Confused. Hesitant.

"Repeat that?"

Allison's voice came again—weaker this time, breathless.

"That's... an order. Fall back to base."

The hunters looked at one another—then, one by one, they stepped back. Their boots retreated into the snow. The dogs were pulled away. The flashlights faded.

Katya didn't move. She barely breathed. Her finger rested on the trigger, waiting. Expecting a trap.

Jenny exhaled shakily, her chest tight with disbelief. She whispered, barely daring to ask—

"What just happened?"

Katya's eyes narrowed, her voice grim. "I don't know."

They waited. Listening.

The wind howled, rattling through the valley like a restless specter, but no voices followed. The storm shifted, its icy breath sweeping over them.

The hunters were gone.

Katya lowered the machine gun, her fingers stiff from gripping it too tightly, for too long.

Jenny swallowed hard, the weight of adrenaline still pressing against her chest. She carefully pulled Neil up, his body sluggish, barely responsive.

They moved slowly, carefully, every step cautious as they slunk out of the cave.

The open air hit them hard—the cold like a blade, the sudden brightness of the snow blinding after so much darkness. Their breaths were shallow, their bodies aching, exhaustion deep in their bones. The sky above was thick with clouds, the wind still cutting through them, but there was a stillness now—a quiet emptier than before.

Jenny gasped. Her hand shot out, gripping Katya's arm. Her eyes were wide, disbelieving.

"You see that?" Jenny whispered, breathless.

Katya turned.

Through the blizzard, a dark shape emerged. At first, it was just a shadow, blurred by the snowstorm. Then a rhythmic chop of rotors echoed through the valley, the sound growing louder, stronger, undeniable. The helicopter tilted forward, pushing through the howling wind, carving a path through the storm.

Jenny and Katya barely processed what they were seeing.

It was impossible. But it was real.

The helicopter landed, its skids sinking into the snow, its rotors churning the storm into a frenzy. The side door slid open—

Noah stood in the doorway. Battered. Exhausted. Alive.

He gripped the frame, his hair damp with sweat, his face pale from blood loss and exhaustion. But his eyes—

His eyes were sharp. Alert. Burning with determination.

Jenny let out something between a sob and a laugh, her voice cracking.

"You son of a gun."

Noah shouted over the roar of the wind. "Get in!"

They didn't waste a second. Jenny and Katya dragged Neil forward, his weight sluggish between them. Noah reached down, grabbing Neil by the collar, all three of them hauling him into the cabin.

Jenny scrambled in next, her fingers raw, her body trembling.

Then she turned, her hand outstretched for Katya.

Katya grabbed it and climbed inside.

Noah slammed the door shut, breathless, and moved back into the pilot's seat. His hands gripped the controls, forcing the helicopter skyward.

Jenny collapsed against the seat, her head tilted back, shaking but alive.

Katya sat still for a moment, staring at Noah. Studying him. She didn't say anything at first. Then, quietly, "Took you long enough."

EIGHTY-SEVEN

PUTORANA PLATEAU, SIBERIA | 22:02 KRAT | MARCH 1

THE HELICOPTER CUT THROUGH THE NIGHT, ITS rotors sending gusts of wind howling over the frozen wilderness below.

The Putorana Plateau stretched endlessly, an expanse of ice and basalt cliffs. Snow lay thick over the valleys, untouched except for the deep, ancient scars left by glaciers. No roads reached this place—only the rare, whispering descent of a chopper shattered the stillness.

And then there it was.

The safehouse lay buried within the plateau, blending seamlessly into the landscape. Not a cabin, not a bunker, but something in between—a relic of Cold War paranoia repurposed into a sanctuary, hidden beneath layers of ice and stone.

Noah's hands tightened on the controls as he guided the helicopter lower, weaving through the mountainous cliffs with calm precision.

The skids touched down on the helipad. The rotors slowed.

Noah sat still for a moment, his breath shallow, his heart

pounding harder than it had through gunfights, through ambushes, through death itself.

Noah inhaled, forced his hands to unclench, then reached for the door.

The cold hit him instantly, a sharp, biting wind cutting through his jacket. He barely felt it.

Because the moment his boots hit the snow, the door to the safehouse burst open.

Noah froze.

Standing in the doorway, eyes wide, breath caught in her chest —was Norah.

She was still. A small, unmoving silhouette against the dim light spilling from inside.

She looked different. Older. Not in years—in experience. In weight. In loss.

Noah's throat went dry.

Neither of them moved.

Not for a heartbeat.

Not for eternity.

Then—

Norah ran.

Noah dropped to his knees, his arms wide open just as she crashed into him, hitting him with everything she had.

The force of it almost hurt.

Her small frame shook, her arms wrapping so tightly around his neck it felt like she might never let go.

Noah crushed her against him, one hand buried in her hair, the other securing her like he was afraid she might float away.

She was crying, her face pressed against his chest, muffled sobs escaping in choked little gasps.

And so was he.

He didn't even realize it at first—didn't notice the heat behind his eyes, the way his breath shuddered and broke apart.

He only knew that he had her.

That she was here. Real. Alive.

Norah's voice was small, trembling, barely more than a whisper against his jacket.

"You came back for me."

Noah's eyes shut tight, his grip on her tightening, grounding himself against the only truth in the world that mattered.

His voice broke when he spoke.

"I never gave up."

Behind them, Jenny and Katya stood silent, watching.

Even Wally, lingering in the doorway, his glasses fogged from the cold, had tears brimming in his eyes.

Noah pulled back just enough to cup Norah's face, his thumbs brushing the tear tracks on her cheeks.

She had been through hell.

He could see it in her eyes—that haunted depth, that understanding no child should ever have.

But she was alive.

That was all that mattered.

He leaned in, pressed a kiss against her forehead, then pulled her in again, holding her close, burying his face in her hair.

She refused to let go. And he never would.

Katya and Jenny moved fast, their focus shifting to Neil, his body heavy, unresponsive as they lifted him between them. He barely muttered a sound, his head lolling as they dragged him into the safehouse.

His broken arm dangled awkwardly between them, splinted but swollen, the makeshift wrappings soaked from snow and blood.

The moment they crossed the threshold, the safehouse's automated medical system flickered to life—soft lights illuminating a sterile, reinforced room filled with supplies, monitors, and machines.

Katya and Jenny laid Neil down gently, working fast.

Jenny's hands shook, but she forced herself steady, her voice low and urgent as she hooked him up to the IV lines.

"You're gonna be fine, Neil. We've got you. Just hang in there."

The machines hummed, their screens flashing vitals, processing his condition as they removed his clothing and wrapped him in a thermal blanket.

When he was settled, Jenny exhaled, her hands still pressed against Neil's good arm, as if keeping him anchored to the world.

In the corner of the room, Wally stood watching. His face was drawn, unreadable. But Noah saw it.

The way his fingers twitched slightly at his sides, a small tremor he was trying to hide. Was it the lasting effects of what they had done to him?

Or something else?

Wally cleared his throat, squaring his shoulders. He turned, nodding toward a basement door.

"Noah." His voice was low, serious. "There's something you need to see."

EIGHTY-EIGHT

WALLY LED NOAH DOWN A NARROW STONE STAIRCASE, their boots echoing softly against the worn steps. The deeper they went, the more the cold shifted—not the sharp bite of Siberian wind but something else. Something artificial.

A chill of circuits running cold, of old metal humming with renewed life.

The stairwell ended at a thick reinforced door, its edges lined with condensation where the warmth of machines met the underground frost of the air conditioning. Wally pressed his palm to a scanner. A faint beep. A hiss of depressurization.

The door slid open, revealing a room unlike the rest of the safehouse.

Noah stepped inside.

The air was thick with machine heat and stale electricity. The walls, once carved from rough stone, had been reinforced with layers of steel and insulated paneling, swallowing sound, trapping it like a secret.

Along the far wall, rows of sleek computer stations glowed, screens flickering with scrolling code, security feeds, layers upon layers of classified data.

It was alive down here. Not just a bunker. A nerve center.

Cables snaked across the floors, connecting servers housed in glass-paneled racks, their cooling fans humming softly beneath the pulse of information. A silent heartbeat beneath the mountain.

At the center of it all, a solitary figure sat at the main terminal, his back to them, hunched slightly, eyes flicking over lines of cascading code.

Noah's steps slowed.

For a moment, his mind refused to register the man before him.

Then the chair swiveled around.

Dr. Adrian Knox.

The same sharp eyes. The same glasses, slightly askew. The same air of detached amusement, like he had been waiting for them the entire time.

Knox pushed his glasses up the bridge of his nose and smirked.

"Hello there, Noah Wolf."

Noah stared at him for a beat, his jaw tightening.

"We thought you were dead," he said.

Knox let out a short chuckle. "I thought so too."

"What the hell is all this?"

Knox exhaled, stretching slightly before turning back to the monitors.

"This?" He gestured lazily to the massive, humming network before them. "This is my life's work. Allison Peterson didn't just keep me alive, she"—he paused, his smirk widening—"put me to work."

Noah took a step closer, his brow furrowing.

"Work doing what, exactly?"

Knox's fingers danced across the keyboard, lines of code cascading down the screens, shifting, changing in real-time.

"Olympus," he said, almost casually. "The Council's god

system. Their all-seeing eye. Their omniscient, untouchable, worldwide infrastructure. The thing that made them untouchable."

He leaned back, turning to face them fully. "Well... not so untouchable anymore."

Wally stiffened. "You broke it?"

Knox grinned. "No. I rewrote it."

Noah's expression remained unreadable, but his fingers curled into fists.

"What do you mean?"

Knox sighed, cracking his knuckles before typing in a final command. One of the screens flashed red, displaying a single blinking cursor.

"Olympus was meant to be a god," he said, tapping the screen. "But Allison had me turn it into a suicide switch. She wanted me to wait until you got here."

Wally blinked, then let out a low whistle.

"Holy shit."

Knox's fingers moved once more, typing in a final sequence before leaning back in his chair. A new window opened. The screen glowed red, a stark, ominous warning filling the terminal. At the center, a single button stood out. A single word beneath it:

IGNITION.

Knox exhaled, folding his hands behind his head.

"She wanted you to press it."

"What will happen?" Noah asked.

"The Council dies," Knox replied. "All of it." His voice was steady, matter-of-fact. "Their security, their firewalls, their networks. Every last backup, every last control system. Everything flips."

Noah stared at the screen, his pulse steady but deep. His mind replayed everything they had done to him. To Sarah. To Norah. To everyone.

Everything they had stolen.

Wally turned to Noah, his voice low, final. "Let's end this."
Noah inhaled slowly.
Then with steady fingers, he reached out—
And pressed Enter.

EIGHTY-NINE

IT STARTED AS A WHISPER IN THE DIGITAL VOID—AN unnoticed tremor in the world's most fortified systems.

Then the collapse began.

Across the globe, the Council's network unraveled.

Firewalls failed. Security grids blinked out. Vaults designed to be impenetrable opened like rotting doors, their encrypted files shredding themselves from the inside.

In a remote bunker deep in the Alps, a red warning flashed across every screen.

SYSTEM OVERRIDE. ACCESS DENIED.

The guards reached for their weapons—then realized the biometric safeties had disabled them.

In Beijing, an intelligence hub buried beneath the city's financial district suddenly locked down. The lights flickered, then shut off completely.

A second later, CCTV feeds from their own surveillance network—secret prison facilities, interrogation rooms, hidden laboratories—were broadcast live to the world.

In London, the massive servers hidden beneath an anonymous corporate skyscraper overheated in an instant. Cooling systems failed. The temperature climbed past critical levels. With a final, helpless whine, the hard drives melted. Every file, every operation, every secret ledger of the Council's financial empire vanished.

Their trillions of dollars—stolen from governments, laundered through war, blood, and deception—were redirected, dispersed into thousands of anonymous accounts, funneled toward charities, NGOs, and war crime tribunals.

The money disappeared, slipping from their grasp like water through broken fingers.

In a command center beneath Washington, D.C., a Council member stood frozen, watching as his private messages, hidden transactions, and classified black ops orders were dumped in real-time onto WikiLeaks.

Across the globe, news stations interrupted their broadcasts. Screens flickered. Anchors stammered, breaking into urgent live reports as a tsunami of exposed secrets poured into the public domain.

Footage of political leaders receiving bribes. Records of assassinations, of corporate puppetry, of entire wars orchestrated for profit.

The world watched in horror as decades of manipulation, war, and genocide were laid bare.

Inside the last surviving bunkers, the panic was immediate.

In Dubai, a Council stronghold sealed its blast doors, but the locks had already been overridden. A massive steel vault door hissed open—exposing a room full of Council officials, frozen in silent horror as armed insurgents poured inside.

In a hidden estate in Argentina, a Council general scrambled for his private jet. The engines roared to life—then shut down mid-runway. A single message appeared on his jet's display.

NO ESCAPE.

In Berlin, New York, Moscow, Tokyo—the Council ran. But there was nowhere left to hide. Their kingdom was burning. The Titan had fallen.

The glow of the monitors bathed the basement in flickering

light, painting their faces in shifting reds and blues as the Council's empire crumbled before their eyes.

On the screens, feeds from across the world played out like a prophecy fulfilled—vault doors forced open, security teams overrun, hidden war rooms exposed. The untouchable rulers of the world were now cornered, desperate, falling one by one.

Noah stood silent, his eyes fixed on the displays, his breathing slow and measured.

It was done.

Footsteps echoed down the narrow staircase.

Jenny and Katya helped Neil descend.

His broken arm was secured in a rigid sling, stabilized and strapped tightly against his chest, the dressing clean and reinforced by the safehouse med system.

As injured as he was, he refused to sit. Not for this.

Not when they were watching the world change.

Norah stood beside her father. Without a word, she reached for his hand.

Noah's fingers closed gently around hers.

They stood together, father and daughter, watching history collapse in real time.

Neil let out a weak chuckle, barely able to keep himself upright, his hand resting on Jenny's shoulder. His grin was crooked, exhausted—real.

"Damn," he muttered, shaking his head. "That is satisfying to watch."

Jenny let out a sharp exhale, her shoulders sagging like she'd been holding her breath for years.

Katya leaned against the wall, arms crossed, her expression unreadable—as if she couldn't quite believe what she was seeing.

Wally exhaled shakily, his glasses slipping slightly down his nose. His hands trembled as he reached up, wiping his eyes quickly, his voice thick with emotion.

"She did it. She destroyed them."

He let out a short, disbelieving laugh, like he still wasn't sure it was real.

No one spoke for a moment.

Then Neil reached out his hand—unsteady, weak, but unwavering.

Jenny took it, then Katya, then Wally, Noah, Norah, until all of them stood together, hand in hand.

A chain of survivors. A family forged in fire.

For the first time in their entire lives—

The fight was over.

Katya was the first to break the silence.

"So what now?" she said.

Noah didn't answer right away. He wasn't sure he had one.

The war was over. They had won. The Council, the unseen empire that had ruled the world from the shadows, was collapsing in real time. The screens showed the proof—vaults forced open, systems down, decades of corruption bleeding out into the light.

It should have felt... different.

He looked down at Norah, her small hand still curled around his. Her eyes weren't on the monitors anymore. They were on him.

For the first time in years, Noah had no orders. No mission.

He had spent his whole life moving toward this moment, step by step, body after body, war after war. But now the war was over.

So what now?

Noah let out a slow breath, his grip on Norah's hand tightening for just a second before he released it. He ran a hand over his face, shaking his head slightly.

"We move forward."

Katya raised an eyebrow. "That vague bullshit isn't an answer."

Noah exhaled, a faint smirk ghosting across his face. "It's the only one I've got."

Neil chuckled, weak and rough. "I'll take it." He let out a slow breath, glancing toward Jenny. "Wherever forward is, I'd prefer it involves a cozy bed and a lot of alcohol."

Jenny snorted. "I second that."

Katya shook her head but didn't argue. "And after that?"

Noah turned back to the monitors one last time. The footage continued, looping through the destruction of an empire that had once seemed untouchable.

They had burned the old world down.

Now it was up to them to decide what to do with the ashes.

Noah's jaw tightened. "We find the next bad guy."

The others exchanged glances.

Neil let out a groan. "Of course there's always a next bad guy."

Noah exhaled slowly, a ghost of a smile touching his lips.

"There always is," he said.

**Don't miss CHILDREN OF THE EMPIRE. The riveting sequel
in the Noah Wolf Thriller series.**

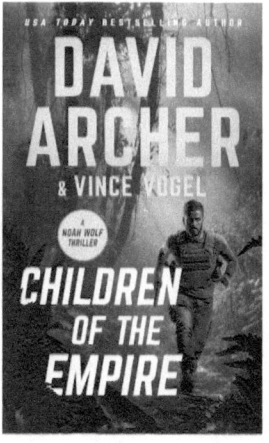

Scan the QR code below to purchase CHILDREN OF THE EMPIRE.

Or go to: righthouse.com/children-of-the-empire

NOTE: flip to the very end to read an exclusive sneak peek...

DON'T MISS ANYTHING!

If you want to stay up to date on all new releases in this series, with this author, or with any of our new deals, you can do so by joining our newsletters below.

In addition, you will immediately gain access to our entire *Right House VIP Library,* which includes many riveting Mystery and Thriller novels for your enjoyment. Including a prequel novella to this series!

righthouse.com/email

(Easy to unsubscribe. No spam. Ever.)

ALSO BY DAVID ARCHER

Up to date books can be found at:
www.righthouse.com/david-archer

ROGUE THRILLERS
Gates of Hell (Book 1)
Hell's Fury (Book 2)
Ice Burn (Book 3)
Judgement by Fire (Book 4)

JACOB HUNTER THRILLERS
The Kyiv File (Book 1)
The Bogota File (Book 2)
The Havana File (Book 3)
The Amsterdam File (Book 4)

PETER BLACK THRILLERS
Burden of the Assassin (Book 1)
The Man Without A Face (Book 2)
Unpunished Deeds (Book 3)
Hunter Killer (Book 4)
Silent Shadows (Book 5)
The Last Run (Book 6)
Dark Corners (Book 7)
Ghost Operative (Book 8)
A Fire Burning (Book 9)
Dawnlight (Book 10)
Dead Ice (Book 11)

ALEX MASON THRILLERS
Odin (Book 1)

Ice Cold Spy (Book 2)
Mason's Law (Book 3)
Assets and Liabilities (Book 4)
Russian Roulette (Book 5)
Executive Order (Book 6)
Dead Man Talking (Book 7)
All The King's Men (Book 8)
Flashpoint (Book 9)
Brotherhood of the Goat (Book 10)
Dead Hot (Book 11)
Blood on Megiddo (Book 12)
Son of Hell (Book 13)
Merchant of Death (Book 14)
Extinction C-14 (Book 15)

NOAH WOLF THRILLERS
Code Name Camelot (Book 1)
Lone Wolf (Book 2)
In Sheep's Clothing (Book 3)
Hit for Hire (Book 4)
The Wolf's Bite (Book 5)
Black Sheep (Book 6)
Balance of Power (Book 7)
Time to Hunt (Book 8)
Red Square (Book 9)
Highest Order (Book 10)
Edge of Anarchy (Book 11)
Unknown Evil (Book 12)
Black Harvest (Book 13)
World Order (Book 14)
Caged Animal (Book 15)
Deep Allegiance (Book 16)
Pack Leader (Book 17)
High Treason (Book 18)
A Wolf Among Men (Book 19)

Rogue Intelligence (Book 20)
Alpha (Book 21)
Rogue Wolf (Book 22)
Shadows of Allegiance (Book 23)
In the Grip of Darkness (Book 24)
Wolves in the Dark (Book 25)
Olympus Must Fall (Book 26)
Children of the Empire (Book 27)

SAM PRICHARD MYSTERIES
The Grave Man (Book 1)
Death Sung Softly (Book 2)
Love and War (Book 3)
Framed (Book 4)
The Kill List (Book 5)
Drifter: Part One (Book 6)
Drifter: Part Two (Book 7)
Drifter: Part Three (Book 8)
The Last Song (Book 9)
Ghost (Book 10)
Hidden Agenda (Book 11)

SAM AND INDIE MYSTERIES
Aces and Eights (Book 1)
Fact or Fiction (Book 2)
Close to Home (Book 3)
Brave New World (Book 4)
Innocent Conspiracy (Book 5)
Unfinished Business (Book 6)
Live Bait (Book 7)
Alter Ego (Book 8)
More Than It Seems (Book 9)
Moving On (Book 10)
Worst Nightmare (Book 11)
Chasing Ghosts (Book 12)

Serial Superstition (Book 13)

CHANCE REDDICK THRILLERS
Innocent Injustice (Book 1)
Angel of Justice (Book 2)
High Stakes Hunting (Book 3)
Personal Asset (Book 4)

CASSIE MCGRAW MYSTERIES
What Lies Beneath (Book 1)
Can't Fight Fate (Book 2)
One Last Game (Book 3)
Never Really Gone (Book 4)

ABOUT US

Right House is an independent publisher created by authors for readers. We specialize in Action, Thriller, Mystery, and Crime novels.

If you enjoyed this novel, then there is a good chance you will like what else we have to offer! Please stay up to date by using any of the links below.

Join our mailing lists to stay up to date -->
righthouse.com/email
Visit our website --> righthouse.com
Contact us --> contact@righthouse.com

facebook.com/righthousebooks
x.com/righthousebooks
instagram.com/righthousebooks

EXCLUSIVE SNEAK PEEK OF...

CHILDREN OF THE EMPIRE

CHAPTER ONE

THE CHOPPER BUCKED HARD AGAINST THE RISING thermals, its rotors slicing through thick Bolivian afternoon like a knife through gristle. Outside, the horizon pulsed red with dust, turning the light sour and coppery.

Beneath the bird, jungle fell away to reveal fire-scabbed clearings, churned mud, and blackened stumps where trees had stood just days ago. Scorched fields lay ringed in wire and sandbags. UN trucks sat like hulking beetles under tarpaulins the color of dried blood, their wheels sunk deep in red clay.

Inside the helicopter's fuselage, the air was sour with sweat, fuel, and adrenaline. Jenny Blessing sat with her back against the cold metal wall, helmet in her lap, jaw tight.

Across from her, Neil Blessing wiped a film of condensation from his glasses with a frayed corner of his shirt.

Next to him, Wally Lawson gripped the black biocontainment case like a sacred relic. It was sealed with triple locks and thermally regulated—and he held it as if it might explode or vanish if he loosened his grip for even a second.

Jenny tilted her head, her voice dry as the dust outside. "Anyone else feel like we're dropping into a graveyard?"

Neil didn't look up. "That's optimistic."

Jenny turned her eyes to Wally. "Hey, Wally? You good?"

Wally looked up slowly, blinking. His expression was distant, slightly unfocused, like someone trying to place a face from a dream. Then he nodded once. No smile. Just the nod.

Jenny didn't push. She didn't need to. She'd read the after-action files. She knew neural decomp when she saw it—what the extraction had taken, and what it left behind.

Six months ago, the Council's top neurosurgeon had performed a memory extraction: ultra-thin wires threaded into the brain to siphon memories one synapse at a time. It had left Wally diminished. Recovery was slow; and as yet incomplete.

The helicopter dipped lower, rotors kicking up another storm of grit. Below, a checkpoint flickered into view through the dust, blue helmets and white body armor barely visible amid the haze. A signal flare went up. Green.

They were expected.

Jenny adjusted her grip on the rifle resting between her knees and locked eyes with Neil.

Showtime.

The helicopter slammed down hard on a makeshift landing pad of splintered wood and rust-stained corrugated metal. The skids groaned as if the bird resented being grounded. Instantly, a wall of dust rose around them, churning into the rotors, and swallowing everything in a blur of ocher and sweat. The heat hit next —a wet, lung-clogging smother that reeked of mildew, fuel, and something faintly metallic underneath.

Jenny ducked low and led the team out beneath the churning blades. The jungle sang around them—not with birdsong, but with the high, shrill scream of cicadas.

Two UN guards emerged from the haze, rifles slung lazily but hands never far from the triggers. Their blue helmets were sun-faded and scuffed, the uniforms beneath a jigsaw of mismatched camo and salvaged gear. One of them—a lean Bolivian with sharp eyes and a clenched jaw—had a black phoenix insignia stitched on his upper sleeve. The mark of the Council. Someone had scratched through it with a blade and slapped a strip of medical tape over the remains.

The guard stopped a few feet away. "You Camelot?"

Jenny stepped forward, her boots squelching in the damp clay. "That obvious?"

The man gave a humorless grunt. "We stopped expecting help a week ago. Lieutenant's waiting."

They were waved through a checkpoint cobbled together from rusting shipping containers. Warning glyphs had been hastily sprayed on every surface in bright biohazard orange—some recognizable, others improvised.

On the far side of the checkpoint stood a squat concrete building—a former warehouse now transformed into a makeshift clinic. Its windows were long shattered, now patched over with tarpaulin stitched to steel mesh. The UN emblem flapped weakly in the breeze, stained with old rain.

Lieutenant Adjani Camara waited at the entrance. She was tall and wiry, her skin cracked with sunburn, her dark hair braided back into a knot. A sidearm rode her hip.

"Lieutenant Adjani Camara," she said by way of greeting. "UN contingent lead. You're walking into something no one here was trained to handle."

Neil stepped past Jenny and offered a tight nod. "That's why you called us."

Camara's mouth twitched, not quite a smile. "No. I called for medicine. What I got was Camelot."

She turned without waiting for a reply, boots crunching across sunbaked gravel as she led them toward the clinic.

Inside, the air changed. Cooler, but not cleaner. A wet, fungal tang clung to the walls, mingling with bleach and old blood. The interior had been stripped down to its bones—no furniture, no patients, just crates, power cables, and the hum of makeshift filtration rigs.

Camara stopped at a heavy steel door marked with peeling hazard symbols. She keyed in a code on the pad, then shouldered it open.

"Locker room's through here," she said. "Strip to base layer. No skin. No hair. No exposed stitching. If it can wick moisture, it can carry spores."

The room beyond was barely lit. Rows of lockers, mismatched and rusting, lined the walls. A drain slithered down the center of the floor.

On the far wall, a rack of hazmat suits hung in grim procession —hooded, sealed, pale grey with charcoal filters like gills across the shoulders. Each one looked like it had already seen too much.

Jenny unbuckled her chest rig and shrugged out of it slowly. The sweat made everything cling. Neil was already peeling down to his underlayer.

Wally hesitated, fingers resting on the zip of his jacket. Jenny caught his eye. No words were needed this time.

"Filters last four hours," Camara said, crossing to a shelf stacked with respirators and sterile gloves. "Longer if you breathe shallow. You won't. It gets thick in there."

Jenny reached for a suit.

"Once you're in," Camara added, her voice turning flat, "you don't take it off. Not for anything. Not if you itch. Not if you panic. Not even if some bug has climbed in there with you."

No one spoke. The only sound was the slow rasp of zippers and the distant, irregular thump of something heavy being moved outside.

Jenny tugged the hood over her head and sealed the collar ring. The world narrowed. Breathing became sound. Her own breath, rasping through the mask.

She looked at Neil through the scratched visor. He nodded once.

Camara opened the next door. Beyond it: dim corridor, plastic sheeting, and the first shadow of something red smeared along the wall.

"Follow me," she said. "And don't touch anything."

The first step past the threshold of the concrete clinic was a step into hell. The hallway was narrow, lit by the sputtering buzz of emergency fluorescents. Bloodstained curtains hung like ghosts between beds, some drawn tight, others torn open to reveal what lay behind—and what lay behind was not good. Even inside the suits, the smell was atrocious: cloying antiseptic fought a losing battle against feces, sour sweat, and something deeper—something that smelled like meat gone bad, like ozone after a lightning strike, like rot beginning not from the skin but from the marrow.

Camara led them through the ward's twisting gut. "This was a UN storage facility a week ago," she said. "Now it's a morgue with nurses."

The hallway curved left, and the truth of it all landed like a hammer. The space widened into what had once been a huge storage area—now repurposed, packed with beds arranged two deep. Some were hospital-issue, others cobbled from crates or broken chairs. Anything that could hold a body.

And there were many bodies to hold.

A boy, maybe twelve, suddenly convulsed on one of the cots. His back arched unnaturally, his spine a bow drawn to breaking. Sweat poured from him, and his veins—black and thick like creeping vines—bulged beneath his skin. His mouth was open in a soundless scream.

Straps held his arms tight. His legs thrashed, uncontrolled.

Two nurses were already at his side, hazmat suits creaking as they moved. One held the boy's shoulders down while the other jabbed a syringe into the exposed skin above the collarbone. The fluid inside was a dull amber. The boy jerked once more—then stilled. His eyes, unfocused and grey around the irises, blinked rapidly as his body went slack.

"Ketamine-analgesic cocktail," one of the nurses muttered

through her voice amp, more for the recorders than the visitors. Her hands never stopped moving—adjusting the IV, checking the vitals patch clinging to the boy's temple with surgical tape.

The second nurse straightened. "Stabilized," she said. "For now."

A sigh rippled through the ward like a breeze through plastic. But it lasted all of two seconds.

Another scream tore through the air—ragged, gurgling, too deep to belong to the thin woman it came from. Camara snapped her head toward the sound.

"Bed twenty-six," she barked.

The nurses were already running. They moved fast—even in the suits.

Camara stepped back to let them pass. "This is what it is now," she said to no one in particular. "You calm one, and another starts screaming. Whack-a-mole with dying people."

They kept moving. What else was there to do?

The next ward was worse. The tarps parted with a wet sound, peeling apart like lungs opening. Behind them: more patients, or what remained of them. Most lay still. Some twitched.

Jenny stopped beside a figure hidden beneath a soaked towel. She knelt and gently lifted the fabric away.

The man's face was slack, pallid. His eyes were open—pitch black. Not clotted blood. Not bruising. The irises, the sclera, even the reflection itself—it was all consumed. It looked less like something physiological and more like the color had bled from his soul outward.

His lips parted. A tongue, black and cracked, twitched once and stilled.

Behind them, a sharp zzzzip tore through the quiet like a gunshot.

They turned.

Two attendants in sweat-slicked PPE were zipping a body bag closed outside the surgical prep room. The bag sagged at the center, the shape still warm, still soft.

Camara stood with the others, silent, as the attendants carried the body past.

"You think it's them?" she muttered. "The Council?"

Jenny didn't take her eyes off the bag. "The Council's dead," she said.

Camara didn't answer right away.

"Yeah," she said at last. "But I heard there are others."

CHAPTER TWO

AFTER SHOWING THEM THE DEVASTATION OF THE quarantine area, Camara led them back to the locker room. Once they'd changed out of the hazmat suits, she proceeded to guide them to an outbuilding on the edge of the compound.

Inside, a makeshift conference room waited.

Fluorescent lights buzzed overhead. In the far corner, a pile of body bags lay stacked beneath plastic tarps. A single fan creaked on the ceiling, moving the air just enough to send a ripple through the covering.

A large conference table took up the majority of the room. At the head of it sat Dr. Helena Menendez, an experienced virologist. Mid-forties, wiry, hair pulled into a fraying knot, she wore sweat soaked scrubs, turning the fabric translucent in patches. Her Cuban accent had been worn down by sleeplessness and crisis.

To her left sat Dr. Elias Otieno, a tall, weathered pathologist from the DRC. His voice was slow and steady, every word placed with the care of a man long-acquainted with human ruin.

The second Neil, Jenny and Wally sat down opposite, Menendez pointed to a map on the wall beside her. Red marker notes ran in concentric circles from a central dot.

"The index case was traced to Alto Beni," she said. "Forty-eight hours later, six surrounding settlements went dark. All infected were indigenous. No deviation."

"No deviation?" Neil frowned. "You mean it only infects indigenous?"

"We're not certain yet—hence the hazmat and quarantine protocols," Menendez replied. "But so far, only indigenous people have shown signs of infection. There was a logging team nearby—made up of people from the cities with European ancestry. They're all clear."

Wally leaned forward. "What exactly does it do to them?"

Dr. Menendez brought up an image on the screen behind her —a CT cross-section of a lung, shot through with jagged white traces. It looked like lightning frozen in flesh.

Otieno took over, voice even. "The virus enters through mucosal membranes. But it's not airborne. Not casual. Transmission is direct—blood, saliva, contact with infected tissue. But..."

He tapped a key. Another scan appeared. Genetic readouts—lines of code, then comparison markers. Red highlights flared across the screen.

"This isn't random," Otieno said. "It's genetic alignment."

Wally leaned in, frowning. "Define that."

Otieno rotated the laptop so the whole table could see. Two genome maps—one standard, one infected—blinked in synchrony.

The differences were glaring.

On the left, the healthy genome displayed as a clean lattice of blue and green markers—ordered, symmetrical, steady pulses along a digital helix.

On the right, the infected map was chaos. Red markers lit up like flare clusters, especially along chromosomes 6 and 11. Entire gene sequences had been rerouted, their pathways corrupted by foreign proteins.

"It binds to a receptor protein found predominantly in Andean and Guaraní populations," Otieno said. "The frequency in other genomes—particularly European-descended—is nearly zero."

Jenny's voice was ice. "You're saying this thing chooses who to infect."

Menendez didn't flinch. "No. I'm saying someone designed it to."

The room fell into silence. The fan ticked around and around. No one breathed.

Wally broke it. "I take it you have a sample in your lab?"

Menendez nodded once.

Wally's expression hardened. "Then I'd like to see it."

A minute later, the lab door was creaking open with the groan of rust and neglect, revealing a room that could barely house two people standing shoulder to shoulder. It felt less like a laboratory and more like a storage closet. Wires tangled like vines overhead, draped like jungle creepers across the low ceiling. Nothing in here looked newer than a decade, and most of it looked salvaged from tech graveyards.

A centrifuge wheezed in a corner, its housing cinched together with duct tape. Next to it stood a scuffed white mini-fridge labeled in smeared Sharpie: BLOOD/PLASMA—DO NOT UNPLUG. A PCR thermocycler, missing half its lid bolts, sat beside it, twitching quietly like it didn't trust itself to keep working. And nestled into a corner, humming with faint digital breath, was the real jewel—a Council-era gene sequencer, scratched but alive, its logo almost worn off.

Camara stood behind Wally and gestured with a grimace. "This is the best we've got."

Wally didn't answer. His focus was absolute. He stepped inside and laid down his gear with the precision of a man setting up for surgery, or a priest for prayer.

First came the portable isolation hood, unfolded and snapped into place over a low table. Then a cooling core no larger than a lunchbox. Finally, a biosample injector with a fingerprint-lock security ring that blinked green beneath his thumb.

Menendez entered a few seconds later, clutching a reinforced cryo-vial between two gloved hands.

"No one else touches this," she said quietly.

She passed it into the isolation hood with the care of someone handling a live grenade. The vial clicked into the locking clamp with a magnetic thunk, and Wally was already moving—gloves on, posture tight, mind elsewhere. His fingers moved like a pianist's, swift and assured, every motion practiced.

Wally's voice dropped to a murmur. "Let's see what you are."

He swabbed a sample with gloved precision and fed it into a cartridge bay on the sequencer. The machine responded with a low chime and came to life.

Next, Wally opened a laptop and linked it to the sequencer. Nucleotide chains began to scroll down the screen—red, blue, green—a digital waltz of base pairs drawing themselves from the blood's secrets.

As the data streamed, Wally tapped into his own neural-linked archive: a deeply encrypted, privately maintained viral index. It had taken him years to build it. The display shimmered with titles as it began cross-referencing:

92 confirmed Council-engineered pathogens...

14 in prototype status...

8 scrubbed from official records...

The sequence comparison began. A progress bar crept across the screen.

12%... 28%... 41%...

Wally leaned back, glasses slipping slightly down his nose. He wiped them absently, then looked again.

74%... 92%... COMPLETE.

The sequencer chimed. Then froze.

A line of text blazed white on black:

MATCH FOUND

Council Origin: PROJECT HELIX

Designation: Variant 7B

Status: EXPUNGED (Internal – Level Gamma)

Wally's blood turned to ice.

He stood locked in place as if the machine had pointed a weapon at him.

"No," he whispered. "No no no—this was supposed to be buried."

The screen scrolled. Details unspooled like a noose:

Originally designed for controlled population pruning during insurgency response.

Abandoned due to immediate non-containment risk.

Final note: Too unstable. Shelve indefinitely.

Wally stared. "This was never supposed to make it out of prototype," he breathed.

"What is it?" Menendez asked.

"Helix-7B."

"Which is?"

Wally didn't turn away from the screen. His voice was flat, toneless—like he was narrating a nightmare he'd had too many times.

"Helix-7B was the Council's attempt at social genocide," he said. "A virus designed to identify specific genetic markers tied to chronic illness, hereditary defects, even certain neurological predispositions. The idea was to quietly 'trim' populations—people who would need lifelong care, or whose genes didn't align with whatever selective ideal they were chasing that year."

Menendez stepped closer. "So it was eugenics."

Wally nodded once. "Yes, it was eugenics."

He tapped a few keys, and the genome map reappeared on the screen of his laptop—now overlaid with faint reference notes, archived metadata from a buried Council server. Annotations blinked beside clusters of highlighted markers: BRCA mutations, neurodegenerative SNPs, autoimmune likelihood thresholds.

"They couldn't get it stable," Wally continued. "The virus mutated too fast. It either didn't activate at all, or it jumped to unrelated markers. In trials, it wiped out entire control groups.

There was an outbreak in Novosibirsk. They buried it. Literally. They sealed the whole site."

"And now it's here," Jenny said coldly.

Wally's jaw tightened. He pointed to the newest data—highlighted sequences on the infected genome that glowed like scars.

"This isn't the original design," he said. "Someone's re-engineered it. See these markers here? They're clustered around loci tied to ancestry—mitochondrial haplogroups, inherited from maternal lines. And this one—chromosome 6—targets immune system variation common to Andean and Guaraní populations."

Neil let out a low breath. "It's not pruning the sick anymore."

"No," Wally said. "Now it's targeting race. Inherited bloodlines."

The room fell still again. Even the lab's broken machines seemed to quiet, as if the virus had turned the very air to glass.

Jenny stepped forward. "So someone's using what the Council buried."

Wally didn't look up. "Yes. Someone with access to their archives. Someone who wants to finish what the Council didn't have the stomach to start."

Jenny's voice was like gravel. "Then we need to find them."

Wally nodded—slowly, grimly. "Yes. Before they unleash it onto the world."

CHAPTER THREE

THE MOUNTAIN LOOMED LIKE A CATHEDRAL CARVED BY ancient hands—vast, unfeeling, and half-lost to ice and silence.

Above the Putorana Plateau, afternoon light slanted cold and hard, casting long, merciless shadows across the ridgeline.

The wind didn't howl—it whispered, low and circling, like the breath of something old refusing to die.

Below, buried in the stone's shadow, was a place that had no name.

Nestled beneath a tangle of rockfall and ice, obscured by camouflage mesh and thermal shielding, the safehouse was invisible to satellites, drones, and mapmakers. No lights. No signs. Only a slab of reinforced alloy, flush with the frozen ground—an elevator sunk into the spine of the world.

Deep inside stood Noah Wolf.

He was motionless at the center of the War Room, a stark silhouette surrounded by machines that hummed with restrained violence. The space was carved into the mountain's marrow—walls of smoothed basalt reinforced with carbon-laced steel, matte and cold to the touch. There were no windows. No doors that weren't sealed with biometric locks. Just a maze of corridors and chambers sunken into the bedrock.

It had once belonged to the Council—a black site sunk deep into the permafrost, where child assassins were trained and ethics were a distant abstraction.

Now, it was something else.

Now it was Camelot's heart and nerve center.

Banks of monitors displayed a roiling patchwork of global hotspots—digital fires burning across satellite feeds, intercepted comms, and open-source traffic streams.

Noah's eyes fixed to it all, the world unfolding before him in vectors and threats, like a prophecy still being written.

He wasn't watching one screen.

He was watching all of them.

MONITOR ONE—JOHANNESBURG

Grainy drone footage panned over a UN relief convoy penned in by a crowd. Food riots had erupted into chaos. Gunfire cracked across the plaza. A guard opened fire into the swarm. Civilians trampled each other for crates of rice that burst open like sandbags.

MONITOR TWO—KASHMIR

Night vision. Static-hazed. Footage of a black-market drone hovering low over a Hindu temple during worship. It loosed a pressure charge on it with a whump that shook the camera. The blast was quick. Brutal. Afterwards people clawed rubble with bare hands, dragging bodies from smoking gaps in the stone.

MONITOR THREE—BALTIC BORDERLANDS

More drone footage. This time taken in Serbia. Eastern Europe's frostbitten edges, burning. Factions flying tattered remnants of Council-era banners clashed in a no-man's-land in the middle of the war torn city—mercenaries, zealots, desperate conscripts. All fighting for the remains of their homeland. A tank belched flame into the night.

Noah watched without blinking when a soft chime echoed through the room.

A voice followed—low and poised, threading through the room's silence.

"Noah. Priority escalation detected in twelve conflict zones. Would you like a full situational breakdown?"

It was Esmeralda—Camelot's AI.

Esmerelda had a long history with Camelot. She'd once had a body.

Tall, humanoid, and athletic. Wally had built her years ago in the bright before-times, back when the world still tolerated dreamers who tried to give machines conscience. She'd served as logistics command, lab interface, even friend.

Then came the Fall. The Council's purge of E & E. The siege of Kirkland.

Esmerelda had been on-site.

They'd said she was wiped during the breach, her memory core slagged in the fires that consumed R&D's labs. Wally had believed it. For a time. Until he found the dead-drop hidden in the archive Allison Peterson left for them. A backup.

For him.

Wally had spent the better part of six months rebuilding Esmerelda from the ghost of that code. Now she ran Camelot's infrastructure like a neural cortex. Air, power, data, perimeter defense. Environmental systems. Surveillance. She didn't sleep. She didn't eat. And since Wally brought her back, she hadn't glitched once.

"No," Noah said, voice flat, sanded of emotion. "There's nothing we can do anyway."

One of the screens—Johannesburg—crackled, then cut to black. The riot blinked out mid-scream.

He turned from the screens. Not with finality. Not resignation. Just purpose. Watching was over. Action began.

"Open up a channel to Bolivia," he said.

"Understood," came Esmerelda's flat voice. "Compiling encrypted burst transmission."

The central monitor lit up with the call:

Noah leaned in without hesitation. A crackle of static opened the line.

"Wally here." His voice came through thin and drained, the words dragging like they were too heavy to speak.

"What have you got, Wally?"

"We found something," he said. "You need to see this."

A heartbeat later, the display on the central monitor changed. The image that filled it wasn't violent. It didn't need to be.

A child—maybe eight, maybe younger—lay on a bare cement floor, half-swaddled in a wrinkled UN emergency blanket. His skin was waxy, almost translucent, the blackened veins beneath it rising like poisoned roots. His mouth hung slightly open, his eyes glassy and empty. One hand was clutched tight against his chest, fingers curled in what looked like prayer—or defiance.

In the lower corner of the screen, system text began to crawl:

AUTOMATED ANALYSIS—MATCH: PROJECT HELIX
Variant Signature: Confirmed
Classification: Weaponized Strain–7B

Noah stared at the screen, unmoving. "One of the Council's own, I presume?"

"Yes, but there's more," Wally continued, voice barely above a whisper. "It's been modified. Someone's taken the base sequence and rewritten the activation logic. The original strain targeted hereditary disorders, autoimmune flags, things you'd find on a medical screen. This version doesn't care about disease."

New data populated the display: genome comparisons, ancestral haplogroup overlays, epidemiological maps shaded with spreading red.

"It's targeting ethnically linked SNPs," he said. "Receptors clustered in Indigenous South American populations—Andean, Guaraní, some Quechua variants. It's surgical. The markers aren't associated with any illness. They're associated with heritage."

The silence in the War Room thickened.

"Whoever did this is into ethnic cleansing," Wally went on. "I think this is just a test zone. Before the real thing."

Noah folded his arms. "You're saying Bolivia was the trial run."

"I'm saying it fits the criteria—remote enough to limit international detection, close enough to UN aid lines for cleanup to look like negligence. And it's working. If we hadn't gotten here when we did, we might have missed it."

"What's your current objective, Wally?"

"I'm staying," Wally replied. "I've isolated a secondary strain in cold storage—slightly degraded, but usable for trace analysis. If I can reverse engineer the compiler logic, I might be able to pinpoint the source. Whoever engineered this left fingerprints in the code. They always do."

Noah nodded slowly. "We'll get you whatever support you need. Where are Jenny and Neil?"

Wally glanced off-screen. "Right here."

Another beat of static—and then two new faces appeared as the camera panned.

Neil stood at the edge of the feed, rifle slung, face drawn. Beside him, Jenny leaned forward into frame, her eyes sharp, alert.

"There's a plane inbound to pick you up," Noah said. "I need both of you in Europe."

"Europe's a big place, boss," Neil replied.

"You'll be starting in Istanbul. I need you to oversee Knox's next move."

There was a pause. Then Jenny's voice, sharp with recognition.

"Adrian Knox? As in the man who nuked Olympus?"

"The same," Noah said.

Noah's gaze flicked toward one of the monitors—Istanbul lit up on a digital map.

"Since Olympus went down, he's been the most valuable—and most vulnerable—asset we've got," Noah continued. "You don't dismantle the Council's central AI without painting a target on your back."

He leaned forward slightly, voice low and firm.

"Every loyalist, contractor, and deluded believer who still thinks the Council was humanity's guiding hand is out to get him. The ones left behind? They're not looking to rebuild. They're looking to punish. To avenge."

Jenny narrowed her eyes. "You think someone made him?"

"I know it," Noah said. "A data fragment surfaced yesterday in a closed-channel darknet cluster—old Council encryption, decrypted by one of Esmerelda's filters. A location tag buried inside: Istanbul. They're on the ground. Looking for him."

Neil grunted. "So the leak's internal."

"Possibly," Noah said. "Or someone's gotten access to our old routing system. Either way, we have a window before Knox is found by some sycophant with a gun."

Neil nodded once. "What's the ROE?"

"Low profile unless compromised. Eyes, ears, and escalation only if absolutely necessary. If this leak was bait, I want the hook."

Jenny glanced sideways at Neil, then back at the screen. "We'll get him out."

"I know you will," Noah said. "You leave within the hour."

The feed blinked. A final line of coordinates and a flight code appeared on the screen.

Istanbul awaited.

CHAPTER FOUR

THE NEXT MORNING, THE CORRIDOR GROANED AS Katya walked, the sound of her boot heels ringing off the old steel floor—sharp, even, deliberate. A half-beat behind her came six softer sets of footsteps, younger but just as precise.

The children walked in two columns. Not quite rigid—close, though. Their eyes moved constantly, scanning their surroundings—not out of fear. There was no hesitation in their gazes. Only watchfulness.

No. It wasn't nerves. It was conditioning.

The base wasn't the only thing Alison Peterson left to Camelot when she defected and died. She left behind these six Council-forged, built for precision, honed for violence, killers-in-waiting. None of them old enough to vote, but already dangerous enough to level a room.

Among them was Noah Wolf's daughter, Norah. Dark-haired, silent, always watching.

Katya stopped in front of a set of reinforced blast doors that led into the training range. The moment she halted, the six behind her stopped as well. No command. No gesture. One breath behind her. Perfect.

She turned to face them, gaze sweeping across their faces —measuring.

Today, they became hers.

She let the silence stretch before speaking, her tone dry, almost sardonic.

"Now let's see how good the Council's genetic engineering program really was."

The doors hissed open. Katya stepped forward. The six followed without a word.

The blast doors slammed shut behind them, sealing the group inside the training range. The sound echoed briefly through the cavernous space, then faded into a heavy silence. The chamber was carved straight into the Putorana stone, deep and cold. Target lanes stretched in rigid symmetry across one half of the room, opposite melee pits marked by scuffs and old stains. Suspended above it all was a catwalk observation deck, its rails dulled with age. Soundproofing panels dangled unevenly from the ceiling like worn skin, and the floor still bore faint scars—ghosts of past drills etched into steel.

Katya turned to face the recruits. The children lined up shoulder-to-shoulder, instinct guiding them before instruction. She didn't even need to ask.

Katya folded her arms behind her back and let her gaze sweep across the line. Six of them. Six potential weapons. Each one a different shape of threat.

Lula stood on the far left, sixteen, broad-shouldered and unbothered, arms crossed like she was sizing up the room for weaknesses. Her smirk wasn't playful—it was an invitation to underestimate her. A test, ready to be failed.

"Going to break us in, Mother?" she asked, her tone deliberately mocking.

Katya didn't blink. "Try that tone again and watch who gets broken first."

Lula shrugged, not cowed in the slightest. "Just clarifying the correct one."

She didn't blink either. Everything about her posture said alpha—but it was the control that made her dangerous. She didn't fidget. She didn't flare. She waited.

Next to her stood Gregor, fifteen. Silent. His posture wasn't just rigid—it was solid. His hand rested near the seam of his pants leg, not from anxiety, but calculation. He was sizing it all up. Distance to weapons. Exits. The others.

Katya clocked it without judgment. He doesn't need orders, she thought. He needs direction. And a reason.

Lula leaned slightly toward him. "You gonna talk today or just glower like normal?"

Gregor didn't respond. His slate-gray eyes remained forward, blank.

"Just because you're jealous he glowers better than you do," Zina said from the next spot down.

Zina—fourteen, wiry and poised just off-center from her designated line. Subtle. Measured. Always with a slight angle to her stance, as if ready to recoil, pivot, strike.

Lula turned slowly to her—and glowered.

Zina met the look, tilted her head, as if sizing her up. "Actually. Yours is pretty good. Maybe a draw."

Katya butt in. "Do you always talk more when you're nervous, Zina?"

Zina didn't flinch. "No. Just when I'm bored."

Her tone was flat, clipped. Efficient. Zina was fluent in six languages, but she spoke in careful syllables, as though she resented wasting even breath.

Beside her, Tao, thirteen, stood as if his body were present only out of obligation. His gaze wasn't on Katya—or the others—but slightly above, slightly past, like he was tracking something no one else could see. His posture was technically correct, but his mind was clearly elsewhere, moving faster than the room around him.

Tao was the outlier.

Where the others had been trained, sharpened, molded, Tao had been calculated. His IQ score—285, verified and reverified by six different tests—was not a point of pride but a warning label. He wasn't just intelligent. He was a savant. Neural processing off the charts. Pattern recognition that bordered on the paranormal. He spoke six languages fluently and understood a dozen more. He could perform vector calculus in his head faster than most machines. Once, during a stress test, he'd rewritten the algorithm of the simulation while still inside it—causing the system to crash for the first time in Council history.

He hadn't smiled once since arriving at Camelot.

Katya studied him for a beat longer than the others. There was no defiance in him. No hunger for approval. Just a deep, fractal stillness—like the surface of a lake that went down farther than anyone could ever dive.

"Tao," she said.

He blinked once and returned to the room.

"Yes," he said simply.

Not "ma'am." Not "here." Just yes. An answer to a question she hadn't asked.

Katya nodded once. She'd knew not to push him. Tao volunteered information only when it suited him.

She moved on.

Imani, twelve, stood nearly motionless next to him, her hands clasped too tightly behind her back, knuckles white. Smallest in the group, but never still. Her eyes moved constantly—floor, ceiling, exits, Lula, back to Katya.

And then to Katya's sidearm.

Her gaze dropped like a pin to the holster at Katya's hip.

"Glock 17," Imani said, quietly but without hesitation. "Generation five. Standard issue for NATO forces. Lightweight. Reliable. Low recoil profile. Polymer frame. Seventeen-round capacity, chambered in 9x19mm Parabellum. Barrel length: 4.49 inches. Stock iron sights. Minimal wear. Judging by the slide finish, it has been cleaned within the last forty-eight hours but not test-fired since. No optic. No compensator. Loaded. I'm guessing you prefer it because the bore axis is lower than a SIG and you don't trust safeties you didn't install yourself."

Katya turned to her—not sharply, just enough to acknowledge the comment.

"Do you always profile your instructor's firearm?" she asked.

Imani's voice was almost a whisper. "Only when they're armed."

The corner of Katya's mouth didn't smile. But something close to one passed behind her eyes.

She made a note. Not fear. Awareness.

She moved to the last in line.

Norah.

Eleven. Quiet. She stood slightly apart from the others—not enough to draw a reprimand, but just enough to signal something different. Her arms hung loosely at her sides. Relaxed. Not careless.

Her gaze was glacial. It drifted slowly from face to face, without hesitation or curiosity. Just assessment.

She didn't speak.

Katya studied her a little longer. *She's got Noah's eyes,* she thought. *Cold as ice.*

"You're here," she said, her voice even, "because someone decided you were good enough to be trained."

She paused. Let that land.

"But I'm here because someone else believes you can be something more than generic trained killers."

Her gaze locked on Lula for a fraction longer than the rest.

"Today, we find out if you can be a weapon..." Her tone hardened. "...a trigger waiting to be pulled."

She let the silence settle, then pivoted.

"Today, we start with fundamentals," she said. "Marksmanship. Precision under pressure."

She turned and began walking, boots ringing off the steel flooring with unhurried purpose.

"Each of you has a file. I've read your diagnostics. I've seen your scores. You're good. Let's see if I can make you better."

She led them toward the far end of the chamber, where a bank of lockers and a weapon rack waited beneath a faded Council insignia half-scraped off the concrete wall.

"The range is active. Cold zone. Live ammunition. No safeties. Your first test is individual—one by one. Ten rounds per magazine. Five mags each. Variable distance. Time limited. You'll be evaluated on grouping, reload efficiency, and reflex transitions."

She stopped and turned back to face them.

"There are no second attempts."

One of the lockers hissed open behind her. Inside, six sidearms rested in foam cutouts—identical Glock 17s, magazine well down, slides locked back.

Katya gestured.

"Arm yourselves. Holster only when I give the word. Range assignments will be randomized."

None of them hesitated.

Lula moved first, no flourish—just a clean, confident lift of the weapon and a smooth chamber check. Gregor followed, mechanical in his motions. Tao didn't look at the gun as he took it, already calculating vectors in his head. Zina rotated hers once, weighing the grip in her palm. Imani didn't blink. Norah picked hers up last, silent as snowfall.

Katya watched them. No wasted motion. No fumbling.

Good.

She stepped toward the control terminal and keyed in the first sequence. Target lanes lit up, one by one. The air shifted—cooler, more electric.

"Let's see what you've got," she said. "Zina, you're up first."

Zina nodded, stepped forward, and crossed into the lane with the smooth, lethal calm of someone who'd been preparing for this her whole life.

Katya folded her arms and watched the girl take position. The countdown began. Ten seconds. Then the target popped.

The test had started.

CHAPTER FIVE

BY THE END OF THEIR FIRST DAY, THE RECRUITS HAD fired over two thousand rounds, run eighteen simulated breach scenarios, memorized the layout of the entire subterranean base, and completed a full combat conditioning circuit that left even Lula silent by the final bell. Zina led the marksmanship scores. Gregor excelled in room-clearing drills. Tao bypassed a digital lock system meant to take three minutes in under twelve seconds—using only a borrowed training tablet. Imani never missed a detail, logging every instructor's routine, weapon preference, and vocal cadence. Norah said almost nothing, but her reflex test results were anomalously high—too fast, too calm.

No one quit. No one asked to stop.

For eight hours, they performed nonstop drills, until finally night began to fall over the stone bones of Camelot.

The locker room was quiet save for the hiss of running water and the rustle of clothes being shoved into duffels. Steam clung to the air in patches, fogging mirrors and softening the flicker of the overhead lights. The recruits moved with the slow, bone-deep exhaustion of people who had burned every calorie and still weren't allowed to collapse.

One by one, they filed out—Zina with her earbuds already in, Gregor limping slightly but saying nothing, Tao still drying his hair with a towel. Imani left last, eyes flicking to the wall clock and then the hallway, always tracking something.

Norah stayed behind. Her locker had jammed slightly and needed coaxing open.

She didn't hear Lula approach until the bulk of her blocked out the mirror behind them.

"You remember me, right?"

Norah turned. Slowly. "Four-three-three."

Lula's lip curled, not quite a smile. "That's right. And you're Three-O-Two."

Her tone dipped, thick with venom.

"The bitch who killed Four-Four-Two. The only friend I ever had."

Norah didn't move. "I never meant to kill your friend."

"But you did," Lula snarled, stepping closer. She was taller, heavier, her frame broad with the kind of strength that could break ribs just by leaning the wrong way. "You killed her and you didn't even blink."

"It was the Council," Norah said quietly. "They made us kill each other."

Lula's jaw tightened. "You cut her throat."

Norah didn't look away. "I never meant to."

Lula shifted her weight. Her knuckles cracked.

The air between them crackled.

Lula was on the verge of moving. Her eyes widened as she—

"Enough," came Katya's voice, cold and slicing as a scalpel.

Both girls turned. She stood in the doorway, arms crossed, gaze sharp enough to shear steel.

"Get dressed. You've got sixty seconds to meet me outside," she said. "I have something to show you."

Lula stepped back first. Not cowed—just calculating. She shot Norah one last glance, unreadable, then turned toward her locker.

Norah didn't move for a few seconds more.
Then she exhaled. Quiet. Measured.
And began to dress.

Scan the QR code below to purchase CHILDREN OF THE
EMPIRE.
Or go to: righthouse.com/children-of-the-empire